DAUGHTERS
of *Jerusalem*

ADVANCED READING COPY

ISBN 978-1-7370520-4-3
Library of Congress Control Number 2023907159

Front Cover art by Noah Gerstman
Cover and book design by Lauren Grosskopf

Pleasure Boat Studio books are available through the following:
Ingram Worldwide Distribution, Baker & Taylor, Amazon.com, bn.com &
Pleasure Boat Studio: A Nonprofit Literary Press
PLEASUREBOATSTUDIO.COM
Seattle, Washington

DAUGHTERS
of *Jerusalem*

A Novel by

GALYA GERSTMAN

PLEASURE BOAT STUDIO: A NONPROFIT LITERARY PRESS

Esther Toledano M. Haim Larusu

LILI LARUSU M. Joseph Ventura

Benjamin
Rachel
Esther
Haim
Leah
Clara
Baby 7
Baby 8
Baby 9
Baby 10
Baby 11
Baby 12
Baby 13
Baby 14
Baby 15
Baby 16
Baby 17
MERCADA VENTURA M. Gabriel Hazan

Joseph
Samuel
Amos
Sara
ALEGRA HAZAN

PART I *Lili*

Chapter One

IT ALL STARTED WITH A PROMISE to God. A promise in return for the life of the baby. For Lili Ventura was cursed. It was plain to everyone in Mala Gozic, her small village in Serbia. By the age of thirty-nine, she had given birth to seventeen children. Actually, that wasn't the curse, though many today might think otherwise. Instead, Lili's curse was that after having had those seventeen children, she was still childless. For reasons that baffled her fellow villagers, Lili's babies would die just a day or so after they were born. Each and every one. All seventeen of them. Thus, Lili had gone through nine long months of nauseating and hemorrhoid-ridden pregnancy and then endured the blitzkrieg of delivery seventeen times, only to have the infant die just a few days later.

The year was 1900, and Lili was pregnant again, for the eighteenth time. One day, she heard of a Greek professor who had come to the capital, Belgrade. "Professor" was the title given to any medical practitioner who had studied more than the minimum required to perform as a doctor, more than the average rube who took care of the country folk with a bottle of potato vodka in one hand and a rusty hacksaw in the other. Furthermore, this professor's expertise was pregnancy and childbirth. Having heard this, Lili put her stitch work aside—she was a seamstress by profession—and promptly set out early the next morning for the capital, barely even consulting her husband, Joseph, to whom she had been wed since the age of fifteen.

3

Their marriage had surprised all, since Lili, short, thin and angular, both in body and visage, was not at all comely. She had small, almost black eyes, whose expression was often fixed and intense, and in which one could read her extraordinary cunning. Above them were thick brows separated by a deep furrow. She had thin and perpetually chapped lips, which she picked at with her teeth, making for a most unpleasant grimace. Her father had always scolded her about it, warning that one day her face would freeze that way, the same as was said regarding crossing one's eyes. But as they had never possessed a looking glass, Lili had never seen how strange the gesture looked. In any event, she had always been confident that despite her looks she would somehow find a husband, and that she had, even a handsome one to boot. Joseph, still a very attractive man after so many years, with his dark hair and blue eyes, was quiet and gentle. To his wife's mind, these attributes were disadvantageous, rendering him ill-equipped to handle the ills and evils of this world, of which she was convinced there were many. As such, when something serious had to be decided, or something difficult undertaken, it was always Lili who took the initiative, made the effort, and bore the responsibility. Even when she had told him about the Greek professor and of her decision to go see him, his response had been: "But isn't it a very long way to Belgrade?"

"Aboltar cazal, aboltar mazal," she had told him in Ladino. "A change of scene, a change of fortune." Ladino was the Spanish-based patois spoken by Jews of Sephardic descent all over the Mediterranean region, from Algiers to Zagreb. *Sephardim*, which means "Spanish," traced their ancestry back to the Spanish and Portuguese Jews who fled or were expelled during the Inquisition of the late fifteenth century, at which time they numbered some three hundred thousand, settling mainly in North Africa, Italy, Greece, Turkey, the Balkans and Palestine. For so many centuries they held on not only to their religion but also to their culture by continuing to speak Ladino and to identify themselves with Iberia. The first ever Jewish periodical, the *Gazeta de Amsterdam,* which began publishing in 1675, was in Ladino. Jews today are still divided into the

two categories of Sephardim and Ashkenazim, or Eastern-European Jews ("Ashkenaz" being old Hebrew for *Germany*). Also those whose origins can be traced to Arab countries are lumped with the Sephardim, though erroneously so, for their common tongue is Arabic, not Ladino.

Determined to see the Professor, Lili hitched a ride with Simon the milk vendor, who let her travel in his cart to the town's outskirts. From there she shared a wagon with some others who had likewise taken it upon themselves, for reasons of their own, to visit the capital. The journey was long, made longer still by the jolting of the carriage over the uneven roads. Bobbing and bouncing as the carriage wobbled over the rocks and stones studding the dirt roads, Lili, though normally outgoing, kept to herself, a brown and nondescript kerchief tied over her brown and nondescript hair and under her chin. Even had she been vain, she would not have wanted to call attention to herself here, among the fair-haired and -skinned Slavs. As a Jew, she was an outsider. Jews had a long history of being alternately tolerated and persecuted in the land of the Slavs, and only toward the end of the nineteenth century, just a few short years before, had they been given civil and political equality.

Lili spent the journey ruminating in silence on the Greek professor and what she had heard of him. She assured herself that he would be different from all the midwives and village doctors she had visited over the years, stronger than all the herbs and roots she had imbibed or inhaled, better than all the chants she had whispered and all the tricks she had performed. This professor would be different.

He had to be. The string of procreative failures she had endured had wrought havoc not only on her body but had cut to the very core of her psyche. In the first place, there was the question of feminine identity. What kind of woman was she? In Lili's world, in Lili's time, women were good for pretty much one thing: bringing men children. Girls would be married off just a few years after they first menstruated, for they were now capable of breeding. As further proof, men could abandon or divorce their wives for such reproductive crimes as bringing them damaged or merely ugly offspring, or for not bringing them sons, the only sex, evidently, worthy of having. Lili knew that a few men in town, and even some women, had already suggested divorce to Joseph. He, however, truly valued his wife, and could not imagine life without her. She was grateful to him for his loyalty, but knew that one day Joseph, too, might become convinced that she was replaceable, that progeny was after all more important than fidelity, or love. This only exacerbated her feelings of inadequacy. What had she come to, Lili wondered, she who had always been so self-reliant, to be worrying about her husband abandoning her? She, the bookseller's daughter, learned, literate, treated as more worthless than the most ignorant of women?

The gossipers in town found further reasons for Joseph to be rid of Lili, further evidence that she was an unwomanly woman. She was unattractive. She was a poor housekeeper. She was obdurate; she did not heed but rather dominated her husband. She had an independent mind and an irreverent tongue. It was perhaps in punishment for her unseemly behavior, whispered the villagers, that she had been cursed. After all, what form had the curse taken, where had it struck if not at the very site of her womanhood? In this manner, Lili's malediction was a masterpiece of cruelty: while it devastated her body, tormented her soul, and isolated her from those who could virtually spot the mark of Cain on her forehead, it also battered her sense of femininity, her very sense of self. If a woman's role in life was to bear children, then what kind of woman was she? And if she was not a true woman, what was she?

Yet Lili's angst was more than just a reflection of inherited cultural strictures; her inability to reproduce left her furthermore in a creative void. All feel the need to justify one's existence, to produce something of value, which in turn makes one worthy of taking up space on this planet. Lili could only feel the hollowness of her life, the lack of her contribution to the universe, the pointlessness of herself. These existential doubts soon took on cosmic proportions. As she gazed further into the remote recesses of ages to come, she realized as never before the weight of legacy. If the scope of one's existence is limited to oneself, what is the point? Am I all there is? Will there be nothing beyond me, nothing to show for my few moments on earth? The world will continue to turn, and I will be forgotten, reduced to the dust of oblivion, as if I had never been here. Why then, she grieved, did God even bother?

But Lili was ultimately a pragmatist. What good did it do to weep? She had learned long ago that God didn't hear one's laments; he barely heard one's prayers. Lili thought of him as a parent with too many children, requiring them to fend for themselves while he took care of even littler or more needy ones. Without leaving her bitter, this rationalization satisfied her intellectually and also emotionally. By the time she was in her forties, she had managed to fortify herself and to truly believe she would be triumphant. It was the only thing that kept her going. She even took pride in her suffering; a lesser person, she knew, would have succumbed to defeat long ago, would have surrendered to the wicked Fates. Lili sometimes imagined that the plagues she suffered were part of a higher moral test, that in the end it would all lead to something great. At other times, though, she considered that this was perhaps merely a way for her to find sense where there wasn't any. Things just were the way they were, and that was it. Whatever the case, one could not allow one's spirit to be broken, she reflected. Otherwise, what was left?

When she and her fellow travelers finally arrived in the city, having crossed the Sava River, which flows into the Danube at Belgrade, they found it to be a wondrous and frightening place. They were, as we would say now, Dorothy in Oz. So many edifices, huge, with sculpted doors and gilded gates. Tall spires and heavy domes loomed over them, as a fortress displayed its serrated walls with gun ports and towers. The buildings around them were high and wide, with many, many windows almost attached to one another, and all so orderly, everything in neat rows, a far cry from the small houses of Mala Gozic, sprinkled here and there haphazardly. Lili, having been born and raised in a little village, was unlike most of her fellow Jews who customarily resided in Belgrade or other large centers, for Jews had historically been forbidden to dwell in provincial towns. But the feudal system of the Ottomans, before the Serb uprisings in the nineteenth century, caused many to move away from developed areas such as mining, artisan and trade towns, and to withdraw to less accessible places such as the remote village from which Lili hailed, and from which she had never traveled so far. Little could she imagine that one day her life would take her farther still, to a world different than any she had ever known.

And the people, throngs of them, moving so fast, wearing such clothes! Joseph was a shoemaker, so Lili always prided herself on having fine shoes. But when a lady emerged from one of the shops and hoisted her dress a little in order to avoid a puddle, Lili beheld the most exquisite red boots she had ever laid eyes on. She made a mental note to describe the color and style to Joseph, who could attempt a reproduction, but then immediately changed her mind. What use was there in her little village for such luxurious footwear? In Mala Gozic, women and men alike wore heavy, practical shoes that could carry one from the butcher's to the baker's, in the snow and in the mud, and not merely across a finely-paved street in Belgrade. In Mala Gozic, shoes were gear, not ornaments.

Lili soon found her way to the hospital and the Greek professor, for whom a large crowd of women had already gathered. He was, after all, a *professor*. After giving her name, she found an unoccupied stretch of wall on which to lean, for all the benches were filled. Amidst the odors of ammonia and "spirit," that is, rubbing alcohol, she gazed at the faces of the women who were waiting with them, and scrutinized nervously those who emerged from behind the professor's closed portal, as if the patient's face would reveal the doctor's magic.

Little by little, through chitchat and the sharing of woes, a warm atmosphere arose in the waiting room, a sisterhood of women, all different and yet here and now united. Was it their shared misfortunes that brought them together, or did it extend beyond that, Lili wondered, as she recalled the cozy buzzing among the rows of women in the synagogue, separated from the men, or the comfort she always felt when she gathered with the other seamstresses in her village, their heads bowed in harmony over their needles and fabrics, gossiping freely with one another. The men would mock the women and their silly banter, never comprehending that it was more than the exchange of useless information, as they saw it, more than just a means of passing time. What import was there to recipes, to news of one's neighbor, to accounts of one's children's first steps, when men spoke of money, of war, of things that really mattered? Lili had often heard men criticize women in this way, saying they spoke just for the sake of speaking, and they were right, but for the wrong reasons. What they could not see was that in women's gossip, the very exchange itself mattered sometimes more than the information exchanged. It was contact. It was a thread that wove them all together, a musical composition in which each had her part, in which each contributed something of herself, a symphony of communication. The world of men was loose, vast, while that of women was minute and tight. Men held each other at a distance, and spoke of things far-reaching, whereas the female universe was immediate and supremely personal. For men, what ultimately counted was success or, more abstractly, honor and glory; for women, what truly counted were the people around them.

At last Lili's name was called and she entered the doctor's office. The examining room used by Dr. Gavros was immense compared to her village doctor's, and so starkly white and clean that the smell of ammonia stung Lili's nose. The ominous metal instruments gleamed as they lay in perfect order on a tray next to a high table, padded and encased in black leather. Dr. Gavros, however, was seated at a desk in the corner of the room. He was a pleasant-looking man in his fifties, with dark, wavy hair, wiry black eyebrows behind thick, black-framed glasses, and a relaxed smile. Lili smiled, too. Why, he was as black as she was! She felt suddenly proud to be so swarthy. He read over the information the nurse had previously taken from her, and then asked why she had come.

"Because every time I have a child, it dies."

He considered this. "What do you mean 'have a child'? Do you mean the full nine months, or it dies two or three months after you become pregnant?"

"No, the full nine months."

"I see." He jotted this down on the same piece of paper the nurse had used as her information sheet. "And how soon after the baby is born does it die?"

"Three or four days, once even five."

"Mm hmm. And before that, was everything normal? The delivery, the baby?"

"Yes, everything was normal, like with any other woman."

"And the baby, was it always normal?"

"Yes... always..." She sighed. He wrote.

"And how many times has this happened?"

"Seventeen."

The doctor looked up from the sheet of paper. "Seventeen? What, you mean, seventeen times you've been pregnant, or..."

"I mean, I've been pregnant seventeen times, I've given birth seventeen times, and then the baby died seventeen times." She leaned forward to make sure he had understood. "Seventeen times."

"Seventeen times," he repeated softly, in amazement. "Well, let's see, if everything is normal during the pregnancy—is it?" he asked, and she nodded in assent, "and everything is normal during the delivery, and the baby is normal, but then a few days later it dies, that means there's something from the moment it's born that is killing it. Let's think what that can be." He was by this point obviously talking to himself, as his eyes seemed to be focused on something far away.

The doctor was tapping his forefinger against his lips, deep in thought. "The child may be overly sensitive to... No, that can't be it." He looked now at Lili and the nurse. "It can't be that the child is overly sensitive to something used to wrap it in, or something used to clean it with, because maybe one or two children would be born so sensitive, but seventeen?

That's highly unlikely. And such a reaction would be visible, you would see that the baby is covered with red spots or something, and you never saw that, did you?"

Lili shook her head. But she saw what he was getting at.

"No, no red spots, but the babies would be very white, or even green, and throw up. A lot. And crying, crying."

"They threw up a lot? Did they have trouble breathing?"

Lili hesitated. Did they have trouble breathing? She tried to recall. "Well, yes, I suppose, but not in the beginning..."

"No, I didn't ask the question right. I mean, when it was clear already that the baby was sick, did it show the sickness first by having trouble breathing or by throwing up? What was the first sign each time? This is important," he added.

It was this last comment that made her hesitate. She paused to think. To remember.

"Throwing up," she decided. "And the skin turning funny colors."

"Mm hmmm... Did you feed the babies anything? Give them anything to drink?"

"No. Nothing," Lili assured him. "Just the breast."

"Just the breast," he repeated. He began now to write furiously, mumbling to himself every now and then, but neither she nor the nurse could understand him. Then he abruptly looked up.

"Mrs. Ventura, you're pregnant now?" She nodded. He asked her how many months, and she told him four.

"Very well. This is what I want you to do. After the baby is born, do not feed it yourself. Get someone else to nurse your baby for you. Under no circumstances are you to nurse it yourself. Do you understand?"

She nodded slowly, surprised by his order not to nurse the baby, and stunned by what such an order implied.

"Professor..." Her voice faltered before she got it again under control. "Are you saying to me that my milk is killing my babies?"

"Yes, I'm afraid that's exactly what's happening, from what you described to me. Your own milk is poisoning your babies."

"That's...impossible!" Lili gasped.

"Unusual, yes," Gavros answered. "Even rare. But it has happened."

Lili sucked in her breath. *She* had been killing her babies! Lili herself! Instead of feeding them with the milk of life, she had been choking them with the ooze of death.

"So do what I tell you," the professor concluded, "and may God watch over you."

The trip back home was a long one. The professor, though professor he might be, was at bottom only a man, and from Lili's experience, that was not much. And she had been disappointed so many times. Seventeen times. Each time she was certain it would be different. Each time she was assured by someone that everything would work out. Why should the professor be any different? They had gone to their rabbi, they had prayed before God, Joseph each time pledging to do something holy, to bring it up as a rabbi if it was a son. Lili had performed rituals prescribed by the womenfolk with their homespun magic, to undo the curse or ward away the demons that stalked them. None of it had worked.

Yet she couldn't stop herself from hoping that this Dr. Gavros would be the one she could count on, the one who would come through for her. That rather than witchcraft or divine aid, her miracle would come from science. Now, perhaps, she could finally put a stop to this cycle of death; she could finally have and keep a baby. Maybe she would even allow herself to love this budding creature in her belly, something that she had long ceased doing. Maybe this time she would let herself stroke her swollen stomach, and even dream a little. A child, a child of her own, imagine that. A little boy, or a little girl. And suddenly in that moment, riding in the carriage home, she knew. She knew the baby would live, she knew the professor would save it, and she knew it would be a girl, a girl like her.

But the months passed, and with them their fears were renewed. Would it really work this time? Or would it be like all the other times?

It was hard to remain optimistic when the townsfolk still believed her cursed. Even the rabbi hinted to Joseph that perhaps their prayers and pledges to God lacked conviction, lacked earnestness. So Joseph went back to the temple, and prayed and promised as never before, while Lili went to consult the old wise women.

These women, three in number, lived in the next village, and were as old as Moses himself. Because of their advanced age, rare in previous centuries, they had seen much, and because of their weighty intelligence, they had learned from it all. Sometimes they imparted their wisdom alone; sometimes they would band together and give a common ruling or diagnosis. Lili was lucky, because this time they were all together in Justa Pereira's house, the eldest of the three. They knew Lili well by now. As all of their earlier treatments for her had failed, they had long ago come to the conclusion that she was cursed, at which point she no longer asked their advice. She had not believed in curses, for she knew that neither she nor certainly Joseph, who would not hurt anyone even in self-defense, had ever wronged another soul. She also refused to believe that she was accountable for any actions committed by her family before her. As far as she was concerned, she expected no one to be responsible for her mistakes, so why should she be responsible for those of others? At least, that was what she would say out loud, to be brave.

But that was many pregnancies ago, and now she wasn't so sure. So she stepped over Justa Pereira's threshold, vowing that come success or failure, this would be the last time. And not just because of her stubbornness. After seventeen pregnancies and deliveries, her body could not withstand much more. Her skin, her breasts, and especially her lower parts had grown weak and tired, flaccid and thin. This would most certainly be the last one, so she could afford to take no chances.

The sages seated before her did not comment on her long absence. They understood well that she had refused to believe in the reality of her curse, and they did not blame her for this. They simply accepted it as part of the course of Lili's life. While they themselves did not believe that one's fate was mapped out and irrevocable, they revered the past and never questioned it. What was, is. But what will be? That was where they came in.

Lili was direct. "Wise mothers, you told me once long ago that I was cursed. Now I must ask you, what can I do to battle this curse? How can I save my child, this one last time?"

Justa answered first. "Lili, you must first understand that you cannot battle the curse. There are demons who do not want you to bear children, and these demons are very strong. They are stronger than you."

Lili's blood froze in her veins. "Are you telling me then that there's no hope? That I will never have this child?"

The crone on the right, Stella Spinoza, smiled. "Oh, you will have this child. This is the eighteenth child, and eighteen is the number of life." She was referring to *gematria*, Jewish numerology.

Justa resumed. "We merely said that you cannot undo the curse. We didn't say you can't have your child."

"But then how is this possible? If, as you say, the demons are so strong?"

"Yes, they are strong, and we are weak. But have you never heard of the weak vanquishing the strong?" asked Stella.

"Why, young David beat the giant Goliath," Justa continued. "How did he manage that? Was he stronger than Goliath? No, but he was smarter," she winked, tapping her balding head with her bony finger. "What you must do is outwit the demons, Lili."

"But how?"

Finally, the last of the three spoke. Esther Azulai derived her arcane authority from her lineage, for she was descended from a line of *tzaddikim*, holy men, who were also scholars in Jewish mysticism, known as the Kabbalah.

"We don't know why there is a curse," she responded, "but we know that the curse is aimed at you. So in order to avoid the demons' power, you must distance the child from yourself. You must fool them into thinking that this is not your child, the child of Lili and Joseph."

"Yes," agreed Stella, "you must treat this child as if it were not your own, but rather one you have bought."

"Bought?"

"Bought," chimed in Justa. "With three pieces of gold. When the child is born, you must bring it to us. We will chant before the demons that they have won, that Lili and Joseph have given up trying to have their own children. The demons will think they have won, and they will be happy. Therefore, when we tell them that you are now prepared to buy a strange child for yourselves, they will be more merciful. But you, Lili, and everyone else, must refer to the child as 'bought,' so as not to risk their wrath again."

Poisoned milk, insincere promises to God, and now an angered Devil. So many diagnoses from all angles of the human condition, but they all pointed to the same thing: that whatever was killing her babies, it was because of her. Well, Lili was never one to shy away from blame, if that was what she merited. If she were the cause of it, she would also be the one to rectify it. She would withhold her milk, she would swear like a saint before God, and she would buy this baby back from damnation.

When the day of delivery came, Lili had her baby, and it was in fact a girl. By that point, she and Joseph had sold practically all the furniture and contents of their house which, along with the meager savings they had garnered through the years from the shoes and sewing, earned them the three pieces of gold. After eighteen pregnancies and childbirths, Lili raised her bleeding and trembling body from her bed and dragged herself, together with Joseph, to Justa's house. The three ancient women received the girl and the gold and recited the necessary incantations. The girl was called Mercada, which in Ladino meant "bought."

In the meantime, a neighbor nursed the baby, and the baby lived. One day, two days, a week. Indeed, Lili's milk appeared to have been the culprit, just as the Professor had surmised. Lili and Joseph, it seemed, were finally to keep their eighteenth child, rescued from poison and bought from hell. Their histories thereafter would have continued on in unremarkable contentment, but for one thing. Mercada had survived not only because she had been "bought" and because her mother's toxic milk had been averted. More frightening and wrathful than the demons, and more knowing and powerful than even the Professor, there remained one more force with which to reckon: God. For while Lili had visited the clinic, Temple of Science, and Justa's house, Temple of Dark Spirits, Joseph had sought salvation in the temple of his ancestors, the Synagogue of the Jews. Each day, as he donned his *tallit,* the blue and white prayer shawl, he thought of the rabbi's subtle admonishment that perhaps their prayers had not been earnest enough in the past. So he prayed with all his heart and his soul for the life of this last child, and promised something to God that he had never promised before: if God allowed the child to live, he swore that he, Joseph, would gather his wife and child away from Mala Gozic, away even from Serbia, and would take them to God's kingdom. He would move his family to the Holy Land.

When, after seeing each day pass with bated breath and still Mercada was alive, even after a week, then two, Joseph could finally relax and give thanks that this child would live. Yet in giving thanks, he was also forced to acknowledge that he could not put off his promise much longer. God had kept his word, and Joseph would have to keep his.

When Mercada was three weeks old, when Lili was at long last beginning to believe that her long nightmare was over, Joseph finally found the courage to break the news to her. They were still at the table at the end of the Sabbath meal. They sipped their tea, the green mint leaves swimming in the clear little glasses, while the uneven tin plates waited to be removed from the table. Lili had made his favorite, *hamin,* a typical Sabbath dish that needed to cook overnight, thus absolving one of having to prepare something during the Sabbath itself, as cooking was forbidden. The hearty mixture of beans, barley, potatoes, a little meat and some hard-boiled eggs filled the house with its warm and enticing smells. Tonight, though, Joseph had had trouble getting it down, rehearsing in his mind how he would tell Lili. He could barely breathe, much less chew. He avoided looking at his wife, focusing behind her on the wall where a braid of garlic bulbs hung above a stack of straw baskets and clay pots. An old jar held some wooden spoons while another was filled with small, pickled eggplants. Joseph sighed. He would miss this place. His world.

Then he took a deep breath and spat it out, with a feeling of release as if finally confessing a horrible crime. He kept his eyes lowered when he told Lili, partly out of shame for bringing even more troubles upon her, and partly out of fear from her reaction. He never denied it; she was the stronger of the two, and it was she who ruled in their affairs. He knew that Lili liked it that way and, though he would admit it only to himself, so did he. She preferred to dominate; he preferred to hand over the reins. People often voiced their sympathies for him, for having such a difficult wife. Joseph, however, though he complained every now and again after one of her tantrums, bore his wife's forceful personality with what seemed to be great patience and acceptance, but was in reality sincere relief. Such forbearance only made him appear more of a saint in his neighbors' eyes, that he put up with a wife who ruled over their home and made all the decisions. Poor Joseph, they would all say.

After his revelation to Lili, Joseph waited. She made no sound, no movement. When he finally looked up, instead of the piercing black eyes he was sure would be boring a hole into his head, he saw that she was smiling. Not that it was a happy smile. It was, he thought, if one could put it this way, a sad smile.

"What, Lili, I tell you this and you're smiling? But I'm serious. I really made such a promise. And now we really have to go."

She still smiled and said nothing.

"Lili, this is God I'm talking about, not some crazy old ladies with hair coming out of their noses," he said, his voice rising an octave. "I can't believe you can laugh away a promise to God!"

"I'm not laughing at God, Joseph, and I'm not laughing at you either, my poor husband. I'm laughing at me," she explained. "I'm laughing because I actually thought that I had paid for having my baby. I actually was stupid enough to think that you could pay for such a wonder, such a pearl, with only three pieces of gold! Or with eighteen pregnancies! But here you are to tell me how foolish I was, Joseph. Here you are to tell me that we shall pay for Mercada with... everything we have come to know and cherish. Our home, our friends, family, everything." She made a sweeping movement with her arm as she in her turn now took in the straw baskets, the chair with the broken back, the candlesticks, the jar of pickled eggplants.

"Oh, Lili, Lili, I... I don't know what to say. I can't say I'm sorry because I'm not sorry, because we have a little girl, after so many years! But I'm sorry it had to be at such a great price. My father always dreamed of the Holy Land. Now his son will see it, like it or not. What have I done? I've heard it's nothing but a desert, with wild animals and murderous Arabs. What will we do there? How will we survive?"

Lili looked into her husband's frightened eyes.

It was Joseph's striking eyes that had attracted him to her, so many years ago, eyes in which could be read a profound intelligence and a gentle soul. She had met him when he had come to see her father about a book, for her father and uncle had been bookbinders. Joseph, an avid reader, had already exhausted the limited supply offered by his local bookshop, and so moved on to the greener pastures of Larusu Brothers Books. He soon became one of their best customers and also one of their best suppliers, for they would buy back used books as well, at a used-book price, and then sell them again for profit.

Lili fell in love at first sight with the handsome boy whose eyes were blue not like the summer sky but lush and dark like an oncoming storm, as rich and lustrous as deep velvet. She remembered him that first time, constantly touching the cap on his head, as if he expected it to fall any minute, and she could see by the fingerless gloves that he bit his nails, a sign that he was a worrier. She was amazed that so breathtaking a boy shared her love for reading.

When she eventually told her father of her feelings, hoping he would aid her in her hopes of conquest, he tried at first to dissuade her indirectly. This was a boy from another village; why couldn't Lili choose someone from her own area? But she was far from stupid.

"You think Joseph is too good for me!" she shouted.

"That's not what I am saying."

"Oh, yes, it is. He is handsome, whereas I am ugly. That's what you think."

He sighed. "No, I am not talking about looks. But yes, you and he are very different. He is quiet and…well, he goes out of his way to be polite and pleasant, while you…you are not quiet at all, and you say whatever you have to say…"

She cut him off. "Well, I don't care! I am as good as he is! Maybe better!"

"Of course you are as good as he is!" cried her father, exasperated. "But that is not how the world is! He will not see your worth. He will see only what is on the outside. Ach, I'm sorry, Lili. I don't want to say these things to you. But sometimes it's harder to be right than kind. And it would not be right if I did not tell you the truth."

Lili was stunned into silence. Though her father had only wanted to spare her wounds and humiliation, he had hurt her more than the taunts or, worse, lack of interest from the boys in her village. True, a flower is a beautiful thing to behold, but weren't the trees just as lovely in the winter, with no flowers and no leaves, naked and shivering? Ruth was the most beautiful girl in her village, for instance, and she was truly lovely, but she was so… dull. As if God had forgotten to sprinkle salt and pepper on her when he cooked her.

Finally, and more importantly, Lili thought, what of the riches of her heart and the depth of her mind? Hadn't her father always told her this? Had he given into conventional stupidity so readily? And would so a boy who read *Romeo and Juliet*? Lili would not believe it. She was sure Joseph would be worthy of her affection, sure he would see beyond the veneer of the skin to what lay beneath. So she made up her mind she would have him. And she did. It was not easy, and it took some time and perseverance, but she did. In fact, it was perhaps pure luck, deep instinct or truly fate that led Joseph to Lili, for they were made for each other. She was the action for his reflection, the doer for his thinker.

Now, sitting at their dinner table, Lili smiled her rueful smile. They were on the verge of a cataclysmic change in their lives, and it was up to her to comfort him. It was always up to her. Joseph's deep blue eyes, lined with heavy lashes, reflected the oceans of dread that were engulfing him.

"Ay, Joseph, don't worry. We will survive the way we've always survived. Anyway, we've already sold so much of our belongings to get the gold— why, we could be packed and ready in an hour!" They both managed a chuckle. "We'll be fine, you'll see. *Aboltar cazal, aboltar mazal.*"

She reached out her hand and squeezed his. He smiled and felt somewhat consoled. If Lili said so, she was probably right, he thought. Everything would work out. Sometimes all you needed was a little dose of someone else's optimism, a dash of their confidence. But in her own heart Lili felt for the first time that she was lying, that this time perhaps they would not be fine. Somehow, she had a feeling that in exchange for the gift and the promise, they would pay with their lives.

Chapter Two

IN THE END, DUE TO SUNDRY problems such as a cholera epidemic in Palestine and a *coup d'état* in Serbia, Mercada was three years old when they finally packed everything and said their tearful farewells to family and friends. The 75 kilometers or so of Lili's journey north to Belgrade from Mala Gozic had seemed endless to her, on the other side of the planet practically, but that was nothing compared to the almost 300 kilometers they had to travel, with all their worldly possessions and a small child, crossing southwest through Montenegro, till they reached the sea. They had to wait two days before they could catch a ship heading south for the Middle East and Africa, with the Terra Sancta as one of its ports of call.

The Holy Land's earliest known name was Canaan, until it was reshaped by the Israelites into the two kingdoms of Israel and Judah, or Judea. The Greeks renamed it Philistia, or Palestine to the Romans. It was intended as an insult, after the Hebrews' longtime enemy the Philistines who had invaded from the Aegean Islands, whence the name Philistine, which means "Sea Peoples." Though the land had always had a reliable stream of visitors, even in the Middle Ages (or rather, especially in the Middle Ages, when maps showed Jerusalem at the center of the world, surrounded by Europe, Asia and Africa) the turn of the century in contrast saw few people having any interest in risking their lives to reside in or even visit a region so desolate. For Jews, to visit or live in the Holy Land, specifically Jerusalem, was considered a *mitzvah*, more than just a good deed, as it is commonly known, but rather a duty or commandment fulfilled, in theory at least. In practice, however, most saw it as just the opposite of a good deed, instead endangering their lives and those of their family. The sanctity of life, they proclaimed, far outweighed the importance of a duty to Zion. Still, among Joseph and Lili's fellow travelers to Palestine there were several enthusiasts, who wanted to return to the land that their Bible said belonged to them: "And you shall take possession of the land and settle in it, for I have given the land to you to possess it," they quoted from the Old Testament. They believed that one day God would send the Messiah to Jerusalem, and they wanted to live in the City of David in preparation for that day. Others, however, were prompted by more secular aims. They wanted to join other *halutzim*, pioneers who, rather than dwelling in the holy city of Jerusalem, opted to live in the countryside and work the land. They were socialists, called Zionists, and their dreams of a Jewish homeland were political, after the first Zionist Congress in 1897 proposed a Jewish homeland in Palestine. Rather than wait for the Messiah, who might never come, these settlers would forge their home through the sweat of their own brow.

Not all those journeying to Palestine were Jewish, of course. Christian pilgrims, mainly Roman Catholic and Greek Orthodox, were also fulfilling life-long dreams by seeking out Jesus's birthplace. A few priests were going to attempt the caretaking of their Middle Eastern flock and the conversion of the uninitiated, while a handful of nuns and monks were preparing to cloister themselves away in Bethlehem convents and monasteries in Nazareth. In a stop-over in Greece, more Christian pilgrims climbed aboard, as well as Muslims who were either returning home, going to visit family, on pilgrimage themselves to pay homage to the spot from which Muhammad started his Heavenly Ascent in Jerusalem, or passing through from a pilgrimage to Mecca. There was only a smattering of Turks, who ruled over Palestine, and a few Europeans, but they were in a different section of the ship entirely, one that had breathing space, clean floors, and even a dining room. Lili, Joseph and Mercada were with the others, on the bottom of the boat, in steerage. Joseph and Mercada grew weak from the stench of the soiled lavatories and the rotting garbage, and from the eternal swaying of the vessel. From such poor conditions, a veritable Petri dish for infections, six people died during the trip, two of them small children. The voyage took almost a week, and then finally, when Joseph swore they could take no more, they arrived at the port of Jaffa.

All those in steerage were placed in a fenced-off quarantined area for two days, to be sure that the bacteria and lice they had brought from Europe would not mingle with the bacteria and lice that lived in the Middle East. Then they were handed out lye soap, told to scrub, and were set free, but not until they had paid their entry taxes. What, then, Joseph protested, were those taxes they had paid when they had obtained their papers? He fretted over the quantities they had spent for their passage, and now for more taxes and transport from Jaffa. They would need the rest for lodging and food, and he could see it was barely enough. What in damnation was he dragging them into? What was this Palestine?

The description of Palestine with which Joseph had been furnished was only partially true. It was in fact a vast desert, made up of sand and stones, all the same pale, colorless hue to his eyes. This desert was peopled mostly by Bedouins and other nomads, whom Suleiman the Magnificent, an Ottoman ruler, had tried to keep out by building in the sixteenth century the famous wall that encompasses Jerusalem's Old City. The Bedouins were feared by the Ottomans and other Arabs, those who dwelt in the city and the countryside, for their reputation as thieves and murderers. An Arab proverb warned that one should change one's front door if a Bedouin discovered where it was. Indeed, the Bedouins saw harvesting and commerce as menial work that was beneath them, and were proud of their rootless nature and fierce warrior heritage, though in truth they were generally peaceful and respectful when left alone. Their generous hospitality, moreover, was legendary. They might knife one to death as soon as he stepped out of their tent, it was said, but while he was their guest, he would be treated like royalty.

Suleiman had had another reason as well for building the wall, having dreamed that if he did not, he would be devoured by lions. Hence the Lions' Gate in the east wall, which leads to the Via Dolorosa. Since the wall was actually built upon the remains of a much older wall, dating back to the Jews' Second Temple, Jewish leaders looked favorably upon the Sultan's undertaking. Ultimately, only the architect himself would prove to be dissatisfied with the results. In certain places, he had deviated from the ancient pattern. When this was discovered, he was executed. So much for innovation.

What struck Lili and Joseph right away was the heat. It was staggering, suffocating. Their sweat dripped into their stinging eyes. They had never felt such heat, coupled with a heavy humidity, as though they were crossing through a thick cloud of steam. They breathed in gulps. They had arrived in August, right in the middle of the hottest season. By the time they would arrive in Jerusalem, practically fainting, they would be grateful for the hilly city's dry and windy heat, far removed from the oppressive, steamy, still air of Jaffa.

But in Jaffa, as their ship docked, Lili and Joseph gazed mournfully at the landscape. Jaffa was a city, but unlike any they had expected. The buildings were all the same lackluster color of sand, for they were all made out of limestone or cement, none of wood, which was logical since there were barely any trees. Compared to the deep forests of their native Serbia, the smattering of a few olive, eucalyptus, and pine trees could hardly qualify as foliage. The architecture, too, was strange, made up of arches, domes, and high, thin towers.

These latter, they would learn, were minarets, towers attached to mosques, with a balcony encircling the top from which the *muezzin* would call the faithful to prayer. His plaintive cry would spread over the city five times a day, according to the laws of Islam. When his wail would break the stillness before dawn, its effect was eerie, capable of sending shivers up one's spine, so much did it seem to evoke the presence of God. "*Allah-u-akbar*," he would chant, "God is great." Then the Muslims would gather in prayer, en masse, in neat rows on their knees. They would be barefoot, having left their shoes outside to protect the purity of the mosque. In unison, they would bow down, pressing their reverent foreheads against the stone floor, and then rise up again as one, like a wave of flesh and blood in a vast and urgent sea of people. Certainly, there had been Muslims back home, mostly in Croatia, but the Slavic lands were vast, and Joseph and Lili had never seen very many in the area in which they had lived.

From Jaffa, they boarded a train to Jerusalem for a forty-mile ride that would take three and a half hours. There were date palms studding the horizon here and there, but they hardly broke up the monotony of the dirt and sand, a bleached, dull landscape devoid of color. Sand, only sand. Everywhere sand. There was not one blade of grass in sight. They silently mourned the sumptuous fields of green they had left behind. Much time would pass before bleak hills of sand would reveal a solitary figure, covered from head to toe in sheets to preserve himself from a passing sandstorm. Or herself? Though the sex could only be determined by logic: what would a woman be doing all by herself in the middle of nowhere? The lone traveler would either be riding atop of or dragging behind him a beast of burden, a horse or donkey. For the first time in their lives, Lili, Joseph and Mercada set eyes upon a camel. It was as tall as a horse, but misshapen, hunched, with a funny face, and it, too, was the color of sand.

Toward Jerusalem, the horizon became uneven, displaying a hilly landscape bordered by gray dirt and tan and white rocks. Eventually they stopped comparing Palestine to their luxuriant Serbia and saw that indeed there was plant life and vegetation to be found. Here and there they saw small fields of little blue wildflowers and thick, bushy trees of yellow mimosa. There were as well patches of poppy fields whose scarlet petals at close range, they would soon learn, looked crinkly and paper-thin, though when touched felt velvety, but from their far-off view provided splashes of deep red, like drops of blood, amidst the beige and white of the land. As they approached the city, they encountered gnarled olive trees with small, gray-green leaves, fragrant pines and long, thin cypress trees. The summer air was heavy with the scent of jasmine and honeysuckle that somehow managed to survive in the arid heat.

Since the sixteenth century, Palestine had been in the hands of the Ottoman Turks, whose influence was felt not only in the architecture, as Lili and Joseph had been seeing, but also in its government. The governor of Jerusalem, Palestine's capital, was called the *Mutasharif,* and was directly responsible to Constantinople. He was advised, however, by a district council, the *Majlis Idara,* in which Latin Orthodox, Armenians, Protestants and Jews participated. Though Jews in Serbia were no longer persecuted by the end of the nineteenth century, Joseph was amazed to find that here they actually held a voice in government.

Lili and Joseph had decided to take up residence in Jerusalem mainly because that was really the only place they knew about. It was the primary city they had heard referred to in the Bible, which was recited every Sabbath in the synagogue, and in the odd travel account or news story. Jerusalem thus seemed the safest bet, at least to Lili's way of thinking. For Joseph, however, Jerusalem meant much more. He wanted to see the City of Peace, the City of David, the City of God. He wanted to live in the city that had housed the holy spirit, the Ark of the Covenant; he wanted to dwell on the hill King David had made his capital. He wanted to be in the holiest place on earth, in the city of his ancestors, in the metropolis of the Bible. If he had to live in the Holy Land, he wanted it to be in Jerusalem.

He and Lili had met a family on the boat who were from Split, on the coast of Croatia—practically their neighbors, now that they had traveled so far. Salo and Dalida Makedri, they had soon learned, had relatives in Jerusalem. Though these new friends had not been able to assure Lili and Joseph that their family would have room for them, they had reasoned that their relatives would at least be able to steer them toward reputable lodgings. So Lili and Joseph had decided to stick close to the Makedris in the hope that they could help them settle in the city.

Lili and Joseph had not really known what to expect of Jerusalem. How does one imagine the holiest of cities? They would soon learn that

Jerusalem was not merely the city of the Jews, as their bible told them, nor of the Muslims, as the Turks would have it; it was the city of the world. From a mere mountain village in Canaan, the Judean king David had claimed it in 1000 B.C. as the capital of the Israelites, and had named it Jerusalem, or City of Peace. Since then, it had been in the hands of the Babylonians, Persians, Greeks, Egyptians, Romans, Muslims, Crusaders and Tartars. Now it was under the control of the Turks. At its heart was the Old City, separated into Jewish, Muslim, Christian and Armenian quarters, built by the emperor Hadrian in the second century in the style of a typical Roman garrison town. Outside the walls, however, there were the German Quarter, the Greek Colony, the American Colony (where many Swedes had settled), the Hungarian Houses, the Russian Compound, and the Arab Abu Tor quarter. There was the Austrian Hospice, and the St. Louis Hospital built by the French, as well as the English, German, Italian and Rothschild hospitals that flanked a main artery called *Hanevi'im*, or Prophets, Street. There was an Arab school for girls, *Talita Kumi*, built by Germans, and the Syrian Orphanage, built by German Protestants but named for orphans of the massacres of Christians in Syria. Nearly every religion, tribe and nation had left its mark on Jerusalem.

What interested Joseph and Lili most, however, were the myriad Jewish settlements. There was Mishkenot Sha'ananim, Yemin Moshe, Nahalat Shiva, Mea Shearim, Mahane Yehuda... By the year 1903, there were about sixty separate Jewish quarters in Jerusalem alone, and seventy synagogues. So many Jews in one place, so many of their brethren! In effect, though Muslims had previously been the majority, by the turn of the century, the population of Jerusalem was estimated at forty-five thousand, including close to eight and a half thousand Christians, a similar number of Muslims, and approximately twenty-eight thousand Jews. (Though estimates vary; Ottoman census figures were often for districts rather than cities; many avoided the census to avoid taxes and military conscription, and nomadic and foreign citizens weren't included.) Half of these Jews were Ashkenazim and half Sephardim (into which category were included the Arabic Jews). Apart from their different languages, these two groups possessed quite distinct customs, traditions, clothing, and cuisines. They lived in separate quarters of the city, worshipped at different synagogues, and buried their dead in different cemeteries. In previous centuries, in fact, it had been a scandal to intermarry between the two cultures. To this day Ashkenazim and Sephardim still build separate synagogues, and to a certain degree follow different religious laws.

Once arrived at Jerusalem station, Joseph and Lili, with Mercada in tow, followed the Makedri family into a carriage, though Joseph would have preferred to walk, fearing for every expenditure. They entered through the Jaffa Gate. To their left was a minaret and two windmills; to their right, the British Ophthalmic Hospital. They passed bakeries and banks, post offices and slaughterhouses, convents, churches, mosques and synagogues. There were workshops for woodwork and embroidery, catering to tourists, and many institutes of learning, from religious establishments like *yeshivot* for the Jews or Muslim *madrasas* to secular institutions like the American School of Oriental Research.

The buildings were all made from the same material, whitish-tannish-grayish and sometimes pinkish stone, a form of limestone that has come to be known as Jerusalem stone. To this day there is a code prohibiting construction with any other material. It was cut in neat rectangles with rough, pocked and craggy surfaces, at times interspersed with clinging ivy. Almost all the buildings had balconies, and long, thin windows, sometimes arched, with shutters. Official structures were surrounded by iron fences in fancy, curly arabesque designs like clovers and fleur-de-lys. The wall encompassing the Old City was formed like a medieval fortress so that on top there was a crown of rectangular spires, with tufts of grass growing amidst the stones closest to the bottom of the wall.

For such a renowned city as Jerusalem, however, Lili noted, it was not as fine as even Belgrade; though it had paved streets, it also had dirt roads and stony fields that passed for infrastructure. Jerusalem was moreover quite dirty and smelly, for there were no sanitary arrangements in the

Old City and few in the new, which accounted for the epidemic that had prevented them from arriving a year earlier. The sultans had not been very rigorous with Jerusalem's upkeep. For centuries, the region had been quite impoverished, so much so that even Napoleon had not bothered to conquer Jerusalem, since there was little industry or crafts produced there, and no fertile rural areas surrounded it.

As for its inhabitants, they were people from a diversity of countries and continents, either living, visiting, or temporarily situated in Jerusalem in some consular capacity. Despite the myriad religious sects, the majority were Arabs, Christians, and Jews. The Arabs, contrary to Joseph's fears, were far from murderous. They were generally well-to-do, a kind of local nobility, having derived their power over time from farming taxes and controlling religious functions. Though the Turks had reigned over Palestine for four hundred years, very few actually lived there, and Turkish did not replace Arabic as the official language. There were also many influential Christian Arabs, and as for Christian Europeans, they were often attached to a church or charitable organization. The Jews, finally, were the poorest and lowliest of them all, made up of craftsmen and small, struggling businessmen, as well as religious scholars in institutions supported by overseas philanthropists.

Whenever disputes arose they were normally between different sects of the same religion: between secular and religious Jews over the opening of a girls' school; between the Ashkenazim and Sephardim over economic or political power vis-a-vis foreign aid or local government; among Sephardim themselves against attempts by sub-communities to break away from the authority of the chief rabbi, the *Hakham Bashi* (*Rishon le-Zion* in Hebrew), legally empowered by the pasha of Jerusalem to represent the Jews; or among Franciscans, Latin Catholics and Protestants, to name a few, disturbed by another sect's missionary proselytizing. Blood had even been spilt between Egyptian Copts and Latin Catholics over rights to the Church of the Holy Sepulcher, to the point that it had to be patrolled by Turkish soldiers. In general, however, every group lived in its own separate enclave, and in peace. Even in the case of a few Jewish families who, due to the overcrowding in the Jewish areas, rented houses in Muslim neighborhoods, they lived side-by-side with their Islamic brethren for the most part uneventfully.

Only in the Christian quarter did Jews run the risk of violence, especially near the Church of the Holy Sepulcher, where they had suffered some beatings and stone-throwing. In the past, pagan Rome's defeat of the Jews was brought on by political rather than religious reasons, after the Jews had rebelled against Roman leadership. Otherwise, the polytheistic Romans generally left them to worship as they pleased. With Christian rule of the Holy Land, which began in the fourth century, came a singling out of the Jews, referred to as "savages." Their legal and religious rights were either curtailed or abolished: they were forbidden to bear arms and were excluded from the teaching profession and from city councils. Synagogues were reclaimed as churches or were simply burned down, while the construction of new ones was prohibited. Things came to a head with the emperor Justinian in 527, who repealed Judaism's label as a legitimate religion, leading to an increased severity in attacks against Jews, including forced baptism.

So when the Islamic Arabs invaded the Holy Land in the seventh century, it was not surprising that the Jews viewed the overthrow of their Christian rulers with joy. Indeed, the Muslims appeared to be, relatively speaking, benign conquerors at first. Having captured Jerusalem in 637, they considered both Jews and Christians as "People of the Book," that is, believers in Allah who had not yet seen the light regarding his prophet Muhammad. (Though elsewhere in Arab lands, religious persecution against non-Muslims, or *dhimmi*, was often entrenched and codified, with Jews and Christians being treated as second-class citizens with little or no legal rights. They usually lived apart in ghettos, were often not allowed to testify against Muslims or even bear witness in court, and could be imprisoned without trial in certain sectors. The history of non-Muslims in Arabia and northern Africa is peppered with sporadic attacks and bloodshed.)

With the advent of the Crusaders in 1096, non-Christians, both Muslims and Jews, were again slaughtered in the name of God. Jews were even burned in their synagogues. (The Soldiers of Christ furthermore ousted the Greek and Arabic-speaking Christians from Jerusalem, whom they deemed too swarthy for Jesus's kingdom.) Though Jerusalem itself was at times no more of a haven for Jews than elsewhere—in 1839 the British consul reported that "the Jew in Jerusalem is not estimated in value much above a dog"—nonetheless, by the year 1903 all the myriad religious groups lived separately and yet together within the same walls, and in relative peace. At times like these, Jews, Christians and Muslims alike recalled that Jerusalem was a city that all held holy.

Central to the hallowed perception of the city was the Temple Mount. It was a sacred place to all three major religions, for the Dome of the Rock, a beautiful octagonal shrine, was built in 685 over the stone Ibrahim had purportedly intended for the sacrifice of Ishmael and was believed to be the spot from which Muhammad ascended to heaven on his winged steed, Al Burak, escorted by the angel Gabriel. Here would be the place from which, on the morning of the Resurrection, the angel Israfil would blow the last trumpet.

The mosque was also called the Sachra, and a beautiful legend is told about it. Once, when it was merely a threshing floor, it was owned by two brothers, one married, the other not. One August night, after the harvest had been threshed and divided, each brother went to sleep beside his pile, as was the custom. During the night, the married brother lay awake worrying about his unmarried sibling.

"I am rich in grain," he mused, "but also in family. I have a wife and children, whereas my poor brother is alone." So he took a portion of his grain and added it to his brother's and then, contented, went back to sleep.

Soon after, the single brother awoke, tormented by what he saw as the unjust apportioning of the grain.

"I received the same amount of grain as my brother, yet he has the mouths of his wife and children to feed, whereas I am only one person."

Thus, he took a portion of his harvest and placed it on his brother's pile and so, relieved, fell back to sleep. In the morning, when the brothers awoke and saw with surprise that their piles were exactly the same as they had been before, they realized what the other had done, and threw their arms about one another. And God saw and recorded the deed of the night and declared the Sachra the place of prayer for all the world.

Leading to the Dome of the Rock, next to which lay the Al-Aqsa Mosque (later to be embellished with marble pillars as a gift from Mussolini), was the Via Dolorosa, the street down which Jesus had walked for the last time, bearing his cross. It was a long, narrow alleyway between high stone walls connected overhead by stone arches every few meters or so. The Church of the Holy Sepulcher, in which Christians of all denominations worshipped, had been built by the Crusaders in the eleventh century over the remains of the original Anastasis Church, constructed in 335 by the first Christian Emperor, Constantine, over the site of Christ's Passion.

But what made it the most revered spot in all of Judaism was a building no longer standing, and all that was left of it was one old, stone wall. It was called the Western Wall, because it had been the western wall of the second Jewish Temple, the first having been destroyed in 586 B.C. by the Babylonians. Herod, Roman administrator of Jerusalem and part-Jewish himself, had ordered its reconstruction in 20 B.C. The temple was finally finished in 64 A.D., sixty-eight years after Herod's death. It would be destroyed, however, only six years later in the year 70, never again to be rebuilt. When Jews were banned by the Roman and then Holy Roman Empires from visiting Jerusalem, they would hold their prayers on the Mount of Olives outside the city just so they could gaze down at the ruins of the hallowed edifice.

The destruction of Jerusalem's Temple had been a major crisis in Judaism, radically altering the practice of the faith thereafter and indeed changing the face of Jerusalem and the name of Judea forever. Up until then, two groups, the Sadducees and the Pharisees, had been competing for control over their Jewish brethren. The Sadducees, hailing from

Jerusalem aristocrats, coined their name from King David's high priest Zadok, and they ruled over the Temple priesthood. The Pharisees, meaning "Separatists," came mainly from the lower classes of smaller Judean villages. Though the Sadducees were influenced politically and socially by their Hellenic conquerors, they were religious purists, maintaining that the Torah (the Scriptures) was the sole legitimate source of Jewish law, and was to be adhered to literally. By contrast, the Pharisees shunned Roman influence in their daily lives yet ascribed to a more liberal view of Jewish law, holding that the Torah called for scholarly interpretation. The battle for power between the two groups was decided with the loss of the Temple, as a result of which the Sadducean priests, whose role was almost exclusively to offer ritual sacrifice in the temple, became obsolete.

Thus, the Torah scholars, or rabbis, eventually took over the leadership of the Jewish community, a coup that truly revolutionized the religion: Scripture now replaced Temple as the focal point of Judaism, and prayer took the place of animal sacrifice as the means of worship. Moreover, the wreck of the Temple would become a mainstay of daily prayers, and its memory was to become incorporated into many moments of a Jew's life. During the wedding ceremony, for instance, the groom crushes a wine glass with his foot and thereby mimics the destruction. As a further reminder, no house in Jerusalem was ever entirely finished; one stone at least would be left out. Strangely, the purported date of the Temple's annihilation, the ninth of the Hebrew month Av, was the very date imputed to the destruction of the first Temple, built by King Solomon. The ninth of Av, therefore, held a doubly nefarious significance and has been thereafter commemorated as a day of fasting. Eerily enough, even to this day, some bather almost invariably drowns in the sea off the coast of Israel each year on the ninth of Av.

The effect of the Temple's ruin was more than religious, however. Having previously stood as the symbol of Judaism, its defeat mirrored that of the Jewish nation. The fall of the Temple was the decisive element in the capitulation of the Jews to their powerful Roman enemy. They were driven out of Jerusalem, sold into slavery or simply murdered. The historian Josephus reported that one million died (though this number should be taken with a grain of salt, as he was later considered an unreliable narrator). Their enemies in other lands saw the Jewish defeat as punishment for an arrogant people who called themselves the Chosen Ones. The notion of the Jews as "homeless" began to take root, presaging the Wandering Jew stereotype that would develop later. Finally, Jerusalem itself, having been severely damaged by the Roman forces, was rebuilt by Hadrian Roman-style and was renamed Aelia Capitolina, while Judea was renamed, as previously noted, "Palestina" to mock the Jews and honor the Philistines whom the Israelites had defeated long before in order to possess the land that they had now lost.

Since the year 70, then, centuries and centuries ago, all that was left of a nation's former strength and glory was the western wall of its ancient Temple. This wall was also called the Wailing Wall, in remorse over the loss, though many thought the reference was to the way people prayed there, and Lili now watched the black-coated Hasidim, of Ashkenaz descent, swaying their bodies back and forth, calling out words every now and again in plaintive, mournful tones, almost as if crying, whereas their Sephardic brethren, colorfully clothed, swayed side to side and recited their prayers in a nasal sing-song. She recalled how the Temple had once housed the Ark of the Covenant, which itself had held the tablets containing God's Ten Commandments. The tablets were the closest thing to God this earth had ever beheld, for it was said that God himself had written in his own hand on those tablets. The Covenant, moreover, referred to the pact between the deity and his human creation; it meant that God would not forsake the Jews so long as they would not forsake him. But all had been lost or destroyed, the tablets, the ark, and the Temple, too. All that was left was one wall. One ancient, decrepit wall to remind the faithful how close God had once been.

It was before this wall that Lili finally stood after having entered Jerusalem. The smallest blocks were at the top, growing progressively larger as they moved down. In between the stones, bits of grass and weeds grew in patches, accompanied by sparse flowers. Pigeons and doves flew into the spaces in between. This relic of a destroyed temple was still teeming with life. As Lili touched it, she understood its visceral significance, she beheld the centuries of devotion in its shadow, she felt with a dizzying fear and thrill the very presence of God. And for the first time since they had begun their voyage, Lili finally understood why they had come. Losing consciousness of all around her save the Wall, she leaned her palms and forehead against the cool stone, closed her eyes and, becoming one with her people, abandoned herself to something bigger than them all.

Chapter Three

JOSEPH, LILI AND MERCADA STAYED, together with the family from Split, in the home of the latter's relatives, in a small house in Nahalat Shiva, one of the new Jewish quarters outside the walls of the Old City. They slept on blankets on the floor, for there was barely enough room for the original members. Within a week, however, they had found a room in a cramped building within the Old City. The toilet and water cistern, both located outside, were shared with two other families, one a recent arrival from Morocco and the other from Italy.

Lili quickly learned to dislike the family from Italy, the Pardos, for they were rude and ill-humored. Those from Morocco, however, the Shafibis, were just the opposite, warm and generous, though they struggled to feed their eight children. The second youngest was about Mercada's age, so she had a playmate, and the mothers, Lili and Bilha, became good friends. Bilha was a small woman, her head always covered by the mandatory kerchief. She smelled of spices, of cardamom and cumin, nutmeg and pepper, since a great part of her time consisted in grinding the fresh spices she would buy at the market. Bilha had been cooking back in Morocco since the age of six, the age at which boys began school and girls began to cook. Potatoes were unsheathed by her in seconds, garlic cloves were crushed swiftly and mercilessly under her wide blade, and cinnamon sticks were pulverized in her trusty mortar. She cooked in the ceramic pots with no handles that had been wedding gifts she had dragged with her from her homeland. She would never understand how the women of Palestine could manage with the tin vessels she always saw on sale at the marketplace.

Bilha had married Selim at the age of eleven. He had been eighteen. By twenty-eight, she had become a grandmother and now, at the age of thirty-seven, had five grandchildren. Though the eldest of her offspring had long left home, they would frequently visit with their own brood, filling an already brimming house with even more noise and movement. It was a happy place. Selim, a locksmith, had taken his two eldest sons into the trade with him. He managed to earn a living, but not much else. They could afford only one mattress, on which Selim and Bilha slept, along with the two youngest, while the rest slept on the many oriental rugs brought from Morocco, augmented here and there with ratty but clean cushions.

The North Africans opened up a new world for the three recently displaced Serbs. Selim boasted that he could trace his ancestry back to the Babylonian exile of the Jews in the fifth century B.C. But he had left Morocco because he could no longer live in fear of the next attack or restriction or tax against the Jews and, wishing to protect his family, uprooted them to Jerusalem. Yet Bilha and Selim would often wax nostalgic about their lost country, telling the three newcomers stories of the *mlach*, the Jewish ghetto in their homeland, where the streets were organized according to trades such as the Street of the Spice Merchants or the Street of the Embroiderers. They told Lili and Joseph of the *B'rach*, the town crier, who would walk through the streets announcing happy events such as a birth or a wedding, alerting as to the search for a missing child, or making public requests for charity. They described the home they had left behind, a house plain on the outside so as not to invite jealousy, but inside displaying walls decorated with beautiful blue ceramic. In the middle of the structure was the patio, a garden full of light. It was hard not to compare this account with the sorry shacks in which they all found themselves now, yet the Shafibis had nonetheless gaily decorated theirs with ornately embroidered tablecloths, and rugs and wall hangings in deep burgundies and bright turquoise. Glass amulets resembling blue eyes hung everywhere, to counteract any presence of the Evil Eye, and for luck, metal plates shaped like hands, called *hamsas,* hung from various walls. They had different superstitions, such as not allowing any food out of the house at Sabbath's end, so that the new week would not deny them abundance. And Bilha would never leave a dish uncovered overnight lest the demon Znun spoil it.

But what most impressed Lili and Joseph were the intoxicating scents that would emerge from Bilha's clay pots or be released from the seeds and leaves she would grind in her mortar and pestle. Cinnamon, nutmeg, and turmeric would flavor the rich stews and soups. The food she cooked was very sweet and very spicy at the same time. The Moroccans used a green herb resembling parsley in its form, but this *cusbarah* (what we call cilantro or coriander) had a strong, fresh flavor all its own. They cooked with little pickled flowers—capers—and ate a light, fluffy grain called couscous. And Bilha made jam out of eggplants! Despite their culinary disparity, the two women found some things in common. Bilha also made *Sarma u vinovom lischu,* or stuffed grape leaves, though she did not spice them with paprika, and she also produced a variant of the *baklava* Lili knew and loved from home, a pastry made from paper-thin filo dough with lots of butter and a choice of nuts, over which is poured a syrup of honey, lemon and water. (Lili had also discovered a Turkish merchant offering *kajmak,* the clotted cream that Serbs plopped over pastries.)

As for three-year-old Mercada, she liked to sit in Bilha's "kitchen" for it was strewn with clear jars containing brightly colored foods that she pickled, from green olives to red peppers to orange foods Mercada could not even identify. Clusters of bay leaves hung from the wall, along with red and green spicy little peppers that she had hung to dry. There were bags of lentils and baskets of chickpeas, jars of candied grapefruit peel and watermelon jam.

It was not that in Mercada's own house there was nothing to eat; it was just that Lili had never been enamored of cooking. It bored her.

Furthermore, she was very clumsy at it. Her thumb bore a scar from when she had practically sliced it off once, instead of a carrot, and her right wrist still sported the dark, crescent-shaped mark from when she had spilled boiling soup on herself. At least it had spilled over her and not on Mercada, as the baby had been right next to her! She shuddered to think.

So while there were some fruits and bread available next door, there were none of the artistic creations over which Bilha Shafibi labored. Even when the Passover holiday arrived, Bilha managed to make the festival's drab cuisine into a delectable culinary experience. Passover always fell in the spring, which filled the surrounding trees with purple blossoms while the almond trees were laden with white and pink buds. The poppies were again in bloom, fresh leaves peppered branches, and the whisper of newly born jasmine hung in the night air. The name Passover, or Pesach in Hebrew, denotes the belief that when God rained down his last plague upon the Egyptians, that of the death of the first-born male of every family, the Angel of Death passed over the houses of the Jews. The Seder meal inaugurated the holiday, during which only matzoth, thin, unleavened bread wafers, could be eaten, to commemorate the Hebrews' haste upon escaping slavery in Egypt. According to the Haggadah, which tells the Passover story, when Moses finally managed to get the Pharaoh to let his people go, they took no chances that Ramses would change his mind again, so they didn't even wait for their bread to rise and baked it as it was. In fact, Jews perform a sort of spring cleaning before the holiday to rid their houses of anything containing *hametz*, that is, any vestige of flour or leavening.

At the end of the holiday, after the eighth day, Moroccan Jews traditionally attach another festival, that of the Mimouna. When Joseph and his family entered their neighbors' home to celebrate the Mimouna, they found the table completely covered with plates of sweet foods such as cakes, jams, honey and yogurt. In the middle of the table was placed a green platter with a raw fish to symbolize blessing, abundance and fruitfulness. But the main course was the *muflata*, a pile of yeast-based pancakes fried one on top of the other, and customarily served to the many guests who drop in for the holiday. Each would pull off a pancake and eat it with butter and honey. It was the first taste of *hametz* to be eaten since Passover, and this initiation to the return of yeast was celebrated by Moroccan Jews. The Moroccans of Jerusalem would go from house to house, paying their visits and eating *muflata* while wishing the hosts luck and success. Sometimes these strings of visits would last until the morning, for doors remained open all night. In Morocco, Selim told them, even the Muslims would join in the holiday and pay visit, bringing with them cakes, honey and pots of fresh yogurt.

Thus, their social life fared well, whereas the financial situation of Joseph and Lili was another matter entirely. Bilha herself was a seamstress, and found it rough sailing to make it pay, since she was in keen competition with others, as it was one of the few avenues open to poor and unschooled women to earn a livelihood. From the outset, then, Lili's idea of pursuing her old craft looked dubious. Joseph, too, was having trouble selling his shoes. The Jews were too poor to buy any and contented themselves with old, ragged ones, cheap slippers or simply with bare feet, while the richer Arabs and Europeans could afford to buy better. He managed to do a few repairs now and then, but they were slowly starving. Joseph could not sleep at night; his hunger and anxieties tormented him. Things had never been so bad in Mala Gozic. Lili restrained herself from remarking that it was his fault they had had to leave their homeland in the first place.

"Lili, what will we do?" was his constant lament. "We have a little girl, and we can't feed her. She's going to die! What will we do?"

It took Lili a few weeks to give him an answer. After she had discovered that she could not rely on her sewing to pull her through, she scoured the city to see what others worked at. Her idea was not to copy another's trade, but to see what was lacking. What was there a need for? One day, it came to her.

It was on a Thursday, the day she reserved for shopping at the marketplace, pronounced "shuk" by the Jews or "souk" in Arabic. This was usually the big day for shopping in Jerusalem, as the Muslim Sabbath fell on Friday, the Jewish one on Saturday, and the Christian one on Sunday. Most of the vendors were Muslims, transporting to the city and then selling the produce that they raised on their farms. Therefore, the market was quiet on Friday, as they celebrated their day of rest. If you wanted to buy your food before the Jewish Sabbath, you had to do it before the Muslim Sabbath, and if you were Christian, you probably didn't want to wait till the last minute on Saturday, especially after the Jews and Muslims had snatched up all the freshest fruit and vegetables.

The Shuk was one of the places Mercada hated most. It was hot, dirty and rank, and sometimes, particularly in the beginning, she would vomit on the spot from the stench of the meat hanging outside, slowly rotting before the eyes of the passersby. Worse yet were the carcasses of the chickens and lambs, for they were recognizable, and it was a special horror for the little girl to see them hanging upside down from a hook, with everything seemingly intact but for the skin that she imagined ripped from their bodies as they screamed in torture.

She remembered the first time they had been to the fishmonger's stall. He had pulled a live fish from a small barrel and then flipped the hapless creature onto a wooden board. It flailed about until the fishmonger whacked it on its head with a huge club. He had killed it, right before her eyes. The man then hacked off its tail with one sharp stroke of a cleaver and began shaving off its scales with a wire brush. At that moment, Mercada saw that the fish was still shaking and squirming. It was still alive! She couldn't imagine its agony. The executioner hit it again with the club and it was finally and forever still. He then returned to the wire brush until the fish was stripped clean. Wrapping it in newspaper, he handed the finished product to her mother and with the same hand dripping with blood and ooze, accepted his payment. Mercada had wailed so fiercely that Lili was thereafter forced to place her order quickly, almost in passing, move to another area of the shuk and then return to the fishmonger and pay him in a flash. It was inconvenient for her because she could not pick out the fish she wanted and couldn't supervise its cleaning, but there was no other way. She did not want to traumatize her daughter.

Even when Lili would stay away from the fishmonger and from the butcher sections, for in any event they had little money for such extravagances as meat, the fruit and vegetable areas or those alleys reserved for nuts and spices were not much more tolerable for Mercada. People shouted out their products and prices, trying to scream louder than their competition, while the masses of sweaty humanity pushed, prodded and stepped on the little girl. It was a torment for her, but her mother would never leave Mercada at home, neither with their Moroccan neighbors nor even with her father. Mercada never left Lili's side. Lili relied on no one but herself.

For Lili, however, her impressions of the Shuk were entirely the opposite of her daughter's. Their poverty and hunger only made the vast abundance of the offerings all the more alluring. It was a cornucopia of gastronomic wealth, and seemingly anything could be found there. Mala Gozic had never had a market of such size or variety, and many farmers from the outlying areas would simply bring their wares door-to-door, rather than conglomerate in one fixed place, expecting customers to come to them. No, the Jerusalem shuk was incomparable, and not only in size. It was also a highly esthetic experience, a kaleidoscope of colors, from the red strawberries, like glistening rubies, or the persimmons as flaming orange as setting suns, to the green pastures of spinach leaves and okra and the almost ebony eggplants, all dripping with dew. And the smells! The heady scents wafting in from the spice alleys, a biblical spread of modern-day frankincense and myrrh, from fresh parsley, dill and mint to dried cardamom buds, roasted sesame seeds and cracked peppercorns. Then there was the warm aroma of fresh-baked pita breads and braided loaves of challah, the pungent cheeses, the exotically fragrant guavas and the intoxicating perfume of just-picked citrus fruit, some still attached to bright green leaves.

Perhaps most of all, Lili loved the human factor. The crowds of eager shoppers, jostling one another to find the freshest produce and the best buys. The elderly women dragging along their shopping bags, stuffed with grapes and olives, or the young mothers with children tagging along, whose petulant whining they checked by filling their little mouths with pistachio nuts or dried dates. But the vendors, now there was a performance. One shouting louder than the next, making their pitch rhyme or delivering it in song, they beckoned to their public *en masse* or by singling out one person at a time. "You, lady, with the little red-headed kid." "You, sir, with the newspaper under your arm." They played as well to one's vanity, addressing old women as young girls, and young girls as beauties, wrinkles and pimples notwithstanding. Even the male customers succumbed to the lures of "Hey, handsome!" and "You! The Boxer!" All this performed amidst a cacophony of languages—the merchants knew them all. It was a feast of sounds, smells, and earthly delights.

One day, in this strange and miraculous milieu, Lili, walking carefully upon the uneven cobblestones, passed a merchant selling figs. As she had never seen a fig before, she asked him, with an Arabic phrase she had by now learned, *Shu ada?* "What is this?" He cut one open for her, revealing the pulpy red fruit inside, and gave half to her and half to Mercada. Mercada was by now an alert and willful four-year-old, scrawny and energetic. She was truly her mother's daughter, especially in personality, though in looks she would turn out to be prettier than Lili, if not pretty in an absolute sense. The girl gingerly bit into the fruit, and soon her entire face was smothered in red fig juice. She looked so much like a clown that suddenly a burst of laughter erupted from inside the merchant's stall. Out stepped his pregnant young wife, to marvel at the comical child.

As Lili saw no other toddlers around, she asked the woman if it was her first child, by holding up her index finger on one hand, and pointing to the woman's belly with another, while arching her brows quizzically to indicate a question. The husband, hearing Lili speaking to Mercada in Ladino, demonstrated his linguistic acumen by answering her in passable Ladino. "Yes," he responded. "It's her first." And then, as an afterthought, he marveled, "But how did you know it was her first?"

Lili hesitated, then made a snap decision.

"Because," she lied, "I'm a midwife."

"A midwife?" said the merchant. "Really? You know how to bring babies?"

"Oh yes," replied Lili. "I've been doing it for years. I learned it from my mother." Lili hadn't even known her mother, who had died in childbirth.

"Well, then," began the merchant, lowering his tone, "can you tell me how many months pregnant she is? I mean, when her belly began to grow, we didn't really notice at first... I mean, my belly grew, too!" he laughed. "You see, I want to know when to expect it."

Her first diagnosis. Her first test, actually. Luckily enough, it was an easy one.

"Well, was she sick at any point during the last few months?"

He considered this for a moment. "Yes, she was very sick to her stomach, about...five months ago."

"And tired? Very tired, even in the morning?"

"Yes, exactly," he answered, surprised.

"Then I would say she's about seven months pregnant. Maybe eight."

"Eight? But look at her! That would mean she's only one month away from having the baby, but she's not nearly big enough." Then a gruesome thought occurred to him. "Do you think the baby's all right, I mean fully formed? Maybe it's too small."

"No, no, the baby's fine, and she's big enough."

"But she's smaller than other pregnant women. Why, my cousin's wife had a baby four months ago, and she was as big as a tent. How do you explain that?"

"Because it's her first." Lili had learned from her own body and then from others' that the first pregnancy often only begets a small stomach since the muscles there are still firm. "You'll see, it will be fine."

"Yes? You're sure?"

"Absolutely. But if you'd like," she added, reeling him in, "I could deliver it for you, just to make sure everything goes all right. I've brought hundreds of babies into this world."

"Oh, would you?" The merchant practically did a pirouette, smacking his palms together. "I would be most grateful! I want to make sure everything goes smoothly."

"Not to worry," Lili assured him. "I'll drop by every now and then to see how she's doing, and when the time comes, I'll take care of everything."

The merchant was so thankful that he gave her a kilo of figs for free. And that was how Lili began her illustrious career as a midwife.

"A midwife?!" Joseph shrieked when she returned home and proudly announced her new profession. "But you're not a midwife! You don't know the first thing about being a midwife!"

She didn't answer him.

"But what if you make a mistake? They'll put us in jail! What will become of Mercada? You're not a midwife!"

"Joseph, Joseph," she cooed, "calm down. There's nothing to it. Babies bring themselves into the world. And don't say I don't know anything about it. I've brought eighteen children into this world. I should think by now I've learned a thing or two. And don't forget how I watched Palomba the midwife, and even helped her once. So don't worry. I'll take care of everything."

And she did. It was touch-and-go for that month, during which they ate little and were threatened with eviction on numerous occasions for the money they owed on the rent. But each time she stopped by to examine her patient, she left with a bag of tomatoes or grapes. Then the moment of truth finally came, and she was awakened just before dawn by the merchant's brother banging frantically on their door. When she arrived, she found that the woman's water had just broken, but her contractions were still spaced wide apart. It was a long day, but when it was over, she had brought a boy into the world.

The news of the birth brought consummate delight to both families, who had been called at the same time as the midwife. They were especially joyous as the baby was a boy. He was quickly washed and then dressed, curiously in girls' clothing. Lili later learned that boys are so highly prized that it is feared they will be harmed by the Evil Eye. As a protection, little amulets are pinned to their swaddling clothes and later hung around their necks, and sometimes the toddlers are allowed to run around unwashed and seemingly untended, that is, are made to appear unattractive so as not to arouse any feelings of envy. What Lili was now witnessing was but another tactic to render the child less appealing, by dressing him as a girl. Girls, evidently, were so undesirable that they were safe from evoking any jealousy.

Thus, the little cross-dresser was passed around to the women who had surrounded the new mother, and then the proud father was called in to hold his new son and accept the accolades of all concerned. He was beaming. Lili herself received many congratulations and blessings for having brought forth the little boy.

She returned home late at night to a frantic Joseph. Women in Jerusalem did not usually venture out alone during the day, much less at night. But when she did arrive home, it was with much fanfare. For among the Arabs, gratitude was expressed less with words than with a show of generosity and hospitality, putting practically everything they owned at one's disposal. Besides the fee they had agreed upon, Lili returned home with a bag each of lentils and almonds, and a plateful of sticky and succulent baklava, sugary and syrupy and smelling divinely of rose water. They could not keep Mercada away from the stuff, of far better quality than any they had ever had in Serbia. It was as if the heavens had thrown them a plateful of ambrosia. As if that were not reward enough, the next day there arrived two heaping crates, one full of oranges, the other laden with eggplants, and a jug of freshly pressed olive oil. The merchant was indeed grateful; they were overwhelmed by his generosity, and Lili wondered if all would pay so lavishly for her services.

But perhaps the greatest gift of all, and the most eloquent and gratifying testimony to Lili's skill, was the request to come visit another pregnant woman, the merchant's wife's cousin, who was due in a month. Or maybe two months.

Chapter Four

FROM THAT MOMENT, Lili slowly picked up more and more patients by word of mouth. She quickly learned Hebrew and Arabic, and soon became the family breadwinner, even when they paid her in product, as many Arab families often owned farms. Eventually Lili's name caught on in the city as well. Soon Jews and Christians began employing her services, and she would return home from consultations bearing a metal pot, a meter or two of fabric, or some soap. Even in difficult deliveries, Lili called upon her memories of everything she had seen done in Mala Gozic, everything she had seen the older women use, and relied also on her own observations and common sense. (She especially counseled her clients to immediately stop breastfeeding if they saw the child wasn't thriving.) All this, along with the hope and faith of her patients, forged a midwife.

One might wonder if there weren't any doctors available at that time—there were—and one might also wonder if there weren't any hospitals then—and there were. But there are always people who are slow to catch on to newfangled advancements, who are reluctant to surf the wave of progress. People like that have been around since the wheel was invented (they preferred to walk), and many Jerusalemites of the early twentieth century would rather have the old standby midwife to a cadre of men in white gowns, suspicious-looking gloves and a table full of very frightening metal instruments. After all, it was a woman's business, wasn't it? They thought better to leave it to the women. This was especially the opinion of the more conservative quarters of Jerusalem, in which the idea of a man, medical diploma or no, having such intimate commerce with a woman not of his immediate family was not only unheard of but was punishable by death. Midwifery was therefore a profession in high demand.

In fact, the sheer ignorance of the time was often what propelled Lili's services to be requested. This was the case involving a woman who couldn't understand why she was getting so fat, until Lili apprised her that her obesity was in fact pregnancy.

"That's impossible, Doña Lili," the young woman protested, using a term of respect.

"And why is that?" she inquired, arching her brows maliciously.

"Because I'm not married."

Lili blinked.

"I've always been told that one must be married before one can have children," the girl explained in all sincerity. "That's what my mother always said."

Again, Lili blinked. "And therefore," she ventured, "you understood that it's impossible to have children until one is wed?"

"Well, yes. That's right, isn't it? That's what my mother always said."

So Lili sat the girl down and exposed the difference between social order and biological imperative. Yes, one *should* marry before having children, but the act of intercourse will produce a child, ring or no ring, rabbi or no rabbi.

"What act of coupling?" This question came from another uninformed, though evidently not uninitiated, patient. She hadn't realized that the act in which she had been engaged was the magic road to reproduction.

"But he said it was just a game!"

"Maybe he didn't know, or maybe he lied." *Either way, he should be whipped,* thought Lili.

In fact, among many Jerusalemites of the time, Lili would learn, especially among those who lived in its outskirts, away from the city, sexual education was often withheld in its entirety. No one ever told them anything. This was not only a result of female oppression; even the men were ignorant. She had discovered from some of her patients that on their wedding nights, the mother of the bride had to insert a piece of cotton in the opening of her daughter's vagina so that the groom would know just which orifice to plunder. Because yes, wives had come to her complaining that they couldn't conceive a child when, after a period of questioning, she discovered that the husband had been penetrating his wife anally in an attempt to procreate. It was like trying to get to Syria from Lebanon by crossing the Straits of Gibraltar, Lili joked to Joseph.

She fondly remembered one mortified country girl in the Greek professor's office, back in Belgrade, who also had discovered that she and her husband had been doing it all wrong. Thinking back to that day, Lili realized how far she had come, from an accursed, childless wretch to the bearer of an army of children. Yes, she had brought into the world hosts of babies, big and small, with tight, curly Ethiopian locks or smooth, pale Polish tresses. It was she who cooled the foreheads of the panting and shrieking mothers, who squeezed their hands and whispered to them, and it was she who wrenched out the little wrinkled, oozing mess, slapped it on its rear to clear its paper-thin, pale butterfly lungs, and heard it breathe on its own for the very first time. It was a miracle, a gift from God to this religion of Life, and she, Lili, was its high priestess.

But her calling was also fraught with great sorrows and defeats. She had attended a young woman, no, a girl really, who brought forth, in sweat, blood and pain, after hours and hours, a beautiful little girl, a perfect creation. But when Lili announced this to the new mother, the young woman wept, and when she stepped outside the room to impart the news to the family, their faces fell. They turned their backs, all of them, husband, brothers, even sisters and mother, and walked away. The husband threatened to take another wife, for up to four wives were permitted to a Muslim husband, though this was seldom practiced since it was too costly for most, and generally outdated. In any case, when Lili came back the next day to check up on the patient, her family had not yet spoken to her, because it was her third daughter and she had still not borne her husband a son. This was not merely the caprice of a misogynistic father but a more or less institutionalized value in a belief-system shared by many of the varied cultures and religions of the area. At the time, for instance, it was common courtesy for two women, upon being introduced to one another, to ask if the other had one boy or two. This was meant to allow the other to proclaim triumphantly that she had more than that, and also to shield her from the humiliation of having to admit to having any girls.

Lili left empty-handed that evening. She was evidently as much to blame as the mother. It was a scenario she would see played over and over again, in Christian, Muslim and Jewish households alike. It galled her. She had been overjoyed to have Mercada. *Quien no tiene hija no tiene amiga,* she had often heard in her youth: Who has no daughter has no friend. How could they show such disrespect to women? How could they show such disrespect to humanity, to God? Wasn't it a woman who bore them, who struggled in agony so that they could walk the face of the earth? Wasn't it a woman who fed them from her very body, who cared for them in their sicknesses, who loved them with a love no crime nor sin could ever wipe away? And what of the mother and sister? How could they turn their backs on her? How could they turn their backs on themselves?

It incensed her especially when she thought of others who suddenly lost their precious, budding child in the middle of the night, as it slipped out in a wave of blood between the mother's legs. Or the poor Tunisian woman of the week before who had waited out the whole nine months' worth of nausea and swollen feet, of fatigue and sore breasts, and of hope and great expectations, only to produce a child who would not cry, whose lungs would not fill with air, whose heart would never beat.

Yet honor, and conversely shame, were all that seemed to matter in the Middle East, more important even than life and death. A girl, sixteen years old, had come to Lili because her husband had been threatening to divorce her if she would not bear him a child (as if she were infertile out of willfulness). Lili made up amulets and prescribed foods and potions for the girl, but nothing seemed to work. Then finally the miracle happened, the girl became pregnant, and her husband came to announce the happy news to the midwife, bringing a bolt of fine cotton fabric as a gift.

But the girl had suffered so much to get to this point that she became wildly superstitious. She would not bathe with the other women in the ritual baths, worried about infection. Similarly, she feared the prodding and poking of an examination and thus refused to see Lili. She took exaggerated care of herself and her baby, which none denied her anyway, and ate enough for a small army, forcing herself to down the food despite her nausea. When she was not eating, she was resting, beaten down by the fatigue. Yet her fears were for naught, for soon she was sporting a sizeable stomach and walking the duck walk, though she had luckily avoided suffering swollen feet. Still, she would not let down her guard and refused to see Lili even though she was fast approaching her "due date," or an approximation of such. She was practically bedridden at the end, for her belly had grown so large that she could hardly bear its weight, and many were predicting a multiple birth.

It was finally almost in her tenth month—with no sign of labor—that her family became concerned and called Lili, despite the mother-to-be's passionate protests. Even when Lili arrived, the girl, in tears, refused to let her examine her, and only her husband's shouts and threats made her acquiesce. Imagine, then, Lili's surprise when she uncovered the girl's belly and found a sack stuffed with old clothes, wound tightly around the patient's midriff. What was truly amazing was that the girl had managed to fool so many people for so long. Pandemonium broke loose when the truth was revealed. The girl had only done it in a misguided attempt to prevent her husband from divorcing her for not bringing him children. But divorce her he did, of course, less from her inability to procreate than from this new humiliation she had thrust upon him. For he was thereafter known as the "Father of Rags," and though he made it clear to all who would listen that his lack of heirs was due to his wife's incapacity, it was nonetheless his own manhood that became the brunt of many jokes for a long while to come.

Another unwelcome aspect of Lili's profession was diagnosing as pregnant an unwed girl. Rather than the cries of joy that accompanied such news for married women, the families of the unfortunate creature, after their worries had been confirmed, would let loose with an avalanche of recriminations, beatings, and sorrow. How did such a thing happen? How could you? Why would you? And now what will we do? But even these queries were eclipsed by the paramount question "Who?" On one such occasion, Lili left just as the parents were getting over their shock and were barraging the girl with their enraged interrogation regarding who was the father. She tried to see her the next day but was barred from doing so. Undaunted, Lili came the day after, hoping that the family had softened a bit. After all, what was done was done.

But as she turned the corner onto their street, she saw a great commotion. There was a crowd gathered, and policemen were standing outside. Then two more police stepped out of the doorway, holding the eldest brother in their grip.

"What's happened?" Lili asked. But no one around her seemed to know. She elbowed her way through the crowd.

"Let me pass," she called out authoritatively. "I'm the family's midwife. I must get through."

This got her as far as the police holding back the crowd. Then she spied a neighbor, and it was he who finally explained to her what had happened.

"It would appear that her brother has righted the wrong committed against his family's honor."

Lili's breath caught in her throat.

"What? What are you saying?"

"The girl committed a great sin, as you know, Doña Ventura, and brought great shame to her family. The only way to wipe out the shame was to... wipe out the girl. And the man who had done this with her."

This, Lili had heard, was known as an "Honor Killing," and had been around since before Islam itself. The Imams in fact condemned it, yet the practice continued, mostly among the ultra-religious sects. Lili had heard stories about such killings, almost exclusively of women, in which a male family member was considered to have the right to kill his female relative if she had brought shame upon the family. Often, even more barbaric was what was held to be the girl's crime. In one instance, a girl was killed because she had dated without her brother's permission. In another, because the young woman had wanted to marry someone out of her faith. In yet another, a girl who had been raped had herself been accused of having brought the shame upon her family. And one person had related that a brother had actually called upon his village neighbors to come and watch as he killed his sister. The neighbors had cheered him on as he did it.

Lili, then, had now come face to face with an Honor Killing. This time, the girl's eldest brother, Hassan, had sought out as well the boy whom she had named. It turned out to be a friend of his, someone who had many times been invited to the house as an honored guest. Hassan had felt outraged. The friend had even come to the house that very night, but Hassan had been unable to lay a hand on him. A guest in one's home could not be touched. Once he left, however, he was fair game.

So Hassan had waited for his sister's offender the next morning as he emerged from his home, stabbing him sixteen times for the sixteen years of his sister. Her lover bled to death on his own doorstep. Then the brother returned home to do the same to his sister. He did not try to hide his deeds. On the contrary, he wanted them publicized; he wanted it known that his family had been purged of its dishonor. Lili never learned whether this apocalyptically warped version of Romeo and Juliet had been perpetrated with or against the parents' knowledge and consent. Views were mixed on the subject.

She would hear of a similar occurrence two years later, even more shocking than the previous one. In the later account, an elder brother once happened to accompany his sister on her weekly trip into town. She had been making the trip for so long that she was already familiar with many of the carriage passengers, and especially with the driver. When she stepped aboard, her brother noticed with horrified indignation that the driver seemed shockingly familiar with his sister. Upon returning her change, instead of dropping it into her hand, he placed it there, and let his fingers graze hers. The brother said nothing at the time, but accused her later at home in front of their family. The next day, he slit his sister's throat. All because a man's hand had brushed against hers.

Thus, whenever Lili was forced to convey the bad tidings of a pregnancy to the family of an unwed woman, she cringed at the possibilities. She would stop by day after day, ostensibly to keep an eye on her patient. Usually, however, once the identity of the father was known, it was a simple matter of making him do the decent thing. A hefty dowry was collected (for she was, after all, damaged goods, even if the damage had been caused by the groom himself), a marriage was hastily thrown together, and the girl invariably delivered a premature baby of a strapping three or four kilos. In one case, though, press her as they may, her family could not wring from the pregnant woman the name of her cohort in sin. Day after day, Lili would stop by, but still the parents had gotten no response as to the father's identity. Her brothers shunned her, while her own father threatened the forlorn creature with beatings if she would not talk. The parents were overwhelmed and flabbergasted that such a calamity could befall their little girl, whom they had sheltered from male influence of all kinds. How had a suitor managed to slip past them? How had she succeeded in stealing away, when they had never let her alone, not for one second?

On the sixth day when Lili came to see her patient, the situation had changed dramatically. Before, the family had let her be privy to their consternation and their inquisition, whereas on this day they completely shut her out. She was not to come visit Dalia, her ashen-faced father informed Lili, not today nor ever. When the latter inquired as to how Dalia's health and progress could thus be monitored, he responded that surely God would decide the matter. She learned shortly after that Dalia had been sent away to live with relatives, and a few months later, the rest of the family packed up everything and moved away.

Two years passed by before Lili heard of them again. She had been called on to treat a pregnant woman, who claimed to have heard of her through so-and-so. When Lili could not recall the former patient, the woman explained that it wasn't so-and-so she had treated, but rather so-and-so's cousin, Dalia. Lili's eyes lit up but, recalling the shroud of secrecy laid down by the family, she kept her cool.

"Ah, yes, Dalia. I think I remember her. She used to live on Saladin Street, with her family before they moved away."

"Yes, that's her."

"Yes, she was a lovely girl," Lili continued. "A pearl. It's too bad what happened to her."

The girl sucked in her breath. "Horrible. Just horrible."

"It's hard on a family when an unmarried girl falls pregnant," clucked the midwife.

"Well, that's surely the least of it!" countered her patient.

This was an unexpected remark, Lili thought. What could be worse than that?

"How can you say that's the least of it?" she ventured.

With this question, her patient saw that Lili did not know the full story, so she hesitated, and then remained silent.

Lili colored with embarrassment. She was not normally the type to pry into others' business, for she understood and respected the value of privacy.

"Please forgive my questions. I did not realize there was more to it, or I should never have asked. I'm truly sorry."

With that, she reverted back to business and continued her examination in silence. When she was ready to leave, however, the woman touched her shoulder, and she turned.

"Forgive me, Madame Lili, for I feel it is I who have given you offense. I did not at all mean to imply that your questions were impertinent."

Again, Lili blushed. "No, no, let's not mention it. It was only my curiosity, because she had been my patient, and I wondered what had become of her, that's all. But I never meant to pry."

"Oh, I understand. I do. It's just that," the patient lowered her voice to a whisper, "it was such a disgrace, such a scandal."

"Yes," agreed Lili. "I'm sure it was. As I said, to have an unmarried daughter become pregnant..."

She cut her off. "No. That's not the worst part. The worst is..."

Lili practically fainted when she heard the rest. It was an absolute abomination. Throughout her entire walk home, past synagogues, churches and mosques, she wondered how God allowed such obscenities. Her body shuddered at the knowledge, and felt tainted by it, like Adam and Eve. Not one, but both! Where were her parents, who claimed to watch over her all the time? But then, who would even fathom such an atrocity, and from one's own sons! It was like Sodom and Gomorrah, a brother, no, two brothers, against one little sister, so innocent, so vulnerable. Had they tricked her, or persuaded her that it was a normal thing? Or had they forced her, had they thrust themselves upon her in the middle of the night and invaded her, in the room the three had shared for so many years?

Little by little, Lili found herself becoming hardened against men. It was not that she hated them; it was that she no longer entirely trusted them. Even a brother would answer the call of the wild rather than the pleas of humanity. In one case, it was even the father of the girl himself who had abused her, though he denied it. How could he even show his face in synagogue? Men, she gradually came to feel, though strong on the outside, were limp and weak on the inside. They had negligible self-discipline and were little more than brawny children. At heart, they had little concern for others, at least when it conflicted with their own interests. Even a father, she had seen, would think of himself before his children, would grab the biggest piece of meat for himself, would use the warm bath water first. During these ruminations, she would think guiltily of Joseph, who was arguably the kindest specimen of manhood Lili had ever come across.

Yet even he could not wipe out her impressions. Kindness, she had often thought, was all too frequently what one called weakness in order to dress it up and make it acceptable. As her father had said, it was harder to be right than to be kind. Anyway, it all amounted to the same thing: a man, no matter how kind, was just as untrustworthy as any other.

Perhaps there was no greater testimony to this for Lili than an episode that occurred about six years after she had arrived in the Holy Land. On this day, a priest came to call. He was somewhere in his forties, balding, with a mellifluous voice. It was not, evidently, for himself he came, he explained to her, but in the name of someone else, who was too nervous to come. He asked if she would go with him and help the poor afflicted person. So Lili followed the robed gentleman through the winding and decrepit alleys of ancient Jerusalem, over stones thousands of years old. They walked past the elderly Arabic men draped in their long gowns, or *jibirs,* their heads covered with cloths called *kaffiyehs,* who seemingly spent their days sitting outside in cafés smoking their hookah pipes or sipping sweet, dark Turkish coffee in dainty little cups. Past the peddlers dragging their limping carts over the unevenly paved streets, Lili and the priest marched silently until they arrived at a church.

Back in Mala Gozic, Lili had always assumed that there was one sort of Christian, as she had only met those who worshipped in the Greek Orthodox church. Living in Jerusalem had exposed her to the dizzying variety of Christ's followers: Latins (Roman Catholics), Franciscans, Georgians, Armenians, Abyssinians, Jacobites, Syrians, Nestorians, Copts. And though they all shared portions of the famous Church of the Holy Sepulcher, each version had its own church or monastery with its own rituals and its differentiating architecture, from the five onion-shaped towers of the Russian Church of Gethsemane on the slopes of the Mount of Olives, bearing twice-crossed crosses, to the Church of St. Anne in the Old City, built in the 12th century by the Crusaders. The latter had only returned to Christian hands about fifty years earlier, having served as a

Muslim seminary under the Ottoman Turks for almost seven hundred years.

Lili had never been in a church, and she halted a moment at the threshold. Not because she feared that her God, jealous, would strike her dead for visiting his competition. It was that, despite the fact that it was built to house a faith alien to her own, it was still, for someone, a house of God. It was still a temple that people revered. It was that reverence that she held sacred. The structure alone, moreover, inspired awe. It was gargantuan, with a ceiling that stretched upwards towards eternity. Never had she seen a ceiling so high, benches so luxurious, walls so festooned. How blue was the stained glass when the sunlight hit it from behind rather than from the front, as she had seen it until now. At the opposite end of the cool expanse was a pulpit made of cedar wood, and near it were objects of value, chalices, mantles, and maybe hundreds of candles! She was surprised and a bit disapproving that so much money had been squandered on a house of God, who supposedly had no need for material things. Yet she was also impressed. Synagogues were usually rather staid and unimaginative structures, though she wondered if that didn't have more to do with the meager finances of the congregations in which she had worshipped.

After taking it all in, she noticed that the priest now stood next to a figure seated on the first row of benches. Lili approached, and saw it was a quaking and swollen-eyed young woman, still in her teens or perhaps her early twenties, and lovely, with long hair the color of cinnamon. Lili needed only a second's glance to make her diagnosis: pregnant and unwed. Nevertheless, she waited politely while the man in robes took her aside and delicately explained, in a hushed voice, the young woman's ill-fated condition.

When he was done, Lili told him that she would check on the girl once a month, and would need to know where the girl lived, unless she preferred to visit Lili at her own home. Some girls did, she told the priest, in order to maintain the secrecy, although sooner or later there was no hiding it.

The priest blushed and cast down his eyes. Lili felt for him, a pure soul unused to the rough and dirty edges of real life, trying to be of aid to those who had fallen.

"She's still so young," he began in a halting manner, "and she's a good girl who's made an error, and she comes from a good family, a well-respected family..."

Lili nodded in sympathy.

"She will be eternally disgraced once it is found out, they all will be disgraced..."

"Yes, yes," she sadly agreed. In truth, though, she did not see the point of dwelling on such misery. Time would heal even this, and people would eventually forget, more or less. It was best to move on.

"She could never marry... And money... money is no object..."

Lili suddenly eyed him warily. What did money have to do with it?

"Yes, sir," she allowed, "but the miracle of creation visits the rich and poor alike."

He let out a long sigh, but his eyes flashed angrily at her. Why was this woman toying with him?

"Madame Lili," he began again, his face grim. "It seems to me that the only solution, though it may be a sad and painful one, is the one that will limit the damage already done!"

Lili's face colored. She finally understood. He was asking her to abort the child.

For a woman who had been so desperate to have a baby, just one baby, as to have gone through childbirth eighteen times, such a request was unspeakable. For a woman who had dedicated years and years of her life to bringing life into the world, such a request was an obscenity. For a woman who had seen with her own eyes the torn-up vaginas and bloody sheets of terrified young women who with knives and other sharp instruments had tried to privately do away with their stain, only to do away with their own lives, such a request was nothing less than pure evil.

And it had been suggested by a priest! Maybe in today's day and age we have seen too many exposés on incestuous rabbis and child-molesting priests to understand what such a betrayal might have meant then. In turn-of-the-century Jerusalem, a city holy to three world religions, a servant of God was considered as immaculate and virtuous as the Virgin Mary, almost. He had to be, because God seemed capable of a lot more miracles and punishments than he is now. Or maybe it's simply that God was seen then to be a diligent participant in men's lives, whereas today it seems that he visits only on weekends and holidays.

For Lili to hear a priest, in a house of God, request that she commit such a sacrilege, was a bitter lesson in the treachery of mankind: that one who wore the veneer of sanctity actually hid beneath his robes the underbelly of a serpent. Her eyes seared into his.

"Father, what you're asking is something I will not do."

His breathing grew heavy, and his eyes widened in distress. "Please, madame, I beg of you. In the name of this innocent child—"

"No longer very innocent, unfortunately," she interjected. "I'm sorry. There is nothing I can do." She turned to leave.

He grabbed her arm. He raised his voice.

"No! Please! You... you must!" His eyes were wild, desperate. At a little distance, the young woman began to sob loudly. The scene had reached a feverish pitch, and Lili was taken aback by the priest's emotion, no longer one of sympathetic pity but now intense, violent, immediate. He still clung to her arm, their eyes only a few inches apart, both locked onto the gaze of the other. And in that gaze, in the nearness of those few inches, Lili saw the truth.

"Father..." she began, but her mouth remained open. "Father..." She looked over at the girl, sobbing now uncontrollably, and then looked back again. At the father.

He saw what she saw. He knew what she knew. He released his grip, and his hand fell limp at his side. He, too, now wept. "Please, please..."

But Lili was already closing the sanctuary doors behind her.

Afterwards when she would tell the story, her tone would be one of contempt, of superior disdain for one who had sinned so shamefully, for one who had presented himself as pure, honorable, a keeper of the faith and shepherd to the groping flock, while all along selfishly committing his crimes, abusing the innocent and betraying his God. When Lili would tell the story, her voice was hard and matter of fact. Her lesson was that exteriors are deceiving, that no one should be trusted. After all, she, too, had a daughter.

But at the time it occurred, at the moment she turned her back on the damned, weeping couple, she could not help but feel the eternal sorrow and irrevocable ignominy she knew they would thenceforth bear. And what would become of the child? Forever after, Lili would carry in her heart the weight of having refused to save them. Yes, sometimes it was harder to be right than to be kind.

Chapter Five

LILI BROUGHT MANY BABIES, maybe a hundred, maybe more, into the world. And since the first symptoms of pregnancy often appeared as illness, she was sometimes called upon to diagnose whether a woman was pregnant or just sick. Eventually, people started coming to her regarding ailments of a non-reproductive nature. Little by little she learned how to treat the sick. Sometimes the spice merchants would instruct her on the medicinal properties of certain plants and herbs, or sometimes she would hear a story of how so-and-so had such-and-such symptoms, which a doctor diagnosed as this-and-that, and for which he prescribed X remedy. Pharmacists were particularly helpful, as she thus would help them sell their stock. But mostly, Lili became adept at home-style remedies. She taught women to tie their baby's hand to its body with a rag if it showed signs of becoming a leftie, which was bad luck. She learned that a half tomato, sprinkled with sugar and tied to an open infection would cure it in a few days. She mastered the use of wind cups, which involved a piece of alcohol-drenched cotton set on fire and immediately placed on someone's back, then covered by a glass or cup, in order to heal a respiratory infection. Sometimes, however, it was negative knowledge she possessed, that is, what not to do in a given case, and this often proved just as helpful as positive medicine. Here again, the knowledge was arrived at through others' experiences and sometimes misfortunes. When a baby has a fever, she learned, do not give it a hot bath, or else it will go into fits. So after a while, her midwife practice had expanded to include the care and curing of the sick. She was a full-fledged healer.

Life continued as usual. Lili tended to her patients, both the sick and the well, in the uneventful routine of the everyday. Every now and then, however, an out-of-the-ordinary case would present itself. One afternoon, a man named Kobi had knocked upon the midwife's door and rushed her to a guest house where a young woman, Samucha, was in the throes of labor. Three hours later, a little girl was born. To Lili's surprise, the baby's final appearance did nothing to improve the expression of both father and mother, whose grimness she had attributed to the anxiety and trauma of labor. When Lili had plucked the little thing out and happily announced it was a girl, the mother had burst into anguished tears, while the father bit his lip and turned away. Even after Lili had wiped it off and wrapped it in a cloth, neither would agree to hold the miserable creature, nor even look at it.

Lili's eyes narrowed. She had no patience for the ignorant misogyny of her time.

"You should thank God above that he has given you such a precious gift, a real pearl. What's wrong with a girl? You were a girl like this once," she spat at Samucha. And then, under her breath, "Some people shouldn't be allowed to breed."

"No, Madame Lili, you don't understand," the father sighed. "It's not because it's a girl. It's because..." He looked down at the weeping mother. "It's because we're not married."

He then explained that he and Samucha had been keeping each other company for a while but had not been allowed to marry until her older sisters did. One thing led to another, however, and Samucha became pregnant. As she was from a very strict family, they could not tell her parents even in order to obtain permission to marry. Somehow, they had managed to hide the pregnancy from everyone, for she had had a small belly under wide clothing. Now the baby was born and were it known, the shame would be insurmountable. Samucha's father might even kill her.

"Please, Doña Lili," Samucha suddenly blurted out, "please take the baby! You must know someone who wants a baby! Someone who will take care of it..." She started again to cry.

"Oh yes, oh yes," Kobi cried enthusiastically. "That would be perfect! Everyone would be happy..."

Lili inhaled deeply. It was not the first time she would have to deliver an infant to an orphanage, and it always left her anxious and depressed, not knowing how the child would be cared for, yet knowing that he or she would likely grow up lonely and unloved.

Kobi sensed her reticence.

"Please try, Doña Lili," he pressed her, still avoiding looking at the warm bundle she held in her arms. The child whimpered, as if sensing it was unwanted.

"You would abandon your child, flesh of your flesh, to an orphanage—" Samucha cut her off.

"No! Not an orphanage. A couple. A husband and wife who can't have a baby of their own. You of all people, Doña Lili, you must know a couple like that. You must!"

As it happened, Lili did know of a couple who had tried and tried to have a baby, but the woman would miscarry each time before the end of the third month. They were extremely distraught, and the young woman was constantly being threatened with divorce by her husband's family. Lili wondered if at this point, they might not just be willing to adopt a newborn.

So Lili agreed, though reluctantly so, for she was unsure of such an undertaking. Would the couple be interested? Would they be offended? Shocked? Still, it was worth a try. It was either this or the orphanage for the innocent little girl.

She thus wrapped the infant tightly and made her way over to the village on the outskirts of Jerusalem where she had visited the young Jamileh three times already, each time to confirm what the girl and her husband already knew. Lili had truly pitied her, for Jamileh's mother-in-law was very harsh with her, constantly berating the girl. In the beginning, Lili had learned from her patient, Jamileh's duties had essentially been the same as those she had performed before leaving her own mother's house, only much more so. Beforehand, she had shared such tasks as grinding corn, kneading dough, churning butter and cleaning chickens with her two other sisters. Now it was mostly up to her alone to do all this, for her sisters-in-law were daughters and not daughters-in-law like herself, while the other daughters-in-law had already proven their worth by bearing sons, thus moving up a rung in the hierarchy.

Matters were of course made worse when Jamileh miscarried the first time. She was then treated even more harshly than before, and when she became pregnant the second time, things did not improve much. Because of her first misfortune she was viewed as too delicate to be trusted to bear children with a normal work routine. Thus, though she was spared much of her previous labors, she was treated as far more worthless for her lack of productivity, compounded tenfold when also the second pregnancy proved unsuccessful. She was the black sheep of her new family, and the ignominy of divorce was constantly being held over Jamileh's head. Even her husband Hosni, who appeared to really care for his young wife, felt the pressure that his childlessness wrought upon his honor. After all, a man with no children was even less a man than an *abu banat*, a father of only daughters. Lili recalled that after the third miscarriage, he had revealed to her that he had prayed to Allah for them to keep this baby, even if it had turned out to be a girl.

It was with this in mind that Lili knocked upon their door that afternoon. As luck would have it, it was Hosni who answered it. Though it was very disrespectful to refuse a host's offer to enter his home, Lili quickly explained that it was necessary they speak outside, alone and in private. Hosni glanced at the baby in her arms and closed the door behind him.

On her way home, Lili gaily saluted all those whose paths she crossed, brimming with happiness at how everything had worked out. She replayed over and over in her mind the wide-eyed look of wonder and gratitude that had crept over Hosni's face when he grasped Lili's proposition. A gift from Allah, he called it, and when Lili told him, as she felt she must, that it was a Jewish baby, he did not balk but thanked Jehovah as well. He then bade Lili wait while he went to fetch Jamileh. The young girl's response was far more tame and quiet than his own, as befitted her subdued and humble character. But her silent tears and trembling lips were far more eloquent than the whispered words of gratitude she uttered to the midwife. Lili pressed her own lips together in emotion as she watched the girl hold the even littler girl, wondering which of the two was the more fragile. Yes, Allah/Jehovah had done well that day, and Lili was glad he had let her share some small part in it.

That had been seven years before. Lili, in fact, barely remembered the wiry woman and stocky man who stood before her. Kobi and Samucha Nahmias, they reminded her, and still she drew a blank. Finally, they recounted their story, and it all came back to her. Ah yes, the unmarried couple and the little baby girl. Since then, they told her, they had been wed, having waited out the marriages of Samucha's older sisters. And thank God, Kobi added, they had been blessed with children; they had a boy and a girl. Lili professed her happiness for them and waited to hear the reason for their visit. They both looked uncomfortable and nervous. Kobi avoided Lili's eyes, while Samucha instead stared at her with an urgency that put Lili ill at ease as well. There was a moment of silence in which the man seemed to prepare himself. He glanced at his wife, whose wild eyes urged him on. So he came out with it. Yes, they had been fortunate enough to have more children, but Samucha had never been able to forget about the baby she had been forced to give up. It tortured her, he said.

At this point, Samucha broke in tearfully, her tone desperate.

"I can't sleep anymore, I can't eat," she burst out. "It's tearing me apart, Doña Lili! What we did was a sin. God won't let me rest. He wants me to reclaim my child. I need to have my baby back, my little girl!"

Lili was taken aback by the request.

"But, but Doña Samucha," she began, "take back the little girl?" Lili let out a deep breath. It was one of those rare moments in which she was at a loss for words. She began again.

"Doña Samucha, Don Kobi, how can you think of such a thing?" They began to protest, but she went on. "Yes, yes, I know what it must be like for you to imagine your child out there somewhere, but you must consider well what you are asking. This little girl has been raised by another family, for how many years already?"

"Seven. Seven years, Doña Lili, that I have been missing her, dying for her," Samucha groaned. "No, with all respect, you can't imagine what it's like!"

Lili inhaled deeply again. She thought of Jamileh.

"Please, Doña Samucha, listen to me. The little girl, I gave her to an Arab couple, Muslims. It's a completely different world she lives in now. And this couple, they had no children. They were desperate. You asked me to give the baby away. It was your wish. How can you do this to them?"

"We were young then," Kobi protested. "We had no choice. But now we do. Now we are married. We have other children, her brothers and sisters. She has a right to know them. Please, Doña Lili, we know everything you've done for us, but please take pity on my wife."

"But what about the other couple?" Lili tried again.

Samucha grabbed Lili's hand and gripped it tight. Her eyes were fierce and her mouth became hard.

"Doña Lili," she said, pronouncing her words slowly and with determination, "this is *our* child. We are the girl's parents. I'm her mother. God knows this. In the name of God, give me back my child. You must do this!"

No one spoke for a moment as the weight of her words sunk in. It was true that the child was theirs by blood. But was that enough? Was a parent, a mother, only the one who had given birth to the child? What of the years of raising it, feeding it, teaching it, loving it? But what of the girl? Would she spend her life in ignorance, not knowing who her real parents were? And what if someone divulged that she was adopted? Would she forever wonder why they had abandoned her? Why she had not been wanted? Could Lili make such a decision for her? But what of Hosni and Jamileh? On the other hand, what of Kobi and Samucha? And what of the brother and sister, who would never know their sister? And what of the girl, who would never know she had siblings? For once, Lili was hard pressed to make a decision. She told the couple she would think on it and that they should come to her in three days.

The next day, Lili walked out of Jerusalem to another village and again knocked on the door of Jamileh and Hosni's home. She had maintained contact with them, for Jamileh had become pregnant a few times more, but was fated to miscarry each and every time. It would thus be all the more heartbreaking to have to tear the one child they did have away from them. But Lili felt they had a right to know and told them of the situation. As she expected, their grief was beyond bear. Hosni was outraged and protested frantically, while Jamileh was dumbstruck, as if not comprehending at first, and then sobbed inconsolably. The little girl they had loved and cared for as their own for seven years was now to be wrenched away from them? How could Allah allow such a thing? Lili was even more unsure what indeed God wanted, and she continued to wrestle with the dilemma all the way home and for the rest of the three days.

Finally, she decided. She thought of the despondence of the losing party. But she knew it was harder to be right than to be kind. When Samucha and Kobi returned, Lili agreed she had no choice but to take them to the girl.

"Thank you, Doña Lili," Kobi said. "We knew you would do the right thing."

"Yes," agreed Samucha. "The child is really ours, under God. It was his will that we return for her."

The next morning was bleak and chilly. It was November, and winter would soon be upon them. The tall, thin cedar trees swayed softly in the wind that kicked up the dust of the dirt roads. The two of them, Kobi and

Samucha, stood at a short distance outside the house as Lili walked up and rapped on Hosni's door. The small man with dark eyes and curls appeared, his face ashen, and called to Jamileh. Her eyes were swollen and ringed in red. Lili asked them both to step outside, and to call the little girl. This they did, and soon appeared a spindly seven-year-old, with bright eyes and a long nose. She looked like her mother. Like Samucha. The little girl was dressed in a long caftan, in the style of her village. She looked at her parents expectantly. When Samucha laid eyes on the girl, she gave a little yelp and clasped her hands together in emotion. She and Kobi drew nearer. They would finally have their daughter back! Jamileh and Hosni stared at them with impotent anger. The excitement of the first couple as well as the grief of the second clashed so strongly it almost rang out, and Lili felt the air would explode with the electricity of so many volatile feelings. She herself was edgy, but also resolute. She had come to a decision, and she had a plan.

Lili finally broke the excruciating silence and when she spoke, it was to the little girl.

"Farida," she began gently, "You see these people? What if I told you they were your real parents? What if I told you this woman here was really your mother?"

Farida's expression turned quizzical. She did not quite understand.

"What if I told you," Lili continued, "that your mother wasn't your real mother, that your father wasn't your real father? That they had only adopted you, but that these people here were your real parents?"

The little girl's face now became one of fear.

"And what if I told you," Lili pursued, her voice now rising, "that these people, your real mother and father, want you now? That they want to take you away with them?"

Farida's reaction was swift. She threw her arms around Jamileh and clung to her with so much force that her little knuckles turned white.

"*Y'ama*! Mother! Please! Please don't let them take me! *Y'ama*! I want to stay with you!" She started bawling, repeating over and over the same words. "Please don't let them take me! *Y'ama*! Mother! Mother!"

Lili looked over at Kobi and Samucha. Samucha's face was pale and stricken. She had thrown her hands up to her throat in a gesture of terror. In all the scenarios she had played in her mind, this was one that surprisingly had never dawned on her. She looked up at Jamileh, who was patting the head of the inconsolable little girl while whispering useless words of comfort. Samucha then turned to Lili for help, which she would not receive.

"That," pronounced Lili to the natural mother, "is your answer. She is not your daughter." Farida's sobs punctuated the midwife's words. Lili stared at Samucha and Kobi, a long, hard stare, until the two dropped their eyes to the ground.

She then bent down to Farida.

"Don't worry, Farida," she cooed. "It was only pretend. I was only testing you, to see if you were a good girl who loves her parents." The child, gasping, turned her forlorn face towards Lili, who smiled reassuringly. "And I do see that you are a very good girl, who loves her parents very much." Lili then stood up and, directing her gaze at Jamileh and Hosni, motioned to Farida. "Now you can go inside with your mother and father, your real mother and father. The test is over."

The three figures on the doorstep hesitated, not yet grasping what had just transpired. Lili's commanding stare, however, brought Hosni out of his stupor. In a flash, he hustled his family inside and shut the door.

Lili then turned again to Samucha and Kobi.

"She is their child. She has been their child all her life." Quietly, she repeated, "All her life." Lili paused again, waiting for it to sink in. "God has given you other children," she added softly. "Go home to them. This one no longer belongs to you."

They stared at her silently. They seemed unable to move, unable to react. Finally, Kobi edged his arm gingerly over his wife's bowed shoulder, and slowly they shuffled off. They seemed to have aged years in those few short traumatic minutes. Lili mutely watched their receding backs. Yes, she thought mournfully, it was harder to be right than kind.

Lili saw Samucha again, years later, in the post office. She had three children with her. She offered Lili a quiet greeting and then looked away from the woman who evoked the memory of a loss. As for Jamileh and Hosni, Lili learned that they had moved away shortly after their last encounter, and their family would not divulge their new residence. They had apparently feared that Samucha and Kobi would reconsider and return for Farida, so they packed up their belongings and fled. They would never again risk losing the only child Allah would ever send them. Lili never saw them again.

In the larger world, a scandal erupted concerning a group of Englishmen who had come to Jerusalem and bought up some property ostensibly to build schools and hospitals. The property they bought was on Mount Ophel, a hill to the south of the city, near the Virgin's Fount. It soon became clear, however, that no school or hospital would come of it, and that the Englishmen had instead been excavating there. These supposed archaeologists, however, were very secretive about their work and their findings, and permitted none to visit the site. Rumors thus began to circulate that they were fortune hunters seeking ancient treasure or worse, the Tomb of David or the Ark of the Covenant. The Jews grew worried over this work and convinced Baron Rothschild to furnish money for them to buy the patch of land attached to that of the English, which they then walled up. The English responded by speeding up their operations.

Then came the spring of 1911, and with it the Feast of Nebi Musa, the Prophet Moses, in which thousands of Muslim pilgrims would file into Jerusalem from elsewhere in Palestine and throughout the Middle East. This holiday came into existence during the Ottoman rule and was held at the same time as the Christians celebrated Easter and the Jews Passover. The Ottomans had always disliked the influx of so many heathen pilgrims into the Holy City during this time of year, fearing that it could lead to an overtaking of Jerusalem by Christians and Jews. Therefore, they encouraged the Muslims to fill Jerusalem with their own numbers while paying homage to the prophet Moses. This period of the year, as a result, was bound to become a tense one, in which religious adherents of three major beliefs would fight for access to their holy sites, located unfortunately in close proximity one to the other. Turkish guards were always stationed around the Church of the Holy Sepulcher, for instance, to prevent rioting, even between rival Christian factions.

This particular year, the worries of the Jews regarding the Englishmen's excavations spread to the Muslims, who began to receive reports that the foreigners had been clandestinely excavating at night in the most sacred sanctuary of the Mosque of Omar, the Dome of the Rock, though the mosque was supposedly guarded at night by sheiks and attendants. The people became so worked up that the authorities, fearing trouble, quickly arrested the military guards who had been appointed to watch over the English. Seeing this, the Englishmen themselves promptly boarded a ship at Jaffa and sailed away. Soon after, it was revealed that they had indeed been working within the Dome of the Rock, wearing fezzes to avoid detection, and had even penetrated into the stables of Solomon! No one knew what their intentions had been, but even had it not been theft, they had defiled a holy place and that was enough. More rumors spread as to who they had been working with, whether the Jews had used them as an excuse to buy the contiguous land, whether the fezzes had indeed been a disguise.

Thus, feelings were running high that Friday, the last day of the Feast of Nebi Musa. In the midst of the more than ten thousand faithful who had gathered on the mosque's grounds, a dispute erupted. No one could say later what the dispute had been about, but it had served as a spark that, fed by the tension, ignited those around it and, like a brushfire, quickly spread throughout the throng. People began fleeing the mosque in panic, shouting about a massacre. Businesses quickly closed their doors and families armed and barricaded themselves within their homes. People began shouting that the sheik had been murdered, as well as the governor, though none of this was true. The Christians feared reprisals, as did the Jews, for the fury of the

Muslims, who thought their holy ceremony defiled, was enflamed. The result was sheer pandemonium, as people ran every which way, swept up in the melee, each fearing the other. Lili, as usual, had been out seeing a patient, and Joseph tore his hair out in worry until she returned, panting from having run home amid the fear and chaos.

Luckily, and perhaps miraculously, peace was restored before any blood was shed. The city breathed a sigh of relief, but the relief was uneasy, for these were the first stirrings of hostilities among the disparate tribes of Jerusalem. A year later, in 1912, the first of the anti-Jewish riots, or *me'uraot* as the Jews called them, would detonate among the Arabs, but it would happen in Hebron. It would take more or less a decade for the Holy City itself to see such intrauterine violence. When that happened, all would lay exclusive claim to the holy among holies, and neighbor would pit himself against neighbor in a fight to the death for possession of Jerusalem, City of Peace.

PART II *Mercada*

Chapter Six

WHEN MERCADA WAS TWELVE, Lili apprenticed her to a seamstress. She wanted her daughter to take up the trade she had left behind in Serbia rather than the one she had adopted in Jerusalem. Though she derived far greater satisfaction from the latter, Lili worried for her daughter. A midwife was always the first to be blamed if something went wrong, or if the baby turned out—God forbid—to be a girl. The midwife was awakened in the middle of the night and was told to follow strangers through desolate streets into unknown homes, in an era when most women did not go out alone even during the day. (Some women, she knew, mocked her behind her back, for women were closely guarded, and saw this not as a curtailment of their freedom but as a sign of their value. They therefore considered those who were not cloistered as neglected or disdained by their men.) A further concern was that the midwife often became privy to the family's dirtiest and most deeply hidden secrets, secrets that were at times dangerous. In short, her business was frequently a sad and sordid one, and Lili did not want her daughter to be immersed for the rest of her life in miscarriages, incest, and murder. A seamstress, on the other hand, worked at home, her hands were always clean, and whatever mistakes she made could be fixed.

"Come see how I sew this hem, Mercada."

"*Déjame,*" she would spit back. "Leave me be. Leave me alone with your sewing."

Mercada was bitter regarding the career her mother had chosen for her, for she had seen and learned much about midwifery over the years. She was not interested in sewing. She could not picture herself sitting around all day, quietly stitching in a corner, repairing others' finery like a housemaid. She wanted to be on the move, to have her work change from one patient to the next. She wanted to feel the power of life in her hands. And if she could not pursue the same trade, then she at least wanted to become something like her mother, strong, unfettered, and able to fend for herself.

Mercada wanted this independence more than other children because she was far more constrained than other children. She had been enrolled in the Alliance Israélite School, a French institution. At the time, French was considered the "international" language, that is, the one used for commerce and diplomacy, by government officials and by the educated. But her studies had suffered due to her mother's paranoia for her health. Having lost seventeen children and knowing that Mercada was the last and only one she would ever have, Lili watched over her to the point of obsession. Whenever Mercada had the slightest cough or itchy throat, the tiniest sneeze or runny nose, or whenever Lili would hear of any classmate falling ill, albeit merely with a stomachache, Lili would haul herself over to the school and drag Mercada out of class.

The teachers would protest. It was a crime, they said, to deprive someone as gifted as Mercada of her education. She was more than intelligent; she was sharp and quick-witted. She not only learned well, but she also reasoned well. And she was blessed with a gift for persuasion, winning any and all arguments almost effortlessly. Like a chess master who can envision mentally his opponent's next move, Mercada would already be planning her retort before her interlocutor had even formulated his original objection. Joseph was no match for her, and always gave in to whatever she decided, though often simply because she was his only child, and he would do anything for her anyway. But with Lili, it was another story. The two women were evenly matched, in intellect and in will. No matter how brilliantly Mercada argued, Lili always had an answer for her, and no matter how passionately Mercada pursued an issue, her mother, unswayed, would staunchly stand her ground.

On this issue, however, Joseph agreed with Lili: his daughter was better off at home than cooped up in a disease-infested room with a gaggle of contagion-spreaders. When it got to the point that Mercada was spending more time at home than at school, though, they realized that this situation was unacceptable as well. They did not want their daughter to turn into an ignoramus. Joseph tried giving her lessons, for he was most erudite, but he was not certain that learning about Galileo and Napoleon was sufficient preparation for life, especially for a girl. Also, he found he had little patience and an even lesser degree of discipline concerning his headstrong daughter. He and Lili thus decided to take on a tutor.

David was the youngest child of parents whose own progenitors on both sides had emigrated from Russia, fleeing from a wave of *pogroms*, meaning "devastation," that were campaigns of violence directed against mostly Jews. Sometimes they were set off by charges of blood libel, in which the Jews were accused of ritually killing Christian children in order to obtain blood to make Passover bread. Such slander was particularly ironic in that Judaism has stringent dietary laws to avoid or at least limit the consumption of even the blood of animals; the act of koshering meat is meant to drain it of as much blood as possible. But somehow people got this blood-and-bread business into their heads—a witch's tale probably disseminated by the ruling authority in order to dodge public unrest—and their revenge would spread like the plague, leaving in its wake mangled bodies and burnt villages. Such pogroms, as well as anti-Jewish laws, led waves of Jews to leave Russia. David's grandparents had decided they, too, had had enough of it, so they had packed their bags, gathered up their children, and sought refuge in Palestine. They had joined not their fellow Ashkenazim in Jerusalem, but those pioneers who lived in the farming communes called *kibbutzim*. They were religious, but not deeply so, not to the extent that they would shut out other types of learning, for these people were highly educated and enamored of the socialist ideas that pervaded *kibbutz* life. They spoke not in Yiddish but in Hebrew, which scandalized their Ashkenazi brethren who viewed the language of the Scriptures as too holy for everyday use.

Unlike his grandparents, however, David's parents were less idealistic and less interested in the *kibbutzim*'s egalitarian life of physical labor. For them, there was only the city, and they had managed to settle themselves well into Jerusalem's society. They had made money, not a lot, but enough to promise a decent dowry for their daughters, and to provide their sons with educations. David had studied in one of the finest schools in Palestine, and had become a clerk for the Postal Service, which was quite an accomplishment at the time. Nineteen years old, he was a gentle, bookish youth, slim-built and handsome, with thick lips, heavy, dark, wavy hair and copper-colored eyes. In his spare time, he gave lessons in French and in English, partly to earn extra money, and partly because he simply enjoyed it. This is how Mercada came to know him.

At the age of twelve, Mercada had a whisper of womanhood about her. Her breasts had started forming a year before, and she had already begun menstruating. In the Middle East in 1912, a girl was already apprenticed, married, pregnant or dead by the age of twelve; that is, she was already a woman. Mercada had become acquainted with various sorts of men, but until then, she had never come across anyone like David. Her usual encounters were with her neighbors, the Shuk merchants, the relatives of her mother's patients, or her father's clients. They were almost without exception all immigrants or manual laborers, all poor and uneducated, penniless, toothless or motherless.

David was nothing like any of them. He was the handsomest man she had ever laid eyes on, and he spoke like a gentleman, in a soft voice with words she could not always understand. His fingernails were clean, his clothes fit him, and his shoes had no holes. He smelled of soap, and his hair was always neatly slicked down with pomade. Most importantly, he was never seen without a book under his arm, whether it was to give a lesson, or simply to read during his lunch hour at work. He had read many books, history books, art books, science books. He knew something about everything. If one had a question on philosophy, he would quote from Descartes; if one asked him something about geometry, he would squint his eyes in concentration and explain the principles of Euclid and Archimedes.

This was that era's ideal of a truly accomplished man, a Renaissance man. Today everything and everyone is specialized. One has to be very good at one thing, rather than pretty good at a lot of things. Concentrate all your efforts in one field, and you can find a job, achieve success, maybe even fame. But scatter yourself to the four winds, dabble a little here and a little there, and you're good for nothing. Jack of all trades, that's how they saw it then; master of none, that's how we see it now.

Though David was a fully complete and polished man for his time, able to speak intelligently on almost any subject, he did have one area that might have been called his expertise: poetry. In David's world and in David's time, poetry was like caviar; one might not like it, one might not even want to taste it, but if it were served at a party, one would be impressed. Thus, David's appreciation of centuries' old elegies was yet another feather in his well-wrought cap. His favorites were of course the French poets, the Gallic language being seen as the perfect sonorous vessel for such literary delights, and if you had the inclination and the patience, he would recite poems to you, in the original French, *bien sûr*. Poems by Pierre de Ronsard warning against the swift passage of time and urging the reader to make the most of today—*carpe diem*! Odes by Victor Hugo mourning the loss of his cherished daughter, drowned at sea, or urging the people to embrace liberty, equality and fraternity. And then there were the sonnets by the blasphemous and censored Charles Baudelaire, on the curves of his beloved's body, and the seething venom of his dark soul with which he desires to infuse her. How could a girl resist? Within a month, Mercada had fallen feverishly in love.

Mercada was not considered pretty per se. Nowadays, one might appreciate her lean, wiry body, but in her time, in her part of the world, it was not in fashion. A beautiful woman was plump, curvy, soft. When they said belly dancers, they meant it. Thinness, by contrast, invoked poverty and insufficiency. A stout girl was one who had money to eat.

The one feature that lent Mercada a bit of allure at all were her eyes. Though small like her mother's, they were an uncommon, deep, dark blue, like Joseph's. But as with all beauty, what makes one truly remarkable is that singularity, that original quality that rises from within. Mercada's eyes, then, were genuinely striking foremost because they rarely looked down or away, but instead straight through. It was plain that this was not a mild, shy girl but a direct, determined creature who wanted to see, who wanted to know, and who would not back down. It was in fact very difficult to lie to Mercada, what with that piercing, penetrating gaze. When she looked at one that way, there seemed nowhere to hide. How could a boy resist?

David had long sought in a woman a kindred spirit; he had yearned fervently for someone not merely to look upon but to commune with, to share his thoughts, to understand him. In Mercada, David felt he had finally found someone on his level intellectually, and was more than impressed with her verbal acumen, her powers of persuasion. No matter what opinion he would espouse, she always seemed to have a counterargument. In fact, it seemed to him at times that when they were discussing a certain theme, Mercada would be both listening to his side and simultaneously preparing her own response. And what a response! She was such a master at persuasion that she could convince one that the sky was liquid, and the earth was a figment of one's imagination. No, he thought, Mercada was perhaps strictly speaking not beautiful. But when she opened her mouth, she was breathtaking. To these charms David had fallen prey.

Lili was quick to realize the love that had materialized between the two. Mercada had become completely useless at home, walking about as if in a fog. If Lili asked her to fetch some quince from one of the crates, Mercada would return ten minutes later empty-handed, having completely forgotten the errand. She had also been neglecting her sewing duties, which was actually nothing new, but no matter how much the seamstress reminded her, or her mother scolded her, the sewing remained unfinished. And though her appetite had waned drastically—she would push her food around her plate absent-mindedly until it finally dawned on her that she was not hungry or that she had never really liked potatoes—her cheeks were always flushed, and her eyes sparkled as never before.

Lili knew that look. That was the look one had when a door was suddenly opened onto an unknown world, a world full of adventure, mystery, lust and lyricism. It was the threshold of an affair, the moment of uncertainty and endless possibilities, ruled only by the sovereign Imagination, whose laws were whatever one chose. The beloved lived truly in one's mind, forged by one's fancy, and starred in scenarios that were spun at night in the dark as one gazed up at the ceiling, unable to sleep. The first kiss, the first touch, invented fights leading to impassioned reconciliations: one became the playwright of one's world, god of one's Eden. For once, the universe was just as one pictured it.

Joseph, too, eventually noticed the far-off look and dizzy grin his daughter was of late sporting. He worried for her health. Was she sick? When Lili explained to him the real cause, he worried even more. If David's family found out, how would they react? One was rich, the other was poor. Enough said. And was Mercada keeping herself chaste? Lili didn't worry about the latter; Mercada had seen too many sobbing, unwed girls to let that happen to her. As for the former concern, David evidently shared Joseph's fears, for he took pains to hide his love from his family. He knew they would look down on an immigrant girl like Mercada, from a completely alien world, whose father fixed shoes and whose mother dealt in blood and private regions.

Indeed, they were worlds apart culturally as well. David's family were Ashkenazim and Mercada's were Sephardim. As different peoples are wont to do, the two groups held each other in complete contempt. The Ashkenazim were traditionally strictly religious, sporting broad-brimmed black hats and coats, no matter what the weather, a costume they had not changed since the sixteenth century. They saw the Sephardim as little better than Gypsies, as the Roma were then disparagingly referred to, or else as Arabs, in their dress and their customs, for they did not distinguish between the Sephardim, whose roots were Iberian, and those Jews from North Africa who had adopted the look and sound of their Muslim compatriots.

Furthermore, as the Ashkenazi ideal was to dedicate one's life to the study of the Torah, the Jewish law, they found the Sephardim (who were in fact more materialistic, or practical, as they themselves saw it) lacking in devotion. From the Sephardim's vantage point, however, this dedication to the Bible rendered the Hasidim, as the Ashkenazim were also known, indolent and impoverished. Their daily survival depended on the *Halukah*, money that was sent in from all over the world by Jewish philanthropists who believed it was a *mitzvah*, a divine commandment, to support those who dedicated themselves to the study of the Scriptures. The Sephardim, on the other hand, though largely poor themselves, were at least employed as craftsmen or laborers. Their families, they clucked disapprovingly, would not starve just so they could sit and study. Not that they did not value education; on the contrary, their vision of faith did not prevent them from trying new methods of education, and they were the first to send their children to schools that taught languages and mathematics along with the holy books, and the first to send their children to mixed classes of boys and girls.

David's family, however, was from a new breed of Ashkenazim, a more modern, secular type. Whereas the Sephardim had looked down upon the pious Hasidim as ignorant and cut off from the world, the modern Ashkenazim looked down upon both for the same reason. These new Westerners were more educated and less religious than the other two clans and tended to be wealthier as well. It would truly be a nightmare for David's parents to match their upper-class son to a poor, undereducated immigrant Sephardiah like Mercada, and David knew this. So they kept their affair a secret, which of course only made things more exciting.

Still, Mercada understood why David was hiding their love from his family, and it weighed heavily upon her. Though one part of her rejected the snobbery of class and ethnic distinctions, another part of her could not help but admit its validity, could not help but feel her own inferiority. They lived in squalor; her mother did look and even live like a Gypsy, she thought; and she saw herself as well as not refined enough for David.

To Mercada's exasperation, Lili could not understand this. For example, once Lili received a crateload of guavas as recompense for a delivery. As luck would have it, neither she nor Joseph nor Mercada liked the fruit. In cases such as these, or when they had a surplus, Lili would bring the food to their Moroccan neighbors. This time, though, she suggested to Mercada that they offer the guavas to David's family. Her daughter's reaction was one of pure horror.

"What?" asked Lili in annoyance. "Why do you make such a face? It's only a friendly gesture."

"A friendly gesture?" gasped Mercada. "All of a sudden? Why not just announce the wedding date?"

"What, just because I want to send them some fruit means I'm talking marriage?"

But in truth, what had dismayed Mercada was the vision of hauling a crate of fruit over to David's well-heeled parents, like a greasy merchant at the shuk.

"You can't bring fruit to people like David's parents."

"So they don't eat fruit?" Lili asked sarcastically.

Mercada was aggravated and humiliated. She remained, for once, silent.

"It's not the fruit," Lili surmised. "It's us. It's me and your father, am I correct? That's what you can't bring over to David's parents."

Mercada flushed. "No..."

"Yes, I see. We are not good enough for them." Lili's voice was now shrill. "Their hands are cleaner than ours, their house is fancier than ours..."

"No!" she interrupted, nonplussed.

"So is your friend Rachel's, but you don't mind our mixing with her parents." Rachel's family owned a pharmacy.

"But Rachel's parents are also your friends," Mercada tried to argue. "Isaac always advises you about medicines for your patients. And Dulce is one of your best friends."

"And they are also Sephardim," Lili concluded. "Is that it? David's parents are Ashkenazim. It's not only that they are wealthier than us. Their skin is lighter than ours."

Mercada, abashed, did not deny it. This was indeed how she felt.

"But my beloved daughter, flesh of my flesh, if my house is shabbier than theirs," Lili now softened her voice, "then so is yours. If my skin is darker than theirs, so is yours."

Mercada blinked, and then burst into tears.

"So that's it," Lili whispered, taking her into her arms. "You think they think they are better than us, than you." She held her child's wet face in her hands. "Well, maybe that's true. Maybe they do think they are better than us. But don't tell me that you also think that. Don't tell me I raised a daughter to be so foolish. Mercada, you cannot let other people determine your worth, for how can they measure? Can they read what is in here?" she asked, as she tapped her daughter's head. "Can they feel what is in here?" she continued, laying a hand over her heart. "Women like us, Mercada, are more than what we seem."

She wiped her daughter's cheek.

"I look at my life, and I feel proud of all I have done. And what I am most proud of is you, though I only gave birth to you. I only made the raw dough, and maybe tried to shape it a bit. But you took the yeast and rose, and formed into your own shape, and continued to rise. I only put in the basic ingredients, but you, you've made yourself into the wonder you are now, and still are becoming."

Lili released her daughter from the embrace and held her at arms' length, in order to look her in the eye.

"But oh, Mercada," she exhaled sharply, her grip rough on the girl's slender arms, "if you haven't learned your worth, then I have taught you nothing! The most important thing in the world is to value yourself; without that you are lost. Terrible things can happen in this lifetime. We never know. You can suddenly lose everything, and everyone. One day we will also have to leave you, your father and I." Mercada frowned; Lili went on. "But the one thing no one can ever take from you, unless you let them, is knowing who you are. This is your most precious possession, Mercada. Don't let anyone, not David's family, not anyone, ever make you give that up. Without pride in yourself, you are truly nothing."

To Mercada, however, these words of her mother's were only words. The harangue fell on more or less deaf ears, for the notions of pride, value and self-worth were too abstract for an adolescent girl, whose universe was still so small. Her mother's speech could not really convince her, impeded by Mercada's newfound insecurity. At the time, she could not know that this, her mother's impassioned diatribe, would turn out to be one of the only legacies Lili would ultimately leave her daughter, a legacy solely of words. Perhaps in the final analysis, the words of vanished loved ones, replayed in the theater of our minds, are all one can ever really leave of oneself. We are all words on a remembered page.

Just like Mercada, Jerusalem was growing. Since the Ventura family had arrived, churches had popped up, including the Dormition Abbey near the southern wall. The Muristan market had been housed within the Old City walls, and many new Jewish quarters had been built outside the Old City. The Bezalel Art School had been established, while the Augusta Victoria Hospital, a huge, impressive edifice, opened on Mount Scopus. The city itself was now spread out to about five square miles. Jerusalem had become a real urban hub whose Jewish population had soared to almost seventy thousand, depending on the source.

The world had never seemed brighter for Lili and her family in their new home. They had a roof over their heads and food on their table. Lili was a well-known and largely respected figure in Jerusalem and its outskirts, albeit among the poor and uneducated, and she filled her days doing what she loved: bringing lives into the world. She was happy with her husband, and proud of her daughter, who had grown to become an intelligent and now educated young woman. She saw traits in Mercada that reminded her of herself—her daughter's stubbornness, her quick mind and even quicker tongue, her independent spirit—and traits that showed Lili her daughter was better than she, for she was charming and funny, and as honest as her father. She was practically a perfect creature, thought Lili, a child who rivaled the angels, a pearl, and she thought it only fitting. She deserved such a child. God owed her. He had taken away seventeen of her babies, and then repaid her for her unmerited suffering by giving her Mercada. And then he made her pay for even that by exiling her to Jerusalem, his city, alone and penniless in the desert. But she had survived, she and her family, and she could only bless the Lord for the way things had turned out. She made a mental note to go at the next convenient opportunity to the Western Wall, to get as close as she could to the Almighty, where perhaps he would hear her best, and give him her thanks.

Mercada, too, had never been happier in all her twelve years. Her universe had blown wide open. She had discovered literature and philosophy, explored history and geography, and she had found David. She was wildly in love with him, and he with her. She felt she merely subsisted during the eternal hours spent away from him. Holding hands with him, the intermingling of their hair as they bent over a page, these were moments of such ecstatic beauty that her breathing stopped when she replayed them in her mind during the interminable hours when she could not sleep. How could she even imagine that only a few months later, her world would be ripped apart?

In December of 1912, a great outbreak of cholera was unleashed in Palestine. Where had it come from? From the festering, rotting garbage that moldered in the streets? Had people simply not known enough to wash their food, to wash their hands? Or had it resulted from the water supply in which clothes were washed, children bathed, animals trod, and people drank?

The water supply in the city of Jerusalem had always been a source of trouble. In the frequent years of drought, water had to be brought into the city by carriers in filthy animal-skin bags, to be sold at high prices. In general, though, the water supply depended mainly on cisterns attached to houses in which rainwater was collected and even this water had at times become totally unfit for drinking due to contamination by sewage water. As previously mentioned, sanitary arrangements were almost non-existent in Jerusalem. The pollution of the drinking water had already brought on various epidemics throughout the years, most recently the severe plague of 1864 that claimed hundreds of victims and forced the city to be placed under quarantine for four months.

This time, however, the limited water supply proved to be a positive. While cholera raged in Jaffa, Beersheba, Jericho and Gaza, Jerusalem remained untouched. The individual cisterns, in which was collected the winter rainfall, provided the security from infection that the common water supplies of the rest of the country did not. Jerusalem was thus placed under a sort of reverse quarantine, cordoned off by Turkish soldiers to prevent contaminated outsiders from entering. The Jerusalem-Jaffa railroad ceased operating. People in the outside villages and towns were dying in droves, slowly wasting away, pale, emaciated, consumed, amidst the nausea and the stench. The Jerusalemites heard of this suffering from vague, far-off reports. They were snug and safe in their isolation.

One day, Lili was called upon to visit a sick man in one of the Warsaw Houses, a Jewish quarter built around 1906 outside the walls of the Old City. He was a cousin of someone whose son she had delivered. But when she found the patient, she immediately realized there was little to be done for him. He was in an advanced state of dissipation. The whole house (all two rooms) told her this, for it reeked a foul, acrid mixture of sweat, diarrhea and vomit. A smell of death. Lili nevertheless attempted some remedies, but soon found them all lacking. She was forced to give up, and solemnly announced to the man's relatives that it was hopeless.

The next morning, Lili awoke feeling miserable, weak and nauseated. She tried to ignore it, but within a few hours she had worsened. She then realized, with a frozen horror, that her patient of the evening before had been dying of cholera, and that she had become infected. Cholera is an illness characterized by acute diarrhea and vomiting, contracted by a bacterium in contaminated food or water. It can be mild to severe and even life-threatening, due to dehydration. When cholera patients are treated quickly, they can recover, by administration of plenty of fluids and also antibiotics, the latter which would only be discovered, by accident, by Alexander Fleming in 1928.

How could it be cholera, she asked herself, panic-stricken. Jerusalem was closed to all outsiders, and the epidemic was elsewhere, not here. Somehow, evidently, her patient had managed to have some sort of contact with the outside world and had brought his disease into the city. And she had been the one chosen to tend to him. She cursed her fate, and her own ignorance. How could she not have suspected? How could she have had such confidence in the infallibility of the Turkish guards?

But all this self-reproach was useless, she realized, come too late. Lili understood she would die. She looked up at the concerned faces of her husband and daughter, the two creatures she loved most in the world, and discovered there was something worse than her own death. If she had become contaminated so quickly, then her family was in great danger. She told Joseph she needed to talk to him alone, so he sent Mercada to Bilha's and Selim's next door. She then explained to him as calmly as possible that she had contracted cholera, that she would soon perish, and that it was urgent that he and Mercada leave the house and stay away until she was gone. It was no use calling for a doctor, she assured him, for she was beyond cure and if the Turkish sanitary authorities discovered her illness, she would be taken away to die in a pesthouse.

Joseph's head reeled. It was like a fantastic story. It took him some time to believe the truth, though she repeated it to him again and again.

When he was finally convinced, he sank into a pool of grief and cried like a child next to his supine wife, giving in to his helplessness. Joseph was always the emotional one in the couple, always the first to panic and to wring his hands in fear and surrender. Once again, and for the last time, Lili found it was up to her to muster the strength to take charge and to see to what needed to be done. With her failing breath, she ordered Joseph to take their child and leave her to die in peace, with at least the secure knowledge that her beloved husband and daughter would be spared and would live on.

"I am already lost," she insisted, "but our little Mercada, who came to us after so many years of trials and suffering, no, she cannot be sacrificed to this disease."

"Lili, I can't!"

She aimed her piercing gaze at him. "You know I am right, Joseph."

"But I can't leave you! I can't leave you to die alone!"

"Yes, you can, and you must. You must be strong. Sometimes it's harder to be right than kind."

Joseph wanted to throw himself over the shivering body of his wife, despite her protests, for one last embrace. He instead rose, turned and walked out the door, without looking back. If he looked back, he feared he would not have the courage to do what he must.

He told Mercada of her mother's fate, while the Shafibi brood looked on. They were audible in their shock and sadness, hands slapping foreheads amidst shouts of disbelief, whereas Mercada was silent, and numb. She was only twelve years old. She could not quite grasp the idea that her mother, that pillar of fortitude, could possibly die. Lili had taken care of so many sicknesses, how could this one have slain her? How could someone who had always been so present in Mercada's life, so large and looming, suddenly be gone?

Joseph, too, sat quietly and miserably, already mourning the loss of his best friend. He thought of her as she had always been, strong and brave, pushing him to do his best, comforting him in his insecurity, standing by his side no matter what. And now he thought of her alone, sick and dying, while he stayed away. For the first time in their lives, it was she who was the weak and he the strong, it was she who needed help and he who could offer it to her. And yet to the very end, it was she who was protecting him, caring for him, and he who allowed her to be their strength.

When he opened the door, only a half hour or so had passed and yet the fetid odor of the disease filled their little hovel. Lili was surprised, confused, and then furious. She spat curses and invectives at her meek and normally obedient husband.

"What are you doing here, you stupid fool? Don't you understand a word I say to you? No, don't come near me." She was ashamed of the state she was in, having soiled herself in bed, unable to gather the force to even get out of bed, much less reach the outhouse. But Joseph did not answer her as he sat on the floor near the bed. He tried to take her hand, but she pulled it away with what little strength she had.

"Oh, Joseph, do you think this is a game?" she said, her voice already breathy and faltering. "It's too late for me, I told you. I'm already gone. It's only a matter of a few hours."

"Then those are the last few hours we will ever spend together," he gently responded. "Would you deprive me of that?"

"Please, listen to me," she pleaded. "If you stay here, you'll die. It's as simple as that." She paused again for breath. "Why can't you understand? Save yourself, my sweet Joseph."

He pressed his lips together tightly in muted pain, and focused his eyes, where with the years the blue had lost its luster, upon hers.

"Lili, Lili," he whispered hoarsely, "why should I save myself? I'm nothing without you. Without you, there is no me. I am not a strong man, you know that," he began to sob. "I won't leave you. I want to die with you. I won't let you go without me. Take me with you."

Lili looked down at the cowed figure beside her. This was her Joseph, who had stood by her through all their fears and adversity, who had never abandoned her even after seventeen botched attempts at giving him a child, who had put up with her willful and domineering character, who had watched her pay no heed to him, who perhaps even thought that she had not needed him. He was the only man who had ever touched her, and he was the only man she would ever love.

She was growing weaker and could already feel her spirit seeping out of her.

"Joseph, what about Mercada? You can't abandon her. She needs you."

"No, Lili, Mercada doesn't need me. She needs you. Without you, all is lost."

He would not be convinced. In this moment of crisis, he had found an inner strength and resolution that he had never before felt. He remained at his wife's bedside, his figure stooped over her wan face as he alternated between holding her hand, placing cool compresses on her forehead, and weeping. He stayed by her side all night, looking into the sunset eyes of his lifelong companion, and slowly watched her slip away. Lili died before morning.

But by then, Joseph's body had started to weaken and fail. Or perhaps his spirit had failed. He soon became wracked with the disease. He would thus not bear the sorrow of Lili's death for long. That same day, come the evening, he too was dead.

Chapter Seven

BY THE AGE OF TWELVE, then, Mercada was an orphan, without father or mother. Moreover, she had no grandparents, aunts, uncles, cousins. She was without family completely.

The burial of her parents occurred that same day, according to Jewish tradition, and was financed by the Shafibis, though the couple's burial plots had previously been purchased by Joseph once they had become financially secure. It was a small affair. Perhaps more people would have attended, since Lili had been a revered midwife and had helped many, had it not been for the fears surrounding her and her husband's deaths. For to the uninstructed populace, cholera seemed a miasma that lurked in the air and that could infect anyone in its vicinity. Afterwards, Mercada returned home, determined to sit *shiva,* the seven days of official mourning with its commensurate visits, where she and her parents had lived, no matter the fear of contagion. In truth, she just wanted to go home. She wanted to go back to the place where they all had lived, as if going back to the place would take her back in time, and all would be as before. She sat on the lone bed. The other mattress had been taken out and burned under the authority of the *Chevra Kadisha,* the Burial Society. She looked down at the floor. It was dirty, and small cobwebs had gathered in one corner. Lili had never been a good housekeeper. But now there were no clothes hanging on the lines outside. There were no pots simmering on the burner, no smells of okra or onions lingering about. There were no sounds. No banging of nails into leather, no Joseph stooped over his shoe anvil. No shouts after her to pick up her stockings, no Lili dragging home a basket of oranges from the market or from one of her patients. No Joseph, no Lili. How had it happened so quickly? How could her world have ended so abruptly? She had not been with them when they had died and had not been allowed to see their bodies afterwards, due to the contagious nature of the pestilence. They had vanished from her life without her having been able to say goodbye, to tell them she loved them, that she would miss them.

Someone rapped gently against the rickety door, and then opened it without waiting for an answer. It was David, who knew enough about the disease to know it was not airborne but rather passed on through an infected person's feces or waters that had come into contact with them. He was thus unafraid. Mercada looked at David but did not get up from the bed on which she was sitting. She had no strength. She hadn't cried. Her eyes were simply blank. Her heart was blank. All had been emptied out of her, all that had been her life had been taken away. Her mother, her father. David sat down beside her and took her hand in his. She stared straight ahead, impassive.

"You're not alone, Mercada. I know it seems that way, but you're not. You still have me."

She didn't move, and she didn't answer. In all the tomes of poetry he consumed nightly, in all the odes and sonnets that stirred his soul, nowhere had he felt such potent grief as he heard spoken in Mercada's silence. Never had a Romantic poet penned anything as eloquent or as somber as was written in her vacant gaze. David felt the greatness of her suffering, and the vanity of his verses.

At that moment, he made a decision.

"Come with me, Mercada. Today is the day we tell my parents about the two of us. Today is the day we announce our plans to marry."

Though Mercada was only twelve, it was not uncommon to marry at such a young age at the time. And under any other circumstances, these were words that would have fulfilled all of Mercada's dreams. But today, now, she couldn't bring herself to be moved. She couldn't manage to care. He again took one of her hands, which she had pressed against the sides of her face as if to keep her head from exploding, and pulled her up.

Everyone in David's family stopped what they were doing when they saw him walk in with Mercada. Some knew of her tragedy, while others didn't even know who she was.

"Mother, Father, you remember Mercada Ventura, the daughter of Joseph and Lili?"

"Yes... of course," responded his mother, Elena Moisovitch, taking a few steps back and moving her daughters back as well. But she looked at her son, not at the girl.

"She lost her parents yesterday. Both of them," he explained. Though his mother already knew that, he thought impatiently. He himself had told her.

Instead, it was his eldest sister who turned to Mercada. "We're very sorry. We didn't know."

Mercada could only nod.

"This is the girl to whom you were giving French lessons?" David's father, Rudy, asked him.

"Yes."

There were a few moments of silence then. They were all patently uncomfortable with her presence there, which David ascribed to Mercada being in mourning; one realizes he should say something, but never knows quite what. What David did not fathom was that his family was not used to having people from the lower classes in their home. And she was a Sephardiah yet, practically an Arab, thought his mother. But the crux of their discomfort stemmed primarily from the fact that the girl's parents had died of a deadly disease that had decimated the rest of the country, and they feared she might be carrying the contagion. Despite David's explanations of the illness, his family, like the majority of people at the time, refused to be convinced it could not be contracted merely by the presence of an infected person. *What was David thinking, bringing in a sick stray like that? Didn't he have any consideration for his family?*

David asked if he might speak with his mother and father in private. Their eyebrows arched in surprise, and his father began to see that they had a problem on their hands. Had his foolish son been teaching the girl other things besides French?

"Then perhaps the girl should wait outside," Elena suggested. She was desperate for Mercada to vacate their breathing space. An awkward silence engulfed the room as David opened his mouth to protest. Mercada, whose heart now felt as dry and barren as the desert itself, didn't wait for David's response. She opened the door and stepped outside.

Elena and Rudy Moisovitch waited for their son to speak first.

"Father, Mother," he began, his heart pounding, "you know that I have been Mercada's tutor in French for almost a half a year now." He waited for them to respond, but they didn't. "Well, in that time, I have come to know Mercada very well, and she has come to know me..."

He could not bring his eyes to meet theirs, feeling their disapproval before they even said anything. He found himself at a loss for words. This confusion and cowardice embarrassed him and made him angry. So he tensed his muscles and came out with it.

"We have fallen in love, and we want to marry."

Elena gasped, while Rudy's eyes narrowed. He had anticipated this.

"So, my dear son, are you telling us that you have made her pregnant?"

Now it was David's turn to gasp.

"Oh, my God, Father! How could you even think...? Why, I would never...! I... I love Mercada!"

His mother's eyes flared, but his father sighed in relief. There were no damages. The situation was still salvageable.

Elena spoke first. "Are you mad? You love... her? Her?!"

David flushed. "What do you mean by that, Mother?"

"What do I mean by that? She's... she's ugly! A skinny little nothing!

And a... a peasant! A Gypsy! In the name of God! Her father was a shoemaker, and her mother! The mother ran around with the Arabs, doing... I don't even want to think what!"

"Her mother was a midwife!" David objected. "What's so ignoble about that? Babies have to be born! Socrates' mother was a midwife!"

"You were all born in the hospital, with doctors! Not witches!"

David's father had remained silent, but now he held up his hand.

"That's enough," he said quietly. "This is getting us nowhere. David, your mother and I will discuss this," he lied, for of course their decision was already made; they only needed to find a way to manage their son. He would buy some time. "Tomorrow we will give you our answer. Now send the girl home."

"But Father, she has no home..."

He cut him off. "As long as she is not your wife, this is not her house."

The conversation was over.

David would have spoken more forcefully but he knew he was partly to blame for their hesitation. It was his fault they hadn't known, all these months, about the tenderness that had developed between himself and Mercada, so he knew it was a shock for them. And he had to admit that it was a shock also because of the prejudices his parents held. But they were wrong about Mercada. She had a soul as genteel and worthy as any Bourbon blueblood. After all, wasn't that why he had fallen in love with her? If his parents respected him, then they would know he would only choose someone on his level. And her charm! She was so witty, so eloquent, everyone who knew her fell in love with her. He knew that once his family got to know Mercada, once they could appreciate her strengths and gifts, they would fall in love with her as he had. Besides, hadn't his father said that she is not yet his wife, implying that she soon would be? It was only a matter of calming his mother, which was probably what his father was doing at that very moment. All this he told himself, and Mercada, as he walked her home one last time, over his parents' objections.

Sleeping in an empty house. Sleeping in a house that is empty. It wasn't that the house was empty. That wasn't the problem. It was that the house that had started out full was now empty. There wasn't enough of her to fill it, she thought. She wasn't big enough, not "there" enough. She was vaporous without her father and mother. There was no Mercada without Lili and Joseph.

She hadn't realized death was there, really there, waiting. She remembered how her father would complain of his eyesight not being what it used to be, how her mother disliked how gray she had become. Mercada hadn't understood then, but she understood now. It was death they were talking about. The slow decay of death. They had seen it coming. She hadn't. Now it would be her turn. Now it would be waiting for her. She now realized that what had stood between her and her own mortality was them. Now, she would be next. When would death come for her? She didn't know. But she did know that come for her it would, and there was no one and nothing to stop it. Her days were numbered.

Even this knowledge would have been acceptable if only the pain would stop. How had her mother and father been able to endure losing all those babies before her, when she was bending and breaking under the weight of this, her own loss? She had heard people say that time heals all wounds but now she could not believe that. The pain was too sharp, too huge, present everywhere and unrelenting. If she closed her eyes it did not go away, not even for a second. It stuck to her like glue, and it was crushing her. It was almost physical, practically making her double over. She wanted furiously for it to cease, to leave her in peace.

But then, after some hours, she didn't want that at all. She wanted the pain to stay, to grow; she wanted the gray cloud to cover everything and everyone. Someone—she couldn't recall who—had told her to try and put it behind her, to focus on positive things. But she thought just the opposite. She recalled the verses of a poem by Baudelaire, "*Sois sage, o ma douleur, et tiens-toi plus tranquille...*" "Be good, o my pain, and be quiet..." She understood it now. She understood why he spoke to his pain that way, in that intimate, private, loving way. She did not want to push her sorrow away. She held out her arms to it. Come to me, my darling, she said. Come to me, my only true love. Take me in your arms and smother me in your wicked embrace. I don't fear you, she told it, I desire you. Cover me, erase me, and erase the whole world.

Where were they? Were they hovering in the air, invisible in the ether? Or were they gone, truly gone? Was there a heaven? Were they with God? What God? Was God just a rationalization thought up to comfort mankind? Was there no God just as now there were no Lili and no Joseph?

Why had she been put here anyway, in this world? What for? Why were any of them there, if nothing mattered? Even if God existed, he didn't care about their loves, their dreams, their sufferings, their plans. What use were families, nations, literatures, histories? What was the point of it going on and on, with different actors repeating roles in the same play, when no one would remember any of them, when all their toil and sweat reverted to meaninglessness, drowned in oblivion? Why had her parents suffered and strived, only to disappear? All for what?

The silence was suffocating. The space smothered. It seemed like silence, but it was really filled with sound, the scratching of the crickets, the creaking of the door, the beating of the wind, the pumping of her heart, the words, the words in her head that kept going, that wouldn't stop. She was sick of hearing herself, but it wouldn't stop. And she was sick of looking at things, things that were nothing. A cold burner, chairs that sat alone, milk going sour, a table that waited for no one. Shoes filled by no one.

Morning came but sleep never did. Still, she lay in bed. Why get up? She heard a knock on the door at some point. She recognized the voices of two neighbors but did not get up. They went away. Later, someone else came knocking. No response, so they knocked again. This time it was a woman whose daughter had been one of Lili's patients. After the third try, she called through the door, identifying herself and telling Mercada that she was leaving some figs on the doorstep. That she would stop by later. Still Mercada huddled in bed, silent. Even when the mourner's group came, including the ten men necessary to make a minyan so that the souls of Joseph and Lili could be prayed for, so that someone of authority (only a man) could say the *Kaddish*, the mourners' prayer, they remained outside for fear of the disease.

The Ottoman authorities, however, put an end to the *shiva* before it could begin. Mercada's house was sealed off. As she showed no symptoms, they decided she had not been infected and let her go. But to where?

Mercada stood outside, on the verge of crying, but then ground her teeth together. No use in crying, she thought. Her mother had always taught her that.

"What good is crying?" she would ask. "The problem doesn't go away, and it only wastes time and strength you could be using to solve the problem. Women like us, Mercada, we don't bother with tears. They are for the weak."

She breathed hard. It was time she started acting like the adult she was now forced to become. Where could she go? Her first, thought, as always, was of David. He would help her, she thought. But when she arrived at his house, David's sister coolly informed her that he was not there. She had opened the door just a crack, just enough to push her face through, while Mercada stood on the doorstep. It was raining. Mercada was wet, and her threadbare dress and shawl clung to her. Batya did not ask her in. Mercada hesitated.

"Well... do you know when he'll be back?" It was well after he usually returned home from work.

At that moment, the other sister, Rebecca, appeared.

"Mercada! Hello! She turned angrily to her sister. "Batya! It's raining outside! Why didn't you ask her in already?" With that, the door swung open, and Rebecca pulled Mercada into their home, clucking over how cold her hands were. Rebecca was the eldest and was already married.

Rebecca now sat her guest down on the sofa and ran into the kitchen to make tea. Batya, red-faced, went to help her. Mercada heard heated whispers from the kitchen but could not make out what they were saying. She had thought of waiting for David, but now reconsidered. Perhaps she should leave, she thought.

Suddenly David's mother appeared at the entrance. Saddled with bags, she had obviously been to the market. The smell of fresh parsley and mint filled the doorway.

"Batya, Rebecca, come help me. Ooh, this rain!"

Then she spotted Mercada. She froze for a moment, and at once her eyes ignited with fury.

"What? What are you doing here?" she hissed. Mercada bolted upright.

"Mother..." began Rebecca. But Elena Moisovitch pushed her two daughters aside and stood away from Mercada, keeping her distance.

"How dare you come to my home?" she whispered hoarsely. "With your pestilent cholera! How dare you, you little Gypsy tramp! And worse, you come here looking for my son? You're not worth the heel of his dirty shoe!" Mercada was frozen in her place. Rebecca whined in the background, and even Batya's mouth was open in shock.

Suddenly, David's mother grabbed a broom from the corner and, holding the end of the stick, beat her on the back, forcing her to stumble toward the door. There, she wrenched it open and in one swift movement, pushed her out of her house, still spewing venomous names and insults. The door slammed behind her, and she heard Rebecca wail behind it, catching only a few words, a reference to David, and to herself as an orphan. She remained there for a moment in her confusion. Then she noticed there were people outside. Despite the rain, they had stopped, and they were staring at her. She felt her ears burn with wretchedness. But she did not look down. She pulled her soaking shawl around her shoulders, and trod home.

Mercada maintained herself this way all the way home, erect, with her jaw clenched against the cold, against the onslaught of the rain, against the dishonor, holding tight the sobs that were building up inside her, climbing up her throat. Only when she reached her front door and was confronted with the seal over her door did she recall she was no longer permitted to enter. She was homeless, she realized, and only then succumbed to her humiliation and grief.

She choked on her tears, in a mixture of hatred for David's mother, anger at herself for having been so blind to their disapproval, resentment at David for his misplaced optimism, and above all shame. Elena Moisovitch did not deem her worthy of her son. Was she so wrong? Mercada was now an orphan, a penniless castaway. She had never been pretty. Mercada wailed at her wretchedness.

David, who would never learn of the scene at his home, would later come to tell her his parents' decision regarding their marriage. They could not marry because, according to the old custom, he was the youngest of his siblings and thus had to wait until his elder brothers and sister married first. Only if they gave him their permission to marry before them could he do it. This they would not do. In many quarters, skipping over a sibling to marry off a younger one would have brought shame to the elder, or worse: it might even prevent him or her from thereafter attracting any suitable mate.

"None will give me his permission! None!" David had lamented. "Yosef at least claims loyalty to my parents, but Batya and Simon! They actually said to me that it would bring shame upon them if I were to marry first! But these are modern times, I tried to reason with them. It's 1912!" Hence this still-revered tradition had effectively and legitimately placed their relationship at an impasse, he bemoaned. Secretly, however, David knew the bowing to tradition was just an excuse. He had never heard his parents mention the custom until he had said he wanted to marry Mercada. He now began to see to what extent his family's true contempt played a part in their objection to David's marriage. But he was graceful enough not to mention his conviction to his beloved, for fear of adding offense to her list of woes. The fact was they could not marry. At least not yet.

In the meantime, her fit over and the sobs having abated, Mercada began to think. She began to remember. She began to fight back. No, David's mother was wrong. Mercada was more than fit to be his wife. Didn't she love him with a boundless passion? Wouldn't she give her life for him? Perhaps she was not the most beautiful of girls, but she was certainly one of the brightest. Didn't David prefer someone who mirrored his mind rather than only his face? For beauty only lasts a few short years and then is gone. Wasn't it more important to find a friend, someone to talk to, someone to understand rather than merely a pretty doll? And wasn't Mercada all those things? Suddenly she remembered her mother's words to her when she had first mentioned the gulf between herself and David's world. Don't let them make you lose your pride. Don't allow anyone to convince you that you are not worthy.

"Terrible things can happen in this lifetime" she remembered her say, and a chill ran up her spine. "You can suddenly lose everything, and everyone. One day we will also have to leave you." How had her mother known? "But the one thing no one can ever take from you, unless you let them, is knowing who you are." Was that what she was doing? Was she letting David's mother take away her worth? "This is your most precious possession, Mercada. Without pride in yourself you are truly nothing."

No! she raged. She would not let that woman strip her of this last piece of herself, of the only thing she had left. She felt almost as if it were something her mother had given to her, before she had died. And she knew it was her duty to preserve it, for her mother's sake, and her own.

Elena Moisovitch would get hers. Two years later, her daughter Batya was forced to confess to her parents, when her bulging belly could no longer be hidden beneath skirts and girdles, that she was with child. Rather than kill her, as Elena threatened, they arranged a rapid marriage to the boy who had soiled her. Those with keen eyes who had observed the changes in Batya's physique, and then heard of the speedy union, quickly concluded what had transpired. Four months later, Batya gave birth to a boy named

Michael, whom everyone outside the family jokingly nicknamed Maher. It was an Arab name meaning "skillful" but in Hebrew the word meant "fast."

When Mercada heard the story later, she felt that God had paid Elena back for how she had treated her. She had accused Mercada of being loose, had called her a slut and worse, knowing she had no parents or siblings to defend her, or protect her honor. But her precious Batya, with two parents and brothers to protect her, would commit her sin, and would bring infamy upon Elena Moisovitch.

Mercada now took stock of her situation. She had no money, and she was alone. No, that was not quite true, she realized. She was motherless and fatherless. She had no family. But there was Bilha and Selim, and their family. They could never replace Lili and Joseph, and Mercada would forever be an orphan, but they were kind and generous and had offered aid and shelter numerous times during the past days. They were her last hope.

When she appeared next door at Bilha's home, the sight of the skinny little adolescent girl standing there was enough for Bilha. Over the protests of her husband and other neighbors, who feared the disease still somehow surrounded the girl even though she still showed no symptoms, Bilha ushered Mercada quickly in, while her daughters gathered round, effusive in their sympathy. Mercada had often fantasized just such a scene, herself surrounded by many brothers and sisters, by many embraces, by the din of a large family where everyone spoke at once. How bitter that it should come to pass in this way, she thought.

Mercada would have to share her sleeping space with her friend, Leah, and one other sister. She didn't mind. She was glad for the company after having endured the crushing silence of her empty home. She soon blended into the family, and they truly treated her as one of their own. She helped Bilha and her daughters as best she could with the food preparation, but they were far more skilled than she was since her mother had not known enough herself to impart many useful techniques. Lili had always preferred to be out of the house, and so cooking for her was always a rushed affair, with little science and even less imagination. Consequently, Mercada would only manage to shuck six or seven pea pods by the time her comrades had completed their piles. This was a source of good-hearted teasing among the women, as they wondered aloud how Mercada would find a husband with such poor domestic skills. Even as a seamstress she was barely competent. Three of the sisters, Leah among them, were also apprenticed to Doña Blanca, and would help Mercada with her stitching in the evenings so she could avoid being scolded by the teacher yet again. Mercada felt something like the black sheep of the family, but she could see they didn't mind her clumsiness, and instead made her feel secure and snug, as if she were wrapped in a plush, toasty blanket.

Sabbaths were especially comforting, for as Bilha's main preoccupation was with food, preparations would begin days before, initiated by a trip to the shuk, which Mercada no longer dreaded as she had as a child. There their sacks would be filled with meats—a luxury afforded only on the Sabbath, with each member receiving a tiny portion—as well as vegetables and grains, to be transformed into intoxicating delights under the magical fingers of Bilha and her daughters. The entire house, what little there was of it, underwent a complete upheaval, the floors scrubbed, the carpets taken outside and beaten, the candlesticks polished, while everyone took their weekly bath and donned their Sabbath garb. The married sons would arrive with their wives and children. The daughters, of course, now belonged to their husbands' families, and dutifully appeared at the tables of their in-laws, visiting instead their own parents on weekdays. By the end of the Friday evening meal (for all Jewish holidays begin the eve before), all would be reeling from their sips of Sabbath wine and general gastronomic overindulgence, amidst a chorus of compliments to the small troop of chefs. Only after removing all the plates and washing them were the women able to relax from their long week. The next morning, while the men went to the synagogue, they were free to rest; the remainder of the food would be kept warm on coals, as it was forbidden to do work of any sort on the Sabbath, including cooking or reheating. Bilha and Selim were stricter in their observances than Lili and Joseph had been. Though Mercada's parents had also respected the Sabbath with regard to cooking and working, Lili would often have to run off to attend a birth. *Pikuach nefesh*, the preservation of life, she would intone, trumped all else.

Mercada felt cozy and almost content. She would have stayed forever with the Shafibi family, were it not for a stroke of misfortune for Zipporah, the eldest daughter. It happened one evening after dinner, as her husband was relaxing, cracking walnuts and tossing them into his mouth. He coughed once. Then twice. Suddenly he began to turn red, then purple, while his eyes bulged out with each desperate cough. A nut had lodged in his throat. He was choking. The family flew into hysteria, the children began screaming and crying, while Zipporah banged wildly on his back to open his breathing passage. She sent her eldest child scurrying for help, but by the time any arrived, he was dead. Just like that. After the funeral and the seven days of *Shiva*, Zipporah was forced to move back in with Bilha and Selim. She was now a widow and had to be cared for by others until her eldest son could begin to support them and the eldest daughter could marry and take in her mother and younger siblings.

With another five mouths to feed, Selim was worried about making ends meet. Yet he never once said anything to Mercada, nor did anyone else in the family. They had genuinely adopted her, and it never entered anyone's mind that she should leave. Still, Mercada realized that she had benefited from their generosity long enough and that now in their time of need she should show some generosity of her own. Since she had been apprenticed to Doña Blanca the seamstress, that was where she decided to try her luck. Doña Blanca, out of respect for Lili's memory, agreed to take Mercada in, but only temporarily. The day Mercada packed her bag and announced to the Shafibi family that she was leaving, she was met with a wave of objections and protests. The family were so sincere in their intentions that they even tried to make her feel guilty for abandoning them, as if they were the ones who needed her. It would have been so easy to give in; the Shafibis gave her ample opportunity, and she wanted so much to stay! But as her mother used to say, it was sometimes harder to be right than kind, even to herself. Mercada knew what was right, what she had to do, and promised she would visit often, a promise she kept. She took leave of her benefactors and moved in with Doña Blanca.

Doña Blanca's household was also filled with children, her own and the students she taught, but it was run in a more orderly fashion than Bilha's and Selim's, and Doña Blanca was a stricter mother and teacher than Bilha. Though not unkind, she was not one to forego discipline when she felt it was needed. As she often said, children are wild creatures who need taming, and while it was natural that they love their parents, it was also necessary that they fear and respect them. In fact, her children and charges did both love and fear Doña Blanca, for she was swift with her punishment, but would always explain why she had been forced to castigate the child. Mercada missed the bubbly chaos of the Shafibi household, though she saw Leah and two of her sisters often, as they were also Doña Blanca's students. Nevertheless, since so many non-family members passed in and out every day in the most natural manner, Mercada did not feel too much of an outsider at the seamstress's either. She tried to earn her keep by doing more than her share of domestic chores, of cooking and cleaning, and she would stay up late at night to do extra sewing. But Doña Blanca had been forthright in telling Mercada that she would take her in only for a short while, and though to her credit the seamstress never said a word to remind her of this, the young orphan knew she would eventually have to find a new shelter.

One day, she was returning from an errand on which Doña Blanca had sent her. It was still winter, and the winds were blowing, whipping up dust and sand from everywhere. Mercada had bowed her head and reduced her eyes to slits, while grasping Lili's old shawl tightly around her neck to protect her from the blustering onslaught. Lili's ragged shawl was of inferior quality to her own, for Mercada's late mother had always made sure that her daughter got the best of what they had. "Just like any other mother," she used to say to fend off her daughter's guilty protests.

Now Mercada wore it over her own shawl. It afforded her hardly any more warmth on the outside, but much warmth inside. Lili and Joseph had left so few material possessions behind, she sometimes brooded, that it was almost as if they hadn't existed at all. So Mercada wrapped herself in the tattered souvenirs of her mother and father, wearing around her neck both the shawl and the one piece of jewelry her mother had ever owned, a thin silver necklace Joseph had once given her back in Serbia. Mercada had gotten into the habit of fingering the chain in times of tension or emotion, like a baby with a favorite blanket. Though it was a plain necklace, with no pendant, it might as well have been a locket with a picture of Lili and Joseph inside. For that was who Mercada saw every time she fingered it, just as she would smell her mother in the folds of her old dresses and see her father's fingerprints in the smudges of his yellowed prayer book.

That day, leading with her head against the gusts, like a wounded bull stupidly hurtling into a surprised matador, Mercada literally knocked into her old friend Rachel. Rachel had lived two streets away from her when Mercada had lived with her parents. Those two streets, however, spanned a distance less geographic than economic; though not exactly rich, Rachel's family had never wanted for anything. The families had met through Rachel's father, Isaac, who was a pharmacist. Lili had often called on him to ask his advice regarding treatment and medication, and she had learned much from the man, who respected her will to learn. Through Isaac, Lili met Dulce, his wife, and the two women became good friends, while Mercada and Rachel, who was only two years older, also struck up a lasting friendship. Rachel's family had been at Lili and Joseph's joint funeral, and also had come to their *Shiva*. After that, her mother had regularly deposited food and necessities for the orphaned Mercada, and she and Rachel had visited her several times at Bilha's and then at the seamstress's address.

That was precisely where they were going when they ran into Mercada, and the three reached the door just as a grey sky cracked open only to spit out a thin, dreary rain. Doña Blanca and two of her daughters were home, as well as an apprentice. The seamstress rose from her seat to welcome the guests and instructed Mercada to put a pot of tea on to boil. After a few minutes of polite chitchat, about their respective families and neighborhood gossip, Doña Blanca stood up to leave the three women alone when suddenly a thought occurred to her. She looked at Mercada and then at Rachel and her mother.

"Oh ladies, I'm so embarrassed. I just realized that I have nothing to serve you with your tea." Loud protests then ensued from both sides, the guests swearing that there was no need, Doña Blanca steadfastly insisting.

"Mercada, *querida*," she said, "you won't mind quickly running over to the baker's and bringing us a small bread so that I can show off my grape jam?"

Mercada minded very much, of course. It was cold and now wet out. And these were *her* guests! But she always did whatever her hostess asked of her. And besides that, it was only right that she play a part in honoring her guests. So she quickly scooped up the coins Doña Blanca gave her and was soon out the door.

When she returned, however, something was different. As soon as she walked in, the three women abruptly stopped talking. They had been speaking of her, Mercada could see, and it was something they didn't want her to know about. Her sudden indigence and the indignities it had wrought upon her, as well as her quick wits and strong will, had made her no longer color easily. *Nil mirare*, she had learned from one of David's books. *Show nothing*. Pretending not to notice, she waited to find out what they were hiding, and was soon rewarded: Rachel's mother proposed to Mercada that she come live with them.

Mercada quickly looked down into her lap. So that's what it was. Doña Blanca had asked them to take her off her hands. Bitter though the thought was, she did not really blame the seamstress. Doña Blanca had taken her in, though she had her own children to support. And she had never once made her feel unwelcome. Mercada raised her eyes to meet

Doña Blanca's, wide and hopeful, happy and even proud of this new and better arrangement.

Then she looked at Rachel and her mother. Dulce was smiling warmly, while Rachel could barely remain seated, brimming with excitement, like a pot about to boil over. Dulce gently took hold of Mercada's hand. She hoped Mercada would accept, she said, so that Rachel might once again have a sister, for Rachel alone survived out of the five children Dulce had brought into the world—two had died at childbirth, one had been run over by a carriage, and the last had succumbed to polio. But Dulce also hoped Mercada would accept, she said, so that she could repay the gift of friendship that her mother Lili, God rest her soul, had given her.

Thus Mercada, having just turned thirteen, said goodbye to Doña Blanca and her family, and packed up her belongings for a third time. That very night, she was already sleeping in a new bed, which she shared only with Rachel and not the throngs of children in Doña Blanca's house. The two girls whispered for hours before resigning themselves to sleep. While she drifted off, nervous and happy at the same time, Mercada fingered as usual the silver necklace her mother had left her, never imagining the role a simple chain would one day play in her destiny.

Chapter Eight

ABOUT A YEAR AND A HALF LATER, in the summer of 1914, a
student in Sarajevo assassinated the Austrian Archduke Ferdinand and
his wife. It didn't seem to the Jerusalemites like much at the time, and
the only difference to be felt was a curious pouring in of Germans into
Palestine. Then all of a sudden, Austria-Hungary declared war on Serbia,
while Germany declared war on Russia and France and then invaded
Belgium, whereupon Britain declared war on Germany. It all seemed like
vague posturings to the residents of Jerusalem, so accustomed in their
part of the world to verbal blustering that never went any further. Yet
practically overnight, all the German soldiers, engineers and even students
and tourists—all the men of military age, in short—picked themselves up
and returned to Germany, many after having just arrived. Foreign post
offices were being closed as documents were confiscated, and the various
consulates were also closing, one by one.

At first the Ottomans declared themselves neutral, but soon sided
with Germany and Austria-Hungary against the Allied Forces, mainly
England and Japan, later to be joined by Italy and still later, the United
States. The seaside towns, such as Haifa and Jaffa, were evacuated, and all
their populations flooded into Jerusalem. Food and other necessities, such
as kerosene and rice, quickly became scarce, and as martial law had been
set, a curfew was in force at night. Hotels were turned into hospitals. All

the young men of Palestine were conscripted into the Turkish Army to fight the English who, along with the French, had already wrested from the Ottomans most of North Africa.

This conscription was a sign not only of war but also of the new Turkish regime that came on the heels of the Young Turk Revolution of 1908. Before then, Jews and Christians were treated as inferior subjects, and even the Muslim Arabs were not considered quite on the level of their Ottoman overlords. With the revolution and the revival of the 1876 constitution, however, all were equal Turkish subjects under the law. The downside was that whereas beforehand, Jews and Christians were exempted from military service by payment of a nominal fee, they were now drafted like the rest. Equality was thus a bittersweet pill. Bittersweet also because Jews and Christians were still not trusted by the Turks to carry weapons, and were instead often used as laborers, to build roads and carry provisions. Such menial services notwithstanding, many families feared their sons' conscription more than anything else, and so would hide them in secret attics or send them off in the middle of the night to flee wherever they could. Some ended up in Europe, while others headed for the Arab countries. As a result, men's work in Palestine was now often being taken over by women.

Rachel's family started off relatively well at the outbreak of the war, with only the four of them to support. Though their supplies became drastically limited, no one as yet was starving. People always needed medicines, and soon they were bartering them for food. Unfortunately, this relatively tranquil state of affairs left them with the luxury of focusing on another worry, that is, a different scarcity. What preoccupied Doña Dulce and Don Isaac even more than war itself was men. Due to the conscriptions and the flight of the frightened, practically the only men to be found in Jerusalem were withered sexagenarians and very young boys. Those in between that remained were spared due to a defect, such as the slight limp that preserved Isaac within the bosom of his abode. In truth, one leg was shorter than the other, but only by a tiny fraction, yet Isaac was able to exaggerate the limp when it suited his needs. In any event, one might be led to wonder why the shortage of men would bother Dulce and Isaac during a time of far greater worries. But the subject of men had always been a great worry regarding Rachel.

For Rachel was ugly. Very, very ugly. Even as a small child, where innocent smiles adorned cherubic features, Rachel's face stood out among those of her miniature peers. Her hair color was a wan cross between brown and gray, its texture that of scorched wire. And as if nature had not dealt her enough black cards, most of her front teeth had been knocked out as a result of having fallen from a tree when she was nine years old. As a result, she wore false teeth that never quite fit right. And that sometimes clacked. And caused her to spit a little bit. To clinch it, Rachel had a problem with her eyes; a seeping discharge would form at the corners, so that she was always wiping them. The doctors had never been able to figure out what the problem was, but they assessed that it did not warrant an operation. So Rachel remained toothless, with frizzled hair and pus-filled eyes. The advent of adolescence had only made matters worse: she had grown tall but not shapely, her legs were long but skinny and her feet disproportionately big. Her face and upper back had become punctuated by the rupturing sores of severe acne, for which Isaac could only prescribe cleansing with alcohol and covering with talc. No matter whom she stood next to, Rachel always made the other look ravishing by comparison.

Yet it hadn't always been so. Or rather, it had, but Dulce and Isaac hadn't been aware of it while Rachel was a child. Yes, they had noticed Rachel's zigzag hair, but they had viewed it as wild and cute. Even after she had gotten her false teeth, the funny clicking sound they made was a sound her parents had come to love, and the consequent slight overbite was for them endearing. Unbelievable though it may seem, all of their daughter's physical faults were for her progenitors quite the opposite, and Isaac and Dulce had always genuinely found Rachel to be simply and absolutely adorable.

In fact, Mercada herself had never noticed Rachel's defects until recently. Joseph had still been alive and had affirmed that her friend had always looked that way.

"But how can that be?" Mercada had exclaimed. "How is it that I never noticed?"

"Because you were her friend," Joseph had replied simply. "Because you saw her with eyes of love."

To explain this remark, Joseph had lapsed into a story, something he had often done, for he had loved to tell stories, especially to make a point.

"One of the kings of Persia," he began, "set out to marry, and as he was the king and deserved the very best, chose the most beautiful woman in the land. It therefore came as no surprise when she gave birth to a child of such surpassing splendor that he soon became known throughout the kingdom for his beauty. Of course, being not only a prince but also a veritable god of comeliness, great care was taken with respect to the boy. He slept, for instance, in a bed specially made, with down feathers from the finest geese in Egypt. He wore special clothes made from fabric spun of the smoothest silk in Byzantium and crafted in Rome. Along with all this, he naturally ate exotic delicacies that even the other royal children and heirs of viziers and pashas never tasted. Such victuals were brought to him every day at the grooming school he attended with other noble offspring.

"One day, a woman came from the countryside to the capital looking for work. As luck would have it, that very day the maid in charge of bringing the prince's food had fallen sick, and so she was hired to replace her for the day.

"When she came to take the meal, she asked, 'To whom do I bring this food?'

'To the prince.'

'How will I know which one is the prince?'

'Easy,' the cook answered. 'He is the most beautiful boy you will have ever laid eyes on.'

'Yes,' concurred one of the housemaids and two of the palace guards, 'the fairest boy there.'

Later that afternoon, the king asked the prince how his day had gone.

'Very badly, father,' he scowled, 'because no one brought me my lunch.'

'What?' screamed the king. He promptly ordered his guards to bring before him the new maid responsible for the outrage.

When she appeared, the king pronounced that she be hanged in the public courtyard for her crime.

'But sire,' she pleaded, 'what crime is that? I have done all that was asked of me!'

'All that was asked of you?' he shouted, furious. 'How dare you? All that was asked of you was that you bring my son his meal, but he never received it!'

'Oh no, sire,' she wept, 'that was not what I was told to do! I was told to give the food to the most beautiful boy in the school. But I looked and looked, and the most beautiful boy I could see,' she groaned, 'was my own, standing beside me. Try as I might, I could find none more handsome. So I did as I was told, and gave the most beautiful boy the food.'

The king, his mouth agape and his eyes wide with incredulity, stared at her in silence for a long moment. Then he smiled.

'Yes,' he nodded slowly, 'I am sure that to you, your own son was and will always be the most beautiful. That is how it is with parents and children,' he sighed, 'and that is how it should be.'

"So," concluded Joseph, "he spared her life."

Thus, it came as no surprise to Mercada that Dulce and Isaac found nothing untoward about Rachel's looks, seeing her with the clouded gaze of parental adoration. And they might have remained with such blissful myopia had they not been suddenly struck by the arrival of a surprise but not wholly unexpected visitor: adolescence. All at once, things were different. Not that Isaac and Dulce suddenly saw their daughter objectively, for this vision would remain forever sucked into the black hole of their private universe. Instead, they began to see other people seeing her. When other girls became the center of attention, surrounded by boys after the Sabbath services, Rachel was cast aside. When other girls began to receive visits from boys with their parents, Rachel's house was quiet. Even at the few parties to which their little cherub was invited, she would remain alone, or stuck making small talk with the parents and chaperones.

Yes, adolescence had struck, and with it, other adolescents, crueler even than children. When Rachel had been taunted by her looks as a little girl, her parents had comforted her with light hearts and the strong conviction that the jibes were only the slings and arrows of outrageous little brats looking to be mean for mean's sake. But faced with these new insults from an entirely new angle, Dulce and Isaac were forced to see the truth: that she had a beauty others couldn't appreciate, an unconventional, quirky sort of look. No one was bothering to seek out the magnificent girl she was on the inside, or her generous heart. And it didn't seem to matter that she knew how to cook and sew and would make a wonderful wife and mother.

They recalled with dread the baker's daughter, Felicité, a most inapt name if ever there was one. Her family came from Lebanon, where they had been wealthy. They had lived in a big house with a servant, and when Felicité was born, it was the servant who would sleep in the same room with the baby, as was the custom among the rich. One night, however, the baby tumbled from the cot and somehow fell on something sharp the servant had left there, piercing Felicité's right eye. The eye was lost forever, and it left a hideous gash. As she grew, Felicité became aware of her disfigurement and the revulsion it produced in others. As a result, she positioned herself so that her hair would fall over that side of her face and cover the eye, which it never really did. The only thing this stance accomplished was to make Felicité bent over like a hunchback and make her walk with a limp. By now she was thirty-four years old and had not married. Obviously, she never would. Isaac and Dulce feared the same lonely future for their beloved Rachel. Who would marry her?

The problem came to a head one Sabbath when Isaac met Don Nissim on his way to the synagogue. Nissim was a *shadchan*, a matchmaker. In Jerusalem in those days, matchmakers were almost always men, for this was seen as a serious affair, a type of business transaction, and women weren't trusted to take on such responsibilities. The *shadchan* would bring young men over to visit the family on the Sabbath, and the parents of the prospective bride would prepare fruit and cakes while the girl would be spruced up to look her best.

Isaac had previously approached Nissim many times regarding a suitor for Rachel, but Nissim had put him off by saying there was time, she was still very young. This was a lie, however, since girls in Jerusalem often married as early as eleven or twelve. Nissim had seen Rachel and knew it would be a tough fight to find someone for her, especially at a time when young men were scarce. This time, however, he agreed to bring one over, for Danny Azulai had become a thorn in his side, or rather the boy's parents had. They had been badgering Nissim for some time to find someone for their Danny, but this, he had discovered, was not an easy thing to do. At the age of eighteen, Danny looked like he might be fifty, for he had gone bald very early, and despite his thick glasses, he was practically blind. This had saved him from the Turkish conscription but did not do wonders to impress the young women Nissim took him to visit, nor for that matter their parents. He took pains to assure them that Danny was a good boy, would be a good provider, but few were convinced.

"Provide for her!" exclaimed one of them. "But he can barely find her!"

This, then, Nissim realized, was the solution to his problem. He would get the two of them off his hands, and would boost his reputation to boot, as the *shadchan* who had managed to find partners for even such lost causes as Danny and Rachel. He had to admit, the two were truly a match made in heaven.

Normally, a young man would be brought to visit in the evening, after the father, and sometimes the mother, had returned from work. Due to the wartime curfew, though, all social intercourse was now done during the day, which was fine since the men were often no longer going to work, at least not full-time, and this way tea could be prepared since it would not yet be Sabbath when fire could not be lit. Nissim was expected to arrive with Danny the next day, and everyone in the house buzzed with excitement. Mercada helped Dulce prepare *tishpishtil*, a sticky-sweet semolina dessert, which now had to be made from carob syrup, as sugar was a luxury few could afford. Rachel fussed over her clothes and hair. Even Isaac helped to tidy up a bit.

Finally, the two men came to call. Introductions were made and tea was served. Rachel was shy at first, winding wisps of her crinkly hair around her finger, while Danny flushed from his shiny scalp all the way to his toes. They spoke to one another by proxy. "Danny is a silversmith," Nissim informed Rachel, while Dulce assured the boy that her Rachel was an exquisite cook.

"She made this *tishpishtil*. Taste it. It's delicious!"

After Nissim and Danny left, Isaac and the three women stayed up late, dissecting the events of the evening, analyzing each shred of conversation. All agreed it had been a rousing success. Rachel glowed.

The next day, Sabbath morning, Isaac met Nissim in the synagogue and immediately pounced. But his enthusiasm was met with the *shadchan's* reticence. The evening had not gone as well as they had thought, it seemed. On their way home the previous evening, Nissim had asked Danny what he had thought of the girl.

"I may not see well," he had responded, "but I'm not blind." Nissim did not tell this to Isaac, but the latter understood that Danny had turned Rachel down. Isaac was flabbergasted.

That... that toad, that hairless, sightless insect had refused his daughter? He thought he was too good for her?!

Not all was lost, however, Nissim reassured him. As luck would have it, Danny had been quite impressed with the other girl, Mercada. He knew that she was an orphan and surely a burden on Isaac and Dulce, and he was almost certain he could make a match without even a dowry, or maybe a very little one.

Dulce and Isaac had taken Mercada in out of the kindness of their hearts, but also for the benefit of their only child, so that Rachel could have a companion. Now they realized that perhaps having Mercada around was no great benefit to their daughter. It would be hard enough to marry her off without Mercada standing next to her, exemplary in her normalcy, making Rachel's unfortunate looks positively ghastly. Worse, once Mercada opened her mouth and her charm spewed forth, all was indeed lost.

Isaac returned home that morning to impart the bad news, and then took Dulce aside for a more detailed and informative report.

"Yes, now I'll tell you, Isaac," Dulce remarked, "I did notice a spark in Danny's eyes when he spoke with Mercada, although at the time I thought it was a reflection from his glasses. Yes, she is a threat and let's admit it, Rachel doesn't need any competition."

"But what can we do?" he asked in desperation. "Can we throw the girl out into the street?"

They both fell silent. No, they could not.

"But can we sacrifice the happiness of our own daughter?" he then asked.

They stared gloomily at the floor. It seemed like an impossible situation.

A few weeks later, a suitor was again expected, a carpenter named Moises. About an hour before he arrived, Dulce took Mercada aside.

"Mercada, would you do me a favor? I want you to take this pot over to my sister Flore's, and be sure to give her this note, too. It's very important."

So Mercada pulled Lili's shawl over the thick new one Dulce had given her, and set out for Tanti Flore's. Fifteen minutes later, Flore was scanning the note to explain the puzzling presence of the pot. Mercada was already closing the door behind her when Flore called after her.

"Oh, Mercada... wait!"

Mercada reopened the door. "Yes?"

Flore had the note in her hand. "Ahh... I was just wondering if... you could help me here for a moment?"

Mercada was surprised, but of course assented. Flore enlisted her to help her make the Sabbath bread, or challah. Making bread was an arduous process then. First, one began with a sack of grains now bought on the black market. One was then required to sort and clean the wheat. After that was done, it was carried to the flour mill, which was located in Mea Shearim, the Hasidic sector, where one waited for the wheat to be ground into flour. Only then did the actual bread-making begin.

Mercada voiced her fears that Doña Dulce would worry about her, and wonder why she hadn't returned promptly, but Tanti Flore assured her that her sister would not mind. She then poured some of the flour onto the table and mixed it with water and old, soured bread used as yeast. Normally the recipe called for eggs, but they were now scarce, and the challah would have to be made as a regular bread. Flore and Mercada took turns kneading the dough and then put it aside to rest. By this point, Mercada feared that Flore would make her wait out the hour or so it would take for the bread to rise and then, after forming it into the traditional braid, would make her accompany her to the neighborhood oven. (At that time, no one owned their own private oven.) But the hour of curfew was fast approaching, so Flore let her go.

By that point, of course, Mercada had realized what was up. That is, she understood Flore was purposely keeping her away from Rachel's house, and probably Dulce had instructed her to do so in the note. She also deduced that it was no coincidence that the two women had cooked up this charade precisely on the evening a boy was expected. They didn't want him to see her, or her him.

She pondered this on her way home. Perhaps they didn't want her to see him because they feared she would be jealous of Rachel and her future happiness. Jealousy was not a thing taken lightly at the time. That the Evil Eye was capable of great harm was a well-known fact. She knew a woman who had been walking with her baby when a neighbor saw them. This neighbor had never been able to bear children. So when she saw her friend's baby, she oohed and aahed over it. The next day, the baby was taken with a high fever, and nearly died. The mother immediately diagnosed the cause: the neighbor's Evil Eye. Or there was the merchant who had just brought in barrels of green beans from his farm. They were firm, crisp, still wet with the morning dew. The merchant to his right complimented him on such fine produce. A few hours later, little worms were swarming over the vegetables. Where had they come from? It was obvious: from the neighboring merchant's Evil Eye. This was why talismans warding off the Evil Eye hung everywhere. They were made of blue glass with a black dot in the middle, to resemble an eye. People would hang big ones on their walls, in all the rooms. They would pin small ones to babies' underclothes. They wore them around their necks, from their ears and on their wrists. One could never be too sure. Was that it, then? Were Dulce and Isaac afraid that Mercada had the Evil Eye?

She barely spoke to any of them that evening, out of hurt, anger and shame. When she and Rachel got into bed later together, Rachel was all aflutter over the boy who had visited, and blithely prattled on, describing his looks and all he had said. After a while, she noticed that her friend was uncommonly silent. Mercada remained resolutely evasive in response to her friend's questions until finally Rachel could only conclude that perhaps the former was indeed jealous of her friend receiving a visit from a boy. And, honest and forthright as she was, she said so.

"You too? You too, Rachel?" Mercada spat out, and then burst into tears. "How could you think I would be jealous of you? You're my friend! You took me in! I'm happy for you!"

"Well, then why do you seem so angry?"

"Because your parents *think* I'm jealous. They think I have the Evil Eye. That's why they sent me out to your Tanti Flore's, to help her make bread for two hours!"

Rachel smiled sadly. "Oh Mercada, is that why you think they sent you out?"

"Well, why else?"

Suddenly Rachel got out of bed and stood before Mercada. Her hair, normally unruly, had become more mussed from the bed. Her skinny legs stuck out from under her gown, and she smiled a rueful, toothless grin, for she had removed her false teeth before bed.

"Look at me," she said quietly. "What do you see? Is there anyone uglier than me? I've always been ugly. I've come to accept it, over the years," she said unconvincingly, "but my parents can't. They're afraid I'll never get married. So when a boy comes for me—someone who obviously doesn't know what I look like," she joked, "they don't want you to be here."

She sat down on the bed and reached for Mercada's hand. "Don't you see? They're afraid that you'll be competition for me. And they're right. You're much prettier than me." She waved her hand as Mercada tried to protest. It was painful to hear Rachel belittle herself.

"You're prettier," she continued, "and smarter, and funnier. Can you blame them for wanting to chase you away for a few hours, so that I might have a chance at happiness?"

Mercada swallowed hard. It was so unfair that Rachel was ugly, she thought bitterly, for she was so beautiful inside, so sincere, so kind. Mercada recalled with shame how she had often pitied herself for not being beautiful, when here was Rachel who truly had it hard. Yet Rachel never whined about her wretched looks, never complained about the insults she received at the hands of the insensitive. She accepted her shortcomings with quiet grace. Mercada's heart went out to her brave friend. She had an urge to wrap her in her arms and protect her from the harsh world. What would become of poor Rachel, she grieved.

Destiny, however, is governed neither by reason nor by justice. Criminals grow rich, fools become kings, and beauties very often wed beasts. Mercada could not have known then that she would have been better off grieving for herself.

In the meantime, the war continued. The Turks tried to take over the Suez Canal in 1915, but the British held on tight. Jerusalem itself suffered no bombardment, but it began to suffer in other ways. Water, always a problem in the city, was being rationed. The Turks closed the spring at the foot of Mount Zion, ladling it out only to those possessing ration cards, which were purchased with a few *kuartikos*, one of the types of currency in use at the time. (Up until this point, Turkish bills and coinage were used, such as paper *lira*, copper *mezidi* and smaller *beshliks*, *kuartikos* and *kabaks*, with the dominant symbol of the *Tughra* on them, which was the intricate signature of the sultan Mustafa III. Forty *paras* equaled one *piaster*. But from 1917 to about 1927, Egyptian money began to be used, though it was also in *piasters*. After that, the British Mandatory Government issued its own coinage, in which one lira equaled one thousand mils. Though British, the coins bore the legend "Palestina" in Hebrew.)

By the winter of 1915-1916, things had worsened. Everyone lived in a state of constant paranoia, for on the slightest pretext one could be arrested as a spy, whether an insignificant, starving pauper or a rich and powerful leader. Even the Mufti of Gaza had been condemned as a traitor, on mere hearsay, and hanged at the Jaffa Gate.

As if political fears were not enough, starvation was slowly gutting the city. A locust infestation destroyed crops, compounding the scarcity of grain that had already become a problem once the normal supplies from beyond the Jordan River and elsewhere were cut off. To make matters worse, the authorities took to requisitioning for the military what little food supplies there were. In the beginning, the city's inhabitants had swarmed to seek out employment in order to buy the small and highly coveted stores of food available. Soon, however, the situation deteriorated to where no amount of money could procure the food. The American Colony, run by Americans and Swedes, opened a soup kitchen to distribute some rations to the starving Jerusalemites. The few hundred who would come to their door with their pails and saucepans rapidly swelled to a thousand by 1917 (the year, incidentally, in which the United States entered the war), and then to two thousand.

It was at this soup kitchen that year that Isaac and his family finally found themselves, for their situation, like everyone else's, had grown grim. There was no more talk of young men for Rachel. Now it was all they could do to put food in their stomachs, and even one meal a day was a luxury. Isaac and Dulce always sent Mercada out to the soup kitchen, for they were embarrassed to go themselves and Rachel was too precious to them to risk being sent out into the streets. So Mercada would go every day, dragging a pot with her, and would fight to receive a meal ticket. She was not wounded that her foster parents never sent Rachel, for she knew that as an orphan she could not expect more. Normally she would have been mortified to stand in line at a soup kitchen. In the Middle Eastern worldview that permeated her existence, what mattered most was to preserve face: better to starve to death than to let others see you beg for food. Pride was to be valued above all else. But these were extreme times, and in any event, everyone else was as stricken as she.

The soup kitchen was soon closed down, however, by the Germans, who claimed it represented American propaganda. The fighting grew nearer, and food was harder to find, even on the black market. Women had been known to try and sell their babies so that they might get some food with which to live another few days. Young girls sold themselves to the German and Turkish troops for the same reasons. Businesses had closed. People began to die of starvation, compounded by an outbreak of cholera, and they fell in the thousands. Even death became problematic, for the Turkish Government's red tape made burial itself an ordeal. People would have to walk miles from one official to the next just to be able to put a loved one to final rest.

Though Dulce always gave Rachel the biggest portion of whatever they found, she never gave Mercada less than she gave herself or Isaac. Still, they were starving. Then they heard of another soup kitchen, this one initiated by the Grand Mufti of Jerusalem, under Muslim auspices. They heard stories about the needy being so desperate that the police used whips on them to keep them from killing one another. But Mercada was more hungry than fearful, and she braved the crowds, leaving the house at dawn. She would have left even earlier, had the curfew not been in force. She discovered that it was indeed a struggle to obtain food there, for the kitchen was soon receiving four and then six thousand people a day. (It became such an institution that when Jerusalem finally fell, the British would keep the kitchen, and its clientele, alive by providing funds for its continuation.) As a result, Dulce, Rachel and Mercada were wasting away, with Isaac in critical shape. The women feared he would not last much longer.

As for the army, the Turks had repelled two British attacks on Gaza that spring, but their casualties were climbing. Reports surfaced that ingenious new ways of killing had been invented, such as poison gas used by the Germans, and huge vehicles of destruction called tanks, employed by the British. The French Hospital had been commandeered by the Turks, and then the Grand New Hotel, near the Jaffa Gate, was turned into one, to supply beds for the growing number of wounded. But for the beds, it would have been unrecognizable as a hospital, for it was filthy and in a state of dire neglect, with little or no soap or disinfectant to be found. Deserters from the army began to enter the city in droves till by the end they would number almost twenty-five thousand. There was much looting. The Ordnance Workshops now occupied the English Schools and were the scenes of cruel punishments for looters or for the Christian and Jewish laborers accused of insubordination. The most popular punishment was the *bastinado*, in which the victim was held on the ground with his legs secured while he was beaten with a stick on the soles of his bare feet.

But all came to an end in December of 1917, when the British, after having captured Gaza and Jaffa, took over Jerusalem. On the ninth day of that month, not one Turk was to be seen in the streets, which were filled with happy and hopeful residents. It wasn't until the eleventh, however, that the Commander-in-Chief, General Allenby, would enter the city. His name had long become legendary, even to the Turks. Due to the trouble they had pronouncing his name, it came out as "Al Nebby", meaning "Said by the prophet," inspiring fear and awe in his enemies. Thus, General Allenby rode on horseback to the Jaffa Gate, dismounted, and entered the holy city on foot, a gesture that won him much respect worldwide. With him were members of the Italian, French and American military attachés.

Allenby stood on the steps of the citadel next to the Tower of David and had his proclamation read in English, French, Arabic, Hebrew, Greek, Russian and Italian. It stated that religious freedom would be guaranteed to all citizens and that their holy places would remain untouched. After that, the VIPs and religious leaders were presented to the General, from the Chief Rabbi to the Grand Mufti. The worst seemed to be over.

Jerusalem was in this way taken over by the English, much to the relief of all its inhabitants, for the English were said to be fair rulers. They had been welcomed, in fact, in other parts of the region as well. The Jews of Palestine, furthermore, had been proud to learn that three entire battalions, containing thousands of Jewish volunteers and named the Jewish Legion, had served in the British Forces. Arabs, too, had fought with them, sick of Turkish oppression, and their fear of Turkish revenge for this cooperation led many to follow the British troops into Palestine. These fears turned out in fact to be well-founded, for the retreating Turkish Army would vent its rage on Arab villages east of the Jordan, making examples of them by burning their homes and slaughtering all the inhabitants. Though the war raged on, it was elsewhere, while Jerusalem was now able to begin recuperating from its ordeal.

In the household of Dulce and Isaac, too, the worst was over. They had survived, and were now able to get hold of food from some relief organizations that had come in with the British. Having overcome their battles for sheer sustenance, however, they were nonetheless still engaged in their private struggle to further their line. They were encouraged by the fall of Jerusalem, which to everyone meant a long-awaited peace and return to everyday living. Soon, therefore, the dating game was inevitably resumed, but it remained much the same as before: a young man came, Mercada left. Alas, however, her banishment was to no avail. The candlemaker never returned. Nor did Rafael, the baker, nor Silvio, Rachel's cousin. (It was not considered problematic at the time for cousins to marry. In fact, in some circles, it was looked on as fortunate—at least one knew the family.) Many young men were sent over, for Rachel's family had a good reputation, and was no longer poor. But the men never set foot twice in Dulce and Isaac's house.

One day, Isaac's cousin's neighbor found a prospect for Rachel, and Isaac readily agreed to receive him. So readily, in fact, that he hardly asked any questions. All he knew was that the boy was from a good family, of Greek descent, and that he worked in his father's fabric store. Only until the boy crossed Isaac's threshold did the beleaguered father think to ask him his name. It was Isaac.

Perhaps this seems a cute coincidence. Even at the time, one wouldn't think it would be of any importance. After all, the year was 1918. The nations of the world had just tried to annihilate one another. In Russia, the universe had turned upside down; they had started a revolution and had even killed the Czar. These were considerable events. But in Jerusalem, there were other, smaller matters, slices of humble, everyday life, yet which loomed massive and fearsome to its inhabitants. Superstition, for instance, still reigned supreme, above even religious worship at times. People didn't always follow all of God's precepts, but they certainly weren't brave enough to disdain bad luck or the Evil Eye.

The confluence of names, then, was a grave matter, quite literally. It was a custom to avoid suitors or fiancées with the same name as one's parent, but as no one could say from where the custom originated, or more importantly why, nefarious reasons were attributed to it, death being the natural conclusion. Thus, a superstition arose that if a person's spouse had the same first name as one's parent, one of the two identically named would surely die. And as luck would have it, of all the men who had come calling, only this one came back a second time, and then a third, and a fourth, too. Of all the suitors, only this one, the one whose name boded so badly for the family, ended up falling for Rachel.

This was not just surprising, but downright stunning, for this young man was actually good-looking. In fact, strikingly handsome. When word got out among the community, people were hard-pressed to explain such a phenomenon. Rachel?! With Isaakito (little Isaac)? No one could comprehend it. *Mazal*, was all they could say. Luck, fate, destiny. People repeated the saying, *El mazal de la fea, la hermosa la desea.* The luck of the ugly is desired by the beautiful. Indeed, Isaakito would prove he truly loved Rachel. When pus would form in her eyes, for instance, he would wipe them for her.

It was too good to be true, and Rachel's father knew he would have to pay for such fortune with his life. He had nightmares for weeks, often waking in the middle of the night shaking with sweat. No one else in his family seemed concerned by such an unhappy coincidence of names, not even Isaakito, who was just as much in peril as the older man. He went so far as to propose marriage, and when he did so, the women didn't hesitate for a second. What was Isaac Senior to do? He was a father after all, and it was his duty to provide happiness for his offspring, whatever the menace to himself. Parents must make sacrifices. *But such a big one!* he fretted miserably. In the end, he gave his blessing, and the two young people were married. Poor Isaac. Instead of dancing on one of the happiest days of his life—the marriage of his daughter (especially *his* daughter)—he suffered during the entire ceremony, convinced that the icy claw of malevolent retribution would seize him at any moment for having spat in the face of superstition. When the groom stomped on the glass with his foot, Isaac nearly bleated in fright. And who would have imagined that Rachel and Isaakito not only lived happily ever after, but that miraculously neither of the Isaacs died. Mazal.

In the meantime, the war came to an end.

Chapter Nine

BEFORE THE WAR ENDED, however, and before Rachel met Isaakito, something happened to Mercada. In the many aborted episodes involving Rachel's suitors prior to Isaakito, Mercada would be sent away as usual. After a while, when the veneer of propriety had worn off and it was plain to all why Dulce and Isaac were sending her off, it was no longer necessary to give Mercada fake errands or to hold her hostage as a temporary servant for one of Dulce's relatives. During male visits, then, Mercada was eventually allowed to wander where she may, though uncommon among young women of those days, and she would take it upon herself to come up with errands of her own. For a long time, for instance, she hadn't been able to wear her mother's chain, as it had broken one day when she was bathing. She had managed to save it, and decided during one of her banishments to consult a jeweler as to how much it might cost to fix.

The day she walked into Gabriel Hazan's jewelry store was the day that changed her life, and his, too. She fixed her unwavering cobalt eyes upon his and, after arguments and cajoling, he was practically begging her to let him fix the chain, and for a ridiculously low price. Gabriel was no match for Mercada when it came to bargaining. If his father, who owned the store, had found out how little he had charged her... But by the time she walked out of the place, Gabriel's head was spinning. He had never met such a girl. He was twenty years old. She was eighteen.

He found her name intriguing—"Purchased," how odd—but she wasn't very forthcoming with information, which only made her more attractive to him. So he spent the next few days asking around, and what he discovered was more fuel for his inflamed imagination. Nobody really seemed to know the explanation for her name, and those that did had already forgotten it. But Gabriel did manage to glean that she was of Slavic origin, and that she was an orphan. This was perhaps the *coup de grâce*, the final stroke that rendered Mercada irresistible to him. Not that her orphan's status aroused in Gabriel any unscrupulous thoughts; he did not for a moment consider it his fortune that she should have no family to protect her or to prove an obstacle in his yearnings. In fact, she had impressed him as anything but helpless—on the contrary, it was he who had been at her mercy that day in his store. But though she had appeared so staunch and intrepid, so cool and hard, he realized she was really a poor, lost soul, a lonely orphan. He wanted to run to her aid; he wanted to take care of her. He wanted her, plain and simple.

Gabriel had been born in Palestine, his father had been born in Palestine, and his father, too, had been born in Palestine. This went back approximately five generations, from which point he could trace his ancestry back to Iraq or Iran, Mercada could never remember which (though the difference was significant, since Iraqis are Arabs whereas Iranians are Persians, a distinction that meant nothing to her, but that apparently meant much to them). Gabriel was a small man, with smooth, light brown hair and gray eyes. His father was a jeweler, and so was he. Nonetheless, Gabriel made barely enough to make ends meet, for he was a true artist, taking great pains to make a beautiful piece. His meticulous eye for detail made Gabriel a slow worker; instead of taking one day to fashion a watch fob, it would take him three or four. And though his specialty was Torah covers, gold and silver casings that housed the Holy Scriptures, there were of course not enough synagogues to make this a big seller.

But the main reason Gabriel could not earn a decent living was because he had no head for business, or rather, no heart for it. He would take pity on people who couldn't pay the full price; he felt uncomfortable hounding clients who owed money. In short, he was too delicate for the job. The same compassion that made him fall in love with Mercada because she was a poor orphan also made him a resounding failure at business.

Mercada eventually sensed this soft underbelly and found it endearing. Of course, she was also flattered by the ardor of his persistence. He asked her if she would permit him to pay her a visit at home, but she refused, feeling it would be insensitive to Rachel's feelings and to those of her parents. Gabriel would not give up, however, and would manage to meet her by chance as she left her home at different times of the day, abandoning his work, or on the Sabbath, when he could lie in wait all day. He would bring her gifts, which she systematically refused. Little by little, though, he wore her down, and Mercada began to return his affections. True, it was not the fire she had felt for David, but it was good anyway.

She often thought of David, and had even seen him, once in the shuk and once on her way home. Though they never spoke, she could see from his eyes that he still felt the same about her, and she did, too. But each time, she would fight back the tears and fight back the urge to throw herself into his arms, or under a carriage. What good did it do her to pine for a man she could not have? She needed to be smart. This Gabriel, he had a business, or rather his family did, and he was kind and sweet and he seemed to care for her. She could marry him with honor and have a name, a place of her own, children. With David, she could have nothing.

After Isaakito entered the picture, and after he and Rachel had wed, Mercada, now eighteen, felt she could reveal her relationship with Gabriel to her stepfamily. They agreed to meet him and gave Mercada their blessing. Gabriel's parents, however, were less enthusiastic. How could they know what kind of family she came from if she was an orphan? And then there was the matter of the dowry. Where would she get it from? But Gabriel was adamant, and they finally relented. If their son was foolish enough to forego a dowry to which he had a rightful claim, then that was his problem.

So a wedding date was set, and as it was customary for the bride's family to bear the brunt of the worries and expense, Mercada, Dulce and Rachel busied themselves with all the fuss and preparations. What a difference from when they had been starving just a short time before! They baked challahs, they baked cakes, they made tishpishtil, baklava and meringue kisses. Almonds were roasted and then candied. Olives were cracked, stuffed and preserved. Meats and fish were marinated, tenderized and spiced, and generally prepared for cooking. Wines and other spirits were purchased. A dress was borrowed, then washed and pressed between hot bricks to render it smooth and wrinkle-free. The synagogue was reserved, and the rabbi engaged.

Three days before the wedding, Mercada ran off with David.

He had heard she was to be married, and had come to see her, to wish her his best. That had truly been his intention. But when they laid eyes on each other, when they came close after having avoided one another for so long... It was agony. David once again cursed his horrible luck, and the stupidity of old customs that impeded him from being happy. How would he survive such a blow? No one had ever made him feel the way he felt about Mercada. There was no one like her, and never would be, he told her. He had pleaded before his family, but they had remained unwavering. Tradition was sacrosanct, they reminded him, secretly relieved that the wretched ragamuffin would soon be out of commission.

Mercada, for her part, was also thrown into a tumult when faced with David's presence. She wrestled with her guilty conscience. How could she marry Gabriel when she felt such passion for David? Wasn't she betraying her intended just by having such feelings? But how could she simply abandon him now, when he loved her so much, and she had agreed to be his wife? Yet what about David's love? Hadn't he loved her first? And finally, what about her? Didn't she have a right to be happy? She had lost both her parents, had been left alone with no money, had been thrown out onto the street, and then by David's mother, and let's face it, even by Doña Blanca. Well, she deserved some happiness for a change. God owed her.

So three days before the wedding, Dulce and Isaac woke to find the bed, now Mercada's since Rachel's marriage, had not been slept in. Mercada was gone, and so were her things. Panic ripped through their home like an autumn brushfire. On the other side of town, David's family, too, discovering his sudden absence and the reason for it, was frantic; his father almost went into cardiac arrest. Finally, Gabriel's family was simply scandalized. What a tramp! We told you! But Gabriel, he died a little inside.

Where had they gone? They never told, and no one ever knew. No one would know what exactly transpired, or what, if anything, they did together. They never said a word. But a day later, they returned, each to his separate home and separate onslaught of incriminations. For Mercada had finally admitted to herself that it was hopeless. They could not be married without the approval of David's parents and siblings, and she could not wait forever. Indeed, Mercada suspected she would be a rotting corpse before they would ever agree to it. She took stock of her situation. Here she was, alone, with no parents. Dulce and Isaac would not take care of her forever, especially now that Rachel was gone. She had to face the reality of her circumstances. Love was one thing; survival another. Thus, Mercada and David spent the only night they would ever spend together in each other's arms, and the next morning she told David goodbye for the last time.

If she had needed any proof that Gabriel truly loved her, she had it when he agreed to marry her, even after what had happened, and despite the uproar of his family. They refused him their permission; he refused to go to work, to get out of bed, to eat. He had never been able to stand up to his family before, and even now, all he could muster was a passive stance, a warfare of self-destruction. But it worked, and he won. As before, his family decided that if he were foolish enough to want this girl, then let him have her, as long as he never came running to them when things went bad.

And they did. Though not, as Gabriel's family had assumed, through any fault of Mercada's. She fulfilled the duties laid out for her, according to the standards of her time. She was kind and honorable to Gabriel. She cooked his food, cleaned his house, washed his clothes, and brought him many children. Instead, it was Gabriel who could not keep his part of the bargain. The sweet indulgence that made him such a lovable fool to everyone else was the flip side to his complete inability to provide for his wife and children. In the first place, owning a jewelry store provided only sporadic profits at best. Weeks, even months would go by before Gabriel would make a sale or render a service. Customers who could afford such luxuries as watches or necklaces were few and far between. He made most of his sales on wedding rings, simple gold bands that fetched only a modest price, and besides, couples didn't marry every day. Moreover, Gabriel could always be bargained down no matter what the price. But finally, it was his legendary compassion that truly did him in. If someone couldn't pay the full amount, or right away, or eventually at all, he could always be counted on to understand. And when his pity moved him to give a client a break, it only meant that Mercada and her children would once again go hungry.

Though most of Gabriel's family were thriving, none offered to help him monetarily, not even when the newlyweds were forced to move to the slums, into what could only be called shanties. One-roomed tin structures that let the rain and roaches through. Against one wall was a small mattress, one of only two pieces of furniture, for in lieu of a separate kitchen, a coal burner fashioned out of an old petrol can was parked on a rickety table against the facing wall. The toilet was a hole in the ground, in a small booth, and it was of course outside, not far from the cistern from which they gathered their drinking and bathing water.

Less than a year after they were married, in 1919, Mercada gave birth to a son, whom she named Joseph after her father. In fact, he even looked like her father, with deep blue eyes. He was a genuinely beautiful child. His creamy skin was like fresh milk with a faint breath of rose, like the underside of a seashell or the glow of certain pearls. And the smell of him. Mercada finally understood what perfection was, and Joseph would grow to become a stunning boy. Though quite shy, he would display a strong intellect, and a profound understanding beyond his years. Having been taught to read and write by his mother even before she entered him into school, he would develop an exceptional passion for books and knowledge in general. Rarely would one see him without a book under his arm.

Things had begun to change in Jerusalem, and indeed in all of Palestine. By the end of the war, the land had lain almost in ruin, mainly from disease, famine, arrests and expulsions. The number of Jerusalem's inhabitants had dwindled down to fifty-five thousand. Sanitary conditions had long ceased to exist, with sewage and garbage filling the streets. Roads had been damaged and were impassable, with electric power no longer functioning. The British had quickly set about rectifying the situation; they had had food transferred to Palestine from Egypt, opened avenues for clean water, fixed old roads and built new ones, and restored electricity. This smooth and orderly British rule, along with the newly restored peace, had sparked new waves of immigration, both among Muslims and Jews.

It was this latter group that began to awaken the uneasiness of Palestine's Arabs, who had heard rumors that the British were negotiating with the Jews to create a Jewish state in the land. Tens of thousands of Jews began arriving, mostly from Russia, and unlike their already established brethren, they spurned the cities. Instead, they carved their homes out of the desert sand and rock, heretofore the haven of Arabs and Bedouins, and radically changed their surroundings. From the arid, lifeless dust they began magically producing fruit trees and vegetable gardens, and created more of the huge communal farms called kibbutzim. They were taking over the land, and the Arabs didn't like it. To further confound the Arabs and also the Jews of Palestine, Britain rewarded the Hashemite royal family, who had aided them against the Ottomans, by giving them Transjordan, that part of Palestine that stretched to the east of the Jordan River. Both the

Palestinian Jews and Arabs were shocked and angered by this concession; the Jews because they had indeed been promised by the British a Jewish state in Palestine, according to a document called the Balfour Declaration of 1917, and the Arabs because they had been convinced that defeating the Turks meant a realization of their own claim to the land, which had likewise been suggested to them by the British.

It was in April of 1920 that long-simmering troubles came to a boil. For a while now, ultra-religious Jews who would come to pray at the Western Wall would bring in chairs and benches upon which to sit during their long hours of prayer. They had also instituted the habit of erecting a barrier that separated the men from the women, as in any synagogue. To the Muslims, these items offended the sanctity of the place, and furthermore raised their fears that the Jews were using these objects as a means of staking their claim to the Temple Mount, over which the Muslims held custody. All this took place around the period of the simultaneous holidays of Easter, Passover and Nebi Musa, that had so often in the past been a time of tension among the three religions.

From this tension suddenly erupted the first full-scale anti-Jewish riot in Palestine. Up until then, Jews had generally been treated with contempt by their Christian and Muslim neighbors, who would pelt them with rocks on their way to the Temple Mount, hurl insults at them in the streets, and charge large sums of money for permission to pray at the Wall. The Arab villagers of Siloam made them pay protection money against the desecration of Jewish graves east of their village, while those who lived near Rachel's Tomb on the road to Bethlehem charged the same for leaving alone the Jewish share of the tomb. Such insults were thought to be unfortunate but unavoidable aspects of the coexistence of different peoples, and were thus grudgingly tolerated.

Yet not since the Crusades had the Jews of the Holy Land been the victims of such widespread violence, and this despite the presence of British troops. Arab mobs, incited by the rumors of Jews usurping their rights to the holy places, rose up and began attacking their Semite cousins in the streets and in their houses, beating them up and looting their stores. The Jews fled through the streets, while those more fortunate managed to barricade themselves in their homes and shops. Young Arab men raced through the narrow alleyways of the Holy City, knives and clubs in their hands, yelling "Death to the Jews!"

Mercada, eight months pregnant with her second child, was home with Joseph, now a little over a year old, when the screaming began. He began to cry, while the child in her womb, reacting to her terror, started kicking furiously. She feared she would miscarry. She could not understand what was going on but knew better than to venture a peek outside, for they had no window, and she would have had to open the door. By the time she could distinguish the cries of the victims from the shouts of "Death to the Jews" she understood what was happening. To the British it may have come as a surprise, but the residents of Jerusalem had had intimations of just such a riot. They had heard the grumblings of the merchants in the shuk and had seen the growing venom of the young Arab men whenever a Jew would cross their path.

Mercada was terrified for Gabriel. Was he all right? Had the riot spread over there as well? He was surely no fighter, her Gabriel, and she knew he would not stand a chance against a knife-wielding attacker.

The commotion outside seemed to last a lifetime, and for some, unfortunately, it did. When it was over, five Jews and four Arabs had been killed, while two hundred Jews and twenty Arabs remained wounded. Gabriel soon appeared, having raced home to allay his own fears for the safety of his wife and child. On his way, he had actually seen someone they had known lying dead on the ground. It was this storm of rage that afterwards prompted the Jews to organize a defense force, called the Haganah, meaning literally "Defense." Its creation was sanctioned by the British military government which, in light of later events, would prove to be greatly ironic.

It was thus in this shadow of hatred and loss of life that a month later Mercada gave birth to another son, perhaps presaging his untimely fate.

They named him Samuel, after Gabriel's father. Samuel was a gurgling, happy baby, and Joseph loved to play with him. When Joseph had been born, Gabriel's family had bragged to all their friends and relatives how their son's first child was a male. But beyond that, they had shown little interest in him. With Samuel, however, they were very different, perhaps because of his name and then his looks, for he resembled Gabriel's side of the family. Samuel the elder especially loved playing with the baby, calling him Little Samuel or Shmulik.

Mercada's in-laws were thus over often, counseling her on how to care for the baby, as if she hadn't already had one, criticizing her for dressing him too warmly, and for the diapers she used, which came out too rough when she washed them. Feeding times were especially difficult, since they lived in one room and there was nowhere to escape their prying eyes when she breastfed. Not that she was shy or squeamish, only annoyed by her lack of privacy and their insults. They carped over the poor conditions in which their son lived, and in truth the little family was barely getting by. But Gabriel's parents and siblings never offered to help, making it sound instead as if it were Mercada's fault somehow. They would never forgive her for running away with David, or for being poor.

Gabriel's family members, on the contrary, were almost all prosperous. His father had been so before he married; Gabriel's grandfather had been a butcher, and later his uncle took over. On his mother's side, too, they were well off. Thus, Gabriel's lack of business sense was perhaps only due to the rich man's son's syndrome: one who was never wealthy strives for wealth; one who grew up wealthy never strives for it, because he never had to. In any event, it was Gabriel's father who had set up the jewelry store where his son worked. But their system was that each pocketed a percentage of the profits only from what each sold. Gabriel's father, a shrewd and almost greedy man, did well; gentle Gabriel did terribly. Mercada had long complained and finally bullied her husband into asking for a different set-up so that he might bring home more money. But Samuel had balked at such a suggestion. Gabriel would never get anywhere in life, he had scolded, by begging, by asking for something he had not earned. Gabriel had accepted the reprimand with embarrassment, and of course dared not ask for a loan after that.

So the young family continued as they had before, on the pittance Gabriel earned, along with a few piasters earned by Mercada for a few odd sewing jobs she had managed to get. But she saw how wan Joseph's little face and skinny body were, and she knew her own aching stomach only meant that baby Samuel would not have enough food. How much milk could she produce on an empty stomach?

One day, suddenly, in a freak accident, Gabriel's father was struck dead. He had been walking back from the store one afternoon, returning home for lunch, when from one of the stone buildings flanking the narrow street, a piece of balcony broke off and careened downwards with the full rush of gravity. It hit the elder Samuel dead on, killing him instantly. His skull had been crushed.

At the funeral the next day, the family was still in shock. It had all happened so fast; they were still incapable of believing it. One of his sisters wept loudly and copiously but the rest were silent and dumb, with blank stares. There is a critical moment in funerals, when the body is being lowered into the open grave, and the surviving family members are forced to confront the wicked truth about death, that their beloved is going to be plunged into the ground and covered up with dirt. Forever. At that moment, when the old man's shrouded body was being eased into the gaping cavity in the earth, Gabriel's mother was struck with hysteria. She rushed at Mercada, who was carrying little Samuel, now six months old, and slapped her, so hard that she almost lost her balance. It was her fault, she shrieked, she had brought them bad luck. Then the widow began to rave, pointing at the baby and shouting that they had named him with the same name, that one had had to die. Rather than restraining her, the other family members suddenly joined in, and began pummeling Gabriel with their fists while a screaming Joseph, who wasn't yet two, was flung away from his father's side in the fray.

It was really only a matter of seconds, not even a minute, before others intervened and it was all over. But it was a moment that would mark the following months and events to come. Gabriel's relatives cut off all ties with him, their flesh and blood, and his little family. No more visits to baby Samuel. He was, of course, too little to understand or even notice their absence, but Joseph, having witnessed the melee, began displaying a nervous tendency. He began regressing, crawling instead of walking, babbling instead of talking, and once again awakening in the night.

Gabriel and Mercada were deeply wounded, more from the violent words and pent-up ill feelings than from the fists. A month went by with no word from Gabriel's family. They had threatened to take the jewelry store away from him, but in the end didn't. Gabriel was nevertheless punished in a different way. Though he had often worked alone before, now the solitary workplace was positively mournful, and business plummeted with his guilt and depression. He tried to visit his family once, but they would not see him. Another month went by.

Then something happened. Or rather, nothing happened. Nothing happened that morning when Mercada leaned over to check on the baby. Nothing happened when she touched his knee. Nothing happened when she shook him. And when she ripped him out of his blankets, nothing happened. He didn't move, he didn't cry. He was blue.

This second funeral was far less eventful, mainly because so few attended it. Gabriel's family didn't come. Mercada had no family. Only a few friends arrived, among them Doña Blanca and members of the Shafibi family, as well as Rachel, Dulce and the two Isaacs. The younger Isaac was a Cohen, from the ancient priesthood lineage of Judaism, and could not, according to religious law, tarnish his inherited purity by entering a cemetery, other than for his immediate family. But he waited at the gates with their two children. It seemed appropriate somehow that so few should attend the burial, since Samuel had only been on earth for eight months. The scarcity of mourners echoed the shortness of his little life.

Gabriel's family had accused him and Mercada of having cursed the elder Samuel, but eventually, long after the baby's death, they would come to feel that the score had been evened, that God had rectified the situation. They softened their stance on Gabriel. He, too, would come to forgive his family, and take pity on his widowed mother. But Mercada's memory was long; until the day she died, she would never forgive them for having cursed her son. They had set the Evil Eye upon him. She was sure they had regarded him with jealousy—one Samuel had died and another was just beginning to live. It had been too much for them, it had burned inside them. It was that poison that had killed her baby.

Mercada was sick over Samuel's death, physically ill. Whatever meager food they had she could not keep down. Her milk dried up, and she cried. But there was still Joseph to worry about. He was a sensitive child and was upset to see his parents crying so much. So Mercada sucked in her grief and bitterness and buried them with her second child.

Public catastrophe echoed the private. A few months later, another riot erupted, this time mainly in Jaffa but also in a few of the settlements in the new Jerusalem, outside the old city walls. This one was much bloodier than the first, claiming the lives of forty-seven Jews and forty-eight Arabs. In response to these skirmishes, as well as to the pressure of Arab groups, High Commissioner Herbert Samuel, an English Jew, ordered a temporary freeze on Jewish immigration into Palestine. The Mandate government also established the Chief Rabbinate to represent the Jewish community, and the Supreme Muslim Council to represent the Islamists. A year later, in 1921, the grand Mufti of Jerusalem, Haj Amin al-Husseini, was appointed president of the Council. This would prove to be a disastrous blow for the Jews, and perhaps ultimately for everyone. Haj Amin was a militant anti-Zionist and Palestinian Arab nationalist who would use his power over the years to foment strife against the Jews and later the English as well. He would eventually travel to Berlin in 1941 to become an ally of Hitler himself.

Chapter Ten

MERCADA DOTED ON JOSEPH, who was twice as precious to her as before, as if she poured into him the love he deserved, and also the love that had been earmarked for his little brother. This became even more the case when she miscarried in her two following pregnancies. She began to think that Joseph would remain her only child until she became pregnant again for a fifth time. Joseph was five years old when Mercada gave birth to another son, Amos, in 1924.

From the beginning, Amos was trouble. He was born a month premature and emerged from Mercada's womb a frightening color blue. When she laid eyes on him, she was reminded of how blue Samuel had been when she had found him dead that morning, and she burst into tears. As if in response, the baby stopped breathing, and the midwife had to shake and smack him. *What a way to enter this world*, Mercada thought. Gabriel, having been thrown out of the house, had gone to the synagogue to pray. It was the custom for all the men to leave the house during a birth and go either to their work or to the temple. If complications struck, a rope was tied from the foot of the bed all the way to the synagogue, no matter how many blocks away. Gabriel prayed feverishly, hoping that the rope would be like a telegraph to God.

The baby lived. But that first encounter with his mother outside the womb would prove to be prophetic: he had made her cry then and would continue to do so for the rest of her life. Even as an infant, Amos was colicky and kept her up night after night with his ear-splitting screams that would go on literally for hours. And he suckled badly, insistently grabbing onto only the tip of her nipples no matter how she tried to teach him, making breastfeeding hurt so bad it brought tears to her eyes and made her hair stand on end. He seemed to have inherited his looks from Mercada's mother, Lili, who had never been an attractive woman. He had her pointy ears and small eyes. As for his personality, however, it was anyone's guess where that had come from. Amos turned into a wild kid, always getting into scrapes, and often perched on the precipice between life and death. Neighbors were convinced it was he rather than all her other misfortunes that had turned Mercada's hair gray at such an early age. By the time he was crawling, he had become a menace to all objects around him, and when he started to walk, things only got worse. Mercada never let him leave her side, fearful of what he would do. They say there are children who do not experience pain and fear as acutely as others, and so are willing to experiment more with death-defying feats. It was as if Amos had a devil inside him, impelling him into mischief, even at the risk to his own life.

Amos's birth, however, brought with it an interesting twist of events. Only a few days after he had emerged from her body, Mercada received a visit from a poor Arab woman. She had actually come seeking Lili, the midwife, and though at some point in her search had discovered that Lili was no longer alive, she decided to try her luck with the midwife's daughter. Though not actually a midwife herself, all had assured the woman, Maryam, that Mercada was just as wise as her mother had been. *Mire la madre, tome la hija,* was a saying in Ladino: Look at the mother and there you have the daughter. So she came to Mercada to enlist her aid in healing her son, whom she held in her arms. He had been born only a week before, but was even smaller than Amos. Mercada immediately informed Maryam that she was no midwife at all and was unfit and incapable of seeing to her baby, named Samir. But the woman became so distraught that Mercada's further refusals caught in her throat. She thought of losing Samuel, of her two miscarriages, and all the pain she had gone through. She also thought of her mother and the seventeen babies she had unwittingly poisoned to death. Mercada and her family were all too familiar with such losses, so she easily empathized with Maryam. She pressed her lips together in hesitation.

"Well, let me look at him at least." Seeing the change in a flash from despair to joy on the young woman's face, Mercada quickly added, "But it doesn't mean I'm qualified to cure him. I just said I would look."

After examining little Samir for any noticeable marks on his body, any wounds or anomalies, Mercada could only conclude that he was undernourished. She asked Maryam how his feeding was going, and the mother assured her that she seemed to be feeding him all the time and yet he cried and cried as if he had gotten nothing at all. Either something was wrong with her milk, or it simply wasn't enough, Mercada surmised. Either way, she would have to let someone else nurse the baby.

Upon hearing Mercada's assessment, Maryam began to cry. That was what her own mother had said. She was in a state of desperation, practically suicidal. Instead of the half hour other mothers nursed, Maryam had been doing four hours per night and still the baby wailed in hunger. In the end, the only liquid he seemed to be drinking from her breasts was the blood seeping out from her cracked and abused nipples. With the passing of each day she would think, "Tomorrow my milk will come in," but each day was the same as the one before. The worst part, even worse than the blinding pain of the infant's mouth clamping down on her raw nipples, were his screams, increasing in hysteria with each barren feeding. It was as if he were being tortured, allowed to be teased into thinking he would drink, and then discovering the fountain was empty. Evidently, something was wrong; Maryam could see that in her baby's behavior. But didn't all mothers have milk? Even the growing realization that perhaps she alone among women possessed empty breasts brought with it a further complication: as bad luck would have it, none of the women in her or her husband's family was breastfeeding at that moment, and the two wet nurses to whom she had been referred had as much work as they could handle and refused to take on even one more baby.

"Well, let's see, I do know of one or two myself whom you might visit..." Mercada began, but Maryam interrupted her before she could finish.

"Oh, Mother Mercada," she cut in, calling her Mother more out of respect than age, for Maryam was not that much younger than she. "I see that you, too, have a small baby in your arms. I do not know those other women you speak of, but I know you. I have heard nothing of those women, but I have heard much about you. Your mother, may Allah preserve her soul, was a great woman. She delivered two of my cousins, so you see she knew my family. They had a great respect for her, and this is why I came to you. I have been told that you, too, are great like your mother..."

Now it was Mercada's turn to interrupt.

"But I learned almost nothing from her! She died before I could learn anything."

"But you are wise nonetheless, and all I ask is that you feed my son as you feed yours. I will pay you, not in money, since we are not wealthy, but in milk and cheeses. My husband's family owns some goats."

Mercada was still shaking her head.

"These wet nurses I know, they are fine women! Why do you refuse to even see them?"

"Because Allah has sent me to you. Will you not do it to honor the bond between our two families that your mother created, to help those in need just as she did? Will you not be like your mother?" Motherhood was almost sacred to the Arabs, and Maryam was going to all extremes to convince Mercada.

The pathos in Maryam's eyes and the choking of her voice had moved Mercada, but it was the shadow of Lili that finally did it. She was all too aware that she had never been as great as her mother and never would be. And yet she felt that it was somehow Lili herself who had brought Maryam to Mercada's door, who was giving her an opportunity to feel what the midwife had felt, to help someone bring life, or at least preserve it.

She sighed. "All right."

Maryam smacked her hands together and pressed them tightly as she began to cry, to thank Mercada, and to bless her for her generous heart.

"You'll leave the baby with me now, but you must visit every day so that he won't forget you and won't get confused that I am his mother. I will only feed him; you will cuddle and play with him and talk to him. I will do this for three months, and then you will take him back."

To all these conditions Maryam agreed, and so it all came to pass. Except for the parts about only three months, and that Mercada would only provide the barest necessities for Samir, devoid of any affection. She found it hard at first and impossible later to put the scrawny little thing to her breast and not look down on him with pity, to change his dirty diapers and not say a word to him, to let him cry without picking him up and comforting him when he was feeling lonely. Three months stretched to six. Gabriel and Joseph also found themselves treating him as one of their own, especially once he was able to respond to the world around him. But it was Amos in particular who struck a bond with the little boy, for they were so close in age that they became like twins, though Samir was a much easier charge than Mercada's own son. They kept each other company, eventually playing together, learning together, and becoming friends.

As for Maryam, she found herself experiencing a mixture of varied and often conflicting emotions. First, she felt relief that the mystery of her baby's trauma had been solved or at least confirmed. This knowledge, however, brought with it shame, for she felt unworthy as a mother. Though she told herself she should be grateful that at least her son would live, she could not help feeling unfortunate that she was cursed with no milk, and in turn could not help feeling guilty that she felt sorry for herself after all her child had suffered. This, too, brought pain when she recalled Samir's passionate wails and the wild jerking of his head away from her breast as she would struggle with him, forcing him toward it. All along he had known what she had not and had tried to tell her! The poor creature, what an introduction to life! On the other hand, Maryam felt relief that she no longer had to endure another day of excruciating nursing and ear-splitting screams of starvation, and of course she felt monstrous for feeling relieved. She truly was an unnatural mother! she berated herself. Finally, she felt jealous that it was another woman who would give her child sustenance, and life. When her baby would look up from the breast that nourished him, he would look lovingly and gratefully into the eyes of a stranger, not Maryam's. Even other women who nursed their own babies made her envious. She worried, too, that Samir would not love her, or would love Mercada more, or would not realize that she, Maryam, was his mother.

As it turned out, Maryam's fears of not being a good mother prompted her to become a superior one, for she made sure to shower Samir with affection, dedicating more than the usual amount of time a mother can or will afford, and more than the usual effort and imagination. And despite her worries and misgivings, she never forgot that Mercada had saved her son, and herself, and viewed it as an act of generosity rather than a business transaction or a mere service rendered and compensated. Even after the six months were over, Maryam would continue to visit and bring Samir, as well as cheeses for Mercada though she was no longer nursing the boy. Maryam felt her debt to Mercada surpassed the amount of cheese she could ever bring her, and Mercada herself had grown very close to the young woman.

The personal events in one's life, as usual, eclipsed those of the outside world, no matter how momentous. At about the same time that Maryam and Samir entered the lives of Mercada and her brood, the Hebrew University of Jerusalem was being inaugurated on Mount Scopus. It was such a grand occasion that Lord Balfour and Lord Allenby arrived to attend the opening ceremonies. The Jews of Jerusalem, as well as others, were deeply moved and proud. Mercada had taken Joseph and Amos to watch the festivities.

"One day you will both study there," she told them, beaming.

On their way home, however, she noticed something different. The homes and shops of Muslims were draped in black cloths, and Mercada suddenly recalled that during the ceremonies on Mount Scopus she had heard a few women utter the Arabs' mourner's cry. She had not paid much attention, thinking only that someone had perhaps recently died. Now she put it together with the shrouds she saw hanging over homes and workplaces. Not everyone in Jerusalem was happy with the inauguration of the Hebrew University. Fearing another outburst of violence like the ones that had erupted a few years earlier, Mercada fled home with her two little boys and stayed put for the rest of the day. As it turned out, nothing happened that day, but it was becoming plain to everyone that tensions between the Jews and the Muslims were slowly rising to the surface. Mercada, reflecting on how she and Maryam had become friends, almost sisters, worried for their friendship, as she saw their clans moving further and further apart.

In the meanwhile, Mercada had a more immediate trouble to deal with, and his name was Amos. One day when he was two years old, she had gone up to the roof of their house to hang wet clothes. As usual, she took him with her. The roof was in reality a secure place for him, since it was bordered by a wooden fence, built there specifically for safety reasons. And because he would be by his mother's side there. Mercada had hung up a few items when she suddenly heard a noise, a braying of horses and a screeching of wheels. Then shouts followed. She whipped her head around in panic but could not see Amos. What she did see, however, was a break in the wood fence. A plank had been knocked loose. She ran over to the gap in the fence and looked down onto the street below, where she could only make out a gathering of onlookers bent over something. Or someone. Amos had found the one loose plank in the fence.

She uttered an involuntary cry and raced down the stairs, impeded by her huge belly. She was eight months pregnant. When she reached the street, the crowd backed away for her to see her little Amos lying unconscious on the ground. The carriage-driver who had stopped short when he saw the boy fall drove them to the hospital where doctors seized him and absconded to the emergency room. She spent what seemed like endless hours pacing in the waiting hall, cursing herself for not having been vigilant enough—this boy needed eyes on him every second! But would he need it anymore? She wondered if she were being punished for having complained about him and his mischievousness, for having called him a little monster. But God, no, she hadn't meant it like that, she had meant it with love. He was *her* little monster. She prayed to a God she wasn't even sure she believed in not to take him away from her.

Still the doctor had not returned. Mercada paced up and down the halls, stopping before one room from which she could hear the moans of a boy. She later learned that he had been the victim of a botched circumcision that had become infected. The Jews circumcised their sons at the age of eight days; the Muslims, at twelve years, at least at that time. Mercada recalled how she had wept at the sight of her sons' blood and the sound of their infant screams, while Gabriel had practically fainted. Yet neither had questioned the ritual itself, and would never have dreamed of not having it performed. It was one of the chains that linked one to one's tribe, and few people in this world are impervious to the need to belong.

After an eternity, the doctor who had admitted Amos emerged. Mercada ran to him.

"Are you the mother of the little boy who fell from the roof?"

"Is he alive?" was her only answer.

"Yes, he's alive."

"Ay! *Gracias a Dios!* Thank God!"

The doctor interrupted her. "I have to ask you something. Do you always put that girdle on him?"

He was referring to a bodice-like garment that wrapped tightly around the chest and abdomen. Lili, overprotective, had always put such things on Mercada to keep her snug and warm, and therefore Mercada put it on her own children, though it was no longer fashionable to do so. She nodded in answer to the doctor's question.

"Well, my dear lady, I want you to know that such girdles are very, very bad for children. They can stunt their growth. Do you understand what I'm saying?"

Again, she nodded.

"However," he continued, "in this case, it was that girdle that saved your son's life. Without it, his whole insides would have exploded like a ripe tomato." (The doctor was not known for his gentle bedside manner.) "So this time, and only this time," he berated her with his index finger, "it was a lucky thing he was wearing it. Otherwise, he would be dead."

"Thank you, Doctor," she answered reverentially.

"But don't use it anymore. Understand?"

"Of course, Doctor. Whatever you say."

Of course nothing! Of course, Mercada continued using the medieval torture girdle on Joseph and Amos. That doctor didn't know what he was talking about! Contrary to the doctor's opinion, it had never hurt anyone she knew, including herself. But it had saved a life. Amos's life. Despite her contrary behavior, Mercada respected doctors and admired their knowledge. Nevertheless, she did not regard them with the same pious, unquestioning awe that others felt. She had learned from her mother that medicine was often a practice of trial-and-error, and that doctors made many mistakes before learning how to do it right. Also, she knew that there were vogues in medical knowledge: one year something was in, the next year out. One year someone discovered a technique or a potion that could cure a disease; the next year it turned out that same technique or potion caused a side effect worse than the disease. So she listened to doctors' opinions but treated them as just that: opinions. When it came to her children, *she* would make the decisions, not some doctor.

A month later Mercada gave birth to a girl, Sara. Sara was as beautiful as Joseph but with none of his shyness. Instead, she was a happy little thing, like poor little Samuel before her. People would stop on the street to look at her, to touch her cheek, to see her laugh. Though Joseph was the child of her heart, her firstborn, a thoughtful, intelligent, gifted child whom she was sure would be the joy of her old age, Mercada had hoped this one would be a girl. A girl with whom she could share things only a woman would be able to understand. A girl like her.

Gabriel especially doted on her. She was his little queen, and he often called her *Reina,* "queen" in Ladino. When he would look at the three little faces asleep at night—the two boys nestled between their parents, Sara asleep in the little basket next to Mercada's side of the mattress—when he would gaze at their peaceful faces, at their cherubic mouths, he felt complete. He had long ago reconciled with his family after the deaths of the Samuels, but they had never set foot again in his house. Nor would Mercada have let them. But it had shaken his faith in his family, and now he was glad that he had one of his own.

Their poverty was extreme. They all slept in one room, and once Sara had outgrown her basket, they all slept in one bed. They had one plate off of which they all ate. It was made of tin, and had a hole in it. For every meal, the hole had to be plugged by inserting into it a piece of squashed bread. The plate was filled for each person in his or her turn, then refilled and passed on to the next diner. As for the toilet, it was outside, like modern-day port-a-johns at fairgrounds, and Gabriel or Mercada would have to wake in the middle of the night to accompany one of the children to urinate. Mercada wouldn't have let them go alone even in daylight. Having lost Samuel and then miscarrying twice made her guard her children as jealously as if they were precious jewels. Just like her mother.

Now that old Samuel was gone, the jewelry business was quickly failing. Sometimes Gabriel sold a bauble for whatever he could get, no matter how below cost price, just so that he would be able to buy some food for his family. But it was always a drop in the bucket, and their misery quickly put a strain on the relationship between the couple. This grew worse after Gabriel's reconciliation with his family, and especially with his mother. By the time he and Mercada had their three children, all but the youngest of Gabriel's siblings had gotten married and left home. The house in which he had grown up was thus quite empty in Gabriel's eyes, and his mother seemed all the more pitiful, not merely a widow, but practically all alone in her old age. When he would stop by, she would pour out all her miseries and fears to him, exaggerating her financial troubles as people are sometimes wont to do, fretting over what would happen once Marcus got married and left home. As it was, she would complain, they had little money left. When he would hear this, Gabriel's heart would break—she was his mother, after all—and if he had been on his way home with money from an infrequent sale or repair, he would give it to her, or the bulk of it. Then he would return home empty-handed or almost that to his starving children.

The first time it happened, Mercada couldn't believe it. That is, she could easily believe her mother-in-law was so selfish as to deprive her son's children of food. But that Gabriel would do such a thing, that he would put his mother before his own children was something she simply could not fathom. By the time he had returned home and explained to Mercada what had happened, even he found it difficult to rationalize. But somehow, when he was listening to his mother, when he had seen her cry, it had seemed the only honorable, humane thing to do. At the time. Yet when he would be home, confronted by his wife, confronted by the sunken eyes of his hungry children, he felt how wrong he had been. Still, it didn't happen once or even twice. On numerous occasions, when he would visit his mother or when she would stop by to see him in his store, his compassion would get the best of him. He could only take into account what he was feeling at the moment.

In truth, it was more than pure pity that dictated Gabriel's actions. He was the sort of person who needed the approval of others. He wanted to be everyone's friend, to be liked by all. He could not sleep at night if he thought someone disliked him or disapproved of something he had done, no matter what he thought of that person. Mercada remembered her mother's words: Sometimes it was harder to be right than to be kind. Gabriel chose the easy way, that of kindness to others rather than righteousness to his own. She had put up with her husband's inability to provide for his offspring, with the poverty that increased with the size of their family. But taking food out of his starving children's mouths and giving it to an old woman who lived comfortably, and who had another son at home to care for her, this was something for which she could not forgive him.

Eventually Mercada stopped having sex with Gabriel. If you can't support your children, you shouldn't have any more, was her way of thinking. But more than that, when she had to look into the woeful eyes of her innocent little infants, how could she possibly think of sex? How could she find remotely desirable the man who had brought such suffering to her little ones?

Mercada recalled her mother's account of the priest who had wanted her to abort his baby. Her mother had been shocked, obviously by the fact that he had been a priest, but also by the very request itself. For Lili, she knew, abortion went against everything she had done, and everything she had gone through to have her own child. But for Mercada it wasn't so simple. Would she be capable of such a thing if she became pregnant again? She didn't know. Yet what she did know was that there was no greater crime than bringing children into this world who would be condemned to suffer. To look into those cold, hungry faces, whose eyes begged you to help them, to relieve them...

As if that were not enough, Joseph's school, one of the finest in Jerusalem, would threaten time and again to throw him out for not having received tuition payments. Mercada had had to personally visit the rector many times, calling upon her famed eloquence in order to plead that he take pity on her child. Luckily, Joseph was a stellar student, brilliant and well-behaved. But Mercada knew she would not be able to rely on the school's charity forever. It tore at her that her gifted son would not get the chance to better himself, to rise above his poverty, because her weak husband would break down at the sight of a deceitful old woman's crocodile tears.

It was autumn, after Rosh Hashanah, or Jewish New Year, and Yom Kippur, the Day of Atonement, 1927. Fast approaching was the festival of Succoth, in which Jews built little shacks attached to their houses and ate their meals in them. It was the season for pomegranates, filled with their little beads that looked like blood-red rubies, and guavas, too, that filled the air with their fragrant perfume as the evenings grew cool. The school year had recently started, and Mercada was returning Joseph home from school with Amos and Sara in tow. She could not leave the two little ones alone and trusted no one else to watch over them. But she had to walk Joseph to and from school. Many Jewish parents took to walking their children home, to protect them from other schoolchildren, Christian and Muslim, who would throw stones at the little Jewish kids, or from those adults who mouthed insults and epithets. Foreign Christians received similar treatment from the native Muslims, who referred to them as "dogs of the north" or simply "sons or daughters of prostitutes." Arabic curses, deeply venomous, were usually indirect, aimed not at oneself but at one's ancestors or tribe. Or worse, at one's descendants: by far the most strongly feared curse is the wish that one never produce offspring.

Mercada, however, had a different reason for walking Joseph to and from school. One day, a year before, he had returned home and told her about a man who had begun pestering him of late. At the time, Joseph was seven years old. He told Mercada that this man would meet him after school, waiting for him at the gate. The first time, he had called Joseph over and told him he would give him sweets if he would go with him. But Joseph had been afraid to leave his friends and ran back to join them. From then on, the man would wait for him after school outside the gate, almost daily, calling to him. He had learned his name from the other boys. So he would call, "Joseph, Joseph, come here! I have candy for you!" Joseph would have to endure the taunts of his friends who would mimic the man's cries—"Joseph! Joseph!" But he was afraid to run home on his own, for fear that the man would catch him and... And what? He really didn't know what the man wanted from him, what he wanted to do to him, but his intuition told him to run. It was this unanswered question that finally prompted the little boy to ask his mother.

"What does the man want from me?"

Mercada had sat listening to her son's story, while she herself slowly turned pale. Joseph was a beautiful boy who had often attracted the attention of others.

"Tfu! Tfu! What a beautiful boy!" people would say, imitating the sound of spitting, to ward off any Evil Eye. But the Evil Eye, it would seem, was not the only eye Joseph had caught.

So the next day Mercada walked Joseph to school, and then was outside waiting for him at the end of the day. The man, however, had not appeared. Joseph was embarrassed that his mother had come to chaperone him. First he had been mocked by the others because of the strange man, and now they jeered on account of his mother. He was not a baby! he protested. He did not have to be walked home! But his complaints fell on deaf ears. Mercada walked him to and from school every single day after that. The man appeared a few times, saw Mercada and quickly fled before she had a chance to confront him. She complained to the school headmaster, and he promised the children would be watched carefully as they left the premises. After those few tries, the scary man never returned.

Still, Mercada would never feel safe again, and would continue to accompany her son for years to come. She thought of her own mother, whose loss of seventeen children had made her obsessed with preserving the one who had lived, how she would rush to school to remove Mercada whenever there was rumor of the flu or simply because she had had a bad premonition. Mercada smiled at the memory. She was both pleased and disturbed to find herself acting like Lili.

On her way home from school on this particular day, Mercada heard her own name called. She turned to face the person she least wanted to see yet most often thought about: David. She hadn't seen him in years, almost a decade. She knew that he still worked for the post office, but now was a high official. She had heard that he had married and somehow had found it in her heart to be happy for him, despite her own suffering. Later, though, she heard that not only had he and his wife not been able to bear children, but that the woman he had married was an illiterate. A friend of Mercada's had told her that she had seen David's wife in the doctor's clinic, and that the woman had had to ask the other patients to tell her which room it was because she couldn't read the signs on the doors. Try as she might, Mercada couldn't swallow it. David, the scholar, the lover of French poetry, the boy never to be seen without a book under his arm, married to an illiterate! How had such a thing happened? How had he agreed to such a match? What misery he had to have gone through with such a wife, someone with whom he could not share his love of knowledge, someone whom he could not really talk to. What loneliness. And no children, no one to pass on his name, no little creatures to hold, to care for, to love. She couldn't decide which of them was more to be pitied, she, in her acrid poverty, or he, in his woeful solitude. Her heart had gone out to him. How unfair the world was.

Now here he was in front of her. He still had a beautiful face, but he had aged. His eyes were surrounded by wrinkles and his hairline was receding just a bit. He smiled at her, warmly, sadly, and they awkwardly exchanged a few pleasantries. He asked about Gabriel, and she lied and told him all was well, though it was evident that all was not well. Mercada, too, had aged, and faster than her old beau. Her eyes mirrored her fatigue, and she had quite a bit of gray now, at the age of twenty-six. Though it was autumn, Jerusalem was cold and unforgiving with its wind and stone, and Mercada had only a shawl around her shoulders, the same shawl she had worn since Lili had left it behind for her. She had mended it over and over again, waging war against the ravages of time, partly out of sentimental reasons and partly because she could not really afford to replace it with a newer, warmer one.

David understood it all immediately. Sara was bundled up against the cold in Mercada's arms, and he tickled her cheek. He tried to tousle little Amos's hair, but the tot scrambled away from him and took to playing with an anthill nearby as David grinned. Mercada felt the ache of his childlessness. Then he turned to Joseph and squatted down to talk to him. Even at the age of eight, he seemed like a little man, answering David's questions with his customary seriousness, carefully weighing his answers. He was at the top of his class, she proudly told David. Mercada looked down at Joseph now, as he and David spoke. Once again, she was struck by how handsome he was, how handsome they both were. David's hair had once curled over his forehead like Joseph's. David asked him what he was learning in school, and Joseph's eyes squinted in earnest concentration as he answered. She remembered long ago, in her parents' house, she and David at the table with their books, she listening to him read from some philosopher, their knees touching, her heart thumping, his voice turning hoarse, her breath catching in her throat...

David then stood up and turned his attention back to her. He repeated how good it was to see her. She smiled. He was moved by her sad eyes, by how hard her life had been and how hard it was now. These things shouldn't befall such people, he thought. Not people like Mercada. She shivered for a second, involuntarily. Her shawl was so thin, she was so thin, and it was unseasonably cold for October. He was suddenly moved to act.

"Mercada, please don't think it rude of me... but we were once so close, I hope you'll understand I only mean the best..."

She looked at him quizzically.

"I want to buy you a coat."

Her eyes widened, and he knew he had offended her. He remembered her steel exterior, her strong sense of pride. "It's just that I can't see you like this..."

She cut him off. "No, David, no. I appreciate it, but... no. I'm a married woman now, and I can't accept such gifts." Her face had colored, but her eyes stared straight into his. He remembered her gaze well, the sort of look that always made one feel unworthy, weak.

Then she smiled and took his hand. Sweet David, so warm, so generous, even after all this time.

"It was nice to see you."

"And it was wonderful to see you, Mercada." His eyes filled with tears. "Really wonderful."

It is said there's nothing worse than a missed opportunity, nothing that burns more or longer than the regret over an action not taken. Even the remorse over an act committed provides the consolation that at least one tried, one dared, one acted. But when it is instead a question of having done nothing, of a moment presenting itself yet one failed to grab it, thinking too much, hesitating... As she walked home, Mercada could not hold back the thoughts of how different things might have been had she gone with her heart all those years ago. She saw, like ghosts, the two of them as they once were, so young, so in love, so ripe with the promise of the future together. How far they had fallen. These thoughts tormented Mercada for days, compounded by her shame that she should desire a man other than her husband, and also that she should feel disappointment with her lot and even pity herself. Her mother would not have had thoughts like these, she scolded herself. Lili would not have dwelled in the past but would have faced up to her present. No, not faced, not accepted; she would have challenged it. She would have conquered it!

And truly, it had not only been Mercada who had given David up, but also David who had given her up, she now thought. After all, he could have married her against the objections of his family if he had chosen to do so. That was what Gabriel had done. But David hadn't. Unlike Gabriel, David had not stood against his family for Mercada. He had not wanted to sacrifice his relations with his family for her. And perhaps he had also not wanted to risk his status and career for her. Mercada thought suddenly of her father, who had sacrificed the most for love. He had not let the love of his life die alone. For he had not wanted to live without her. He had given his own life for love of her mother. Mercada's father, and also her husband, showed their love in their actions, in their sacrifices. David, she now understood, had ultimately shown it only in his beautiful words.

She would never see David again.

But the fates would not give Mercada time to even hatch a plan to wrench herself and her loved ones out of their misery. Once more, she found herself rushing to the hospital with Amos's limp body. This time he had been run over by a horse, and the carriage wheels behind it. It had been part of a game he had been playing with some older boys, she had learned. He always played with older boys. The ones his age were too tame for him. This was another reason Mercada was pleased when Maryam would visit with Samir, for Samir was a stabilizing influence upon Amos and would follow Amos's lead only so far. He was brave, yes, but reckless, no. This time, however, Samir was not present to talk sense into Amos. The older boys had invented a game in which one waited for a carriage to ride by, then jumped out of an alley and ran across the street before the carriage ran the player over. Not content with once or even twice, Amos was on his third pass when his little legs stumbled. The animal and wheels had crushed him. The poor carriage driver was hysterical, he hadn't even seen the boy. He had jumped out of nowhere! No one had had to call Mercada. She had heard the screams of the driver, of the passersby, of the horse, and from within the little shanty she knew: Amos.

Again, she flew to the hospital with him. The doctors there remembered him from last time a year before. They rushed him into a closed room, shouting orders at nurses. Mercada waited for what seemed like hours until a doctor came out to speak with her. As it is, doctors don't put on bright smiles when they come to talk about a loved one, but this time Mercada could tell it was worse than the first accident. The doctor wouldn't speak to her unless she sat down. This did nothing to ease her fears; on the contrary, it brought her to the verge of breaking down.

"Just tell me! Is he dead?"

"Please sit down, Mrs. Hazan." She finally did as he wanted, so that he would tell her something. As she sat down, he took her hands in his.

"He's dead, isn't he?"

"No, no, he's not."

"Oh, *Dios santo!!* Blessed God!"

"But... but he's very bad. Very bad."

Mercada held her breath. "How bad?"

He looked her straight in the eye.

"Mrs. Hazan, do you have other children at home?"

What did her other children have to do with this? Nevertheless, she answered yes.

"Madam, concentrate on them. Forget this one. He's a lost cause. I don't think he'll make it till tomorrow."

It was as if all the breath had been sucked out of her body. She realized in retrospect that at that moment she had gone into a panic, but as she had never really experienced true panic before, she had not recognized it at the time. She had always expected a moment of panic to be characterized by screams, cries, hysterics. Instead, everything had become a blank, no sound, no sight. Looking at the doctor before her, all she had seen was white, as if she had become temporarily blinded. She didn't know how long she had been like that, but she "awoke" to find the doctor hitting the back of her hand and repeating her name loudly.

"Mrs. Hazan! Mrs. Hazan!"

"Yes?"

"Are you all right?"

"Yes."

"Are you sure?"

"Yes."

"All right. Now, I want you to go home and get some rest—"

Mercada took a deep breath, regained her composure, and then cut him off.

"No," she croaked, but then tried to calm herself. "No," she repeated, more firmly. More determined. Forget Amos? That's what the doctor had said. He's a lost cause. But this doctor didn't know who he was dealing with.

"No, Doctor, I'm going to stay right here," she said evenly.

"But Mrs. Hazan, I tell you, there's no hope. We can't perform miracles!"

She shook her head. "No, you can't perform miracles, but I can. I'm going to stay with my little boy for as long as it takes until he gets better. And he will get better. You'll see, doctor. Now, take me to him."

So stay with him she did, practically night and day for the two and a half months in which Amos was hospitalized, mostly with Sara in tow until Gabriel could retrieve her. And he did indeed survive. On the day Amos was finally allowed to leave, the doctor asked to speak with Mercada alone in the hallway.

"Mrs. Hazan," he said quietly, "I just wanted to shake your hand. I had told you there was no hope, and here you are with your little boy, ready to go home. You were right, and I was wrong. I don't know how he made it, but I'm glad he did."

"He made it because I wanted him to make it," Mercada replied simply. "He knew I was there waiting for him. Sometimes people die not only because something is wrong with their bodies but also because something is wrong with their spirit. They don't fight their sickness. They let themselves die." She thought of her father. And she thought of herself; when they both died, she had almost died of a broken heart. "Well, sometimes people get better not because their bodies are so strong but because their spirit is. They want to get better. They fight. You may know more than me about many things, doctor, but this, this is something that I know. This is something my mother taught me."

The doctor just shook his head in wonder. What could he say to that?

He would see her again, though. Amos would make sure of that. He was like a cat, working on using up his nine lives. The doctors would come to know him well. They would realign the shoulder he would dislocate in a scuffle with a group of boys; they would set the leg he would break when he would fall out of a tree; they would set his nose after he would smash it while trying to show Samir and Sara he could fly. His body would sport scars even the most battle-weary soldier of fortune couldn't hope to brandish. It was not that he was a bad kid; it was just that he had so much energy, he couldn't really control himself. And he was simply too curious. *What would happen if...*he was constantly wondering. If he never showed guilt or fear about anything he did, it was because he couldn't feel those things the way others did. That his mother would die a little inside after each of his episodes just didn't penetrate into his brain. All he understood after a mishap was that it hurt, and that he would have to try something else for fun. And he never failed to find something else.

But Amos was also a miraculous child, for no matter what happened to him, he was almost always up and about in a few days. There is a saying that God takes care of fools, drunks and little children, and Amos certainly proved the last true (and maybe the first). He would lose some blood, shed some skin, break some bones, but he would always be ready for more. Even in an accident like the one with the carriage, when no one had thought he had a chance, not even the doctors, Amos had amazingly come through. The doctors were mystified, and grew to love the wild, crazy kid who would enter their doors wailing in pain, like a broken cat, only to be grinning mischievously a few days later, itching to get into trouble again. He was not really a cute child, especially not after the broken nose and the scar that crossed his upper lip when he fell down a well, but there was something about his eyes that made one laugh. When he was happy, they absolutely beamed, and when he was angry, they were a study in comic frustration. But he was never angry for long. In fact, he was never there for long. Once one's head was turned, he was out of sight.

Amos's impish charm was small comfort for Mercada, who felt that her son's antics were shortening her life. She loved him passionately, but was constantly forced to show her anger, to rain punishments on him, to deprive him of his hotly prized freedom. When she would confine him to home, his agony was almost palpable. He whined, he cried, he screamed, he literally bounced off the walls.

One such afternoon, Mercada found herself standing over a huge pot of soup, stirring mindlessly. Amos was like a pent-up animal, gnawing at her already frayed nerves, and she fantasized about a year from then, when she would put him in school with Joseph. She looked forward to this with a longing verging on the obsessive. Finally, someone else would have to share in the chore of guarding him. At the same time, she fretted over his entry into school, wondering how any institution would manage to contain him. Or how long they would try.

As she stirred, she looked down at her son and daughter. Amos had pulled the blanket off the bed and was pretending it was a horse as he dragged his sister along the floor. She howled with laughter. Mercada knew she would have to wash it now, but at least the two were harmlessly occupied. No sooner had she thought this, when Amos pretended the horse was bucking, sending his sister reeling onto the floor. Mercada ran to the now screaming child and felt the back of her head where she had fallen to see if there was any bleeding. She shouted angrily at Amos and sent him "to bed," even more of a limitation than being stuck home, a true torture for him. But he obeyed her and sped away, fearful of reprisals from his mother.

It turned out Sara was all right really, she had only gotten a bump on her head. So Mercada rocked her little girl in her arms till the sobs had subsided to little petulant gasps.

"I fall," she stated.

"Yes, I know, *querida*, but now it's all right. Mama made it all better." Though the main language spoken in the household was Hebrew, Mercada tried to speak some Ladino with her children in order to honor her heritage.

"Amos fall me."

"No, Amos didn't mean it, Sarita." Mercada called Amos over.

"Come here and tell your sister you didn't mean it. It was an accident, wasn't it?"

He perked up, relieved that punishment had been foregone. He walked up to the two, and slowly reached his hand up to pat Sara's head, as if even he were afraid of what he might accidentally do.

But Sara wrenched her head away angrily. "No! No Amos! Amos bad!"

Mercada tried to smooth things over but Sara would not be convinced, so she decided to separate the two for the time being, telling Amos to go play out back while Sara would stay with her inside. The arrangement suited both children just fine, for Sara loved to cling to her mother and watch her cook, while Amos could think of nothing better than to be outside and free from his mother's surveillance. Still Mercada peeked outside every fifteen minutes or so, especially if he was too quiet. She had to go out the front door and around back each time, but she worried that he might fall down the outhouse cesspool or into the cistern. Instead, he was relatively tranquil, having found a cockroach in a corner to toy with. She returned to Sara, to whom she was telling a story while she brought the soup to a boil.

A moment later, she heard a loud banging. When she shot out the doorway, she saw Amos had taken possession of their tin plate—how had he gotten it without her noticing?—and was proceeding to smash the cockroach with it. Mercada leapt at him, smacking him on his rear and shouting at him. Was he mad? Didn't he know they ate off that plate?

She was examining the gooey mess of the ex-cockroach stuck to the bottom of the plate, emitting sounds of disgust and reproach, when from the kitchen, they heard a loud noise. It was a sound they would remember forever, the two of them. They would hear it over and over again, for years to come, in their nightmares, or sometimes even when they were awake. It was a crash, and a splash, followed by unearthly screams such as Mercada had never heard in her life. Sara, left alone for only a moment, had reached up to grab the pot, to see the soup that was inside it. She had brought the hot cauldron down upon her, along with the boiling liquid. Almost all of her little body had been doused with the fiery broth. Mercada tried to grab her in her arms but she would not be touched from the pain. Instead, she shrieked and shook. Then her eyeballs went white and she seemed to lose consciousness.

Two neighbors rushed in upon hearing Sara's screams. Mercada shouted for a carriage as she gathered her shaking little girl in her skirts. Her skin was still so hot! The one neighbor ran out shouting to all who could hear for a carriage, while the other neighbor tried to stave off the damage.

"Oil! Butter!" she cried. "For a burn, you have to smear her with butter!"

Mercada looked up at her wild-eyed. She could not focus. Instead, she kept shouting for a carriage.

The neighbor grabbed a bottle of olive oil from the counter.

"Yes, Mercada, don't worry. They're getting you a carriage. But we can't lose time. We have to treat the burn."

With that, she poured the oil over Sara's limp and swelling body and began smearing it over her exposed limbs. Mercada, panting, blindly followed suit and also started smearing the oil over her beloved child.

But in an instant, she regained her composure. What was she doing there when her child was dying? She grabbed Sara off the floor and rushed out the door. She ran like an insane woman, screaming out the word "carriage" as she stumbled along, until finally one passed by and sped her to the hospital.

She wept in the outer room as she waited to hear from the doctors. How had she left Sara alone? Mercada flayed herself with recriminations. Why was she so cursed as to have to visit these walls so often? she thought pitifully. Every time it was for Amos, but now… *Why?* she thought. *Why did it have to be the girl?* Suddenly, she realized the implication of the thought, rising to the surface before she could tamp it down, a horrible, unnatural thought. *The girl, and not…the boy?* Mercada put her hand to her mouth in fright, as if to stop herself from saying it, from even thinking it. But you can't put a muzzle on the mind. No! She loved all her children! Please, God," she began to beg, when a doctor emerged. He knew her well by now. His expression made her turn pale as he sat down beside her.

"Doña Mercada," the doctor began, gingerly, "your daughter has been burned very, very badly. Severely."

"Is she alive?"

"Yes."

Mercada sighed.

"For the moment," he added.

"Oh, God, Doctor..."

"Dona Mercada, I want to ask you something. Why did you smear the child's body with oil?"

"Oil?" She hardly remembered what had transpired since she heard those hair-raising screams.

"Yes, with oil," he repeated. "I'm sorry to tell you that that was perhaps the worst thing you could have done. For such an aggravated burn, you have to leave the skin exposed to air. Otherwise, infection might occur. I'm afraid your daughter is in a very bad state. We'll see what we can do."

Had Mercada been a weaker woman, she might have fainted. That would have been a blessing, at least a respite. But she could not leave her body. She could not escape the horror. Sara might possibly die, and she, Mercada, had caused it. She had left her alone with the soup—how could she have left her alone?!—and then had followed what that ignorant neighbor had told her. She had poisoned her own daughter! Was there a more profane woman on this earth?

Sara remained in critical condition, and when Gabriel had come to see her, she was more hideous than when she had been brought in. The swelling had been replaced with something else, something indescribable. Her skin had sloughed off in parts and the flesh beneath had wrinkled and puffed and melted over her very skull and bones. She looked like red clotted cheese, as if she had had severe boils. One eyelid had become molded shut over the eyeball and seemed to drip down so that it hung a centimeter or two below the level of the other. Her nose had all but disappeared. Sara did not look human anymore. Their little girl, the little angel with the lake-blue eyes, the vision of loveliness for whom people would stop and stare on the street, had been disfigured into a ghoul. She was unrecognizable. Gabriel stood stock still at the doorway, frozen in his place, and then began to cry. But Mercada just sat and stared at the atrocity she had created.

Gabriel stayed only a little while. He could not stop crying. His little princess. Mercada, however, stayed the whole day and the whole night. She complained to the nurses about the open window, but they insisted it was what the doctor ordered and eventually the doctor himself was called in to reassure the distraught mother that fresh air was the best cure for her child. Though Sara would never be pretty again, though in fact she would be forever ghastly to look upon, she might at least live. Mercada clung greedily and selfishly to that hope.

Two days later, Sara came down with pneumonia. Her body had been too broken down to fight off infection. The open window had finally pushed her over the edge, Mercada was convinced, and the doctors informed her and Gabriel that their daughter would not last long. Gabriel and Mercada were thus forced to bear the unbearable, to watch their child die. They sat beside their little girl, who was heavily drugged with painkillers. Surrounded by the wails and moans of other sick children, she lay there, very still, her one working lid at half-mast, as if she were slowly drifting off to sleep, which in a way she was. Mercada tried to rein in her own anguish so as not to frighten her daughter, but the tears came rushing down relentlessly, and she could not stop her lips from trembling. Gabriel choked down his sobs so that it sounded like he was babbling. Sara could not speak, and her fingers could barely return her father's grip on her hand. Only her eye could talk. Sara fixed a longing, quiet gaze on Mercada, as if saying "Mother, help me. Stop the pain. Take this mask off my face. Make me the way I was before." She looked weak, weary and truly pathetic, in unquestioning incomprehension of her condition, and unsuspecting ignorance of her fate. In the din of diseased children, Mercada could only hear her daughter's faint, halting breath, and held her own in wait for the final one. When it came it still caught her unprepared, as Life released Sara from her suffering and made her free. She wasn't even two years old.

Sara's death haunted the family. Her facial expressions, her preferences, her manias were a part of the family routine, and now of its lore. Her little dresses were like ghosts. They reminded all of the person who might have been. She had already been a someone, with her moods and mannerisms. The way she would form her mouth into an O shape and open her eyes very wide when she saw something new that interested her. How she would follow Joseph around, adoring him, literally looking up to him with her huge eyes. How she would laugh at Amos's antics, performed just for her. She hated to take baths. She was afraid of bugs. She loved carrots. She narrowed her eyes when she was angry, wrinkled her nose when she did not like something. The way she mispronounced Vs as Bs and Gs as Ds: *halav* (milk) was *halab* and *dag* (fish) was *dad*. Sara had been an individual, with all the portent and promise that a being holds. Rather than bemoaning only their own loss, her family grappled with the abrupt elimination of a person.

For Mercada, when Joseph and Lili had died on the same night, she had felt that the bottom of the world had been ripped out from underneath her. When Samuel had died, it had nearly killed her. But none of those losses compared with the death of Sara. She lost her senses, and would have thrown herself into the grave when they lowered the small, sheathed body, had Gabriel not held onto her. She lunged at one well-wisher who had suggested that perhaps it was a blessing in disguise that Sara had died rather than have lived with such a disfigurement, and again Gabriel had had to restrain her. She neglected Joseph and Amos; she could not find the strength to care for them. This time it was Gabriel who showed strength in the face of adversity. He dressed them in the mornings. Mercada silently despised his calm strength, attributing it to his lack of suffering.

"You're only a father," she said to him. "You can't understand what I'm going through."

He didn't answer her. He began to drink.

She hardly spoke. Instead, she thought. First, her thoughts were almost exclusively those of self-recrimination. She had killed her daughter. She was damned. If only she hadn't left the pot! Or the oil! Why had she listened to that woman? And then the doctors, who had insisted on leaving the window open. They had killed her. No, it was her fault again. She had never let doctors tell her what to do before, why had she listened to them this time? Even if she herself hadn't killed Sara, she hadn't saved her either. Her mother had been a midwife; how had Mercada not known how to rescue Sara? Hadn't she learned anything from those years of following her around? Surely something would have sunk in besides how to pluck a baby from between its mother's legs. Her mother had been a healer, for God's sake.

When Mercada moved beyond blaming herself and took a look at the state of her life, she felt she was looking into a vacuum, a black hole, empty and pointless. She had no desire to live. She wouldn't eat. She wanted to let herself die.

Eventually, she began to come up for air. If time doesn't heal all wounds, it at least places a fuzzy layer of gauze over the pain so that one can function. She stopped pushing away her sons. Though she felt she could not comfort them, nor could they comfort her, she knew she could not abandon them. She knew they needed her. This was what helped her emerge from the deep gulf of her despair. Bathing them, feeding them, dressing them and walking Joseph to school with Amos beside her slowly brought her out of her grief, and back into the merciless world she knew.

She thought of Lili. Her mother, too, had suffered—seventeen babies! —but had always brushed herself off from her misfortunes and got back on her feet. She would be looking down on Mercada from heaven perhaps and would not approve of what she saw, Mercada knew. And she was right. Mercada was still a mother. She still had children to raise. She had to be strong for them. Sinking into her grief was something she could no longer afford.

But she would never be the same. She looked like a woman in her forties, though she was only twenty-seven. Her smile would forever wear a tinge of sadness, and she would never allow herself to forget about Sara or Samuel. Especially not Sara. Not that she could ever forget her. For Sara would appear in her dreams or nightmares regularly the rest of her life.

Chapter Eleven

IT WAS 1928. The Jews of Jerusalem were readying themselves for Yom Kippur, or Day of Atonement, the holiest day of the Jewish calendar. It would be spent in complete fasting and almost constant prayer, remembering and asking forgiveness for sins committed during the past year. Mercada's first impulse was to refuse to go to temple, to refuse to beg God for forgiveness for sins she could not believe she had committed, especially when she felt it was instead God who had sinned against her. But she again looked at her two sons and decided to keep up appearances for their sakes. And in her heart, she almost dared not cross this deity who had shown himself so willing and capable of spewing fire and brimstone upon her. So she went to services after all with Gabriel and their two sons, now aged nine and four, while he prayed and she chased after their boys.

Unlike Mercada and Gabriel, who were not devout, it was customary for the very religious Jews of Jerusalem to pray not at a synagogue but at that last vestige of the Temple of the Jews, the Wailing Wall. The Jews themselves called it simply The Wall (*Kotel* in Hebrew). Disturbed by the fact that men and women prayed side by side, whereas in a synagogue the sexes were separated by a partition (ostensibly to prevent any lack of concentration), a group of very orthodox Jews again introduced a screen at the wall, so that this holiest place of worship could resemble their other temples. The Muslims, meanwhile, knew exactly what to read into this gesture, and the Mufti of Jerusalem, Haj Amin al Husseini, president of the Supreme Muslim Council, declared that the Jews' aim was to take possession of the Mosque of Al-Aqsa, located directly above the Wall. So the next day the British police promptly removed the screen, right in the middle of the Yom Kippur services, while people were engaged in prayer. To add salt to the wound, over the next few months building operations were carried out near the vicinity of the Wall. The Jews saw these operations as intentional attempts to prevent them from praying there. Such skirmishes, forging a deepening mistrust, were further symptoms of the cancer that was growing between the two peoples.

A nascent animosity was similarly surfacing between Gabriel and Mercada. During Yom Kippur, one is not permitted to eat, drink or, among other things, engage in sexual intercourse. This was normally not a problem for Gabriel and Mercada. In the first few months after Sara's death, Mercada did not want Gabriel to touch her, and he, too, felt no desire to come near her. In fact, they rarely had sex even before the tragedy. Either they were too tired, too weak, or too depressed. Moreover, Mercada had vowed to herself that if she could help it, she would not bring any more children into poverty.

But after those few months, a radical change came over her. Mercada was struck by a sudden need for another baby. It was inexplicable, uncontrollable, and soon became her *idée fixe*. So one night she rolled over onto Gabriel and whispered to him to give her another baby. Her urgency surprised and frightened him; he found it unsettling the way she suddenly clawed at his clothes, taking him over. It was even worse that she made no pretense of feeling any passion for him, that she made plain that her fire was fueled by pure pragmatism. At first, he couldn't get an erection, making her frustrated, angry and even more intimidating as they struggled in silence, their movements clipped and limited so as not to wake the children asleep on the other side of the bed. Gabriel felt at that moment that he was anyone, less than anyone, a mere thing, a tool, a means through which Mercada's raging need could accomplish its will.

He felt ashamed that his body acquiesced to her rough demands, that his penis reacted to her despite how small she made him feel. It got so bad that after a while, around bedtime, he would automatically become edgy and apprehensive that she would strike again. He would lie in bed tensely, expecting and dreading when she would slide her hand under his night clothes to prepare him, mechanically, for her siege.

This lasted a few months, until to the relief of both, Mercada became pregnant. Almost two years since Sara died, Mercada gave birth, in 1929, to another baby, another girl. She herself had not eaten for several days, due to the scarcity of food in their home. Even worse, she had drunk very little, for they were in the midst of a drought and water had become a precious commodity, once more brought in by train from the coast. Nevertheless, the baby was somehow born a healthy three and a half kilos, about seven pounds. They named her Alegra, meaning Happy, in an attempt to influence her fate.

Alegra proved to be no beauty, not at all like Sara or Joseph. Instead, she looked more like Amos, with small, raisin-like eyes that always darted around. She was born with one of those egg-shaped heads that babies get from being squeezed out of the womb, but Gabriel saw nothing of all that. Squinty-eyed, egg-headed, and with hair growing on her back and out of her ears (though it all fell out within a few weeks), Alegra was an angelic vision to her father. As he had done with Sara, Gabriel doted on her. She was his little girl. He would bring home little toys for her, though toys were an unheard-of luxury at the time, as they barely had enough to eat. This time, however, almost everyone around them was impoverished as well. As it happened, a few months after Alegra was born, the stock market crashed in far-off America, a country so powerful that everyone in the world was suffering the effects of its economic cataclysm. But Gabriel was impervious to Mercada's remonstrations. He had lost one little daughter; now he felt entitled to spoil the other.

Like Amos again, Alegra soon exhibited an inordinate amount of energy, but she was more controlled, more calculating in her actions. By the time she reached the age of two, she displayed the keen mind that characterized her eldest brother Joseph, ten years old when she was born, but with none of his gentleness or shyness. Once she was speaking, it was evident that the little girl had also inherited Mercada's quick wits and even quicker tongue. But above all, it was her mother's iron will that showed through. Mercada could not simply scream at her or threaten her in order to get Alegra to obey, and "Because I said so" never worked, even at the age of two. Instead, Mercada had to reason with her, had to lay out the possibilities and eventualities of a given situation and let her daughter select for herself the best option. Of course, Mercada would present the case in such a way that the most attractive or logical course of action was the one she wanted Alegra to choose. This would work for a few years anyway, until the girl was too sharp for the game. Nonetheless, only by allowing her to choose for herself, to act upon her own decision, could her mother ever get anywhere with Alegra, who would never just do what she was told. It was maddening and exhausting for Mercada, but she had to admit she would have it no other way. A woman, she knew, needed to think for herself in this world, for there were many who would see her broken and chained.

As for the situation in Jerusalem, a month before the stock market was to take its dive in New York, the margin of tolerance between Jews and Arabs would likewise give way, with catastrophic consequences. In August of 1929, Muslim Arabs all over Palestine rose up and launched attacks on Jews, most seriously in Hebron and Safed. The Jews returned the attacks so that the violence escalated and lasted almost a week, when troops finally had to be rushed in from Egypt in order to quell the riots.

August is the season of extreme heat, and the air was sweltering. Jerusalem was a furnace. It was dusk, night was falling, and the temperature was only slightly beginning to cool off and become bearable. Gabriel had just gone out with Amos to buy some milk. It was Joseph, then, who heard it first, a ruckus of some sort happening outside. Hearing male voices raised, he initially thought it was simply two men fighting over who knows what. It didn't even occur to him that there was any physical violence, because arguments in the Middle East erupted often yet rarely got past the point of verbal abuse. But when it began to sound like the fracas had escalated, Joseph assumed they were having a fistfight, and like all the others in his house and in the building, leaned out the door to see what was going on. What he and Mercada first glimpsed were two girls who had been sitting on a bench a few meters away and were now cowering behind it, their bodies crouched and their faces full of fear.

Joseph thought, *Ha! Girls! Always scared. What do they think, that someone's fist is going to come flying all the way across the street?* He stepped out a bit to look to the left to see if he could spot anything. There he saw a man lying on his back on the ground with another man kneeling on top of him. He couldn't see the one on top, but the one underneath was dressed in smart clothes. He was shouting not to hurt him, or something like that, something about not having money.

"Get inside!" someone on the street shouted.

At first Mercada thought it was a brawl over the bottom one owing the one on top some money. It couldn't have been a hold-up, for no one would be so brazen as to rob a citizen in the middle of the street in the middle of the day with so many witnesses about. The man on the ground sounded very scared; his voice was high-pitched, and he spat out his pleas in a rapid-fire string of desperate words. All this Mercada didn't quite think but rather vaguely noticed, thinking it through much later when she had a chance to process the events.

Suddenly a young man jumped out into the middle of the street. He had his left arm outstretched and was waving it, and they all saw that he had something in his hand. Mercada realized it was a gun, though she never got a good look at it. The newcomer was screaming something at all of them, at the top of his lungs, but Joseph didn't catch any of it until the end, when the armed man called them something vulgar, akin to sons of whores (literally, the vaginas of their mothers). It was at this point that Mercada realized this was not a robbery, not some personal argument between the man on the ground and the other two. She and everyone else finally realized that it was not about the man on the ground. It was about all of them. The young man hated them all, all of Mercada's neighbors and friends, family and acquaintances, all of them perched on the balconies and crouching behind benches and mailboxes. They were all interloping, invading, usurping Jews, who were trying to steal Arab lands.

He just might shoot us, Mercada suddenly realized. He just might kill us. She grabbed Joseph by his shirt and slammed the door, backing away from it toward the wall, as far as she could go, scooping up Alegra as Joseph scrambled to find a place to hide. Everyone who passed their door made their pulses surge and their hearts race. Each time they imagined it was the man with the gun. But it was the neighbors and people off the street, shouting as they scurried past to stay indoors and lay on the floor. It shortly became a full-fledged riot. Mercada waited in trepidation with her children for an assailant to come in and point his gun at them. She spotted on her wrist the bracelet Gabriel had given her for her birthday. *Oh no!* she thought feverishly. She didn't care about losing the bracelet, but feared it made her too noticeable. She didn't want to attract attention. Except that money and jewels were not what they had come for.

She thought of Gabriel and Amos, who had gone out to buy milk. How long since they had left and she had caught wind of the commotion outside? Had they managed to get to the other street by then? Had the gunman seen them? Had they seen him? Were there more gunmen? Her mind was dizzy with fear and confusion. She could only faintly remember the man who held their little lives in his hand, though she had looked straight at him from her perch. She could only remember that he was young.

Suddenly Mercada's thoughts were interrupted by a short but fairly loud cracking sound. It was a shot. Oh God. They were really shooting. And then another one. The shots sounded absurdly tame, like little firecrackers. Someone is shooting! Will they come in and hunt us down? She might die here, she thought, and then her mind switched to another, even worse thought: her children might die. From that moment on, the only thing that filled her head was her children. Over and over again, their names repeated themselves: Joseph, Amos, Alegra. She didn't even think anymore about the prospect of her own head blown open, and she had to admit she didn't think of Gabriel, either, or anyone else. Only her children. Joseph, Amos, Alegra, over and over, like a mantra. She finally discovered that she had been wrong to doubt her maternal feelings during those moments when guilt would wash over her for not loving them as much as she thought she was supposed to, for wanting to be free, for letting them cry a little in the middle of the night because she wanted to sleep longer and risking that the cry might mean something serious. For not playing with them as much as she should have. For all the times she resented them and their wants and their needs....In that moment, however, facing down a madman or possibly a horde of them, Mercada realized she was a mother after all. In possibly the last seconds of her life, it was all about her children.

Gabriel and Amos did return, for the scene outside their home was repeating itself all over town and would last for days. When Gabriel saw what was happening, he grabbed his son and raced home, managing to avoid the armed man around the corner from his house. For days the family sheltered at home as the rioting continued. The boys did not leave the premises to go to school, nor Gabriel to go to work. He did not even venture out to buy food. Instead, the little family huddled together, and though they heard many blood-curdling screams and learned what bullets sounded like, they managed to remain safe within their little home.

The violence had stayed outside, until one night. Little Amos, five years old, awoke in the darkness, stirred by an unfamiliar sound. Like a cat, his senses were immediately alert, and he strained his eyes to see a vague form in the area of the doorway. The little light that filtered through presented to the boy's eyes a figure of a man, looming large and sinister, who had obviously just broken into their home. Unthinkingly, Amos screamed. Mayhem ensued, with the rest of the family waking and then screaming themselves. As fate would have it, Amos's shrieks frightened not only his parents and siblings but also the intruder himself, who as a result jumped back outside and fled.

It was an image that would stalk the little boy for years to come, invading his sleep and haunting his dreams. He wondered what the man had wanted. Had he come to kill them? As he grew older, he wondered if perhaps the man had meant to rob them, but seeing they were too poor to possess anything worth stealing, had changed his mind just at the moment Amos had awakened. Or had he come to rape his mother, who had just given birth? Or to steal the baby, like in stories? Or to steal Amos himself? Maybe the intruder had simply been a frightened innocent, trying to find shelter from the violence. This was the one possibility Amos wanted to believe, but his doubts and fears pursued him. And why had the man run off at the mere cry of a little boy, a harmless, worthless little kid?

What tortured Amos the most, however, was the thought of what might have happened had he not awakened in the middle of the night. He had saved his family, and not for the last time, as it would come to pass. Still, the knowledge of his act of rescue brought him little comfort. He was no hero. He had not meant to do it; he had not been brave. On the contrary, he had shouted out of terror. It had been pure chance, sheer luck that the trespasser had balked. It chilled Amos to know that all their lives had hung in the balance, only to be spared by the involuntary shout of a fearful kid such as himself.

In the aftermath, over a hundred Jews and an equal number of Muslims had been killed, while over three hundred of each had been wounded. It had been almost a decade since the first riots had taken place. Before then, Jews and Arabs, Muslims and Christians, had lived, if not in perfect harmony, then at least without bloodshed. Though they had not always been friends, they had at least not been warring enemies. All that had changed, and as far as Mercada could understand it, the enmity of the Arabs had grown acute when they began to view the Jews as their rivals for the land. Though the Jews had been the majority in Jerusalem for at least as long as Mercada herself could remember, Muslims outnumbered Jews in other Palestinian towns and cities. And while under the British Mandate, Jews were allowed more religious and political freedom than ever, she saw that the Arabs were always given the upper hand, the final say-so in decision making. This, though, was not enough to appease their worries that soon these Jews would try to take over Palestine entirely, and they were prepared to kill before they would let that happen.

During this time, then, the Hazan household, like those of all Jews, tried to lead its day-to-day existence peacefully, and kept to a low profile. Muslims and Jews lived even more separately than before. Mercada was sure that had her mother been alive, she would no longer be engaged to tend to Arab mothers-to-be. Instead, each community kept to itself, and most people lived in a self-imposed curfew, staying within the confines of their homes as much as possible and centering attention on their own individual families and lives.

It was in this atmosphere that Maryam's family loudly disapproved of her visits to Mercada. Though the situation had cooled off and returned temporarily to something resembling normal, Maryam's family warned her that it was no longer safe for her to venture into Jewish sections. Not only that, they scolded, it also looked bad, as if she were a friend to the Jews and not to her own people. Maryam had shown enormous fortitude in defying them, and she continued her visits to Mercada for as long as she dared. But when no one would accompany her anymore on her forays, and when her husband and brothers finally put their foot down, threatening to lock her up if she insisted, Maryam was forced to give in. She and Mercada had themselves begun to realize that they were perhaps putting their children at risk every time they crossed the city, from both angry Jews and Muslims. The relationship between the two women was forced to come to an end.

Two years went by, and other relationships were suffering. Mercada was pregnant again, in her seventh month. One evening she was preparing a huge pot of *hamin* on their coal stove. She had already put in the hard-boiled eggs, which would turn a delicious nutty brown, as well as the cow intestine—poor people couldn't afford real meat—which she stuffed with rice, raisins and pine nuts and then sewed up with needle and thread. The whole thing had just started to cook when Gabriel offered to take Alegra out for a walk. Mercada, however, knew his real reason for the outing: he wanted to get something to drink.

Sometime after the death of Sara, Gabriel had started drinking, and despite their poverty, or in fact because of it, he had begun to drink more and more. The fights between the couple became more frequent and more intense, Mercada accusing him of drinking away his children's food money, while he countered that it was she who drove him to it. He had even struck her, not once but a few times. Those who knew them began to look down upon Gabriel, for Jews rarely indulged in liquor and Muslims were absolutely forbidden by the Quran to touch it. Gabriel sensed the disapproval of neighbors and shopkeepers, and this only made him drink more, for the stupor relieved his guilt and self-hatred. It obliterated not only others' disdain but also his own, at what he had become.

The *hamin* would have to cook over a slow fire all night. Ever since the soup had spilt over Sara, Mercada was nervous, even superstitious, about leaving a hot cauldron for any length of time. So when Gabriel offered to remove Alegra from this danger by taking her out, albeit for a short while, Mercada grudgingly consented. Amos and Joseph were old enough to be trusted around the pot, at least Joseph was and he would keep Amos in check.

At the age of twelve, Joseph was almost like the father of the household. He watched over the two younger ones, helped Amos with his studies and sometimes helped Gabriel at the store. Mercada found herself relying on him more and more, and on Gabriel less and less. At first it was because the boy was simply around more than his father and seemed to understand better the hardships of his mother's daily existence. Furthermore, when Joseph was in the store with his father, Gabriel would not give customers huge bargains on jewelry just to be a nice guy, and he would not give his mother money when the two of them stopped by on the way home to visit her. Most importantly, Gabriel wouldn't drink around Joseph; at least, he wouldn't take a drink around him, though he would often arrive home drunk. He couldn't stand to see his eldest son look at him when he reached for a bottle. Joseph didn't need to say anything to keep him in line. He only had to be there, to look at him. His presence, his serious air of a little man, reminded Gabriel of his responsibilities and made him ashamed.

But this time, Gabriel had been alone, or alone with his favorite little girl, and when they returned, his eyes were glazed and she was sporting a brand new pair of little slippers her father had bought for her at the shuk.

The two boys looked at their mother in silence. They knew what would come next. It was a scene they had witnessed many times before.

"*Estás loco?* Are you mad?" Mercada hissed. "Are you mad?! You look at her feet, but do you look at her stomach?" She raised Alegra's dress to reveal the girl's abdomen. "Do you see her stomach? What about your sons? Instead of putting food in their mouths, you put trinkets on Alegra's feet?"

She pulled one of her daughter's new shoes off and inspected the sole.

"And you had to let her wear them home, didn't you? Now we can't even try to return them." She stared at him hard and cold. "And you're drunk."

At this, Gabriel, who had borne all the previous criticisms without comment, became enraged.

"How dare you insult me in front of my children," he exploded. "I am the man of the house and I do what I want!"

"Man?" Mercada cackled. "You think you're a man? A real man doesn't let his children starve while he goes out and gets drunk! A real man doesn't take the food out of his children's mouths and buy himself liquor!"

He fixed burning, seething eyes on her, this shrewish, scornful woman with her bursting belly who would only yell at him, and mock him and ridicule him in front of his own children, this woman who truly hated him, and who had become his worst enemy. In that moment, he lost control.

He slapped her. Before he understood what was happening, Mercada was pummeling him with her fists. He only meant to push her off him but, in the melee, he fell on her. She shrieked in pain, cradling her bloated stomach while his children screamed in terror, trying to pull their father off their mother.

It was only a moment, and then it was over. Gabriel felt an intense fatigue as he allowed his children to drag him away from his wife. He sank to the ground amidst their bawling. Never had Gabriel felt so alone as he sat on the floor and witnessed the group that had formed around her. They were still crying, panicked, as they tried to pull their mother off the floor. They had their backs to him, as they helped her up. A more symbolic pose could not have been struck. Gabriel was suddenly filled with an enormous sense of despair. How had everything come to this? How did he come to find himself in such a position? For he loved his family more than even himself. If he drank it was because he could not face the suffering he was inflicting upon them. If he drank, it was because he loved them so much it hurt.

Mercada had by now sat up, and suddenly she gave a shout. Down between her legs, there was blood. A lot of blood. She thrust herself up with one hand, the other pressed between her legs, and stumbled out the door. The children, still tearful, followed. Gabriel was left alone.

When Mercada returned the next day, the children were with her. Had they gone with her? Had they spent the night with a neighbor? Gabriel didn't ask and hadn't bothered to find out. They were better off away from him, he had thought. He himself had never left the floor; he had spent the night slithering in his ignominy, like the serpent's punishment for his crime against Eve. Mercada's belly was no longer swollen. She had lost the baby. No one spoke to Gabriel, Mercada out of hatred and the children from fear. The neighbors had heard the whole brawl. Soon everyone knew. The hospital staff likewise had immediately understood what had transpired. Some of the nurses had even gone so far as to enjoin Mercada to leave that bastard of a drunken husband, as did her old friend Rachel when she had heard. Lying flat on her back in the hospital bed, Mercada herself had wondered why she stayed with Gabriel. For a few moments, she had felt sorry for herself, and longed for her mother. Now there was no one to protect her. On the contrary, it was she who was supposed to do the protecting, of her children. She recalled again her mother's words, reminding her not to lose her pride, not to abandon her self. Was that what she had done? Did she no longer believe in herself? Was that what Gabriel had accomplished? She wished him dead.

But no, she had to admit, it wasn't all him. He hadn't started out this way. It was events, it was life that had beaten him down. He had been too weak to fight. Now he was letting himself die, drinking himself into his grave. But he was also abandoning his family, he was letting them all die! Yet what could she do about it? Could she leave him? Then what would become of her and her children? It would bring dishonor upon them. And they would be even more vulnerable than they were now. A woman alone, little children alone, that was even worse than having a drunkard for a husband and father. Though he barely brought money home, still he was better than nothing.

But finally, Mercada had to admit to herself that it was also for Gabriel's own sake that she could not leave him. She remembered him as he had been, soft and gentle. He deserved better than the life he was now living. No, she could not leave him like that, a broken man. She looked down at her deflated stomach and clenched her teeth. Nor, however, could she forgive him. He had murdered her child. And he had beaten her. In front of her children. No amount of despair could exonerate that. She would continue to live with him; she did not see any choice. But Mercada promised herself she would never let him hurt her or her children again.

She returned home, and no one in the Hazan household ever spoke of it again. The children soon went back to normal and reclaimed their usual relations with their father. They wanted so badly for things to be the way they had been that they made it so. Mercada, too, eventually began to speak to him again, and later to treat him normally, if not affectionately.

The episode thus died with the unborn. The two never made love again. And ironically, somehow Alegra's new slippers had disappeared without a trace, never again to be seen.

In some ways, Mercada was convinced, this was what finally did Gabriel in. His alcohol abuse was manifestly sucking the life out of him, but that time he had beaten her, the time he had killed their baby, was to leave more of a mark on him than on anyone else in the family. He continued drinking and also took up smoking, yet another drain on their finances. Mercada never yelled at him anymore about his continued use of alcohol, nor about his newly adopted vice of smoking. What had transpired that night had not made him see the light. On the contrary, it had only made him sink deeper into his self-destruction. She knew there was nothing she nor their children could do to stop the downward spiral. As she had once told Amos's doctor, some people die not because their bodies are sick, but because their spirits are.

Joseph was now running the store almost single-handedly, but it was a losing proposition. It broke Mercada's heart to see her gifted son deprived of his education while he waited in an empty shop for customers who never came. As for her own resources, people would bring Mercada articles to be sewn, more out of pity than need, but still there was hardly any food in the house. She could not understand how her work did not provide her children with sustenance whereas Gabriel managed throughout his incapacity to get his hands on liquor and cigarettes. He was now drinking Arak, an anise-flavored brew that was almost pure alcohol. It was cheap, and it got him where he wanted to go straight and fast. He neglected his family and he neglected himself. Sometimes he did not even come home.

After one of his nights out, Mercada could not contain herself. She was angry with him for having abandoned them and, though she wouldn't admit it, she had been worried about him, for his sake and her own. She had thought he had gotten killed, that he had drunk himself into unconsciousness or that he had been assaulted by thieves or murderers.

Even a drunkard for a husband seemed better than none at all, and Mercada knew in her heart that she would deeply mourn were Gabriel to die. She could still see the tender, trusting man she had married beneath the wreck that stood before her, his head bowed.

"Where have you been the whole night?"

Gabriel could only mumble his apologies between sniffles—he had recently caught a cold.

"I'm sorry, I... wasn't thinking. You're right, dear."

"Oh Gabriel! You're always sorry. Look at you. You're killing yourself. Look at your children."

He stood motionless before her, silent.

She sighed. It was no use. It didn't matter what she said. She couldn't change him. You can't change anyone.

She didn't speak to him the rest of the evening. They went to bed in silence, like warring parties. Gabriel hated Mercada's silences, but he hated her screams worse, so he, too, remained silent as he let his decrepit body sag into the mattress.

As usual in the morning she did not mention his state of the night before, and this was all the forbearance he asked. They both awoke in a bad mood, for Gabriel had kept them awake with his sneezing and sniffling. Nonetheless, Mercada crawled out of bed to prepare him breakfast, which consisted of boiled, black coffee (the milk was saved for the children), along with a piece of bread and some hard cheese. Mercada had learned to ask for old bread and to buy the cheese when it was moldy; the merchants would almost give them away. At home, she would sprinkle a little water on the bread, heat it over the flame and it was almost like fresh. Similarly, she would pare away the green outside of the cheese in order to expose the edible part underneath. But when breakfast was ready, Gabriel still hadn't budged from bed. He complained that his cold had gotten worse, that he hadn't gotten any sleep, and that he felt too lousy to go to work.

Mercada was unsympathetic. She had heard this story before. And who was going to provide for the family while he lounged in bed? she asked. He was the father of three children; it was his obligation to support his family.

So Gabriel, half-blind due to runny eyes, dragged his shaking frame out of bed, into clothing, and out of the house. Though his body felt like that of a torture victim's, he preferred even so to be away from the accusatory stares of his family. When he came home for his midday meal, he could not touch anything on the plate and simply climbed into bed for his siesta. This did not happen altogether infrequently, for alcohol curbed the appetite, so Mercada did not comment. It meant she and the children would have a little more to eat. A half hour later, however, Gabriel awoke in a cold sweat, shivering, with a wracking cough, and by then Mercada could see that this was more than mere drunkenness or even the flu. She grabbed Alegra and went to fetch the doctor, who diagnosed Gabriel with pneumonia. He was taken to the hospital, a hospital they knew so well by now, and where they were so well-known. Mercada came every day to see him, along with Joseph, Amos and Alegra. The latter two roamed the halls, seeking out mischief, while Joseph followed them, watchful.

A few days passed, and still Gabriel seemed no better. He did not appear to be fighting the illness; he looked so tired. His mother and one of his brothers had come to see him, after a long period of neglect brought on by his reproachful behavior and their dislike for Mercada. Gabriel's mother and Mercada had eyed each other with cold hostility, but neither had said anything for fear of disturbing the patient. He was so weak that even harsh words seemed like they would push him over the edge. After another few days, the doctors were pessimistic, and Gabriel, without having been told, knew he was dying. He accepted the knowledge, almost with relief.

Mercada broke down in tears, less from the news itself than upon seeing his surrender. She wept for him, for the sad, miserable life he had led, which he was so willing to leave. She wept for herself, that she now would have to go it alone, and for the guilt over having been such a harpy, for never giving Gabriel any peace. She wept for her children, who would be orphans, who would miss their father, who perhaps would now truly starve. She hated him, too, for his selfishness, for having brought this upon himself. And she remembered how he once was, poor Gabriel, so kind, so good to everyone, that was his curse. He could never say no to anyone. He wanted everyone to like him. It was hard work to go through life with such a delicate heart, with such a burning desire to please, to be loved. Gabriel had finally become worn out.

"It's funny," he now said, in between halting breaths. "I'm going to die of pneumonia, the same thing that killed little Sara." Mercada tried to protest, but he kept talking, and she acquiesced, fearing she would miss something he had to say. This time she let him have the last word.

"Mercada, I know I've been a terrible husband. I know I've only brought you misery." He coughed, then continued. "Still, I have one request of you. Listen to me. Please promise me," he squeezed her hand with as much force as he could muster, "that you won't bring Alegra to my funeral. She should not come to the cemetery. I don't want her to cry. Promise me." She promised.

An hour later, he was dead. They buried him the next morning, while Alegra remained with a neighbor. Gabriel had not had many wishes fulfilled while he had lived; instead, this one wish was fulfilled after he died. His youngest child would never cry over Gabriel, and eventually would barely remember what her father had even looked like.

Chapter Twelve

GABRIEL'S FAMILY DID NOT sit Shiva with Mercada and her children but sat it separately in the house of Gabriel's mother. Mercada knew they held no love for her, but was nonetheless dismayed on account of her children, Gabriel's children. She suspected that his family stayed away for fear of having to fork over money now that she was a widow with three orphans. Instead, neighbors filled the vacuum, coming by with their food and sympathy.

But people were talking. What was the matter with this family, that calamity visited them with such frequency? First the little boy, Samuel, then the two miscarriages—

"Miscarriages? I hadn't heard about those."

"Oh yes, two of them, then the horrible death of the little girl, Sara—"

"*Que Dios nos guarde!* May God preserve us."

"Not to mention the baby she lost in the seventh month, the one they say died because he beat her up..."

"Yes, yes, everyone's heard that."

"And now Gabriel. And the little one not even two years old."

"You know, so many bad things, that's not just bad luck."

"No, God doesn't strike one family so many times for no reason."

"No, He doesn't. They must have done something. I tell you, that Mercada is cursed."

People began to avoid her. They would cross the street when they saw her. They would keep their children away from hers. Mercada found herself alone, for most of her friends had abandoned her, out of fear more than anything else. She heard the rumors and wondered herself if she had done anything for God to have rained down so much suffering on her. Those around her believed that such strings of misfortunes were signs of a curse, and though misguided, in a way they were right. It was indeed a curse that brought such troubles to Mercada, and this curse was poverty. It was poverty that drove Mercada to harass her husband. It was poverty from which Gabriel had sought refuge in alcohol, resulting in his own death and in the death of his unborn child. Poverty had forced them to live in a shack so small that the kitchen was in the middle of the one room, where a little girl would topple a pot of boiling soup on top of herself and die such a hideous death. Poverty was even likely to blame for Mercada's miscarriages as well—how could she nurture a fetus if she herself was starving?

Mercada was ragged with grief and worries. How would they survive? She was a widow at the age of thirty-one. Joseph was twelve, Amos seven, and Alegra was two years old. The store went back to Gabriel's family, since he had never made out a will. His younger brother took it over and that was that. Mercada continued her sewing at night, and during the day took in other people's laundry. Her hands were rough and calloused from all the washing and scrubbing she would do with the harsh soaps, but it wasn't nearly enough. Having moved away from her old neighborhood, she had lost touch with friends who might have helped her. Many avoided her on purpose; they had their own families to support during these years of the Great Depression and they could not spare aid to others.

She also began selling flowers that the flower merchants would give her to sell in the streets for a tiny share of the profits. Again, it wasn't enough for the four of them to survive. So Mercada began collecting flowers on her own, on the rocky slopes outside of town. Sometimes she would take Alegra with her; other times if it was raining or if she deemed it too cold, she would be forced to leave her with a neighbor. Mercada had come to rely heavily on the kindness of strangers. She had no choice. She could not risk letting her children get sick by dragging them with her, but she could not stay home with them and let them starve.

And it was not just for food that they needed money, but for rent, clothes, even school. Joseph's and Amos's school began demanding tuition that had been due for some time. She again appealed to the rector's pity. Weren't the two boys now orphans? Wasn't she a widow with a baby practically still suckling at her breast? And Joseph was such a gifted student, how could the rector deprive him of an education? He loved school, he loved books. She convinced the rector to let her boys stay on, as a form of charity, for free. He was moved and so he gave in to her, again. But how long could she rely on his pity? She needed to be strong, and no longer fearful, yes, but she also needed to be smart. She needed to come up with a plan. What would her mother have done?

Mercada finally decided it was time to swallow her pride and visit Gabriel's family. Practically all of his siblings were financially stable. They would surely be able to help her in some capacity. Gabriel's brother Saadia, for instance, had a jewelry store like the one Marcus had taken over after Gabriel's death, while his sister Dina's husband had a butcher shop in Mahane Yehuda and lived in a villa in Bayit Vagan, a rich suburb. Another brother was a lawyer.

Mercada, desperate, went to see Saadia first, but not to ask for charity. She did not want to abase herself nor insult her brother-in-law with such a request. Instead, she had come up with a plan that would show him she was worthy of his aid. Rather than a gift, she had decided to ask Saadia for a loan, which she would pay back as soon as she could, so that she could open a bread store. It was becoming fashionable for homemakers to no longer make their own bread and carry it to a neighborhood oven, but rather to buy loaves ready-made in a bread store. Mercada had spoken to the owner of one such communal oven, and also had made agreements with a certain purveyor of flour. In this way, Mercada explained to Saadia, she proposed to support her children, his brother's children. She laid down the plan before him, in detail. But at the end of her proposal, he told her no, he could not afford to make a loan at this time. Business was bad, he said, averting his eyes. He was sorry.

Gabriel's sister likewise turned her down, claiming to possess no money of her own. All she had, her husband Maurice gave her. As for him, Dina said she could not make such a request upon Maurice, for whom Gabriel and Mercada were not really blood relatives. Even for her he would not do it, she said, lowering her voice. He had had a bad experience with his first wife, and thus was reluctant to be so trusting with the second.

Mercada, along with everyone else, knew the story of Maurice's first wife, with whom he had had two children. While married, he had been drafted by the Turks during the First World War. To support their two children, his wife, Mazal, had turned their house into a restaurant. Turkish soldiers would go there to eat. There was nothing to it. But one day a neighbor told Maurice, who was home on leave, that she thought she had seen a man kissing Mazal. And that was all it took. Maurice heard this and, allowing his wife no chance to defend herself against the untrue accusation, left her and their two kids. What could be more important than his self-respect? After Mazal died, he reclaimed his two children and set out to remarry.

As a result, Gabriel's sister, Dina, was seventeen years old when the *shadhan* brought her to Maurice. Dina and Maurice married, and she became stepmother to the boy and girl. The way people told it, she turned the little girl into her personal maid, but the child, starving for maternal affection of any sort, adored her anyway. As for the boy, the treatment he received at Dina's hands was even grimmer. One day she noticed that they had run out of bananas. So she sent Maurice's son, who was eleven by then, out to buy bananas in the shuk, which was located in the Old City. This would not have been such an outlandish request had Dina not sent him out precisely during one of the riots, the one in 1925. The Old City, moreover, was where most of the violence was taking place, and everyone at the time knew it. Trekking down the meandering, narrow alleyways, the boy suddenly found himself surrounded by a mob of irate youths. He was alone, and eleven years old. He never stood a chance, and was stabbed to death.

No one could understand how Dina had sent Maurice's son out during the massacre, especially not for something as frivolous as bananas. Rumors spread that she had sent him out on purpose, so that he would be killed. Perhaps she had not wanted him to become a rival against her own children, whom she had had with Maurice. Years later, during the War for Israel's Independence, one of Dina's sons would be killed liberating the Castel heights, on the road to Jerusalem. People said it was God repaying her for what she had done to Maurice's son. An eye for an eye, a son for a son. Divine justice.

Mercada's situation had become so dire that eventually she came to the attention of a German couple, the Holzbergs. He worked in a bank; she was a schoolteacher. Both were in their thirties and had no children. One day, they came to call. She was surprised to receive a visit from the couple, whom she had never heard of. Nevertheless, she invited them in and offered them a cup of tea. She was grateful for their refusal, as she only owned one cup. She was, as the saying goes, poor but proud, and the look they exchanged between themselves as they sat on the mattress—there were no chairs—in the barren room that housed her entire family made her blush with humiliation and resentment. What did this couple want with her?

Mr. Holzberg spoke to Mercada in a Hebrew clipped with a slight German accent, and in the German style, came directly to the point.

"Mrs. Hazan," he began, "my wife and I have heard of the loss of your husband and the difficulties you now face in trying to raise your three children. Your little girl is only two years old, still a baby. My wife and I cannot have children."

Mrs. Holzberg, silent the whole time, only blushed. He did not seem to notice.

"I am a banker," he pursued. "I earn a good salary, and we live in a nice house. My wife is a teacher, and she is wonderful with children." Here he paused for a moment. "We would be willing to take your little girl and raise her as ours."

Now it was Mercada's turn to color. Again, he seemed not to notice. He pressed on.

"With us she can have a long, healthy life. We would love her and provide her with a good education. If she stays with you, she will be doomed to a life of poverty and suffering. We can save her from her misery, if you would accept."

Mercada had placed her hand over her mouth. It was a reflex, as if she were trying to hold herself back. Joseph, who had been reading, and Amos, who had been occupying himself by picking up sticks without allowing any of the others to be moved, were now silently staring at the three adults seated on the bed. Alegra blithely grabbed at Amos's sticks, taking advantage of his momentary lack of vigilance, completely unaware of her starring role in the events taking place.

Mercada stared down at her. Her head was dizzy from the man's speech, and from so much hunger and fatigue. She stared at the little girl who perhaps would also starve, and who at any rate was surely malnourished. Alegra would grow up in poverty and suffering, Holzberg had said. Would she grow up at all? Mercada asked herself, recalling with customary pain the fate of Sara. Suddenly she noticed Joseph and Amos. Their eyes were now wide with apprehension. They seemed almost to have read their mother's thoughts, if one could judge by the look of horror on their faces. They said nothing, but their looks were enough to bring Mercada back to reality.

"Give away my child?!" she suddenly snapped, her voice having risen an octave. The Holzbergs winced at her tone. Mercada tried to regain her composure. She was deeply offended and also frightened by how desperate her situation was that people were coming to her offering to take her children. She remained silent for a long moment as she wrestled with her nerves, remembering once again *nil mirare*, never display one's feelings.

"Mr. and Mrs. Holzberg," she began smoothly, though trembling inside, "I understand your pain in not having children, and I am grateful for the generosity you exhibit in offering to give my daughter a better life. But I would be going against the laws of God, and certainly against the nature of my heart, if I were to give away any," and she looked purposely at her sons, to reassure them, "of my children."

"But Mrs. Hazan..."

"Mr. Holzberg, please do not argue with me. Yes, we are poor, and yes, we are hungry. But we will not always be poor and hungry. I won't let my children live like this, and I won't let them die like this, either. I cannot accept your proposition. I'll die before I give up my children. I have nothing in this world and no one but them."

With that she rose and the couple, understanding this cue, did likewise. Mrs. Holzberg had tears in her eyes and he, with a dejected voice, thanked Mercada for her time. Suddenly she felt sorry for them. She had seen them as aggressors, greedy child-thieves trying to take advantage of her misery. Now, for the first time, she saw them for what they were. Two lonely people with barren lives, living in a house so silent that only their footsteps echoed in the hallway. To them, she was the rich one, with the smudged, tiny handprints on the peeling walls, the perpetually runny noses and the chaotic squabbles over the right to lick the spoon when she cooked. Even the maddening whining, the relentless *But why*'s and *It's not fair*'s, the continuous mopping up of spills that seemed to reproduce when she turned her head, and the breathless pursuit of her fleet-footed children, moments that used up what little patience Mercada still had, would have been precious treasures to the young German couple.

"Though I can't help you," Mercada began, "I know someone who can. Have you heard of Mrs. Zucker?"

Mrs. Holzberg's eyes, wet with tears, only blinked, while her husband answered that he did not know the woman.

So Mercada explained to them that Bella Zucker ran an unofficial orphanage where she cared for abandoned babies or those born out of wedlock, and for older children whose parents had abused, neglected or likewise abandoned them. Mercada was surprised the couple had not heard of Bella Zucker, for she would often visit door to door, or else would have one of her assistants do it, asking for charity for the orphans, since it was a privately run institution with no government aid or sponsorship. Mercada herself had once gone there to help, before Gabriel had died, since she could not offer her charity in money. It was a sad, cold place, livened up here and there with drawings the children had made or pictures cut out of books and pasted on the walls. They all slept three or four together on mattresses on the floor, but they were bright and chipper as only children can be, ignorant of their misfortune. Still, Bella Zucker had told Mercada that those children who had forgotten or never known their parents would often ask about them, where they were and why they had left them. She couldn't bring herself to tell them the truth, she confided, so she would tell them that their parents were in America, that land of promise and abundance. She said they had gone there to make lots of money and would soon return for them with plenty of toys.

Mercada had smiled sadly.

"I just had to give the children hope," Mrs. Zucker explained, "that they weren't abandoned and that their parents really would return for them. Actually," she continued, "my stories turned out to be prophetic. One boy, Daniel, learned to play the violin while he was here with us." Bella in fact tried to educate the children in various fields. "One time we threw a party for some visiting foreigners who had come to see how we were running the orphanage. One couple saw Daniel, heard him play the violin and decided to adopt him."

"What a heartwarming story," Mercada sighed.

"But you haven't heard the best part," the Zucker woman crowed. "Guess where the couple was from? America!"

Thus, the Holzbergs left a little less disheartened than a few moments before, vowing to visit Mrs. Zucker that very day. Mercada would look back on this moment as perhaps the first time she had demonstrated her talent for making connections between people, which would serve her well in the future, though in this case she derived no merit. At the time, however, she spent the rest of the evening comforting her sons, reassuring them that no one would ever take any of them away from her. But she could not reassure herself. So this was what she had come to. Strangers offering to adopt her children, as if she were dead. She was obviously as good as dead. Gabriel had only been in his grave for a month and already their distress was becoming legendary. She thought bitterly of her late husband's family, none of whom had found it in their hearts to help her. And when, a year later, she held a paltry ceremony for Joseph's Bar Mitzvah upon his turning thirteen, they did not come. They were supposedly her family, but she got more support from strangers, from neighbors who would drop off their old bread or vegetables that were going bad.

Their suffering thus continued, and not just physically. Mercada had to look into the dark-circled eyes of her small children, for starvation impedes sleep, and it was all she could do to keep from killing herself. The children would furthermore be affected psychologically by their hunger. Amos, for one, would eat too quickly, even as an adult, out of a subconscious fear that his meal would disappear or be taken away from him. And they would retain indelible memories of the shame of their poverty. One day during a bout with fever in which she would become slightly delirious, Alegra would imagine herself knocking on her neighbors' door, knocking and knocking. It confused and frustrated the little girl that she was in her dream, since she knew they were home. Still, they would not answer her knock; they wouldn't open the door.

"Maybe," she mumbled, eyes half shut and forehead blazing, "it's because they are sick of us, sick of us always knocking on their door and begging for food." It was a humiliation she had never spoken of, had never wanted anyone to know about, even her mother. But Mercada, mopping her daughter's brow, saw how she suffered from their destitution and disgrace. Even a little girl knows what shame is.

But shame took a back seat to starvation. Mercada discovered the existence of a social service run by an American organization that once a week gave out free sacks containing flour, rice, oil, sugar and noodles. It was a godsend, but this was a step Mercada had heretofore not taken. She had asked for provisions on credit, and had allowed her children to accept food, but she herself had not asked outright for donations. Even standing on bread lines during the war had been different—everyone had been starving then. But now the disgrace was only hers. Once she had made up her mind to swallow her pride, she had tried on two occasions to enter the establishment, but each time ended up stepping up her pace and passing it by, her head drawn and her eyes to the ground. It truly was degrading to be poor! She could not bear the thought of people she knew seeing her walk into that place, seeing her begging for charity. She was wracked with guilt that her pride was preventing her from providing for her children. What a selfish and unnatural mother she was! Each time she would walk up to the building with little Alegra and then walk on past it, dragging the little girl as she quickened her step. This time, the third time, she had to do it. But how? How could she bring herself to do it?

"If only," she thought miserably, "I could empty my mind. If only I were too stupid to understand what a shameful thing it is to do. If only I couldn't understand it," she thought, looking down at Alegra.

The little girl looked up at her, expectantly. She had walked this way before with her mother, and wondered why she would become so agitated. Why would they venture out only to return home again, having bought nothing, having visited no one? Alegra was only four years old, almost five. She did not understand. She did not, Mercada realized, understand! She squatted down to the little girl's height and quietly explained to her what she wanted her to do. She then stood on the corner and kept her eyes peeled upon Alegra as she walked down the street to the American relief house. Mercada's heartbeat quickened when her daughter disappeared past the door. She had an almost unnatural fear of having her children out of sight, a neurosis surely inherited from Lili, whose history of botched reproduction had always rendered parting from her only surviving child acutely stressful.

Alegra, on the other hand, was overjoyed to be allowed to stray from her mother's side, to be liberated from her watchful gaze. She strode purposefully inside and walked straight up to a tall woman standing by a table.

"Why, hello, little girl," the woman said to her.

"Hello," Alegra answered. She was about to say that her mother had told her to pick up a package but stopped herself. She wasn't a baby! She was doing this by herself. "I want a package."

"Did your parents send you?" the woman asked.

Alegra sighed in frustration. "My mother. My father died."

The woman's face fell. "Oh, I'm so sorry." She pulled a sack out from behind the table. "Do you think you're strong enough to carry it? Shouldn't your mother come in and help you?"

Alegra fumed. "No! I'm not a baby!"

With that, she grabbed the sack out of the woman's arms and, struggling to keep her balance and also to save face, invoked all her strength to walk carefully out the door.

Mercada felt she hadn't drawn another breath until Alegra reemerged, struggling with the weight of the parcel. Her mother relieved her at the corner, showering her with kisses for having been such a brave little girl to go in there alone. Alegra grinned with pride.

And so it was that Alegra, in her own little way, came to support the family. Each time the ritual was the same, except for her smile of pride at the end. Even at the age of four, Alegra was soon made aware by other children's taunts that her forays to the American center were not something of which to be proud but rather embarrassed. In the end, she did understand, despite Mercada's plan. Still, Mercada forced her to do it. There was no choice. Alegra thus not only learned to become a tiny breadwinner, but also came to learn, as had the rest of her family, that poverty equaled humiliation.

And worse. They would all soon discover that from physical poverty, it was only a short slide into moral decay. It was a few days before Yom

Kippur, the day of fasting and asking forgiveness. The meal before the fast was therefore of great importance, for it was meant to sustain one for the twenty-four hours of mandatory abstinence. The shuk was thus packed, teeming with harried shoppers filling their sacks with fresh produce and other bounty.

Mercada's treasures were much more modest. She had found on the ground two ears of corn that the merchant had thrown away. They were already going bad, and no one would buy them. She had leapt upon them before two old women, who had spotted them before her, were quick enough to pounce. Her next stop was at the meat stalls, where she would be thrown a few chicken claws with which to make soup. Even meat bones were too valuable to be spared, for they would still fetch a piaster or two. Finally, she spent the little earnings she had on a bag of potatoes, which would at least fill her children's stomachs.

Mercada then set out to leave with her meager merchandise, all of which would have to serve as a holiday feast. On her way out, she noticed a woman selling freshly killed chickens, not in a stall but in the middle of the shuk, where people were crowding past her. There was a great hubbub around the woman, what with people shoving in order to get through, and the woman herself was not even watching her wares. Why, someone could just walk off with one of her chickens and she would not even notice, Mercada thought absentmindedly.

Suddenly the thought struck her. *She* could walk off with one of the chickens. Her face burned hot at the idea. Stealing! It was stealing! How could she even imagine such a thing? And what would happen if she got caught? The scandal! They might even put her in prison! But what would happen, she mused, if she didn't get caught? She pressed her lips together as her stomach raged. Oh, a chicken, a delicious, tender chicken. Boiled, it would provide at least two meals, both soup and meat. Mercada could practically smell it, and saliva automatically rose to her mouth. With a whole chicken, she could put real food into her children's concave bellies. She recalled the pathetic sight of their sunken eyes.

She took a deep breath and began her approach. Her heart beat so fast and her ears roared so loud she thought she would faint. Mercada could not find the calm necessary to see if she was being watched, if the woman or anybody for that matter saw what she was doing. Instead, she bent down and blindly grabbed from the crate. It took a few moments before she was conscious of holding a chicken, which she quickly stuffed under her shawl. Soon followed the woman's screams as she discovered the theft. Mercada froze with terror, but she was already at a safe enough distance for anyone to suspect her. The woman's cries tore her heart out, and her own shame made her mouth tremble. But she made herself picture her wretched children again, and thus garnered the strength to think past her guilt.

Indeed, the children were overjoyed at the prospect of dining on chicken, and afterwards licked their fingers clean. At least Amos and Alegra did. Joseph, however, ate solemnly in silence. He had been the only one to ask his mother how she had obtained such a feast. It wasn't that he hadn't believed her when she said she had found it cast aside. He was fourteen years old, on the brink of maturity. He believed what his mother told him. He did not even think to question her. But he also noted the deep crimson that set over her features when she answered, and he felt the heaviness in the air afterward. He sensed something wrong; he couldn't say what. What he did understand was that he could not remember the last time they had eaten a chicken. The feast only emphasized all the more their usual hunger, a hunger they almost took for granted. For the first time, Joseph realized there was something he could do about it. He could get a job.

At first Mercada was against the idea. She worried that it would get in the way of his studies. Still, he could get a job after school, but how would he do his homework? What bothered Mercada more than the question of school, however, was the very fact of childhood itself. He was her little boy. She had always taken care of him, not the other way around. It was her duty to provide for him. But he was fourteen already. By the age of fourteen, she recalled, Mercada herself had been left alone, forced to survive on her own. And as she stared into Joseph's large, serious eyes, she had to admit that the life he was living was not the carefree life of a little boy anyway. He really was a man, like it or not. He had no choice, and neither did she.

But finding a job proved more difficult than they had imagined. She had tried to get him a job working for Gabriel's brother in the store he had once owned, but Marcus said he was barely making ends meet as it was and could not afford to hire anyone. It was the same story with the other family members. Mercada had hoped to employ Joseph at least with a jeweler, banking on his experience helping Gabriel when he was alive, but she met with similar refusals. She even tried to find him an office job, but at the time such jobs were considered too prestigious to be offered to a mere boy. And Joseph, his growth stunted by starvation, looked far younger than his fourteen years. His mother, having entertained thoughts of finding her son a clean, safe post in which he would be able to sit and perhaps even study part of the time, discovered this was not to be. Toward the end, they began seeking out work in manual labor, but even this was impossible to find.

The lack of work was beginning to demoralize both Joseph and Mercada to the point of desperation, for their situation was worsening. They had again gotten to the point where their only meal was breakfast. One day, on their way home from another fruitless search, the little group stopped into their neighborhood grocery store. Shoshana, the proprietor, turned her head the other way when they entered, for she knew they had come once again to "buy" food on credit. She had warned Mercada that their tab had gone unpaid for too long already, but each time Mercada would convince her to keep it going. When she would cry and point to her starving children, no matter how angry Shoshana was, she always ended up giving in.

She saw Mercada enter with her brood, gritted her teeth and prepared for another embarrassing argument. This time, however, Mercada began before even picking out any food.

"Ms. Shoshana," she called her, for the Hebrew term *G'veret* does not indicate married or unmarried status, "I know I've asked much of you in the past, and you've always been so kind to us, so understanding. God sees how good you are, and he will repay you for taking pity on me, a poor widow, and my small children who are orphans. In the Bible God tells us to take care of the widows and orphans just as you have, Ms. Shoshana. If it weren't for you, we would surely have starved by now."

The shopkeeper already felt her resolve weakening, and it made her angry. How could you fight against words like that? How could you say no to that? And she always brought her children in, looking like little skeletons. She knew it broke your heart, and that's why she brought them, Shoshana thought, frustrated.

Mercada continued. "But I don't want you to think that we are not appreciative. I don't want you to think that we will continue to accept your kindness and mercy without giving you anything in return."

Shoshana raised her eyebrows.

"You have been generous with us, Ms. Shoshana, and we want to be generous with you. So I am offering to have my Joseph here, who is already fourteen years old, a man, work for you in the hours after school."

The shopkeeper tried to protest but Mercada would not let her interrupt.

"Ask his teachers, ask anyone who knows him," she went on quickly, "they will tell you how responsible he is, organized, serious. He has been a great help to me since I lost my husband and was left alone to raise my small children, including this little one." She pushed Alegra in front of the hapless woman.

"Now he has become the man of the house, since I can't support them by myself. I need his help, we all need his help," she stated, pausing for effect. "And since you could use his help, we would be honored if you would let us try to repay our debt to you by letting Joseph work here."

"Ms. Hazan," Shoshana began painfully, "Mercada..."

"Please, Shoshana, please. Don't say no. I'm begging you. Please just give him a chance—"

But the shopkeeper was shaking her head.

Mercada's voice was taut, shrill. "Ms. Shoshana, just give him a week, just to try him out. If you're not satisfied, then we'll forget about the whole thing. But please, in the name of God, for the sake of my starving baby, please give him a chance!"

Shoshana looked at Mercada's crimson face, and then at the children. Joseph, too, was blushing deeply. She knew she had already lost the battle when she found herself finding reasons why she should accept the offer, or rather request. Shoshana had no children of her own and her husband, who was much older than she, was sick and frail. The running of the store had been up to her alone for some time now, and perhaps she really could use some help. So Joseph went to work for her every day after school except for Saturdays, the Sabbath, but including Sundays, and Mercada was able to pay her tab little by little.

Their situation was better than before, but even so they still never had quite enough to eat. And hunger, well, it brings out the worst in people. There is no pride, there are no scruples, when one's very life seems to be on the line, and how much more so when the lives of one's children hang in the balance. Thus, it happened that one day, Mercada went into Shoshana's store while Doña Pardo, a neighborhood woman, was at the counter. Mercada began filling her satchel with the usual items she could afford on Joseph's salary and their own store credit. Shoshana had gone to the back of the store to fetch a bottle of olive oil for Doña Pardo and just as Mercada looked up from the cheeses, she saw Doña Pardo grab some eggs from the basket on the counter and shove them in her coat pocket. First one, then two, then three, before Shoshana finally turned around. She came back to the counter and began adding up the woman's purchases, without any mention of the eggs. She hadn't seen Doña Pardo take them.

Mercada's pulse began to race. Dona Pardo had stolen those eggs! She had slipped them into her pocket and then calmly walked out. Mercada kept her eyes lowered, focused on the cheese. It was wrong to steal. What that Pardo woman had done was criminal. But if she had done it, then surely Mercada could do the same. After all, she had starving children to feed, and they hadn't eaten eggs in an eternity. How quickly one is able to justify an immoral act. With what ease we can convince ourselves of anything. Her face turned hot when she thought of her mother looking down on her from heaven. "It is harder to be right than kind," she always said, and indeed Mercada was finding it impossible these days to do the right thing, rather than treat her children with kindness.

Mercada chose the rest of her purchases and then approached the counter. As Shoshana was adding up her bill, Mercada studied the back section and finally found something suitable to request. Shoshana looked up and without a word turned to fetch the product. Then, barely breathing, Mercada delicately picked up an egg and stashed it in her skirt pocket. She had done it! And what was more, Shoshana was still reaching for the candles she had asked for. There was still time, time for one more. And so she lifted yet another egg from the pile, shifted it to her left hand, and then dropped it into her other pocket. She wondered if she had time for a third, but her heart was thumping so loud she couldn't bear it. Why risk getting caught? Two were enough, better than she had ever hoped to get when she had entered the store.

Shoshana added up the rest of the items, while Mercada guiltily reassured herself that what she had done was wrong, yes, but not so wrong as it might have been had she not done it for the sake of her children. Was it more morally right to let them starve, to have their growth stunted? True, Shoshana was their benefactress and did not deserve to be betrayed this way, Mercada admitted abashedly to herself, but for Shoshana the loss of a few eggs was not as great as the need of Mercada's children.

She might have truly convinced herself with these arguments. But as she turned around toward the door, her eyes locked onto those of her son's. Joseph had just returned from a delivery. Mercada did not need to wonder whether he had seen her commit her crime, for the look on his face left her in no doubt. She felt a wave of nausea well up within her, realizing that even death by starvation was better than being exposed to that look. They both stood there, frozen, until Mercada finally walked out of the store. Neither had said a word to the other. Mercada went home, cooked the two eggs and fed them to Amos and Alegra. She would not have dared serve them to Joseph.

She didn't know what kind of reaction to expect when he would return home that evening. Would he confront her? Would he accuse her? Or would he avoid her eyes and let a wall of coldness come between them? How would he express his disappointment, his loss of respect for her? How would he react to her breach of trust? The hours stretched on interminably as Mercada was beset by these questions. How could she have let herself fall so low as to steal? She had stolen that chicken right before Yom Kippur, Yom Kippur of all days! And now she was repeating her crime, before the eyes of her own son. The person to whom she was closest in the whole world. Joseph had become her helper, her surrogate husband almost, her best friend. Now she had disgraced herself before him.

These self-recriminations were interrupted by the sound of the front door. Joseph was home. Amos and Alegra ran to greet him, as they did every night, as they would were he their father. He hugged them gently, released himself, and then walked up to his mother. Without a word, without a look, he put his arms around her and hugged her tightly. In no other way would he have been able to say to her "I understand you, I forgive you. I haven't lost respect for you. We are still friends." For once, Mercada found herself speechless. Tears streamed down her face, silently, while Joseph pressed his cheek against her neck, and held his arms wrapped around her.

The episode, however, did not end there. The very next day, Moses, or Moshe, Kaplan came into the store, as Joseph was helping to stack orange crates. He was a regular client of Shoshana's. This time, though, he did not come in to shop. He had something important to tell Shoshana, he said, and wished to speak to her in private, that is, away from Joseph. The boy's curiosity was piqued, and he couldn't help but hear a few words of their conversation since Kaplan, like many old folks, did not hear well and supposed that everyone else was the same. So he spoke—and whispered—loudly, and Shoshana, in order for him to hear her, was forced to do the same. Imagine Joseph's horror when he heard that Mr. Kaplan had discovered someone stealing from Shoshana. The boy even thought he heard mention of eggs! But what he couldn't catch was the name of the culprit, for the blood rushing to his ears was roaring like a tidal wave. His mind raced madly, trying to recollect if Kaplan had been in the day before. Had he seen Joseph's mother leaving the store, with lumps in her pockets? Another sickening thought occurred to him. What if that hadn't been the first time his mother had stolen? What if she had done it before, and Mr. Kaplan had seen? And now if Ms. Shoshana knew!

Upon returning home that evening, Joseph, who had never ever wanted to speak to his mother of the previous day's events, took her aside and told her what he had heard. The two then spent the rest of the evening racked with nerves, aghast at their crime, and its hideous consequences. Once again, Mercada bewailed, disaster was upon them, just when she had thought she was in the clear, that she had escaped harm. She deserved it, she knew, but she couldn't help feeling sorry for herself. She was an honorable woman, and the fact that she had stolen only showed how dire her situation was. Couldn't anyone understand that? She imagined what Shoshana was thinking of her, how the woman who had taken pity on them and gone out of her way to help them would now feel such outrage at having been betrayed. How could Mercada ever face her? And what about the punishment? Under the Turks, they would have cut off her hand! Would she now go to prison? Who would care for her children? They would die!

But the next day, when Joseph appeared for work as usual—what else could he do? —Shoshana said nothing. And the following day, and the one after that, nothing. Joseph expected at any moment that Shoshana would whirl around and accuse him, while Mercada waited in anxious dread, expecting the woman to appear at her door or accost her on the street in front of everyone. But the days went by and nothing happened.

Perhaps Joseph had misheard? Or perhaps the thief was someone else. After all, Doña Pardo had stolen; perhaps it had been her. Or someone else even. What was eventually clear was that Mercada had been spared. Her crime remained hidden, and if her own guilt and the loss of her son's innocence hadn't been enough to prevent her from ever stealing again, the terror of near detection was more than sufficient.

This would not, however, be the last of their scrapes. In the case of the eggs, their poverty had brought them to the brink of imprisonment, at least in their eyes. But in another episode, it nearly led to a death. As in 1929, another uprising occurred in 1933, toward the end of October, this time with the difference that the rioting was now aimed not only against Jews but at the British government in Palestine as well. Mercada had been out of the house, with Alegra in tow, when the gunshots began. Her first thought was of Amos and Joseph, who were both in school, though by then Joseph had graduated to the College Terra Santa while Amos was still in the École Alliance Israélite. So she dashed over to the Alliance, and then to the College Terra Santa, literally dodging bullets. By the time she had retrieved her two sons it was too dangerous to brave the trip through the alleys to return home. Mercada thus began banging frantically on doors. From within the first house, someone screamed "Go away!" despite Mercada's entreaties, and at the second door she and her children beat their fists against it again and again, with no response. Finally, the people in the third house opened their door and they darted in. The occupants then scrambled to push pieces of furniture against the door and to block the windows. Mercada and her boys were helping with the heavier pieces, while Alegra sobbed on the sidelines.

Amidst the pandemonium Mercada suddenly noticed that Amos was missing. The two women had only turned their backs away from the children for a moment. Her panic was tinged with fury. It was just like Amos to take advantage of the chaos and his mother's momentary break in her surveillance, she thought, to run off into the fray, as if this were merely one of his games! He had always been wild and reckless, and Mercada had always feared that one day it would do him in. Him and her. She realized with dread that this might be the day. She was driven mad by her fears.

She made everyone move the furniture away from the door and immediately dashed outside to see if Amos was anywhere within earshot, barking his name like a wounded animal. No one answered. Another burst of gunfire erupted from the next street. She stood panting and crying in the emptiness. There was no way she could venture forth any further. It was not her own death she feared; but if she died, who would care for her children, the last two survivors of their accursed family?

She returned to their temporary sanctuary and clutched them to her breast, Joseph staunchly trying not to cry while his little sister wailed. Mercada imagined Amos lying in a pool of blood, his skull cracked open by a bullet or his throat opened into a long, crimson smile by a scythe. Or she envisioned him captured by someone merciless who would tie him to a chair and torture him, who would cut his head off...

They remained cowering in the little house, fearing at any moment that the door would burst open and their enemies would kill them all. They continued to agonize over Amos's fate. He had been gone already an hour. Mercada, Joseph and even Alegra all thought of the little nine-year-old alone out in the streets amid the savagery. Restless Amos had surely gotten more excitement this time than he had ever bargained for, the poor little fool. Or else he was already dead.

Suddenly someone began banging furiously on the door. The small group gasped in unison, imagining their fears of invasion realized, when a tiny voice shouted from outside to let him in.

"It's me! Amos!"

Mercada rushed to draw open the bolt on the door, and Amos scurried in. His little family converged upon him with their hugs and cries, their questions and accusations. How had he done such a thing? Why had he done such a thing? He withstood their caresses for as long as he could, then pushed them away to show them his booty.

He had brought with him a threadbare blanket that his mother recognized as theirs, and which he had filled with various odds and ends. Mercada gazed in disbelief at her cooking pot, at the tin plate with the hole in it. Her shawl, too, the one her mother had left her, was in the pile, as well as Gabriel's prayer shawl, which was now Joseph's. Joseph grabbed it from the pile and clutched it, his only souvenir from his father, and suddenly began to cry. Soon all were crying as Amos beamed, proud of his feat, the lone rescuer of the family's meager possessions. They had so little, and he had feared that what with the possibility of looting, they would remain with nothing. Mercada stared at him as she realized that this boy who had so often seemed impervious to the feelings and concerns of those around him, had been thinking of his family all along, had in fact been thinking only of his family and not of himself and the danger he had been in. Moreover, he had understood all too well the depths of their misery and the importance of their few derisory belongings. Like Joseph before him, Amos had been robbed of his childhood and burdened with the bitter realities of a life of poverty. He had risked his life for his family's welfare. He was their hero, once again.

The rioting ended after two days. In its aftermath, both Jews and Arabs buried their dead, and then slowly proceeded to return to their daily lives.

Chapter Thirteen

MERCADA CONTINUED TO BE plagued by her inability to support her children, despite the kindness of Shoshana the shopkeeper. Even their outer trappings bespoke their need. While hunger was something that could ostensibly be hidden and denied, clothes were another matter altogether. Joseph and Alegra owned only two outfits; Amos had more, having inherited one or two of his older brother's trousers. Moreover, all their clothing was always acquired too large so that the pieces would serve for a long time, necessitating large cuffs and hems temporarily sewn in. The effect was always uncomfortable and ungainly. Even when the clothes finally did fit, they were by that time faded and threadbare. While the two younger siblings paid little attention to these limitations, Joseph felt mortified by the jeers of some of his classmates who mocked him by claiming they could predict a month in advance what he would wear, since his outfits alternated on odd and even days. They all wore shoes that were too large for their feet, so that they would grow into them and not have to purchase new ones, for they owed the shoemaker as well. They would stuff newspaper in the tips so that the shoes would fit, and when holes appeared in the soles, Mercada would cover them up by placing over them old cigarette packs she would find on the street. Mercada herself braved the cold Jerusalem winters bereft of not merely a coat but even undergarments. They would make do with what they had and when that wasn't enough, they would borrow on credit. In a short while, in fact, Mercada seemingly owed everyone, from the fabric merchant to the coal supplier. She ruminated endlessly for an idea of how to earn money. If only she had a skill, a talent that others would pay for!

But it was living on credit, the staple of the needy, that paradoxically eventually led Mercada to discover her true vocation, and would finally rescue her from her misery. She had always been an adept persuader—hadn't she persuaded her sons' schools to keep them for free? Hadn't she persuaded Shoshana to take Joseph in? Didn't she use her powers of persuasion almost daily for one favor after another? Similarly, Mercada found herself resorting to her wiles when she could not pay her debt to the milkman. They had been arguing for a bit, and when she began her customary lament that her children would have no milk to drink, the man countered that everyone had it rough, and that his own children had not had chicken for months. Her tongue working faster than her brain, Mercada immediately offered to get him a chicken. He eyed her suspiciously.

"You, get me a chicken? How can you get me a chicken if you can't even pay me for milk!"

She herself did not know. She hesitated. *Nil mirare*, she reminded herself. Show nothing.

"You leave that to me. But if I get you a chicken, will you cancel my debt?"

"One chicken, for how many months of milk?"

"Stop thinking of what already was," she countered. "The milk is gone, and you know I have no money. You can refuse me more milk, but then you will have to find someone else to sell it to, or it will go sour. And then you will have nothing." He opened his mouth to retort so she hurried on. "But think instead of the chicken your wife will cook! I bet she is a good cook. Mmmm, I can already smell it. A steaming bowl of chicken soup. Your children, do they like the legs or the breasts? Or the liver, roasted over coals…"

She went on like this for a bit until finally the milkman gave in. A small victory, but now Mercada was left with the predicament of how to obtain a chicken with which to pay him. Luck, however, was on her side, for once. It was Mercada's habit to visit the baker every Tuesday, when he would agree to give her a loaf or two of two-day-old bread, which he could no longer sell anyway. It was also Mercada's habit to chat with the merchants; she was well-liked, and they found her witty and entertaining. On this particular Tuesday, the baker was in a foul mood. Problems with his future in-laws, he confided.

"Already?" Mercada wondered aloud. "But they're not even married yet, your daughter and their son."

The baker became taciturn, his features grim. A wedding, an unforeseen problem...Mercada did a quick calculation.

"Let me guess," she prodded. "They want a bigger dowry."

The baker's eyes widened in surprise.

"And the reason they want a bigger dowry..." she let the sentence hang, as she fished.

The baker's blushing frown told her she'd made a catch.

"Might she already be...in the family way?"

"How...how could you have known that?" he sputtered.

Her only response was a modest smile.

"You truly are a very sharp woman, Ms. Mercada," the baker gushed, and laid out his problem in full. His future son-in-law's father, it seemed, was suddenly demanding of the baker an exorbitant dowry for his son to marry the baker's daughter, because in fact she had become pregnant. No matter that it was the man's son who had caused her condition. She was now considered damaged goods and he knew he had the baker in the palm of his hand. The man had stood firm against the other's ill-fated attempts at negotiation. After the baker had summarized his predicament, he eyed Mercada appraisingly. Now it was his turn to do some quick calculating. He might have failed to win over his future in-laws, but few were as versed in the art of persuasion, he knew, as Mercada. To this, he could testify from his own experience of her haggling.

"Perhaps you can do me a favor."

"If it is in my power, I will gladly help you in whatever small way I can," Mercada replied graciously.

"Maybe you could have a word with this man, on my behalf. I would be so grateful."

"Of course I will speak with this man on your behalf, and do my best to persuade him. I will do this for you, because you are both honorable and generous, and I know that you would repay my efforts with, perhaps, a few loaves of fresh bread?"

"Oh, of course, Ms. Mercada, should you prove successful, I will gladly offer a fresh loaf of bread."

"I will accept a loaf of bread even if I am not successful," she replied, "for my effort, since lawyers are paid for their time and words, even if the judge decides against their case."

"Lawyers? But—"

"And if I am successful, three loaves."

"Three! But Madame Mercada, you are not a lawyer! You cannot charge me like a lawyer."

"Charge you like a lawyer?" she laughed. "I hardly think a lawyer would charge you only three loaves of bread." She smiled condescendingly. "But you can hire one and find out."

Stymied, he fumed. And gave in.

Two days later she achieved what the baker had not been able to. The future father-in-law had agreed to lower his dowry demands, acquiescing to Mercada's arguments. She had addressed herself to his high moral character, to the honorable reputation of his family, which she stressed many times, in order to both tickle the man's vanity and remind him of his son's poor behavior. Mercada also painted a rosy picture of the marriage at hand, all but referring to the union as a *fait accompli*. Then she suggested how postponing the event due to haggling over the dowry would risk the discovery of his prospective daughter-in-law's stigma, that would of course reflect badly on his son, as well as on the rest of the family. The sooner the matter resolved, the safer their secret would be. "Their" secret, not "her" secret. Mercada ended by congratulating the man with regards to the young woman, listing the attributes of the prospective bride, whom she barely knew, to such a degree that by the end of their conversation the man was brimming with excitement that his son had found such a catch, and that he himself would gain not only a daughter but also a grandchild. A true bargain! He would be paid more than the original dowry price, so as to make him feel he had won the bargaining, but less than the inflated request.

That very afternoon, Mercada returned triumphantly to claim her three loaves of bread, which she offered the butcher in exchange for a chicken, which in turn she bestowed upon a shocked and impressed milkman.

A week later, hearing the fabric merchant complain that his landlord was threatening to raise his rent, Mercada proposed to speak to his landlord and prevent this in exchange for a few meters' worth of fabric. She sewed Joseph a new shirt.

When she was trying to persuade a seamstress to sew a coat for Joseph (Mercada had never been skilled enough to make a coat), the seamstress agreed on condition that Mercada place her daughter, too, in the Alliance school. Mercada struck a deal with her that she would get her daughter into a good school, perhaps not the Alliance, for they were already pushed to their limit, but a good school nonetheless, and thus she would get her coat. It turned out to be harder than Mercada had expected, for the girl's records showed her to be a poor student, and few schools were willing to accept her, though the parents had money to pay. But Mercada finally persuaded the Evelina de Rothschild School for Girls to accept her, on the argument that if the girl was no genius, then she was a perfect candidate for a school that included in its curriculum courses in domestic economy, laundry work and first aid to the injured. She proved to them that theirs was the only school that could provide such a girl with at least a respectable profession. So the seamstress got her little girl into a decent school, and Mercada got a coat for her Joseph.

Mercada realized she was on to something. People were taken with Mercada's slippery tongue, and showed begrudging admiration even when she used it against them, usually to gain something on credit. Soon she started offering it to obtain not something from them but for them. Little by little, it became more than her tool; it became her very profession. Mercada was delighted with this twist of events and could hardly believe her luck. No, it was not luck, she knew, but truly the power of the tongue. The episode involving the seamstress's daughter greatly enhanced Mercada's renown. Suddenly she no longer needed to seek out business; it came to her. People who had heard of her cunning would call on her to aid them when they had a dispute over services rendered, when they could not obtain the best doctor for an operation, even when they were having marital troubles.

But the "case" that served to seal her reputation was the one involving a man named Robas versus his employer, which happened to be the National Bank itself. This Robas had had to quit his job for personal reasons; but having worked there for almost ten years, he felt he was owed dispensation pay. Legally, however, only one who had been fired, not one who had quit voluntarily, was entitled to such remuneration. This was what two lawyers had already told the man. Mercada, however, agreed to take on his appeal, and so appeared before the man's boss one morning.

"I had told Mister Robas," she began, lying, "that he was better off bringing a lawyer for something like this, but when he told me what an honorable man you are, sir, I thought maybe I could come and speak to you on his behalf, as his friend."

The manager frowned.

"I am only permitting this meeting," he replied, "because I do not want to show disrespect to a lady, but I already explained to Mister Robas that the bank has its rules."

"Of course, sir, but a manager such as yourself must surely have to make difficult decisions from time to time."

"Perhaps, but this is not a difficult decision, Ms. Hazan. Mr. Robas left our company for a spurious reason—*spurious* means *frivolous* or— "

"Oh," Mercada cut him off. "I thought it meant something false. But I'm sure you know better."

The manager hesitated, unsure. "As I was saying, Mr. Robas made a rash decision to leave and now that he recognizes his *faux pas*—that is French for— "

"*Mistake*," she finished. "Yes, I know."

"You speak French?" he asked, evidently taken aback.

"Oh, just enough to get by," she offered modestly.

"And where may I ask did you study the language?"

"I never studied the language, but my son went to the École Alliance Israélite and from hearing him I learned a bit."

The manager raised his eyebrows. "Your son went to school, and you learned."

"Something like that. As King Solomon said, 'From all my students, I learned.' One must simply be open to all avenues." Mercada smiled meaningfully.

The director understood the meaning but plunged on. "In any event, what I want to remind you is that Mr. Robas left us not even due to an emergency but because he decided to follow his sweetheart to America."

"I am sure Mr. Robas would not consider being with his future wife as anything less than of dire importance." She smiled again.

He smiled back. "Ha. I'm sure that is true. There is always a woman involved. As the French say, *Cherchez la femme.* That means— "

"Yes, I know. *Follow the woman.* So you understand Mr. Robas's situation. It is common enough that the French even have an expression for it."

The manager sputtered at his inadvertent mistake.

Mercada dove in. "As Pascal wrote, *Le coeur a ses raisons que la raison ne connaît point.*" Seeing the director's befuddlement, she continued. "As I'm sure I don't need to translate, *the heart has reasons that reason itself doesn't know.* How can we blame a young man for not following his heart and his destiny? How can we stand in the way of his future?" She then expounded upon the former employee having so faithfully served the bank.

"I am sure there exists some way we can come to an agreement," Mercada stated. "As you yourself so wisely said, Mr. Director, *Follow the woman.* That is exactly what Mr. Robas is trying to do. With, I am convinced, your blessing."

To make a long story short, within thirty minutes Mercada had persuaded him that Robas deserved some sort of recompense.

As she rose to leave, the bank manager spoke once more.

"Madame Hazan, when you came in you said that you had told Monsieur Robas he would have been better off hiring a lawyer."

Mercada nodded.

"Well, let me assure you, my lady, you are worth ten lawyers. You tell that to Mr. Robas."

After this episode, Mercada's reputation was sealed. Where bona fide lawyers, and more than one, had seen the case as hopeless, Mercada had triumphed, and not merely regarding a simple inter-communal squabble over seats at a synagogue or the price of a donkey, but instead involving the National Bank, no less, and regarding a liquidation payment that the bank legally did not owe! People who had previously crossed the street to avoid her when they thought she was cursed or simply when her indigence was all too apparent, now made a point of greeting her, as they would a well-respected member of the community. Almost any problem that surfaced would be met with the suggestion to go see that Mercada Hazan. People offered tales as evidence of her success: one man's brother-in-law's business had been saved thanks to her; another's cousin had obtained a desperately needed operation due to Mercada's machinations. Her feats had become almost legendary, and Mercada began to feel that she could in fact solve almost any problem, by dint of her savvy tongue.

Mercada at this time also decided that as he was the eldest and had for a long time already held the position of breadwinner and man of the house, it was time Joseph got a job, a real job, not just as an after-school helper and errand-boy. He was sixteen already. He had gone to school for as long as she could manage it. She opted once more for city government, which carried with it a great deal of prestige and power. Before, he had been too young; now he would be eligible. She knew one of the directors of the city municipality, a Mr. Frank, whose son had attended the Alliance school with Joseph. She used this as her means of introduction to his office and soon managed to obtain for Joseph a post in the tax department, under the provision that he would have to work there for six months before getting paid, and then would receive a salary per month of four lira, equaling about one pound sterling. They were finally able to move out of the slums and into a small home, with electricity and an indoor bathroom.

Chapter Fourteen

NOT EVERYTHING, HOWEVER, would prove within her power to solve. When Alegra was six, Mercada went to place her in the École Alliance Israélite. Joseph had attended the Alliance school till he was thirteen. With his bar mitzvah, he was forced to change to the College Terra Santa. For some time, Mercada had managed to maintain both Joseph and Amos in the school for free, by wielding her winning words. She would appeal to the dean's pity by reminding him of their poverty and then of the boys' father's death. With Joseph, who was such a good student, she could convince the dean that it would be a crime to throw out such a gifted and model student, that one day he might become the pride of their school.

Amos, however, was another matter. He was a poor student, with no interest in learning, and he was a troublemaker. He had set fire to the school outhouse, had brought a dead rat into the classroom, had gotten into countless fights, and had been kept late at school so many times as punishment that Mercada was used to making the two trips to accompany home first her eldest, and afterwards her second son. Later on in his career of delinquency, Amos would persuade other kids to skip school with him, and they would hang out in cafés and learn to smoke cigarettes.

Mercada even found him one day by chance in a café known to harbor *hashashniks*, men who smoked hashish. Mercada had always been wary of the *hashashniks*, fearful of the influence they might have on her children. For this reason, she never let her children play outside where she could not keep an eye on them. In an era before television and even before they could ever hope to own a radio, the children were forced to spend their leisure time at home, with the meager supply of toys. And when nightfall arrived, they could no longer do their schoolwork or play because, in the days before electricity arrived, they never had enough kerosene to light a lamp, and candles were scarce. It was thus quite a martyrdom to be imprisoned at home, but Mercada was deaf to their complaints. She had seen too many neighborhood children tempted by the aromatic smoke and the happy, glazed look of the *hashashniks*.

So when Mercada had caught Amos in that cafe, she had thrown a fit. She had dragged him out of there in front of everybody, to his burning disgrace and the onlookers' great amusement, and when they had gotten home, she had given him the beating of his life. She had never laid a hand on Joseph; she had never had to. He could at least be reasoned with or punished in other ways. But Amos was wild and capricious and was unmoved by scoldings or threats. And it only got worse as he got older.

Thus, while Joseph helped her case before the school dean, Amos harmed it. This time, moreover, her appeals for free schooling came on the heels of another one of Amos's pranks. He had been caught in the library making paper airplanes out of the torn pages of some of the books. The rector was still furious, and thus remained adamant in his refusal to allow yet another of Mercada's children in, for free yet. His tone now, moreover, was insulting.

"Madame Hazan," he sneered, "haven't we taken in enough of your family's poor children?"

Mercada was taken aback by his venom, and in turn could not hold her own tongue.

"Monsieur Laredo," she spat back, "I think you forgot how poor you were at their age when you came here from Bulgaria with barely the clothes on your back." The administrator colored, for no one, especially one who had climbed to such a highly respected position, liked to be reminded of his humble roots. She saw that she had hit her mark, and so Mercada backed off and opted for a more graceful finale.

"But you, sir," she continued smoothly, "obtained a brilliant education, which you have wisely turned into an illustrious career. Maybe one day my children might also climb to such heights. If, that is, they are given the same opportunities."

As usual, her persuasiveness was delicate and masterful. Perhaps, had the book desecration not occurred so close to this meeting, and had the dean been a bigger man, big enough to see beyond the insult toward the compliment, her tactic might have succeeded. But she had offended him, and he would not forget it. He refused to let Alegra attend. It was the first time in a long time that Mercada had not been able to obtain something she desperately wanted by the force of her argument.

She was not to be beaten, however, and marched directly from the Alliance School, with Alegra still in tow, to the Evelina de Rothschild School for Girls, an equally respectable institution. She knew the headmistress from having rendered a service for her, something to do with a highly sought after seamstress who would not take on a job for the headmistress's daughter until Mercada had intervened. It thus took little time to talk the headmistress into accepting Alegra into her school, and for minimal tuition fees. Mercada walked out of the school with her head held high, proud of herself once again for prevailing against defeat, using only her wits as her weapon. She congratulated herself in succeeding in sending her youngest child to a reputable school and was furthermore delighted that Alegra would learn fluent English. Though French had always been considered the language of diplomacy, Mercada was sure English would prove to be perhaps even more useful now that the British held a mandate to govern Palestine. Even the *Palestine Post*, a newspaper established in 1932 by the Jews of Palestine, was in English.

Alegra had remained silent during the entire transaction. She had had her heart set on attending the same school as her brothers, and now balked at the prospect of having to face an alien environment entirely alone. Still, she kept her fears well hidden. Though she could not know what *nil mirare* meant, she had learned from her mother not to reveal her thoughts and emotions. Many was the time she had had to accompany Mercada while she attended to her business. At first, she had asked questions and even interrupted her mother during one of her negotiations, pointing out an error in her argument. Mercada had colored, and Alegra had known she had misspoken. But Mercada had kept her cool and resumed the transaction. Only afterwards did she explain to her daughter why she had said what she had said, inaccurate though it might have appeared. She also took the opportunity to illustrate the merits of holding one's tongue.

"You know, according to my father, may God rest his soul, even life and death are in the power of the tongue. Do you want to hear a story he told me about the tongue?" she asked. When Alegra nodded, Mercada began her story.

"One day a king became very sick and needed a special herb to be cured. It so happened that a farmer making a delivery to the court had this very herb growing in his field, and he promised to bring it to save the king. On his way to his field, the various parts of his body began an argument over which was the most valuable. The legs claimed that they were, for they were the ones taking the farmer to the field and then back to the palace with the herb, which would result in a generous reward. But the hands protested that they would be the ones to cut and carry the herb, and thus they deserved the reward. The eyes, however, asserted that without them neither could the hands find the herb nor could the legs bring it back. The ears disagreed, saying that they were the most essential since they had been the ones to hear of the king's plight in the first place. And so on. But then the tongue spoke up." Mercada paused for effect.

"And? What did it say?" Alegra, who had been following the story raptly, asked.

"The tongue spoke up and declared that it alone possessed the supreme power of the body. That it possessed the power of life and death. Well," she addressed herself to her daughter, "what do you think the other parts said?"

"I bet they said no."

"Worse. The other organs all laughed at the tongue. Life and death! Why, the tongue couldn't carry, couldn't see, couldn't hear," they said. "It was hardly the most important part of the body! The tongue then remained silent, while the others continued their debate and ignored it. Finally, the farmer returned from his field with the sought after herb and was ushered into the palace and into the king's bedchamber.

"'What is it you have there?' asked the king, surrounded by his doctors, counselors and guards.

'What I have here,' answered the farmer, 'is a poisonous grass that will kill you within a few minutes.'

"What?" Alegra gasped.

"That was exactly the reaction of the king," Mercada said. "'What?!" he shouted. 'A poisonous grass that kills? Take this man out to be hanged at once!' he ordered. The guards grabbed the unfortunate farmer and dragged him through the palace corridors to the courtyard gallows. All of the body parts were now in a frenzy.

"'Why did you say such a thing?' they frantically asked the tongue.

'Because I can,' it responded coolly.

'But it's not true!' they protested, panic-stricken.

'It doesn't matter. As long as I say it, people will believe it to be true. You all may have the ability to see, hear and walk, but I alone create reality. Now do you believe that I possess the power of life and death?' the tongue asked the others. They vigorously agreed and begged the tongue to save them. That's when the farmer suddenly spoke up.

"'No, wait! I misspoke! It's not poison grass, it's a medicinal herb that can save the king! Take me back to the doctors and they will vouch that it's true.'

"The guards weren't so sure by now, but the farmer begged.

"'If I am wrong, then I will be put to death anyway. But if I am right, then the king will be saved.'

"So he was brought back to the royal bedchamber where the doctors examined the grass and found it was in fact capable of healing their sovereign. Rather than being hanged, the farmer was richly recompensed with expensive delicacies and fine furs. The end."

Ironically, Mercada now realized, her father had used this parable to ingrain into his daughter the importance of holding her tongue, since he felt she was always too quick to speak her mind. This was also Mercada's intention in retelling it to Alegra. But she now had to admit that what it had taught her instead was how valuable a gift her tongue had become for serving her, protecting her, and now even providing for her.

Alegra did learn the lesson, however, and kept her tongue, but only in front of others. At home, she made her opinions well known, chafing, for instance, against the restrictions placed upon her free movement. By the time she was eight, she and her mother, had fought many times over this. It infuriated her that while both of her brothers were out of the house most of the day and even at night, Alegra was always supposed to be home. Not even alone, she complained; they enlisted neighbors to keep an eye on her when her mother and brothers could not be there. They saw their behavior as something good, as treating her special, coddling, pampering and protecting her, the youngest, and the only girl. But Alegra felt like an animal caught in a trap, willing to chew its own leg off in order to be free. They expected her to sit home and learn to sew and cook, she fumed, and even at the age of eight, she could see they were preparing her for her role as wife and mother, expecting her to stay under their care until a husband would take over. She would move from one prison to another. She and her mother, especially, fought bitterly over this.

"You never let me do anything! You never let me go anywhere!" Alegra would shout.

"You're only eight."

"Amos said he went out alone when he was eight."

"That's different. You're a girl. Girls can't wander around alone," Mercada would try to explain.

"That's not fair!" her daughter would yell. "You're a girl, too! Do you think that's fair?" she would challenge Mercada.

"You're right. It's not fair," her mother agreed. "But the world isn't fair. There are bad people out there. You don't know what it's like."

"How would I know? You never let me out! Never let me out of your sight!"

"It's for your protection, *querida*."

"I don't want your protection! I don't need to be protected! I'm not Sara!"

Mercada was taken aback. "Who mentioned Sara?"

"You!" Alegra retorted. "You never stop talking about Sara! Sara this, Sara that! *She had the most beautiful eyes, people would stop on the street to look at her...She was so smart, she started talking at nine months...*Sara Sara Sara!"

"Well, she was your sister."

"No!" Alegra cried. "She was never my sister! Can't you understand that? She died before I was even born! I never met her! She was never a part of my life, except as a ghost who haunts this family and because of who I can't do anything or go anywhere! But I'm not Sara!"

"I know you're not Sara," Mercada said quietly.

"And anyway," Alegra had to add, "Sara died at home. With you here. So what difference does it make if I'm here or out?"

Alegra saw her mother's face and immediately regretted her words. But she couldn't help herself. She had not been lying: Sara was a shadow over her, a cautionary tale her family had taken to heart and for which Alegra was made to pay with her own freedom.

Little could she know that her long-sought freedom from her mother would come sooner than she had thought. One day, as Mercada was accompanying Alegra back from school, they passed a construction zone where an apartment building was being renovated. They heard a shout but before either could react, a huge cement block came hurtling down and fell upon the pair. They were rushed to a hospital, the very same one to which she had brought Amos over and over again through the years, as well, of course, as Sara. And though Alegra's face was bathed in blood, it would be revealed that she had only broken her nose. The brunt of the damage had fallen upon Mercada. Her kidneys and spleen had been crushed and one lung had been punctured. The doctors and nurses, who knew her well and were almost like friends, were themselves shaken and saddened over her condition. They found they could not hide their emotions behind their customary professional distance. The main doctor, with tears in his eyes, confided in Joseph, the eldest, that he did not think Mercada would make it. The nurses even hugged him. This made him feel all the worse. If the nurses were embracing him, he knew, it must truly be hopeless.

Mercada's children stayed by her bedside. Joseph, the most voluble, tried to coax his mother not to give up, to prove the doctors' prognosis wrong.

"You're a survivor, *Ima*. Look at all the hardships you've endured and still you made it through. You'll make it through this, too!"

Mercada tried to smile through the pain. Talking was difficult, but she knew she had to make the most of the little time left to her to instill in her children the strength they would need to survive her.

"There are some things even I can't fix," she said soothingly to her three children. "That even my mother, a woman smarter and stronger than me, couldn't fight against. When it is our time to go, then it's our time. My poor mother, she couldn't even say goodbye to me. She had to isolate herself so as not to spread the cholera. Now that I am a mother, I can see how much fortitude she needed to keep herself away from her only child."

Joseph breathed in heavily, willing his tears back.

"No, don't cry. Don't cry for me. I have been so lucky. I had wonderful parents, and when they were taken away, I had wonderful friends who helped me, who took me in, who cared for me. And of course, my greatest fortune was to have you, my beloved children."

"But you suffered so…" Joseph protested.

"Life is suffering, my dear boy. But I did well also, didn't I? Didn't I manage to feed you all and clothe you and put you in the best schools, all on my own? I may not have a law degree, but I was almost as good as a lawyer, wasn't I? Isn't that what everyone said about me?"

"Don't talk about yourself in the past!" Amos suddenly piped up.

Mercada sighed and again tried to smile. "It's my time to go, my boy. But know this: all my suffering was worth it because you all came into my life, my beloved children, my pearls. You are my legacy, you are the proof that I was on this earth, and that what I did was good. Now it is up to you to continue my work. You three must take care of one another. My children, you are not immigrants like me, not strangers but Jerusalem-born. A war is coming, mark my words. You must be strong. You must stand together. Because you will be forced to fight.

"Alegra," she now called to her daughter, who had remained quiet in a corner of the room. "Remember when I told you the story that my own father had told me? The one about the tongue being the most important part of the body?"

Alegra could only nod, not trusting herself to speak.

"Well, I was wrong. It's not the tongue that's the most important part. It's the heart. If you stay together, the three of you, if you hold onto each other, if you love one another, nothing can stop you. A lone stick can be snapped. A bundle of sticks can't. Be that bundle. Stay together. Together you are strong."

These would be the last words she would say to her children, or to anyone. Mercada died soon after, but she had found a measure of tranquility before dying. She had succeeded in resurrecting herself from abject poverty and pariah status. More importantly, she had lifted her children out of deprivation and humiliation, and she had prepared them for life, even for life without her. Thus, Mercada died in peace, surrounded by those she loved most in the world and to whom she had dedicated everything.

Joseph, eighteen, Amos, thirteen, and Alegra, eight, were left to bury their mother in what they expected would be a quiet funeral. But to their amazement, scores of people came, bakers, butchers, seamstresses and shopkeepers, bankers and doctors. People she had helped through her negotiations did not forget her. Nor did those who had helped her. The Shafibis, her old neighbors, came, as did Isaac, the pharmacist, with his wife Dulce and their daughter and son-in-law Rachel and Isaakito. Doña Blanca the seamstress attended, along with Monsieur Laredo, the dean of the Alliance school. Shoshana the grocer was there. David came, alone. Only Gabriel's family were absent.

The crowd of mourners was a testament to Mercada's impact on the lives of those who had had the fortune of knowing her. She had been a lowly immigrant and soon a young orphan, impoverished and rejected, but she had risen in the eyes of her fellow citizens to a renowned, respected and, most crucially, much beloved figure. It was a funeral fit for who Mercada had become: a fixture of Jerusalem.

PART III *Alegra*

Chapter Fifteen

RELATIONS BETWEEN ARABS and Jews worsened still further. In 1936 the Supreme Arab Committee, with the Mufti as president, declared a general strike. Arab shops closed and the residents refused to pay taxes until Jewish immigration stopped. At this time the population of Jerusalem was one hundred twenty-five thousand, of which over seventy thousand were Jews. The English were becoming impatient and exasperated with the continued strife between the two groups. As a result, Lord Peel, in what would be known as the Palestine Royal Commission, recommended to the League of Nations in 1937 the partition of Palestine into two states, Arab and Jewish, with Jerusalem and other holy sites remaining under the Mandate. The Zionists, represented by David Ben-Gurion, elected head of the Jewish Agency in Palestine in 1935, and Chaim Weizmann, president of the World Zionist Organization, though angered by many of its provisions, such as the part regarding Jerusalem, nonetheless accepted it on the whole. The Arabs, however, under the Arab High Committee, flatly refused the entire idea. Before the English had arrived, the land had belonged to the Muslims, though they were Turkish at the time. They rejected the proposition that any of it belong to Jews.

Thus began a wave of intimidation, sabotage and murder, that dragged on. Arab extremists directed their violence not only against Jews but this time also against moderate Arabs. Jewish buses were bombed;

shops owned by Arab "traitors" were burned. At first there were only a few instances of Jewish reprisals. Then the self-named *Irgun Zva'i Leumi*, National Military Organization, shortened to *Irgun*, began perpetrating large-scale attacks on Arabs and Arab property. The Arabs in their turn escalated their actions, murdering Jews and uncooperative Arabs, while the British tried to quell both parties, both diplomatically and militarily. But when supposed Arab reactionaries tried to assassinate the British Inspector-General of the Palestinian Police Force, the English declared the Arab Higher Committee unlawful. The mufti had to flee to Lebanon and the Arab mayor of Jerusalem was deported to the Seychelles Islands. The deputy mayor, who was Jewish, consequently became the first Jewish mayor of Jerusalem.

1938 brought still more bloodshed. Even a few members of the highly influential Nashashibi family, who had been head of the Arab National Defense Party, were murdered for having withdrawn from the Arab Higher Committee. Finally, in May of 1939, the British tried to appease Arab tempers by putting out what would come to be known as the "White Paper," that severely restricted Jewish immigration and land purchase. This, of course, led to mass protests and yet more violence, this time from the Jews, and specifically by the Irgun, which set fire to the Department of Migration.

Then Germany invaded Poland and the world was once again at war. This led to a suspension in fighting between the Jews and Muslims of Palestine, while the British were forced to turn all their attention toward Hitler. All public buildings that had belonged to German institutions were taken over by the British.

Joseph, now twenty, had become very successful in his work and admired by his bosses. They were especially impressed with his knowledge of languages, for he spoke Ladino, Hebrew, Arabic, French, and English, the last of which he had mostly taught himself. When a foreign VIP would come to visit the Municipal Government offices, Joseph would be called in to serve as translator. As a government worker he was now drafted to aid the British forces, but thanks to his linguistic acumen was given a desk job translating foreign dispatches.

Meanwhile, Amos had been desperate to join the Jewish Brigade, but at fifteen years old was rejected as too young. When Joseph, now head of the household, learned of his brother's attempt, he had reprimanded him severely. Weren't there just the three of them left? he had railed. Did he not recall their mother's last words about remaining together? What if he was killed? And what about Alegra? She was still a child, and Joseph could not raise her alone. Amos was needed at home, he told him. He forbade his younger brother from trying to enlist again.

Amos felt hurt and slighted by Joseph's belittling of his daring. As always, Amos felt that Joseph did not appreciate him and saw Amos as their mother had: the troublemaker, the disappointment. More and more as he matured, he thought of Gabriel, his late father, and began to see him in a new light. He saw not the villainous drunkard, as he had long been portrayed by the rest of the family, but a downtrodden victim, a man who had tried to do his best but who had been forever carped at by his critical and overbearing wife. Gabriel, too, like Amos, had never been able to do right in her eyes. For Amos, this had become a self-fulfilling prophecy; he was always doing the worst thing one might expect. But he felt that donning military fatigues would finally earn him some respect. Everyone else seemed to appreciate his intentions. Yet though he might be commended, awarded medals, with all listening raptly to his stories of smoke and gunfire, only his brother, he thought with bitterness and regret, would remain unimpressed.

The British placed Jerusalem under martial law. Food and supplies were rationed. Once again it was Alegra who would prove to be their breadwinner; at ten years old, her youth made her the best candidate to melt the hearts of those who had food to spare. She would set out almost before dawn to stand in food lines or scavenge and plead in the black market. But hours of searching and waiting would nonetheless yield little. Prices soared. People began trying to grow their own vegetables but could not perform the same miracles with the arid dust of Jerusalem as the pioneers had managed in the kibbutzim. Kerosene rations were severely reduced. Those who were fortunate were able to do some cooking by electricity, though current would be cut off sporadically. Others tried cooking on wood fires, with wood they would scrape together by digging in gardens. On the positive side, the strife between the Arabs and the Jews declined due to common restrictions and hunger. Neighbor had to rely on neighbor.

The day after his sixteenth birthday, Amos went to the conscription center and lied about his age, claiming to be eighteen. He was drafted on the spot, given military fatigues and a rifle, and told to report for duty the next day, to be put on a transport headed for Egypt. When he told his siblings what he had done, Joseph was livid. He could not understand such zeal to throw oneself into the arms of death, and to die for another's cause yet! Amos, he had seen, had long been itching to don a uniform, another thing he could not understand. Hadn't Amos always resisted others' authority? He certainly resisted Joseph's. And didn't a uniform signify that one was under the orders of another? But he recalled his younger brother's fascination with guns, possessing in his palms the power to kill in an instant. Amos dreamed of being one of the heroes in the books Joseph had read aloud to him and Alegra, he thought. Maybe he also dreamed of medals. Yet what Joseph experienced of war was not heroism and battles but bread lines and hunger. And every day brought news of another fallen boy. Worse, they were hearing stories about mass killings in Europe. And now Amos had thrown himself into the thick of it.

Amos would only return home at the end of the war in Europe, a twenty-year-old man. His uniform bore medals for bravery. His face, too, was now decorated with a different sort of badges of honor, a cut through the right eyebrow, a piece of his right ear missing, and he had the tranquil, arrogant look of a military man who had made it back home. He told Joseph and Alegra tales of his battles. Alegra avidly ate them up, and Joseph found himself fascinated despite himself.

The war in Europe had ended, and with its end began arriving hordes of Jews, filling boats and ships that the British were once again reluctant to let enter the ports of Palestine. Those who were finally granted permission to enter bore tales of such fantastic horror that they would have challenged even the nightmares invented by Edgar Allen Poe.

After it was all over, the body count was off the charts. Not hundreds, not thousands, but millions. Could this be true? Millions? Had the Nazis really killed practically all the Jews of Europe? One third of the entire Jewish population of the world?

The skeletal beings with their hollow expressions had made it to Palestine against all odds, and they were a grim, determined lot. Having survived the worst that one man can throw at another, they were fearless, oblivious to pain, and alone in the world. Their families having disappeared, there was no one who would miss them, and so they had nothing to lose. Thus, a new breed of steely warriors was forged, from the very young to the elderly, who would do battle with the inhospitable desert land in order to bring forth fruit, and eventually with any force that would dare to rise against them or threaten them again.

Their tales of persecution would fill the Jews of Palestine with outrage, inspiring the younger generation to conspire against what they saw as their British oppressors. They were sick of their ancestors being burned alive in Inquisitions in Iberia, massacred in pogroms in Russia, raped by Cossacks in the Crimea, and now executed in gas chambers in Central Europe. The Jews were always helpless, always considered foreigners no matter where and for how long they lived somewhere, never seen as rightful residents and thus never merited anyone's protection. They were expendable, and this point was never driven home more than by the Holocaust.

The refugees likewise decided that it was time the Jews finally fought back against those who would do them harm, and to this end they needed their own land. Indeed, they were not allowed into other countries: European countries and the United States had greatly tightened their restrictions on Jewish immigration, and the British refused them entry into Palestine for fear of more Arab unrest. Moreover, the Jews of Europe could not even return to their pre-war homes, as these had most often been taken over by strangers who would literally kill to keep their newly acquired properties; many Jews, after having survived years of torture and escaped death, would return to their homes to be summarily murdered by the new inhabitants.

No, they really had no place to go, and thus they made up their minds to fight for what they believed they deserved. The Jews would have to reclaim, in no uncertain terms and once and for all, they said, the land of their forefathers and mothers, the land God gave to them millennia ago, the land of milk and honey. Though the arid desert appeared anything but a land flowing with milk and honey, it was all they had, the only place they could call home, and they vowed to drive out from it both the English and the Arabs.

The Jews of Palestine, however, were divided on the issue of the British. Many, like Amos, had fought on their side against the Germans, and Joseph worked for the British Mandatory government. Nonetheless many Jews, especially the young, like Alegra, were fed up with being ruled by the British, who according to them often showed favoritism toward the Arabs. The Arabs, of course, saw it as quite the reverse. The land was theirs. They had merely shown tolerance by letting Jews live there. Now there were all these European Jews attempting to settle there, and it angered them. As the Arabs would later see it, the fact that these Jews had nowhere else to go, the fact that the West was turning them away, was merely used as a political tool to further the aims of the Zionists and endanger the rightful claims of the Arabs.

The Palestinian Jews were divided on the issue of the Arabs as their natural foes as well. On the one hand, the new attitude on the part of the Arabs regarding the Jews as usurpers made relations between them and their old Jewish neighbors uneasy once again. But the Jews had lived with them sometimes for generations and had often developed bonds of friendship and cooperation. Yet the Arabs, and to a lesser degree the Jews, had always been clannish peoples who trusted only their kin and those like them. The raids upon other clans, which the Bedouins had had to practice in order to survive in the unforgiving desert, necessarily produced a fortified kinship and clan mentality. In a world in which you were constantly under attack by others, you had better be able to rely on those around you for support. For the Jews, constantly pushed about and exiled, the same fears and the same reliance upon family and tribe developed. Thus, while the Jews and Arabs of Palestine had often lived in peaceful coexistence, they would never entirely allow themselves to trust each other, and were always prepared to view the other as an enemy at seemingly the slightest provocation.

Adding to this mistrust were once again the English themselves. They sowed insecurity among the Jews by curtailing Jewish immigration—as if these Brits were anything but a temporary presence in Palestine, thought the Jews, to claim the right to decide who would live in the land! The English also appointed Muslim Arabs—and worse, extremists like the Mufti of Jerusalem, who had flown to Germany to side with Hitler! —to positions of political power.

Yet whereas the Jews would note the English restriction of Jewish immigration, the Arabs were preoccupied by the very failure of the Mandate government to prevent such immigration. To the Jews, not enough of their folk were allowed to enter; to the Arabs, far too many were let in. They viewed with growing apprehension both the increasing numbers of Jews as well as their talk of Zionism, a Jewish homeland in Palestine. It was not their fault, claimed the Arabs, that the Jews had been expelled from or murdered in Europe. The Holocaust was not their doing. Why should they have to pay for it by giving up Arab land? The Jews were slowly settling in the desert of all places and buying up Arab lands in the towns and villages, even buying up houses in Jerusalem, while the British, it appeared to them, were doing nothing to prevent this.

Here, then, was the crux of the British problem: they were forced to make promises to both sides. To them, this seemed feasible; to the parties in question, these promises were mutually exclusive. In fairness to the British, they had appealed to the United Nations to help them solve the problem of the two nations living on one land. They thought the Jews and Arabs could divide it. Yet somehow it ended up looking like the British had, upon their eventual withdrawal, promised Palestine simultaneously to both the Jews and the Arabs. With God, history and Her Majesty's Empire as guarantors of ownership for both parties, really, who would not have predicted the outbreak of war?

The Jews tried to stockpile weapons in advance, but the British would raid their caches and throw the Jews into prison. In 1945, as the end of the British Mandate drew closer, the opposing Semites could plainly view the other's plans for war.

Amos had returned from the battlefields of North Africa having finally discovered something he was good at. Now the thought of having to hang up his uniform filled him with a sense of emptiness and loss. So he decided that if he would have to give up his soldier's fatigues, he would replace them with a policeman's uniform. After all, there was little difference between soldiering and policing as far as he was concerned. You had to obey orders, show discipline and get the bad guys, as simple as that. With his service in the Jewish Brigade and his many medals, Amos was speedily accepted into the police force. This was one more feather in his cap as far as his neighborhood acquaintances were concerned, and he was treated with the respect accorded one of authority. Now when people knocked on their door with problems, it was Amos and no longer Mercada they were seeking. They wanted not words but deeds, not persuasion but the brute force of the law.

Once again, Alegra was entranced by Amos's heroics. Though her mother had often taken Alegra along when she plied her own trade as a bargainer, cutting deals between two parties, Alegra had been bored by her machinations. Talk, talk, talk was all she did, her daughter thought. Words, words, words, who cared? Alegra was more interested in action. She hungered after Amos's stories of beatings and bullets. He was a fighter! It was deeds, not words, that got things done, she was certain. If Alegra had to follow in anyone's footsteps, it would be Amos's. Not her mother's, she thought, who had tried to interest her in her negotiations, nor those of Joseph, who was studying to be a lawyer in the evenings at the Hebrew University, on a government scholarship, following in his mother's footsteps since Mercada had been all but a de facto lawyer.

But the plan for Alegra's future, she knew, had always been marriage and motherhood, like her mother and grandmother and all the women before them. Now that she was sixteen, it hung like a demonic shadow over her unless she could come up with a means of escaping her purported destiny. As a young woman, Alegra was expected to be pursued by suitors, but as fate would have it, her beauty was marred by her swollen nose that was constantly running, as well as her mannish voice, both the result of the accident that had killed her mother and broken Alegra's nose. Unfortunately, the doctors had botched the operation to fix it, and left her nose crooked, which was only revealed after the bandages came off. They said it was too late to do anything about it.

Joseph was glad his mother had not lived to see the way her only daughter had been scarred.

Alegra could never be pretty with such a swollen, crooked proboscis, he thought. She would always look like a prize-fighter rather than a princess. Worse yet was that her voice was affected, and had transformed into a hoarse, raspy whisper, like those of the villains on the programs they would listen to with their new radio. Moreover, Alegra would forever have a post-nasal drip, which would force her to constantly wipe her nose with her sleeve or, when fortune permitted, a handkerchief. But the true damage was that the injury had affected Alegra's spirit. From a carefree, happy child, she had turned overnight into a self-conscious little creature, convinced of her own inferiority. The jeers of the other children at the English school had formed a shell around her. She would sit at the back of the class and speak only when compelled to.

Nonetheless, by the age of sixteen, Alegra was not really ugly; she was simply considered a tad too masculine. She had male friends, but no male admirers. She herself didn't fret over this but instead used it to her advantage. As men would not be breaking down the door for her if she sat at home, the only solution was that she should go out into the world and find a husband herself, she told her brothers. These were modern times, she argued. Girls no longer stayed home but found employment outside, and this was only to Alegra's benefit; perhaps in this way she would meet someone who could get to know the real Alegra and see past her face. Her brothers allowed themselves to be convinced, mainly because they tired of arguing with her. She was permitted to go out and seek employment, and she took advantage of her newfound liberty little by little until she was able to absent herself all day and wander through the city unfettered.

By now, Alegra had conquered or at least concealed her sense of physical inferiority through an outgoing and almost aggressive personality. Before anyone could laugh at her voice, she would laugh first. Before anyone could reject her, she would reject him first. In fact, she pretended to have no romantic inclinations; she was all business, one of the boys, someone you could roughhouse with and whom you didn't have to handle with care. Because of this attitude, she made more friends among boys than girls, and she had to admit that she felt more comfortable with them, having grown up with two older brothers, than with girls of her age, who dwelt too much on their looks and on finding a mate.

By the time she was seventeen, Alegra had obtained employment in a bank. At first this had reassured Joseph and Amos that their sister had gotten a steady, safe desk job, for Alegra seemed to be spending so much time with boys that she was acting like them, coming home with dirty, scratched knees and her hair messed. The first time she had returned looking that way, Amos had been home and had assumed the worst.

Had it been Joseph, he would have questioned her before jumping to conclusions. Amos, on the other hand, had reacted without thinking. He had slapped her hard across the face as soon as she had entered their house.

"How could you lose your honor like that?" he accused her. "Now who will want to marry you?"

"Marry me?" Alegra repeated, bewildered. She touched the tender spot on her cheek where her brother had struck her. He had never lifted a hand against her before, so she was more shocked than angry. "What are you talking about?"

"I'm talking about your honor," Amos repeated. "A girl who is not a virgin is looked upon as if she were a whore! That's how people think, and you know it!"

He would have continued haranguing her had Alegra not burst out laughing.

Now it was Amos's turn to be surprised. "What are you laughing at, you miserable girl?"

"At you! Is that what you think, that I've lost my virginity? Why?" She looked down at her rumpled clothes and skinned knees. "Because I'm a mess? But I'm always a mess!"

"Oh Alegra..." Amos sighed with relief.

"First of all," she continued, "you should know me better than that. I'm not stupid. I wouldn't dishonor myself."

Amos began to smile.

"And anyway, who would want to rape me? Look at me!"

He stopped smiling. "Don't talk like that." He hesitated. Rather than take on the thorny issue of his sister's self-confidence, he chose to focus on the dangers out in the world. "You don't know some of the things I've seen. Men are dogs, Alegra. They will sleep with anyone. Even old women." He had been trying to show that no one was safe from predatory men, but now realized the implication of his words. "I don't mean you are not—"

"Not what? Or should I say *not who?* Not Sara?"

He blanched. "That's not what I meant."

244 | Daughters of Jerusalem

"Yes, the beautiful Sara. If only she had lived instead of me."

Amos grimaced. For Alegra, Sara was the beautiful angel to whom she would always believe she was compared. But to Amos, she haunted him in a different way. For he would always remember that it was because of him that his baby sister had died. No matter how many Nazis he killed, no matter how many murderers and rapists he captured, he would never be able to wipe that stain from his soul.

But Alegra was too tired to argue, and with a wave of her hand dismissed Amos's agitated expression.

While Alegra was being accused of surreptitious trysts with the opposite sex, Joseph was just as much a conundrum for his lack of such, at least to his brother and sister. He was handsome, both acknowledged, with his huge blue eyes and straight teeth, his tall and slender build. He was intelligent, well-read, warm, generous and well-mannered, and soon he would finish his law studies. Though he had many women friends, there was never a specific one he would bring home. Alegra was particularly fond of Hannah, who was extremely educated and well-read (everyone called her a walking encyclopedia) and could add dimensions to the discussion of the political situation in Palestine, dimensions that Alegra sometimes had not considered. In the end, Hannah would never marry, for all the men with whom she would ever come in contact were beneath her intellectually. Except for Joseph, she thought.

But Joseph was not interested in Hannah, at least not in that way. He never seemed truly interested in any woman in particular. They were all just friends. Yet he professed many times to his sister how much he wanted to marry, and even more how he wanted to have children, for he loved little kids. He struck Alegra as being quite lonely, amidst his many friends. He longed to find someone special, he admitted to her, and wondered if he ever would find the right girl, if she was really out there for him.

Alegra scoffed at his doubts, and reassured him he had everything to offer, that no girl in her right mind wouldn't want him, if only he would want her.

"But is it so horrible to be unmarried?" she couldn't help asking. "Is it always so wonderful to be married? Look at how things ended with our mother and father."

"They were poor," Joseph protested. "That would curdle any marriage." He didn't like to dwell on his parent's relationship. Once he had overheard his mother and brother arguing. In a moment of fury Amos had accused her of being the reason his father had died, that she had driven him to drink. Mercada had stood with her mouth open; for once she had been at a loss for words. But Joseph saw that Amos had not enjoyed his victory and had stormed out of the house in anger and shame, not returning until later when both pretended nothing had happened, each awkwardly avoiding the other's gaze.

Alegra folded her arms and gazed evenly at him, for she did not agree. Sometimes hardship strengthened a union. But she decided to take another tack.

"Then look at us. Look at our lives," she said. "We have the freedom to take a trip to Ein Gedi with our friends at a moment's notice. We can stay out dancing till late. We wouldn't be able to do those things if we were married with children."

"There is a time for everything, Alegra—"

"And now is the time to live a young person's life!" she interrupted. "You feel like going to a party, you go. You want to leave, you leave."

"But what about being in love, Alegra?" Joseph asked her. "Don't you long for that feeling?"

"You know what feeling I long for?" she told him. "You know the feeling you have before going out on Saturday nights? Bathing, getting dressed, shaving in your case. You know what all that excitement comes from? From knowing that anything can happen. That there's a world of possibility and mystery out there."

Here Joseph would smile. "Aren't you concerned about your future?"

"Remember that phrase you taught us when we were younger?" she answered. "*Carpe diem*, seize the day? When we concentrate on the future,

246 | Daughters of Jerusalem

or even the past, we disregard the present. We neglect the moment. So let's enjoy this time. Let's live it. Seize the day!"

Indeed, Alegra could think of nothing worse than to be saddled with a husband and tied down to household chores and worse, motherhood. She especially envied Amos, with his dapper uniform and his brushes with danger. He was her hero. At her age he had been out fighting Nazis in foreign countries! She longed to escape the confines of her little house and little life, to go out into the world and fight, as she so often told him.

These remarks often made Amos laugh with a bitterness he tried to hide from his siblings. Perhaps when he had been a soldier, his life had been exciting and dangerous, and he had fought against a hateful enemy. But now, as a policeman, his work consisted of jailing drunks and breaking up fistfights. The English officers got the serious calls, like raiding illegal arms caches or intervening in shootouts. As fate would have it, when he got to his squad room after refusing yet another of Alegra's ardent pleas to accompany him on what she envisioned as his nail-bitingly thrilling rounds, he found that he had been posted to run a raid on a hotel known for its use by prostitutes. He clenched his teeth at the futility. He did not see the point of such raids. Just let people do whatever dirty things they want to do in privacy, as long as they don't hurt anyone, was his opinion. But orders were orders.

He and his group burst through the front entrance of the hotel and quickly ran up the stairs, breaking open the doors amidst the shrieks and protests of women in various stages of undress and various positions of intercourse, while their clients scurried to cover their faces or genitals. The clients needn't have worried, for the government's policy was to let the men run home and only to arrest the women. It was a crime to sell one's body, not to buy another's.

It was Amos who kicked open the door at the end of the hallway. What he saw made him pale with disgust, the sight of two men touching each other, kissing one another. And then Amos recognized one of them. He quickly grabbed the door handle and slammed it shut, swallowing hard and trying not to panic. His head whirled and he feared he would vomit. He looked around to see if his comrades-in-arms had noticed. But they were all busy harassing the prostitutes and the normal perverts. Amos followed the other policemen downstairs, not taking his eyes off any of them, should any decide to return upstairs.

He did not return home that night, nor the next, sleeping instead at his headquarters. He could not erase the scene from his mind; it haunted him when he closed his eyes, the two of them, in bed together. He thought with a resentful sneer what his mother would have said if she had known that her beloved favorite was a monster. And she always complained that he never went out steady with one girl! That he played around instead of settling down and marrying!

Joseph had at times considered choosing one woman to be his girlfriend, to please his mother when she was alive, and a few of his female friends had made it abundantly clear that they were interested in the position. But he could not bring himself to imagine it in more than the vaguest of terms. He could not imagine dedicating himself to a girl, spending every day and every night with her. Most of all the nights. He could not imagine bedding down with those mushy, flabby feminine forms, leaking fluids from all orifices. Just the thought filled him with revulsion. And he could not imagine ever giving up those stolen moments of contact with the hard, tight flesh of young men like himself. He was riven with shame and anguish by what he saw as his own perversion and had lived in terror of being revealed, that something or someone would give him away. In his early youth he had been practically consumed by the conviction that surely he was the only one whose dreams were invaded by the wrong object of love, whose desires were awakened by the sight not of ample buttocks but of bulging muscles, not of overflowing breasts but of swollen groins.

It thus came as a great relief to Joseph to discover that he was not alone in his uncommon passion. He would never forget the first time he felt his veins become throttled and choked as he leaned into the hips of another man, practically losing consciousness at the final violent moment of eruption and unbelievable pleasure. It was literally a secret brotherhood in which young men like himself, suffering and eager, knew to recognize each other at almost a glance. It was all they needed and all they could risk in a society that would not merely cast them out but would probably have them killed, a threat to the common order and to Middle Eastern machismo. So Joseph lived his life of hidden yearnings and secret rendezvous while the girls he befriended fantasized about bridal dresses.

Was it a blessing or a curse that it had been Amos who had discovered him? Had it been another policeman, he would have been thrown in jail or beaten to death. Probably both. But Joseph wasn't sure that death wouldn't have been better. Now Amos, his own brother, knew. How could he ever face him again? Would Amos report him? Joseph would lose his job. He would go to jail. He would have to kill himself. He thought he *should* commit suicide, and entertained the notion for a second, but realized he was only flattering himself. He did not have the courage to do it. He was weak, not like Amos. Were Amos in his shoes, he would be able to kill himself without batting an eyelash; he had proven his mettle in the war. Joseph had always envied his brother's blind strength, his certainty, his bravery. He never lingered over a dilemma.

"Your problem is you think too much," Amos had once told Joseph. "*Quien mucha pensa, no se la fada Yerusalaim, ha ha.* [Whoever thinks too much will never reach Jerusalem.] You have to act, not think. Once you think too much, you're powerless."

It was true. Amos was always forthright and decisive. He always knew what to do, never hesitating. He was, in short, a real man.

But what was a real man? Joseph knew Amos must despise him. But did Amos ever imagine what it was like to become the man of the house at the age of twelve? To become the breadwinner at fourteen? He had been the one to look out for everyone, Amos, Alegra, even their mother in her final years. Who did they think listened to her tell her stories over and over and kept her company in her loneliness, fear, grief and desperation? Amos? Alegra? No, it was him. Hadn't he wanted to go out with friends and enjoy himself? Of course he had. But then he'd see his mother, always dressed in black, sitting alone, and he wouldn't have the heart to leave her. He'd make up an excuse so she wouldn't know he was staying for her. Didn't Amos think that required strength? To put away one's own wants and desires for the benefit of someone else? He had been sacrificing himself all his life. But that was something Amos would never see, never even notice. And when Amos had joined the military, who took care of their little sister? Once again, it was him, Joseph, who stayed back, who took care of her.

Yes, everyone thought him weak like his father, may God rest his poor soul, but on the contrary he was strong. Joseph never let himself sink into despair like his father did, escape into liquor. No, even in the depths of their poverty, he was strong. He confronted his family's crises, he held the flood waters back, he was their rock. Without him, they would all have been submerged. He didn't need to fire a gun to be a man. He supported his family. That was a true man, was it not?

Joseph wandered the streets, thinking, thinking, ravaged by guilt and fear. He could not imagine what to do. How could he go home? How could he face Amos? Why did this have to happen? Why couldn't he have been normal like everyone else? Why had God made him this way? He cursed himself and lamented his predicament. But in the end, he decided to be a man and go home and face his brother.

When he entered their home, however, he saw that Amos hadn't returned. He waited up as long as he could but finally went to bed. After all, he had to go to work the next morning. Assuming he still had a job.

When Amos did finally return home, he mentioned not a word about what he had seen. He behaved as if nothing had happened, avoiding Joseph's eyes. Joseph went to bed, having understood that his brother had not turned him in, and that he was safe from prosecution. His job, too, he was relieved to realize, was still his.

250 | Daughters of Jerusalem

But his relationship with Amos, often tense due to their conflicting natures and places in the family, was from then on almost nonexistent. Amos would not look at Joseph, and for months avoided contact with him, leaving the room or the house when Joseph appeared. This was how Amos always exhibited anger toward someone: he could never look the person in the eye, out of fury and disdain. Joseph suffered from Amos's silence, but it was worse when Amos was not silent. Once he almost threw it in Joseph's face during an argument the two brothers were having, with Alegra right there in the room. Joseph had paled with fright, but Amos only smirked and did not act on his threat.

Amos also suffered. He told himself that the golden boy image of Joseph had been a sham all along, for Joseph was worse than a degenerate; he was a criminal against nature. Amos had finally turned the tables on his brother; it was Joseph who was the rotten one, not him. Though in truth Amos would have preferred never to have witnessed the scene, and never to have known of Joseph's sin. Nonetheless, though he felt finally liberated from his role as the black sheep of the family, the changed roles gladdened him less than he would have imagined. He felt conflicted, for Joseph had been like a father to him for so long. He had gotten Amos out of scrapes, had intervened on his behalf, had worked to earn money to support him and Alegra. Amos felt angry and betrayed but also felt a sense of debt to his older brother. He knew he should be grateful to Joseph for all he had done. Yet this new information about Joseph made Amos wonder what else he didn't know about him. He felt that much more alone. Another myth of goodness and purity had shattered. Nothing was true; no one was honest.

Chapter Sixteen

SKIRMISHES BETWEEN THE JEWS and the Arabs had resumed after the war had ended, along with the guerrilla activities of Jewish anti-government groups like the Irgun. Even the Haganah, the Jewish Defense Force that the British had approved, clashed with the regime's troops upon confiscation of Haganah weapons after a search. In July 1946, Jewish nationalist groups, labeled terrorists by the British even though they did not target civilians, blew up a wing of the King David Hotel, which had been housing government and military departments, incurring a heavy loss of life. The British forces consequently decided to prevent further attacks by enclosing themselves in barbed wired areas in the New City, outside the walls of Old Jerusalem. These areas, which the British claimed for themselves, chasing out the Jewish inhabitants, came to be known as "Bevingrad," after Ernest Bevin, the unpopular British foreign secretary.

The main conflict, however, was between the Jews and the Muslim Arabs for control of Palestine. The nearby Jewish settlements of Atarot and Neve Yaakov to the north of Jerusalem were being abandoned, as they were surrounded by Muslim villages. In fact, all of Jerusalem was flanked by hundreds of Arab towns, putting its Jews in a precarious position. The Old City, along with some neighborhoods in the New City, found itself under a sort of siege in which Jewish supply convoys were attacked by

Muslims on the main Jerusalem highway, the only road from the coast. British armored cars were supposed to patrol the highway, but the British did little or nothing to prevent the attacks by Arab bands. People on both sides of the conflict were desperate to return to their families in other cities and towns, or simply to escape Jerusalem. Yet travel from Tel Aviv, for example, to Jerusalem was only possible in British police armored cars and even that only at a very high price, that few could afford.

The Arabs intended to disrupt the Jews' lines of communication, isolate and then starve them into submission. Farmers in the surrounding Arab villages were also suffering from the siege, for their food lay rotting only a few miles away, deprived of their Jewish consumers. Many Arabs were in fact against the fighting and some said so outright, but they were powerless to affect their military leaders. The Christian Arabs especially did not dare to protest too loudly, for some Muslim fanatics began saying, "After Saturday comes Sunday," that is, after the Jews' turn comes the Christians'.

Snipers from both camps shot at each other all over the city, within and without the walls, for the British were unable to patrol everywhere. Concrete forts were being built and trenches dug; roadblocks were converted into barricades; streets were torn up for anti-tank traps. These were no longer clashes. This was war, what the Jews would later call the War of Independence and what the Arabs would refer to as the *Nakhba*, or catastrophe. The British were relinquishing their Mandate, unable to quell the growing strife between the Zionists and Arabs. As a solution, the partition of Palestine had been decided by United Nations Security Council Resolution 39 in January 1948. On January 30, Gandhi would be assassinated by a Hindu extremist opposed to another partition, that of India, into a Hindu state and Pakistan, a Muslim one. Similarly, the partition of Palestine was loudly rejected by the Arabs of Palestine and the neighboring countries. Indeed, the United Nations resolution would serve not to diminish the conflict between the Jews and Arabs but to fan its flames for decades to come.

Attacks and atrocities on both sides abounded. In February of 1948, Arabs stole a British army truck, loaded it with explosives and blew it up outside the offices of the *Palestine Post,* causing loss of life and destroying two adjacent buildings. Later that same month, a large residential and commercial block on Ben Yehuda Street in the heart of the city was blown up by a truckload of heavy explosives. Sixty people were killed, and hundreds injured. The entire street was destroyed as well as some of the surrounding streets. Abd al-Qadir, founder of the Organization for Holy Struggle, claimed the bombing was in retaliation for an Irgun attack in Ramle, an Arab city. But when it was learned that a pair of British deserters had participated in the attack, the Irgun gave orders to shoot British soldiers on sight. Eight were fatally shot the same day. Ben-Gurion, now head of the World Zionist Organization, condemned the Ben Yehuda assault as well as those perpetrated by the Irgun.

Indeed, the Arabs, too, were suffering their share of the brutalities of war. In April, the Irgun captured a village called Deir Yassin. Over 250 people were reported killed, among them women and children. Many Jerusalemites were stunned by the accounts. Deir Yassin had been one of the few peaceful Arab villages around Jerusalem. They claimed that when a militant Arab band had earlier tried to make its base there, the villagers had driven them out, with the son of the *Mukhtar,* chief of the village, losing his life. But the Irgun maintained that for months attacks had been launched from the village on the surrounding Jewish areas, in which many had been murdered or wounded. They were thus unapologetic about their victory, parading their prisoners, including the Mukhtar and his family, through the streets of Jerusalem. Few people cheered at the sight of the three truckloads of prisoners with their arms in the air coming down King George Avenue. The Haganah, which was the general Jewish army, quickly forced the Irgun, a splinter group, to give them all up and then handed them over to the British.

Not more than a week later, the Arabs provided their own demonstration of brutality. A convoy of doctors, nurses, scientists and staff, along with hospital patients, was ambushed on the way to the Hadassah Hospital on Mount Scopus. Almost eighty were killed, including the hospital head. The hospital staff and patients had been trapped under fire for seven hours. The bodies were burned beyond recognition. After this episode, Hadassah was evacuated, and emergency hospitals were set up within the walls of the Old City itself.

The sole hope of the Jews for victory against their rivals for the land seemed to rest upon the Haganah, though it suffered from too little equipment and weapons, as well as too few members compared with the Arabs. Hardly a day went by that the siblings did not hear of the death of someone they knew. Friends caught snipers' fatal bullets; the butcher's wife was attacked and killed on her way to the bus station; one of Joseph's friends was shot to death while on patrol duty for the Haganah. Living in the Old City was both more and less perilous than in the New, for many hostile Arabs fleeing villages overrun by Haganah forces had taken refuge in the Old City, contributing to the swelling of their numbers there. Yet the twisting and snakelike alleys always provided a turn by which one could hide from gunfire, and the British Mandatory Army routinely patrolled the Jewish Quarter to prevent disturbances. Still, the British could not be everywhere at once, and the family had frequently found themselves taking shelter in the courtyard behind their building. But nothing, they knew, could shelter them from a direct shell hit. Somehow, they all managed to maintain a façade of calm. Amos, of course, had experienced mortar fire when he had served in Egypt, so he managed to maintain a dignified, if anxious, silence during shelling. Joseph also tried to present a stoic front, aware that he was the head of the family and convinced that the other two looked to him for security. Even Alegra held her own, impressing her brothers with her ability to think rationally under such dire circumstances.

In fact, the situation had eclipsed any fraternal discord in the household; instead, they constantly discussed the rapid decline in the state of affairs now that they were home together so often. Alegra was no longer working at the bank and Joseph was no longer needed on a regular basis for translations. Amos still reported regularly for duty but acknowledged that police headquarters were in disarray and everyone there admitted the police were incapable of stemming the violence. He worried over what would happen once the British left, for the mandate's termination was announced by the UN General Assembly in November 1947, to be effected at midnight, May 14, 1948.

"The Arabs will surely run us into the sea," Joseph fretted as they sat in their kitchen in a rare quiet moment.

"It's not like the British have tried very hard to prevent that scenario," Alegra retorted.

"Well, at least they've provided some protection," Amos countered. "Didn't they negotiate that truce at Nebi Daniyal?"

"Yes," Joseph answered, "but only through the Mayor of Bethlehem, and only because he's a Christian."

"And those were English soldiers who arrested those Haganah boys and left them in the Arab neighborhood in Bethlehem, where they were slaughtered," Alegra added, her temper rising.

"That's only a rumor," Amos cut in. "But it was British soldiers who rescued those Jewish taxi drivers from the Arab mob in Haifa. They themselves could have been killed, but they did their duty anyway."

And so it went. Though Alegra most often argued against the British, the other two were generally a bit more ambivalent. For when the English had first arrived in Palestine, as Amos reminded them, they had been welcomed and admired by the Jews, since they had rescued them from the Turks and had brought with them a civilizing, European influence that the Jewish residents of the Holy Land greatly prized.

And at first the conquering British army had behaved in a manner that was deserving of admiration, for they cleaned up the dirty cities, rebuilt roads and infrastructure and in general created order from chaos, bringing Palestine into the twentieth century. But as time wore on, the pressures of the opposing factions in the land took their toll upon the British as well. When they did not take sides, they were viewed as cold-hearted, and when they did, they were prejudiced. Both Arabs and Jews swore the English were slanted toward the other. And once the British began curtailing and then stopping Jewish immigration into Palestine, especially once the atrocities committed by the Nazis in Europe were known, the Jews viewed them as their bitter enemies.

Alegra swore that the British were inhuman and that they viewed the Jews and Arabs alike as vermin. She never forgot an episode years before, during which she had been playing ball with a group of other Jewish children. She had been six at the time. When the ball was kicked too far and fell into a puddle of dirty water, Alegra had rushed to retrieve it. A British soldier standing next to it had picked it up just as she approached. He returned the ball to her, and she turned to rejoin her comrades. But suddenly he ordered her to stand still. She froze, surprised and frightened. Then she felt the soldier slide his hands up and down her back. His hands had become soiled from the dirty ball, so he had wiped them on the back of her shirt, as if she were a walking rag. Even at that tender age, Alegra had understood the humiliation, and forever reviled the contempt of the type of man who would use a little girl as a dishrag.

The other siblings were somewhat more forgiving of their overlords, Amos especially, as he was torn between his service to the British both as a soldier and police officer, and his sympathy with the Haganah. He had even gone so far as to warn a known Haganah member of an impending arms raid. When he and his team had arrived, all they found were schoolbooks and innocent faces. That night, Amos had not been able to sleep, conflicted between his fidelity to his sworn duty and to his brethren. Worse, however, was his frustration and indecision, his feeling of being perched on a fence, and outside the action with his hands tied.

In the turmoil of the times and due to the danger of even setting foot outside, Joseph and Amos had decided that they should now be the ones to venture forth for provisions, which at this point consisted of products such as powdered milk and egg, the real things having long run out. Still, food and necessities needed to be purchased, and this often entailed waiting on long lines, providing perfect targets for snipers. Many a food line scattered in hysteria at the mere crackle of a car engine backfiring. At first, the arrangement that Joseph and Amos both go out had been strongly debated. Wouldn't it be better, Amos proposed, to lose one brother rather than both? But neither he nor Joseph could accept the notion of allowing the other to go in his place, so they always went out together.

Still, Alegra could not stand to be cooped up at home, and often came up with excuses for her forays outside, claiming for instance that she had forgotten to tell her brothers to get candles, which had become a necessity due to the unreliability of electrical power. Sometimes she simply went out on the sly, when Joseph and Amos were out. For Alegra didn't feel fear as strongly as other mortals. It was an emotion that stood next to, but not in front of, her other emotions. It did not block out the others; it merely coexisted. So when Alegra attempted something dangerous, she felt the fear, but also the importance, the necessity of it, and the excitement. She had the fearlessness of Amos married to the reasoning of Joseph. She needed exhilaration in her life but was still mindful of the risks she took. In any event, she was never one to sit on the sidelines when important events were taking place, perilous or not.

It was during one of her escapes that heavy gunfire began close to where they lived. In fact, it was the sounds of shots that had prompted Alegra to leave the house. She couldn't live with herself, she thought, if she stayed home and safe while someone else was perhaps in danger and needed help. In her imagination, she saw a person lying in a pool of their own blood. Maybe a child even. Maybe Joseph or Amos! Alegra did not see herself as the baby of the family, as her brothers did. She knew herself capable of acts of strength and courage. It was always she who would shoo away snakes and approach snarling dogs when her childhood friends would cower in fear. It was she who would step in when she felt a classmate's teasing had crossed a line. Though she had never really been a leader—she was too independent for that—she had always been someone others could count upon. She felt a sense of duty to help out those in need.

Mercada had often bemoaned her daughter's protective nature. Countless were the times she had been called in to school when Alegra had misbehaved, only to discover that the girl had come to blows for defending a bullied child. She would of course justify her daughter, and had indeed been proud of her for these actions. Nonetheless, she would have preferred Alegra to not get so involved, to look out more for herself.

"Why does it always have to be you who comes to the aid of the defenseless?" Mercada would ask her, only half in jest.

"Because if not me, then who?" would be her intrepid child's response.

Once Mercada was gone, Alegra's brothers, too, unknowingly diminished her by labeling these sentiments as maternal instinct.

"Alegra is like a mother hen," Joseph would often say, not unkindly. "Always looking out for those who can't defend themselves."

But Alegra would counter: "I'm not mothering. It's not because I'm a woman. It's because I'm a human being acting as a human being ought to act."

Now, in the midst of situations of real peril, with guns firing and people dying, how could anyone expect Alegra to sit at home? Thus Joseph and Amos returned home one day, managing to literally dodge bullets, when they saw that their sister was not there. Joseph took a deep breath and put his hand to his forehead, while Amos's eyes widened. Without a word, they spun on their heels and set off, marching grimly toward the clouds of smoke. As they approached the melee, they clung to the walls of the buildings, sweating in fear, their eyes darting about searching for their sister, for anyone pointing a gun at them, for a shelter to run to. Their throats hurt from the smoke and also from their alarm; they could not remember how to breathe normally. Both were secretly glad for the presence of the other. Misery truly does love company, and it would have been even more frightening and would have appeared even more deadly had either been alone.

The two stood side by side, pressed against a doorway that offered little protection, their eyes tearing from the smoke and their ears ringing from the close gunplay.

"I don't see her," complained Joseph.

"With this smoke," Amos whispered hoarsely, "we can't see a thing. We'll have to get closer."

"We can't make a run for it, though. We'll get killed."

"We'll have to go back and then around to the other side of the street. Maybe we can see better from there. Damn that Alegra!" Amos spat out between clenched teeth.

"Yes," Joseph agreed. "I hope she's all right."

So they turned around and retraced their steps to the end of the street, and turned the corner to reach the other side of the skirmish from the back. But at that moment, they spotted four Arab men moving in their direction along that street. At the same time, they themselves were spotted by the foursome, whose kaffiyehs, the traditional Arab headdress, were wrapped around their faces to protect them from the searing smoke. Both groups were frozen for a split second at this unexpected confrontation, and then Amos and Joseph darted back around the corner as the four men shouted and pointed their rifles. The crack of gunfire ripped through the air as the brothers dashed frantically up the street, scrambling for cover. Joseph felt his heart stop as he blindly kept up with Amos, whose limbs had suddenly taken on the speed and agility of a trapped animal. He could not think, only react.

Their assailants then turned the corner. Another shot rang out. With each firing, Joseph's hair stood on end. They rounded a curve, which brought them a few moments of respite during which they couldn't be seen. Still they could find no shelter. Finally, they reached the end of the street. Around the corner was where the fighting was raging. They would be killed as soon as they jumped out into the open. But they would also be killed where they were; their enemy would soon appear around the curve. Where to run? Their blood was pumping furiously, interfering with their brains. They had both accelerated into a full-blown panic. Joseph turned to face his sibling. His hands gripped Amos's shoulders.

"We're going to die." He was trembling.

Amos stared at him, his eyes wide. He couldn't answer. Amos's reaction to fear was always to shut down, not to feel. He was like a dead man already.

"I love you, my brother," Joseph rasped.

If Amos had tried to respond, he couldn't have. His throat was caught. He couldn't breathe.

At that instant, their foes were upon them.

Suddenly it was as if everything began to play in slow motion. The four men didn't shoot them immediately. Instead, they surrounded them and threw them to the ground. The two brothers cowered beneath them, waiting for the bullets or knives. Joseph began to whimper. He could not muster any dignity, and had it occurred to him to beg for their lives, he most likely would have. The two brothers, contrary to the cliché, did not see images of their lives flash before them in that moment. In fact, they did not see much at all, as if all the blood that had come flooding and throbbing up to their faces had swept away their sight. Joseph felt only a pulsating fear, a white hysteria. Amos felt empty. That moment before their deaths seemed interminable, almost worse than the murder itself. They heard the four men speaking or shouting, but they could no longer understand, their minds could no longer process the words. All they could really hear were their own heartbeats, booming so as to burst their eardrums.

One of the men stepped forward and bent over Amos. Amos closed his eyes. So he would be the first to go, he thought, as nausea overtook him. The man grabbed his arm and pulled him up. Amos stood up and opened his eyes, facing his aggressor. Despite his fear, he would try to die like a man. His adversary then unwrapped the kaffiyeh from around his face.

Samir! It was Samir, his boyhood friend, the baby Mercada had rescued from starvation by acting as his wetnurse. Amos blinked uncomprehendingly, his senses still eclipsing his mind.

"Leave these two alone," Samir commanded.

His comrades shouted in surprise and began to protest loudly. Samir put one hand up to silence them, his face almost expressionless in his determination. He spoke calmly.

"I said leave these two alone."

"Have you lost your mind? Or your nerve?" asked one. "These are our enemies!"

"No," Samir replied. "These are my brothers."

Amos and Joseph slowly began to comprehend what was transpiring. Samir was going to save their lives. They listened as he briefly and quietly explained who they were, and how their mother Mercada had nursed him so that he might live. His friends listened. One shook his head in seeming disbelief. But all took a few steps back, signaling their acquiescence. If the mother of those two Jews had truly suckled Samir when his own mother could not, then she was tantamount to being his mother. And though they may have been brothers in enmity like Jacob and Esau, they were nonetheless brothers. Samir's comrades understood that he would not brand himself with the sin that Cain had committed against Abel. They turned around and began to walk away.

Samir helped Joseph up, who had remained crouched on the ground in uncertainty. He then faced them both, his eyes sad and serious.

"Leave this place. It is very dangerous here for you. This land belongs to us. You will have to go. You must understand that." He made a movement as if to leave, but Amos's voice suddenly piped up as if from somewhere outside himself, almost involuntarily.

"We were looking for Alegra."

"She's not here," Samir assured him, and indeed they would find their sister safe and sound upon their return. "Go home." He turned to go, and then returned as if in afterthought.

"But," he added, "I have finally repaid your mother. Just as she gave me life, I have given you yours. Now go in peace, my brothers. *Salaam aleykoum*. But go."

He left them there, pale and shaking. They could not react immediately.

They simply stood there, confused, staring straight ahead, unable to digest what had just happened and seemingly incapable of moving beyond it. Finally, Amos turned to Joseph.

"Let's go home."

"Yes," Joseph said, but made no movement.

Then, hesitatingly, and completely out of character, Amos slipped his arm through Joseph's. It was a gesture more eloquent than any words he could ever have uttered. Thus connected, they proceeded home.

Chapter Seventeen

BY EARLY APRIL 1948, the situation in all of Palestine, and especially in Jerusalem, was critical. The city dwellers looked like scrawny children from having their diets so severely curtailed. Somehow people still managed to find cigarettes—a phenomenon that had bewildered Mercada when Gabriel would find money for that but never for food—yet the combination of the nicotine, the nerves and the lack of sustenance made them look even more withered and rachitic. Death hovered everywhere, as a slow wasting away or a quick bullet. Where houses and buildings once stood now loomed amorphous heaps of stone and rubble, amidst the bloom of flowers, indifferent to the stupidities of men.

The British Mandatory government had for months been trying to evacuate the Jews from the Old City, or at the very least to disarm them. At this time, it was estimated that Jews numbered less than two thousand whereas the Arabs made up approximately thirty thousand of the Old City's residents, without counting those that had newly come in from Syria and Iraq to aid the Arab cause. Militarily, battles raged everywhere, sometimes for days on end as was the case with the Castel, a strategic height overlooking the main road between Jerusalem and Tel Aviv. Its name derived from the Latin *Castellum*, as the Romans called it, and was fought for dearly. In the end, the Arabs won it, though the Area Commander of Arab Jerusalem lost his life for it.

What was surprising, in fact, was that the Jews won any victories at all, considering their disproportionate numbers, especially when compared with the influx of some eight thousand soldiers from other Arab nations, along with ex-Nazis, mercenaries, and even British deserters. Furthermore, the Jews' shortage of munitions and food took its toll on them. Yet win battles they did. First, they captured Kolonia, named after an old colony of Roman legionnaires. The villagers themselves having left during the battle for the Castel, it had become occupied by armed groups who would launch attacks on the main road. This victory was followed by one in Tiberias, during which the entire Arab population there, numbering six thousand, fled, some to Nazareth and others to Transjordan. A few days later, the port city of Haifa fell to the Haganah.

Once word got out of their defeat in Haifa, many Arabs began to leave Jerusalem as well. The Arab National Committee began to threaten punishment for those fleeing Jerusalem. Yet as many Arab leaders had themselves already fled, there was little that could be done to stop the evacuation. In many cases this was brought on by the leaders' own doing; in order to stir their soldiers on and to prevent any neutrality on the part of villagers, they had depicted their enemy as fierce barbarians. The operation at Deir Yassin had only contributed to this image, and now many Arabs were afraid to fall into the Jews' hands. If further reasons were needed, they were also astounded at their foes' might and cunning, as were the Jews themselves, despite being greatly outnumbered and outgunned.

To many Jews, the Arab flight only cemented their belief that the land truly belonged to them and not to those leaving, who to their mind did not have enough connection to the region to stay, to fight and die for it. Yet the Arabs fled mainly because they were able to, because they didn't have to stay and fight or die but were able to take refuge in the lands of their neighbors, the very neighbors who had all along supported them and promised to defend them and to ensure their recovery of the territory. Those who fled most likely did not see it as abandoning their cause, but rather as leaving matters in the hands of their mightier brethren.

For the Jews, however, there was really no option but to fight or die. Where else could they go? The Palestinian Jews only knew Palestine as home, the North African Jews could evidently not return to their former Arab homes, now officially enemy territory, and the Europeans no longer had homes or families to return to after the Nazis tried to wipe them out. Moreover, who would fight for them? Unlike the Palestinian Arabs, no one else would come to their aid, no kindred nation nor even foreign mercenary, who viewed theirs as a lost cause. The real secret of the Jews' prowess and success was thus that there was no other option but to be brave and succeed.

Yet the war still raged and the British were still the ruling body, empowered by the rest of the world to govern according to their own laws, at least until the end of the mandate, which was nearing. And as they themselves were often under attack by both rival parties, they were very strict about implementing security. Buses, trucks, food convoys and even private cars, both of Arabs and Jews, were routinely stopped to check for weapons and explosives. Even their own vehicles had to pass through their checkpoints. This was usually merely a formality, though the theft of military vehicles by the warring camps often made such surveillance necessary. Every now and then their suspicions would be aroused by something irregular in a British transport. If, for instance, the driver of a truck appeared to be swimming in a uniform two sizes too big for him. Or if he seemed tense and sweating. Or if he were merely small and dark. Of course, not all English were tall and blond, and the Middle Eastern heat made everyone sweat, especially those used to the rains of Surrey or the winters at Bournemouth, while the ever-increasing violence of one Semite against the other made everyone tense; a mortar did not recognize an Englishman from a Jew or Arab. And as one hapless soldier explained, a uniform that did not fit right was merely another casualty of war.

"Yes, the uniform," he said, his face sour. "This was the only size they had left when I arrived, thanks to those bloody thieving Jews and Arabs. Better not be a heavy sleeper. They'll steal the bed right out from under you!"

266 | Daughters of Jerusalem

The checkpoint soldiers chuckled. In a land where the Jews and Arabs looked and sounded indistinguishable from one another, at least you could tell who was British, once he opened his mouth. Hence, they let Alegra through, a supply of illegal weapons stored in the back of her truck.

In the beginning, on her earlier missions for the Haganah, Alegra was forced to work guard duty, often relegated to women and older men. Sometimes they were armed, sometimes not, and the dreary task of remaining stationary and idle for hours on end would greatly disappoint and frustrate her. Eventually she was transferred to smuggling arms on buses. She and her comrades would appear as a normal busload of people traveling into Jerusalem. On the way, they would stop at a strategic point to pick up heavy sacks filled with the dismantled parts of sub-machine guns and pistols, hand-grenades and ammunition. The women's role was to hide them on their bodies. Alegra would stash revolvers under her armpits and gun barrels under her skirt. Old women were especially prized for this sort of work, for who would suspect the old babushkas who could barely make it up the steps of the bus without heaves and grunts? When the bus would be stopped for a search, the soldiers would glance under the seats and perfunctorily frisk the young men. But when they approached the women, many of whom looked slightly pregnant by this point, their harsh stares said, "Don't you dare lay your hands on me!" and the British were too gentlemanly to press the issue.

Yet Alegra was frustrated by these missions. Even in the Haganah she was treated as if she were a frail child. She knew how to fight; she had learned how to shoot. Why was everyone still treating her as someone to be protected rather than as a protector, fit only for less dangerous work? It was hard for her to stomach allowing others to risk their lives while she stayed largely away from harm. Luck, however, if one could call it that, came to Alegra's aid, for she was eventually called up for more interesting work when one of her group leaders finally realized the potential she represented. What had always been her humiliation and at the root of her insecurity proved to be her passport to adventure and glory: her voice.

The husky rasp that made her a comic figure when it emanated from her slight, girlish frame, along with her mangled boxer's nose, became the key to her disguise as a man. The perpetual post-nasal drip that had plagued her all these years only added to the image, for the sound of her mucus-laden snorting and the sight of her wiping her nose with her sleeve was so unladylike as to dispel any doubts. Short hair for women was the style of the period, so Alegra's cropped locks only appeared an exaggerated variation from the norm; and as far as a man's hair was concerned, it was a time of war, and few soldiers could be expected to trim theirs with regimented punctuality. As long as she slathered pomade on it, it looked short enough to pass. Yet the *coup de grâce*, the element that made her the perfect imposter, was her flawless English, without the trace of an accent, which had been ingrained in her at the famous English School in which Mercada had succeeded in placing her years before. In fact, Alegra awakened less suspicion among the British than she did from her own family, who harassed and questioned her regarding her irrepressible need to absent herself from the house for hours. Luckily for her, she had always had the soul of a stray cat, so when of late she would reappear caked in dust and grime, her siblings were already used to it. Still, they were not stupid, and living in such close quarters lent all an almost X-ray vision, or at least the capacity for spotting small and seemingly insignificant details. But their suspicions leaned toward the area of amorous affairs, and though the thought of Alegra running around wildly and unrestrictedly with young men often produced passionate arguments and threats, her brothers were more worried about her physical safety during the siege of Jerusalem, and less about her maidenly virtue. The times were extreme enough that survival itself could not be taken for granted, and so concerns regarding virginity fell by the wayside.

Thus, the idea that Alegra was a high-ranking Haganah operative never even dawned on either of them, so used to viewing women—especially

Alegra, the baby of the family—as the object of protection rather than the protector. And as the Haganah maintained such secrecy regarding its members, her identity was well-insured. Though the Haganah was not an outlaw group like the Irgun, its members obeyed strict rules of secrecy, using only first names taken from the Bible as aliases, and were banned from keeping photos or letters. Rarely did a Haganah member know more than a handful of others. The hiding places of their weapons were even more guarded, known only to chosen officers, because the British government, which had originally backed the foundation of the Haganah, began to grow fed up with the clashes between the ragtag Jewish defense force and the Arab bands, and with their own increasing inability to control the situation. The government regularly implemented searches for Haganah arms, stating that it alone was responsible for safety and that the Haganah had become a "menace to peace." Those caught bearing arms were hanged.

It was through her work with the Haganah that Alegra met Leon Meyer, who would change her life. He was actually with the Irgun, but a decision by the World Zionist Council had recently decreed that the splinter group function as a unit under the direction of the Haganah. Leon had only been in Palestine for three years, having arrived from a German Displaced Person's camp after the war. He was originally from Poland and had spent the war in different concentration camps and even a death camp, Treblinka, built solely for extermination purposes and from which he had narrowly escaped; in fact, he was one of only a few who would ever make it out of there alive. Leon had arrived in Palestine on one of the clandestine ships filled with desperate refugees who waited for days and sometimes weeks on board because the British refused them entry. But the determination of these displaced people eventually overcame such resistance. After all, they truly had nowhere else to go, for no other country would take them. Most, like Leon, had lost all their family to the Nazis, and this made them fierce and reckless. Having no one to care about means having nothing to lose. Leon, too, had become hard. Only when he would talk of his family would he betray any softness or weakness, his voice faltering and his eyes becoming glassy with tears. All of Leon's features were thick and coarse, from his large green eyes, lovely and sad, rimmed by heavy lids, to his full lips and even fuller nose. He was both funny-looking and handsome at the same time.

Being from Warsaw, it turned out that Leon had known the family of one Heinoch, and sought him out when he arrived in Palestine. Heinoch himself had arrived before the second World War. Little, in fact, in Heinoch's background had made him a proper candidate for life in the Holy Land. First of all, his father had of all things owned a brothel in Warsaw, a Jewish one, so that his "pious" Jewish clients did not have to indulge in non-kosher meat. As for Heinoch himself, he was always getting into trouble. When he got into yet another fight with a neighborhood boy and bloodied his nose, his father decided that if the boy wanted to beat people up, he should do it professionally. Thus, he sent his son to the Macabi, or Jewish Youth Center, to train in boxing. Heinoch had finally found a way to channel his aggression, and to receive praise and renown for it as well.

But one day he and a group of friends from the neighborhood were accosted by a group of Polish officers who began to taunt them, calling out "There goes the Jewish army!" The mockery stung, as it alluded to the might of the Poles and to the customary cowering of the Jews, long deprived of rights such as property ownership. With Heinoch amongst them, both to jump at the provocation and to provide the security of a seasoned fighter on their side, the small group challenged their rivals and a fight ensued. In the melee Heinoch killed one of the officers. His fists truly had become lethal weapons. It was only a short while, then, before the Jewish section was swarming with police looking for Heinoch. But he remained hidden until he could make his escape. Where, in the absence of foreign relatives, did a Jew go? This was how Heinoch alighted in the Holy Land.

Thus, Heinoch was a born terrorist, and had become a high-ranking member of the Irgun, into which he quickly initiated young Leon. Heinoch, code named Jacob, was to provide the connection between the new refugee and the strange Haganah girl who disguised herself as a man and whose true name only he knew. Alegra, secretly known as Judith, found herself quickly smitten by this boy who could alternate between teary-eyed sentimentality and passionate brutality. He hated the Arabs without having ever known them, and Alegra found such cold certainty disconcerting. Even she, who could be fierce against her enemies, could understand them as well, for she had lived with Arabs all her life.

Once, after a training session on how to clean a gun, Leon had eyed his weapon with satisfaction.

"Wait till the Arabs see this," he had said.

Alegra, who had managed to sit opposite him, had gazed at him in the candlelit room.

"But why do you hate them so much?" she had asked him, diffidently. She was never timid, except when she was around Leon. Nevertheless, she had pushed on. "There are good Arabs and bad Arabs, just like there are good Jews and bad Jews."

Another Haganah member, Noah, had answered her.

"It's not that we hate the Arabs. It's just that there isn't room for both of us."

"Why not?" Alegra had countered. "We've lived together for generations. In peace."

"Don't be so naïve, Judith," another had retorted. "Things change. Villages grow. Populations grow. And one day, both want to build a house or a farm on the same spot. One day both want to plant their flag on the same spot. There's only room for one people."

"Anyway," Noah again had cut in, "they're Arabs. They can go to any Arab country: Syria, Lebanon, Iraq, Egypt. Where can we go?"

Then Leon had spoken. "It's either here, or Hell. And I'm not going back to Hell."

For Leon, Alegra's qualms were typical of the Haganah, which he deemed too soft compared to the radical Irgun. The Haganah abided by too many rules, paid too much heed to humanitarian concerns. War was pitiless; the world was pitiless. He once recounted to his comrades-in-arms the first time he had laid eyes on a black man, after the war was over, in Degendorf, Germany. Leon had never seen any blacks growing up in Poland. He had only read about them in school, in history class, his favorite subject. He had felt disgust and sadness upon reading of the enslavement of Africans in the United States. He knew what it was like to be a second-class citizen: though he and his parents before him had been born in Poland, they were always treated as foreigners in their homeland, because they were Jewish. How much better he would come to understand, only a few years later, the plight of the American slaves. Even the racial purity laws of Nuremberg were said to be modeled upon the Virginia slavers' racial categories. Learning about the Civil War and the Emancipation Proclamation, which freed the slaves, had given young Leon hope.

Therefore, it was with both shock and outrage that his first glimpse of a black man was as one came crashing through a glass window, thrown down to the street below. It seemed the man, a U.S. soldier, had had the temerity to think a dance being given in honor of American GIs included those of dark skin as well. A few of his compatriots offered to enlighten him regarding his error by heaving him through a third-story window. This man, who had risked his life at the behest of his country, who had fought with surely as much valor as any one of them, Leon brooded, was not considered worthy enough, human enough, to attend the same social event.

Up until then, Leon had looked upon the American soldiers who had rescued him in Majdanek, the last camp in which he had been reimprisoned after his escape from Treblinka, as his heroes, angels sent from a heaven of civilization. They had treated the inmates with kindness and magnanimity; like gods tossing ambrosia to brutish mortals used only to swill, they had given them chocolate. And Leon had worshiped them like gods, in their hulking, muddied tanks, flicking their shiny Zippo lighters. They had finally come. Good had finally triumphed over Evil. But the defenestration showed him that Americans were no angels, and no less disappointing than others.

Alegra felt a deep sadness as she listened to Leon tell his stories for another reason as well: she had fallen in love with him and knew that he would never return her love. She was all too aware of her physical shortcomings, and acknowledged it was no compliment to her looks that she could pass so easily for a man. She believed she could never hope to win Leon's affection, and felt this all the more when, like a knife slicing into her heart, he would talk about his eldest sister, the beautiful one. Even her name proclaimed it, for Shayna, in Yiddish, meant "beautiful."

"It was the perfect name for her," he would vaunt, "because she was so pretty that people would stop in the street and turn to stare at her. She was a redhead," he went on, "not the carrot-colored kind with freckles, but with hair the color of cinnamon, and thick lashes as dark as honey. Her hair showed off her eyes, which were green, very green," he assured his listeners. He spoke of her as a lover would, and allowed himself to describe her looks in such passionate detail and with such yearning only because she no longer existed. She was now a ghost, one that haunted her brother with the memory of all that had been and all that was lost, and that haunted Alegra with all that she herself could never be.

Leon recounted how Shayna's looks were so breathtaking that she inflamed the heart of a young Polish officer. When the war broke out, her officer came for her. He came to take her away, to marry her and provide her with Polish papers. She refused, and chose to stay faithful to her heritage, remaining with her family on their way to their doom.

Leon never failed to break down in tears at the end of this story, no matter how many times he told it. And though he felt strongly about his religion, for his entire family had perished on account of it, he once admitted that he could not agree with Shayna's decision to preserve her heritage at all costs.

"After all," he quietly acknowledged, "the most important thing is to survive. I would rather she had been a live Christian than a dead Jew."

Leon had many more stories, mainly about the tortures and terrors he had suffered at the hands of the Nazis. This was how Alegra and her cronies learned about the Holocaust. If they hadn't known it already, they knew now that they had to win their war over the land. There was indeed nowhere else to go.

Alegra managed to maneuver herself into running a few missions with Leon. He had come to occupy her thoughts so much that she felt she had to have him, that she at least had to make a stab at it or else go mad. Since she knew she could not win him with her looks, she thought she might impress him in some other way. She would indeed find a way.

Chapter Eighteen

THE IRGUN ENGAGED not only in attacks against the British Mandatory government but also served as spies, placing its members in government offices as cleaning personnel. One day one of the Irgun agents overheard that a British arms shipment was to be moved from Acre to Jerusalem, but with little security attached to it so as not to attract attention. The Haganah and Irgun decided to attack the shipment. Heinoch, the commanding officer of the raid, chose members of his squad for the incursion, among whom was Leon. But a few more were needed, to be chosen from the regular Haganah.

When Alegra got wind of the plan, she volunteered to her immediate commander, whose code name was Isaiah, to take part in the assault. But Heinoch refused Isaiah, explaining that though she may be brave, and skilled at passing for a slight Englishman, what was needed in this case was brawn. They were going to overtake an arms transport by surprise, but also by force. In short, it was a job for a man. Alegra thus found herself relegated to the sidelines while the plan of action was mapped out, a straightforward ambush from an isolated point on the only road out of Jerusalem.

The crew, consisting of ten troops, among whom was Leon, and Heinoch, their commander, arrived before dawn on a ridge of one of Jerusalem's surrounding hills, hidden by scrub pines and acacia bushes and under cover of a moonless night. Each was armed with a pistol, a canteen of water and a backpack with spare bullets. It was a long wait, hours and hours of waiting, as they nervously sipped at their water and fingered their firearms. In the darkness they trembled in the arid cold, but as the hours wore on and the sun rose, they began to sweat from the stifling heat. And from nerves. On a wait such as this, one both feared and longed for the enemy's approach.

When the team finally did spy the first truck in the British convoy as it appeared around a bend, it was with a mixture of nausea and relief. They jerked themselves awake and jumped to their feet, whispering urgently to one another to prepare themselves. The trucks, covered in dark tarpaulins, proceeded at a cautious speed. Heinoch's unit waited until the middle truck was right below them, at which point he signaled the charge with a hand motion. They all jumped down, one after another, guns raised, still trying to maintain silence despite some slipping along the rocky terrain. They were soon spotted, but none of the British soldiers had the wherewithal to fire a shot, so taken by surprise were they. In fact, they surrendered easily, having recognized their defeat, and the attacking band silently rejoiced at such a painless and bloodless victory.

But it was a trap. The English had recently become aware of the spies in their offices. Rather than round them up, they decided to feed them false information and thus net the bigger fish. The ambushers therefore became the ambushed. As soon as the army's reinforcements appeared, flanking their trucks from both sides of the road, the Irgun squad realized they had been set up. Heinoch screamed out orders to retreat, and the fighters rapidly took to their heels. But a young recruit froze in panic. The others shouted at him over their backs to run yet he just stood there, trembling and sobbing as though he had been shot. Leon knew not what possessed him, but without even thinking he, too, stopped, turned and ran back for the boy. When Leon grabbed him, it was as if he had awakened the boy, who suddenly tore past him and fled to safety. It was Leon, instead, who stumbled, lost his footing and was soon in the gunsights of his captors. He was arrested. All the others had escaped.

Alegra was sick with the news, as they all were. Leon had been taken to Acre prison, to await sentencing, most likely hanging. They knew he would be interrogated in order to give up the others, especially the leaders, such as Heinoch. Would Leon be tortured? Unlike the others, who only knew their commander as Jacob, Leon knew Heinoch's real identity.

An emergency meeting was called and attended by both Irgun and Haganah members in one of the latter's hideouts, an abandoned farmhouse on the outskirts of Jerusalem. In hushed voices and by candlelight, they debated their options. Could they break Leon out of prison? Even if they managed to get to him, they themselves could be captured. There was no point in risking the freedom of others, in exchanging one prisoner for another.

Alegra, who had been privy to the discussion, finally spoke up.

"I can do it."

The others stopped arguing and looked at her.

"You can do what?"

"I can break into the prison. I can go disguised as a British soldier. I've done it before."

"You've passed through checkpoints," one of the members, code named Absalom, reminded her. "It's hardly the same as infiltrating a well-guarded prison."

"Yes," Heinoch added. "It's one thing to go past a few guards; it's another thing to enter a hornet's nest full of them."

"Plus, there are Arab prisoners there, too," warned Isaiah. "If any of them recognized you, they wouldn't hesitate to rat you out."

"Why would anyone recognize me?" Alegra coolly asked.

"Because you're from here!" Heinoch retorted. "Because you grew up among them! But forget about that. It's just not possible." He dismissed the idea with a wave of his hand.

"How about an overt attack?" proposed another female recruit, code named Deborah. "A few explosives to create an opening, we charge in, we take them by surprise?"

"Or set up an explosion as a diversion…" offered Absalom.

"No, no," Heinoch argued. "The place is a fortress, not a little shack. It would take more explosives than we have access to," he explained. "We would have to coordinate with other groups. It would take too much time, and he could be hanged next week. Anyway," he decided, "it still doesn't solve the problem of the sheer numbers of the British soldiers. Even with the element of surprise, it wouldn't work."

They continued their debate and seemed to have abandoned and forgotten about Alegra's idea. But she hadn't. She knew it could work. It had to. Heinoch was right about one thing, though. Time was something they didn't have. The more they discussed and argued, she thought, the more time was being wasted. She wondered if Leon would even be tried, but if so, summarily. Then it was a quick step to the hanging platform. She left her unit to its discussions and walked briskly home. She knew what she had to do.

Alegra was in luck. No one was home. She dashed into the room shared by her brothers and opened the wardrobe that held their clothing. There it was, right on top of the pile: Amos's police uniform. He had two, in rotation. It was far too big for her, but she didn't have the time to go through the Haganah channels and get a smaller one, and anyway they might have asked too many questions and then refused. Unfortunately as well, Amos's uniform was that of a Jewish policeman and not of a British soldier, so the role she had played a few times before would not help her prepare for this disguise. She would have to play it differently this time. She summoned Amos in her mind, conjured up his attitude, tried to remember his routines. It would not be too big of a switch, she convinced herself. After all, it was harder to pose as a British man in front of other British men than it would be to pretend to be a Jewish man in front of a Brit. At least she had half of the disguise—the Jewish part—already down pat. And as she had heard an English officer remark once, all Jews looked the same to them.

She made one more all-important stop and then was on her way to Acre prison, having gotten rides here and there, the uniform tucked away in her rucksack. No one thought it odd any longer that a young woman would be traveling alone such a distance. The war had broken down many conventions. Alegra had thought through her plan on the way there. She would need a plausible excuse to gain entry. She toyed with a few possibilities. Bring in food? Men always fell over themselves when it came to their stomachs, she thought, but quickly realized the garrison would have food brought in officially in bulk. Then it hit her. She would turn her weakness into her strength, that is, she would use her foreignness as her weapon. So when the sentry asked the diminutive Hebrew policeman his business there, Alegra was ready.

"I've been summoned as a translator," she rasped, "to help with the debriefing of the Jewish prisoner." She was sure Leon had remained silent during any preliminary rounds of questioning but in any event, he could not speak much English.

"I have no orders to let through any Jewish policemen," he replied.

"Well, he was only just captured," she pointed out, wiping her nose on Amos's sleeve. "I was the first one they could find." She lowered her voice conspiratorially. "And the sooner your officers get names and information out of them, the better."

The soldier on sentry duty hesitated.

"But if you want to keep your superiors waiting…" Alegra said, shrugging her shoulders.

The sentry thought quickly. It made sense. And indeed, he would not want to be the one to keep his superiors waiting on such a matter as this. Besides, this lone, skinny little Jew would hardly be capable of staging a break-out or an invasion, he reasoned. So he checked the policeman's bag for weapons and lightly frisked him just to be sure. Alegra was glad she had taken the time to bind her breasts down and stuff a pair of socks down her pants. The sentry let her pass and even told her where the prisoner was being kept.

One can imagine the fear that would have gripped Alegra during her passage through Acre prison, surrounded everywhere by her enemies, but only if one did not know her. Her ability to keep a cool head in compromising, and even death-defying, situations arose from her focus not on the risk but on the reward. She never dwelt on how a mission could fail but rather on its success. In other words, she thought not of herself but of the others, those who would benefit from her risks, those whom she might save. And if the endeavor did run into a snag, she was good at improvising, at dealing with it and moving on toward her goal. She would never just succumb to defeat. She would always fight.

Alegra had learned from the master negotiator herself, her own mother, that in order to convince someone of something, one had to be convinced oneself. So it was with the veneer of calm and confidence that she approached the desk of the prisoner's guard and told him that she was there to translate.

"I received no mention of a translator coming," he said warily.

"Well, I was sent for by my unit commander, Captain Giladi, who received the order from your Lieutenant Grace," Alegra bluffed, whereupon the guard's eyebrows rose. Was he impressed? Was it disbelief? She pressed on. "I was told to await the lieutenant's arrival at 3:00 sharp. Here, at the prisoner's cell."

The guard checked his watch. It was 1:15.

"Well, you're early then, mate."

"Just in time for a spot of tea? I don't mind telling you I'm parched with thirst, old chap."

If the guard had harbored any lingering doubts as to the veracity of the soldier's story, they were quickly dispelled by the latter's excellent English, hardly a trace of an accent, for Alegra had taken care to let a little of the Semite show through, for authenticity's sake. As for Alegra, she harbored no doubts at all that an Englishman would never refuse a "cuppa." She also relied on the fact that he would make not a cup of tea but rather brew a pot—the only civilized way to make it —and would join her in partaking of it. It was therefore easy enough to create a momentary diversion—how clumsy of her to knock over the stack of files on his desk! —in which to sprinkle the hashish into the guard's cup. Growing up in a neighborhood overrun by hashashniks, long deplored by Mercada, had proven useful, for Alegra knew exactly where to get the stuff. The problem with drinking it as opposed to smoking it, she was told, was that it would take longer to take effect, but the positive side was that the stupor would be stronger and longer than if smoked. She was glad for the dirt-black strength of the tea, hoping it would mask the heavy dose she had been forced to use. After all, she couldn't wait for hours.

It only took an hour before the guard's eyes started to glaze over. Still, she waited. Soon he started to mumble to himself, and finally to hallucinate. Gently she removed his keys, and then strode calmly and slowly along the rows of cells, as if she belonged there, until she found Leon. His eyes widened in shock at the sight of her, and she put her finger to her lips to signal silence. Together they half led half dragged the guard to the cell and stripped him. Leon donned his uniform. They locked the guard in and made their way through the prison. Hallway through hallway, up and down stairs, they walked in silence.

Heinoch and his crew were wide-eyed at Leon's sudden reappearance at their hideout, in a British uniform yet, with Alegra by his side in her Jewish policeman's uniform. And they were open-mouthed at his news that it was she who had sprung him and how she had managed it.

"Judith?" they asked in disbelief, staring at the scrawny young woman. "Judith? But how?"

Isaiah and his band, too, were at a loss for words. Their impressions ran the gamut from incredulity to fury to delight and finally relief.

Yet the British, too, were reacting to their prisoner's escape. It was a slap in the face to them and their authority, which already felt to be crumbling about them, so they worked furiously to determine and then find the culprit. And though Alegra had taken care to take with her the document she had signed an on which the guard had written Amos's name and badge number, she had not counted on the guard's acute memory.

When he was finally lucid, he recalled that the uniform bore the name Hazan, A. He remembered it because the name had suggested the word "hazard" to him. He recalled thinking, "A. Hazard. A hazard," which he had thought quite clever. And that was all it took.

Soon, an army squad was banging on the Hazan family door to arrest one Amos Hazan, British police officer. Amos was open mouthed as they pulled him from the house, with Joseph demanding to know the charge.

"Aiding and abetting a prisoner to escape?" Amos sputtered. "That's nonsense!"

Even as the evidence was presented to him, the British police uniform, the name that the guard remembered, he still maintained his innocence.

"It must be a mistake," he assured his questioners.

But it was when the guard himself was brought forward to identify him that he began to realize what had happened.

"Is this the man you say came for the prisoner?" the guard was asked.

He hesitated, and came up very close to Amos to peer into his face.

"He looks something like him, I suppose. Not really sure. But the name, I'm sure of that."

"You see?" Amos cried. "He doesn't recognize me. Anyone could have stolen my uniform!" And that was when Amos had his first inkling of who that might have been.

"But he's changed his voice. Haven't you?" the guard sneered. "I knew that raspy voice was a put-on, trying to hide what you really sound like."

Amos paled. It couldn't be. It couldn't be. The interrogators had accused him of working for the Haganah or the Irgun. Alegra? That was why he couldn't find his uniform! His little sister, whom he would never have suspected of undercover military activities. A rebel infiltrator had been in his own family and he had not even known it! And because of her now he was in prison. They were threatening him with hanging. But once Amos put two and two together and realized it had been Alegra who had perpetrated the breakout, he turned silent and refused to answer any more questions. He was thrown into a cell, the very one that Leon had occupied.

Joseph, in the meantime, set out immediately to speak to the powers that be. There was no time to lose. He went to speak with his brother's superiors at the police precinct, but they were just as mystified as he, and told him it was out of their hands. Joseph then appealed to the Governor's office, even trying to throw himself upon the man's mercy. That had so often worked in the past for his mother. People in power, she had told him, loved to be reminded of their superiority by one's own obsequiousness. He recounted to the Governor's aide that Amos had grown up orphaned of their father when he was a child, and then of their mother when he was a teen...But the aide said the Governor would not intervene in prison affairs. So Joseph sought out the prison and demanded to see the prison commander, who made him wait outside of his office for an hour. Joseph accosted him as soon as he opened his office door. The man was curt and cold as he explained that Amos would be tried before a tribunal and that it was up to them and not him to decide his fate. He was not about to break anyone out of prison himself, he added smugly. Joseph protested at the absurdity of the charges. Amos was a police officer! He upheld the law; he didn't break it. But his pleas fell on deaf ears.

Finally, Joseph visited Amos in his cell. He had been jailed in the very prison he had ostensibly ridiculed, and now security was even tighter. Joseph barely recognized his only brother. He seemed like a small boy again, too little in the prison uniform meant for a much bigger man. He was sitting on the prison cot with his head in his hands, a forlorn posture. But when he looked up, it was his expression that took Joseph aback. He had expected Amos to look angry and outraged as he himself felt at this preposterous allegation. But instead, he looked calm, even resigned.

"Amos!" Joseph tried to rouse him. "We won't give up! Remember what our mother said. We must be strong. This accusation is outlandish! You, of all people, breaking the law. Why, did you even know this Irgun member?"

"No," Amos answered simply.

"There, you see? It's completely illogical. I'll ask one of my law professors to recommend someone to represent you. You'll see. We'll get you out!"

"No, Joseph. I thank you, but no."

"What do you mean, no?"

"I don't want to be released."

"But…but you didn't do this."

"No, I didn't."

"So?" Joseph said. "I don't understand."

"But I know who did," Amos said. He looked up at his brother, who had remained standing.

Joseph now raised his voice. "I still don't understand! Why would you protect someone and forfeit your own life? Who could be that important to you?"

Amos remained silent and stared at his brother, willing him to comprehend.

And he did. Joseph placed his hand on his chest and sucked in deeply. "No," was all he said.

Amos grimaced in response. "Now you know why I can't contest the charge."

"But they'll hang you."

"Well, if one of us has to hang, better it be me."

"Oh Amos," Joseph sighed, and sat down next to his brother on the cot. He put his arm around him and hugged him. They had not touched since the day they had almost been killed. But Amos did not stiffen. Instead, he let himself be folded into the arms of the man who was his older brother and also his surrogate father. The man who had cared for him, supported him, raised him and loved him.

Joseph began to weep. "This is so wrong."

"No," Amos responded, his mouth above Joseph's shoulder. "It's actually so right. Don't you see?" Now he pulled away from the embrace and held his older brother at arm's length so he could speak to him face to face. "One baby sister died because of me. But now, now I can save the other. I can finally wash away my sin. It's like…a gift from God. I can save my baby sister this time."

When news of Amos's arrest came out, it was Alegra's turn to be shocked. She had removed the documentation with Amos's name! She had been so careful! She had succeeded in her mission, only to doom her brother! She had saved one beloved only to destroy another! She appealed to the Irgun and the Haganah, but they could not find a solution. Alegra's rescue of Leon was itself miraculous, and even that success had had a nefarious consequence. Moreover, Alegra's feat had been won by ruse, for the Jews could only compete against the British with trickery; any other weapon would find them sorely outmatched. The British would not allow themselves to look foolish twice. All rescue appeared impossible. Even time was their enemy. Amos would soon be tried and almost certainly hanged.

But part of the reason Alegra had run first to her comrades in arms was because she could not face Joseph. Did he know it was all her fault? It didn't matter. She could not go home. She felt so alone, even though she spent the night with fellow Haganah members in an old warehouse. She did not sleep, her tortured thoughts torn between ruing her own failure to protect her brother and trying to come up with a plan to save him. The next morning, Alegra knew she had to see Joseph. He would need her in a moment like this and she could not let her guilt prevent her from joining him. As was so often the case, Alegra focused on the needs of others, rather than her own.

When she arrived home, he was not there. She hesitated, not knowing whether to wait or not. Her first impulse was to flee, to not waste time waiting, but she knew that was really just an excuse to avoid Joseph. She forced herself to sit at their kitchen table. She ran her hands over the scarred surface, noting where a burning candle had left its mark and a pomegranate had spilled its juice and left a stain. After a few moments, Alegra picked up the day's *Palestine Post,* which was folded and lying on a chair in the corner. She expected to read of Amos's arrest but saw he was not mentioned. She was galled to see the world turned and continued on as if nothing had happened. As if Amos's arrest wasn't important at all. Instead of his supposed crime topping the headlines, the paper focused on the United States' suggestion of the day before, that the United Nations Organization reconsider its decision to partition Palestine, reportedly for being unenforceable. Palestine was to have been partitioned into two nations by this time, but the United Nations opted "to consider further the problem of Palestine." Nevertheless, David Ben-Gurion announced that they would proceed with the plan originally set up by the UN. Amos was not even mentioned in a small column. He would have had to compete with the daily deaths from shootings and mortars.

Incredibly, she read, the newspaper deemed more important even the rations for the upcoming Passover holiday, citing the numbers: two pounds of potatoes, two eggs, four pounds of matzot. The preparations for Easter were of course noted as well, and these were extensive. Whereas the Jews of Jerusalem would have to make do with negligible rations for their Seder meal, the English had brought in special consignments of holiday treats for Easter celebrations. Though spring lamb would have been impossible, they were nonetheless regaled with canned oysters, jars of mincemeat, Scottish shortbread and the likes, as well as crates of fine wines and whiskies.

Finally, Joseph arrived. Still intent on procuring Amos's freedom, he had been out seeking the aid of his former law school professors. Joseph had stopped cold when he saw his sister, and stood in the doorway. Alegra, for her part, had stood as well. They faced each other in silence. From Joseph's expression, Alegra could see that he knew of her role in Amos's capture. Silently, Joseph closed the door and stepped inside.

"Joseph…"

"I know," he answered her softly.

"I never imagined…" she began. "I took all the precautions."

He sighed in response. She was so much like Amos, he thought, so sure she was right, so convinced of her actions. So quick to act, the both of them, rather than pause to think.

"But I'll make it right," she now said. "I'll turn myself in. It's me they want, not Amos."

"Alegra, are you mad?" Joseph responded, alarmed.

"It's only right," she assured him.

"Right? How is it right? For you to die instead of Amos? What does that solve?"

"But he's innocent!" she cried.

"So? Do you think Amos would want you to be killed in his place? Do you think he could live with that?"

"But it's the only way to save him!"

"Alegra," Joseph said, "I'll find a way. Please. Don't do anything. I still have some contacts in government and have been going to my old law professors. Please, let me handle this from now on."

Alegra wanted to believe him. She wanted to believe that Joseph, like their mother before them, would solve the situation with words. He told her to return in the evening, when he would hopefully have news. Alegra reluctantly agreed. Yet not an hour later, she was already plotting.

Two days later, Passover began, and then it was Easter Sunday. The joyous sentiments created by spring's arrival were enhanced by the holiday feasting. The British government offices were closed, and those who could not take time off, such as guards and prison staff, were nonetheless treated to special food and drink by the administration. Rather than reflecting the sacred spirit of the holiday, however, the prison where Amos was being kept was soon imbued with a party atmosphere, becoming heady and raucous, with much boozing among the guards and jeering from the inmates. Prostitutes were brought in surreptitiously for the celebration, though only for those on the correct side of the bars. A good time was had by almost all, until a nasty rumor that the governor was arriving threatened to cut short the festivities. The rumor was soon proven false, but only after the prostitutes were quickly hustled out and the liquor hidden away. No unauthorized personnel were allowed on the prison premises, after all, no matter how welcome they were. The guards were still ostensibly on duty, and thus expected to remain sober.

In the aftermath of all the revelry, no one could really say at what moment it had become clear that prisoner #6-2483-5, also known as Amos Hazan, had gone missing. It took only a second to recall that the only people to have exited the prison were the horde of prostitutes, and it took only short leap from there to deduce that the only way anyone else could have abandoned the premises was mingled within said bevy of prostitutes. What took a little more time and patience was pinpointing the jolly fellow who had brought the women in. Eventually one, then another of the partygoers were summoned and questioned. The officials had meant to drag out of them the name of the pimp or at least of the guard who had hired him. Many had to admit shamefacedly that they hadn't really scrutinized the would-be pimp, much less checked his documents. What red-blooded Englishman would notice a bloke in a crowd of available women?! The man had merely appeared with his harem. Each guard thought another guard had hired him.

This time, it wasn't Alegra Hazan, alias Judith, who had donned the garb of the opposite sex to fool the British, but rather Amos Hazan, whom she had persuaded, during the height of the revelry, to slip into a dress and throw on a wig. An expertly placed scarf hid his moustache and the rest of the disguise was accomplished by the attractiveness of the real prostitutes who surrounded him on their rushed flight from the purportedly approaching authorities. Alegra, though now masquerading as one of the prostitutes, had once again infiltrated the prison, even at the risk of being recognized. She could not allow her brother to hang.

Amos would remain hidden within the bosom of the Haganah, moved from safe house to safe house, hoping to elude the British for another month, when the mandate would legally end on May 14, 1948. The Haganah leadership viewed Amos's presence among them as a coup. As a former British police officer, they realized he could provide invaluable information to the Haganah. Amos gave them intelligence on a planned raid, on secret meetings between British and Arab agents, and on general police workings. He furthermore began helping to train new recruits in handling weapons and in hand-to-hand combat, in preparation for the war to come. The neighboring Arab states had already announced that they would invade upon the official partitioning of Palestine.

Amos's rescue also led to his finally meeting Leon, for whose escape he himself had been incarcerated. Leon was grateful for Amos's unintended part in the affair and was impressed with his stoicism in facing a death sentence. Amos, too, was affected by Leon's tales of survival in Europe against all odds, and by his feats as an Irgun member. They found they had much in common, and were fast becoming friends. Alegra, seeing them together, wasn't sure how she felt about their budding friendship. She shouldn't have been surprised, she knew; they were so alike. Still, she felt a twinge of jealousy that Leon seemed to feel so brotherly toward her brother, and she didn't fully know whether it was because Leon appeared to get along better with Amos than she herself did, or whether it was because Leon showed more interest in her brother than in her.

On May 14, 1948, David Ben-Gurion declared independence for the State of Israel in what was then the Tel Aviv Museum. In front of 250 guests, whose invitations had been kept secret for fear the Arab armies would invade sooner than expected, and broadcast live on the first transmission of the new radio station, Kol Israel, the Voice of Israel, he read the proclamation. Ben-Gurion would soon become Israel's Prime Minister, as would two others who had signed the document, Moshe Sharett and Golda Meir. On the wall behind him hung a portrait of Theodore Herzl, founder of the Zionist movement for a Jewish homeland. Also behind Ben-Gurion flew what would become the official flag of Israel. Throngs gathered outside the museum, filling the nearby streets. They made the most of their celebrations for they knew that within the next few days, the armies of Egypt, Transjordan, Iraq and Syria would invade.

When Alegra heard Ben-Gurion's declaration, sitting in a makeshift barracks surrounded by her Haganah comrades, the room erupted in cheers. Alegra's cheers were perhaps among the loudest, for now she knew that Amos was finally safe. She and her brother faced one another and, uncharacteristically for both, threw their arms around each other. They then ran outside to revel with the rest of their countrymen and women who had taken to the streets, shouting with joy, many singing the Hatikvah, "The Hope," which would soon become Israel's national anthem. Alegra found herself hugged by strangers while crowds danced around her. When British trucks were spied pulling out of the city, the shouting of the throngs became even more raucous. Hands grasped at Alegra's as she was pulled into the circle dance called the Hora. Even that was deemed not close enough and soon the dancers had their arms around each other's shoulders. Tears filled Alegra's eyes. But even through the mad din she recognized the voices calling her name. She turned.

There before her stood Joseph and Amos, side by side, jostled by the crowd, beaming. She threw herself upon them and they in turn grabbed her. The three huddled close, heads touching.

"We've done it!" Joseph cried. "We've created a nation! We finally have a home!"

"No, you've done it," Amos said, staring at Alegra. "It's thanks to you that I'm here. It's thanks to you and the Haganah that we're all here."

Alegra smiled. Yes, she thought, it was thanks to her and to her comrades. It was thanks to all those who had believed, who had hoped, who had fought and persevered. Lili and Joseph, Mercada and Gabriel, had all faced seemingly insurmountable challenges and made countless sacrifices so that the three could be standing there, celebrating a new beginning. It was thanks to them that the three siblings, their progeny, were now here. Now Israelis. They had a country. They had a home. And they had each other.

AFTERWORD

AS MANY OF THE EPISODES in this novel are based on stories my
mother told me about her mother and grandmother, people have asked
me how much is true and how much I've made up; which characters are
based in reality and which are inventions. I thought my answers would
be straightforward but realized that the answers are a little of both. For
instance, Lili is based on my great-grandmother, Esther Arouesti, who
immigrated to Jerusalem from Serbia with her husband and small child.
Esther did indeed bear seventeen children who died from her milk, as a
specialist from Greece told her. She did also decide one day to become a
midwife, telling her distraught husband not to worry, that babies delivered
themselves. And they did die of cholera when their daughter was twelve
or thirteen. All this, then, is true. But from these bare facts I created a
Lili whose thoughts I could hear and whose emotions I could feel. Could
I possibly know what kind of person she had been or even what she had
looked like? No. I made all that up. Similarly, the stories my mother
handed down about what her grandmother had seen as a midwife were
mostly true, but embellished greatly by myself.

As for my grandmother, my mother's mother, her real name was
Clara but her nickname was truly Mercada, which I have discovered was
not uncommon. I invented the three wise women, but historians of the
Sephardi culture attest that ransoms (*regmemientos*) would be paid in order

to deceive demons thought to have brought about the deaths of previous children, and these "ransomed" babies would have the moniker Merkado or Merkada tacked onto their names. My grandmother, too, had been "bought" so as to deceive the evil spirits intent on relegating her to the same fate as had befallen her previous seventeen siblings. She also ended up alone at the start of her adolescence, and did marry a down-on-his-luck jeweler, Isaac Mizrahi (not to be confused with the designer) who merely continued her life of poverty. The part about his physical violence was my imagining what could and often does happen in situations of stress and hopelessness. But he did die early as well, leaving her a widow with five children. Moreover, Clara also bore a son who died of polio as an infant, and a daughter named Sara who did in fact die of third-degree burns she endured from a spilt pot of boiling soup.

From this point on in the novel, however, most of the characters are whole inventions. Alegra is certainly not my mother. Just the thought of my mother as a secret Haganah agent makes me laugh, though she was brave in other ways. She traveled alone to visit her brother in Guatemala, where he had settled, and then went on to stay for a few months in New York, again, on her own. And though she had two brothers, Avram and Shlomo, neither are Joseph or Amos; neither studied law nor served in the police force.

As for Leon Mayer, he was partly based on my father, Michael Gerstman, a Holocaust survivor. The horrors Leon recounts were from my father's own lips, but that is where the resemblance ends. My father didn't make it to Palestine until many years later when it was Israel. Just when he was supposed to board a ship for Palestine from the Displaced Persons camp in Germany where he had been sent after the war, his x-rays showed a spot on his lung. Fearing he had tuberculosis, the authorities wouldn't allow him on the ship. By the time the next one arrived, it was headed for the United States. As my father's sister, and only surviving relative, had settled in Brooklyn, he went to join her. He met my mother right before she had intended returning to Israel. They married after seven weeks of dating and remained happily married until he died fifty-nine years later at the age of ninety-four. They used to hold hands when they walked together. In any event, all the parts about Leon's military exploits were whole inventions, as were the prison escapes.

My grandmother died in her mid-eighties. She had lived alone for many years, her children having moved to other countries or having died. They all wanted her to live with them, and indeed she would stay a few months with one, or with another, but always insisted on returning to Israel. She maintained that she didn't want to die "outside." She wanted to die in Israel and so she did. After my father retired, he and my mother moved to Israel, allowing him to realize, after all that had befallen him during the Holocaust, his dream of living in a Jewish country, where he is now buried, and enabling her to return home. My mother will be ninety-four this year. She is almost blind so she can't read this book. Perhaps she will be able to listen to it, though her hearing is impaired as well. But what matters is that it exists. And that she is proud.

Galya Gerstman
San Jose, Costa Rica, 2023

ACKNOWLEDGEMENTS

THOUGH I BASED THIS WORK on the stories my mother told me, it is nonetheless a work of fiction. However, my mother's mouth was not my only source, especially in providing historical background and picturesque details of the place and time. I consulted Bertha Spafford Vester's *Our Jerusalem: An American Family in the Holy City, 1881-1949*; Raphael Patai's *The Arab Mind*; Arthur Koestler's *Promise and Fulfillment: Palestine 1917-1949*; Albert Hourani's *A History of the Arab Peoples*; Yitzchak Kerem's article, "Superstitions of Sephardic Jews in the Balkans"; Charles D. Bell's *Gleanings From A Tour in Palestine and the East*; and A. Goodrich Freer's *Inner Jerusalem*, among others. Any errors in scholarship or historical inaccuracies are entirely my own.

I would also like to thank Mark Schreiber for his friendship and aid in all things, from editing to marketing to buoying my resolve. Without him, this book would be nowhere nearly as good. I also thank Lauren Groskopf, at Pleasure Boat Studio, for choosing to publish this book, and for her toil and patience.

Thanks as well to Ruth Roman and Diana Rawlinson, my intrepid readers who scoured my work for errors large and small, and to my brother, Noah Gerstman, who, along with being a reader, contributed a painting of his as my cover art.

I am indebted to my family, Jaime, Isaiah, Claire and Jacob, for cheering me on, supporting me and believing in me. And finally, I thank my mother, who over the course of my lifetime told me the stories of her mother and grandmother in Old Jerusalem. This is the product of those stories.

GALYA GERSTMAN is also the author of the novel *Texting Olivia* (Pleasure Boat Studio, 2021) and has had articles published in Scary Mommy, Motherhood Later, and other sites. Galya taught French Literature at Tel Aviv University before relocating to Costa Rica to raise a family. She possesses a PhD in French Literature from Columbia University and a BA in Creative Writing from Barnard College.

CPSIA information can be obtained
at www.ICGtesting.com
Printed in the USA
JSHW020946130723
44480JS00006B/21

9 781737 052043